*For Jane, my wonderful wife*

## ACKNOWLEDGEMENTS

To keep its exciting sport fresh and vibrant, the PBR has changed its format in a number of ways over the years. In my novel, I have tried to remain true to the spirit of the PBR. Where necessary, however, I have taken liberties to fit the needs of the story. My apologies in advance to those who live the bull riding dream, in whatever capacity, and know where my imperfections lie.

I owe a debt of gratitude to the following people who have either encouraged my writing efforts or contributed specifically to this, my first, novel: Iva Martin, Michael Kohler, Lorraine Thomas, Elizabeth Stauffer, Larry Ward, Ross Murphy, Andy Zhang, all of my English grammar and writing teachers, and, of course, Jane.

# Murder at the PBR

# CHAPTER ONE

I was standing not twenty feet away from them the night John Henry killed Cauy Hall in Billings, Montana, helpless to do anything about it. Everyone said (and I agreed wholeheartedly) that had Lane Lowick been there, he would have saved Cauy. But that night, Lane Lowick, himself, had been dead for six weeks to the day, the grim result of a hit and run accident in Laughlin, Nevada.

Lane and I had been best friends since high school, and PBR traveling partners for some three years until his untimely death. Like modern day nomads, we were a pair of Texas-bred good ole boys, drinking and wenching our way from one city to the next on the lucrative Professional Bull Riders circuit. Take the Saturday night in Columbus, Ohio, three weeks before Lane's death. I'd finished in the money so Lane and I celebrated in a way that had become our long established pattern — picking up susceptible free spirits at a raunchy cowboy club. I danced, held hands and came onto an attractive redhead on the front side of her twenties; Lane caroused with a similarly ripened and equally appealing bottle-blond. So how did I wake up the next morning in bed with the bottle-blond, Lane with my redhead? Can't explain it, but neither Lane nor I uttered a peep about the switch as we drove to the next event. Things like that happened to us with astonishing frequency. More than a few of our compatriots thought us a little wild.

The Professional Bull Riders circuit, or PBR as we call it, is a dream come true for a handful of talented and courageous cowboys willing to climb onto the backs of the meanest and orneriest bulls nature and breeding programs have combined to propagate and stay there for the longest eight seconds anyone can imagine. The TV people have billed it as America's first extreme sport. From experience, they are not wrong; cowboys in our line of work get seriously hurt—even killed.

The circuit is a recent off-shoot of the rich rodeo heritage which itself evolved out of long cattle drives to railheads like Dodge City and Abilene where cattle were shipped to Kansas City and Chicago and, from there, to points east. The period lasted only about twenty years following the Civil War but branded a lasting impression upon our nation's mythic psyche. Anyway, after the drive, cowboys enjoyed showing-off their roping and riding skills to one another, their sweethearts and anyone else willing to watch them, often while hyped up on liquid stimulants and their own brazenness. Bull riding, first called steer riding, was the only event with no direct connection to any actual cattle drive necessity. But like a precocious child, it developed early on because there always seemed to be a few cowboys around with a loose enough cinch in the saddle anxious to give it a go.Bull riders today come from all over the world, in all sizes, shapes, work ethics and sets of values. We have cowboys on the PBR circuit from Canada, Mexico, Australia, Brazil, as well as both U S of As—the one east of the Mississippi River and the one out west.

Our events take place over a twenty-five-weekend schedule, disseminated throughout the year in various cities around the country. Bull riding, we love to say, is the fastest growing spectator sport in America. Because of its phenomenal rise in popularity, paydays for bull riding cowboys have become more than something to sneeze at. Oh, not what baseball, football and basketball players make, but with sponsors and guarantees, it'll do.

As a world-class bull rider, I was making great money and spending every dime of it. However, I was on the injured list because of a separated shoulder and a fractured clavicle the sports healers said would keep me out of action until the new season, the first of the year.

My injuries were the consequence of a mauling I received from Terminator the final night of a late-season event at the World Arena in Colorado Springs, Colorado, the week after Lane was killed. I could claim I got hurt because I was still upset at losing my best friend, was distracted and had lost my concentration. It wouldn't be true. Bull riding injuries, serious ones, can occur even when you do everything right. In this case, I was struggling to get to my feet following a "wild-get off" when the bull knocked me face down in the dirt. As the animal ran over me, his two hind feet landed squarely on my upper back thereby tearing two or three muscles that held my right shoulder together besides fracturing the clavicle that supported my riding hand. Bulls have no compunction about kicking a man when he's down.

Terminator, while a rank bull of the highest order, was not usually so vicious after bucking a cowboy off his back; just getting rid of the alien object up there seemed to be goal enough for him. That I had ridden him for the full eight seconds, something accomplished by anyone only twice before in two years, may have served as the catalyst for his unusually belligerent behavior. Everyone told me that had Lane been there it would never have happened. I knew they were trying to be consoling—cowboy style. The truth is, under those circumstances, Terminator probably would have mauled me anyway—Lane or no Lane.

Lane had been one of three bullfighters on the circuit, referred to by friends of bull riding as the clowns of the rodeo. And a star in his own right. He was as much a fan-favorite as the most popular riders, his autograph sought with as much favor as that of the current World Champion's.

He, like me, had been a high school bull rider, but only

mediocre in the sport, compared to the competition. He also tried bareback riding, then saddle bronc riding and even suffered a short stint with bulldogging before finding his true calling when he slapped on some grease paint one night and stepped in as a substitute bullfighter—at San Jose, California, I believe it was. A fearless daredevil in his work, he saved bull riders with feats of agility and skill the other bullfighters could only wish they could pull off. But he was such a cowboy the other bullfighters never held it against him, deferring to him with near-reverence, appreciating him as much as the bull riders and the fans. In a few short years, he was acknowledged as the best bullfighter in the business, touted by many as the best ever.

American bullfighters are not to be confused with their Spanish and Mexican counterparts. American bullfighters do not kill the bulls. Instead, dressed in clown garb and face, they protect and save bull riders who have leaped off, fallen off or been thrown off a bucking bull. To do it they jump, shout and run around to draw the bull's attention, or toss their hats across the bull's line of vision to distract the animal and, if necessary, plant themselves in front of the bulls and take the blow meant for the fallen bull rider. It is dangerous work. But those who do it love it, relish the adrenaline rush when the danger is at its height, receive an overwhelming sense of satisfaction from what they do and are more respected by the bull riders than anyone else on the circuit. Lane the epitome. I still can't believe he is gone.

Having said all of that, I would be derelict if I did not take up for my friends, the bullfighters. It wasn't because of negligence by any one of them that I received my injuries. That was just pure orneriness on the part of ole Terminator, a major reason we need bullfighters in the first place. As I've said, I did ride him that night for the full eight seconds required by the rules, to score a ninety-two and a second place finish in the event, which moved me up to fifth place in the world standings at the time. Unfortunately, my injuries from that "wreck" had knocked me out of the World Finals in Las Vegas, little more than a month away at the end of October, and my forced lay-off had since dropped me to ninth in the rankings from where I continued to nose-dive. However before Vegas, were, after Billings, four remaining events on the schedule: Fort Worth, Texas; Albuquerque, New Mexico; Atlantic City, New Jersey; and Phoenix, Arizona.

Even six weeks after Lane's death, the memory of the events leading up to what happened continued to haunt me like a lingering cold. In Laughlin that weekend, we were staying in our usual fifth rate motel — a step or two (or more) below anything Triple A would consider rating. It helped us live cheap and spend more of our resources on the important things in life — women and…the pursuit of women.

I had fallen into a sound sleep the night before and hadn't heard him come in. I'd had one of my frequent "it's-obvious-this-isn't-going-anywhere" dates. Charlene had been attractive enough, young enough, smart enough, cowgirl enough. She just hadn't been — enough. Yet it was just as obvious that the boot was on the other hoof as well. I hadn't been enough for her.

Lane was asleep when I awoke so I left to get myself some breakfast. Upon my return, the sound of the door opening aroused him.

"Make some damn noise why don't you," he growled in his West Texas drawl. That said, he turned toward the wall and fell asleep again. When he awoke an hour later, he complained of a terrible headache.

Now only one thing gave Lane headaches. Wine. He could guzzle beer by the case. Oh, he got drunk but a good night's sleep had him up and stomping around as if he hadn't been imbibing anything stronger than Kool-Aid the night before. Same with hard liquor, which he didn't care all that much for and seldom touched. Wine, on the other hand, *always* gave him a headache. One sip wouldn't bother him and sometimes he could survive a glass. But anything more and he'd suffer a humdinger of a migraine the next day, such that not even a hand-full of Excedrin (or any other brand) would dent the thing. His only solution—sleep, and lots of it. He would have to sleep it off.

When I returned from lunch, he was seated on the bed, feet on the floor, head in his hands.

"Who was she?" I asked in my version of the Texas dialect. I knew he'd been out the night before with something choice. Nothing else explained it. He had wanted to impress her with his idea of style and class, and drinking beer would have conveyed the wrong image. Of course, if his date had been anyone remotely connected with the PBR, she would have already caught his act.

I concluded he'd been out with someone he'd met the day before, shortly after pulling into town. For no PBR people, employee or groupie, came forth after he was killed claiming either to have been out with him on Thursday night or had waited for him Friday after the go-round when he was killed. Since he was killed on the parking lot of the Laughlin Fairgrounds, we surmised he was on his way to meet some blackjack dealer or showgirl who simply assumed he'd stood her up. He never shared his plans for the evening during the few hours before the Friday go-round when his head was relatively clear.

It wasn't that I hadn't tried to pump him. *Him*, for information about his date, not his stomach for, well...you know. Besides, it wasn't his stomach that was the problem. It was his head. Anyway, I asked him about the filly he'd been trying to "break."

Despite the rage going on within the boundaries of his skull, he'd managed to fork out a roguish grin before swiping a hand and collapsing on his pillow.

"First date?" I asked.

"As first as it gits," he replied, turning on his back and

rubbing his forehead with the fingers and thumbs of both hands.

"So you didn't get far, huh?" Now we all know what I was doing. That guy thing. Baiting. To get him to cough up the details, I treated him like he'd never had a chance, as if he'd never gotten to first base. Of course, I knew he had tried. Lane was the type of guy, possessed the confidence, who would try to make the ride without asking in which direction the critter spins. Haven't I already said he was a fearless daredevil?

"Well, ole buddy," he retorted, "I'd score the ride a ninety-eight."

"A ninety-eight!" I couldn't believe it. Lane always did this. (Then so did I.) But a ninety-eight? That was the highest score he'd ever awarded. His previous best was a ninety-four.

"And do you know why I score the ride so high?"

"I'm all ears."

"Cause of the degree of difficulty."

"A rank one, huh?"

"The rankest." He was sitting up in bed now. His head still had to have been throbbing, but telling what happened was offering him some measure of relief. "At first, she didn't want to get rode. But you know what they say 'bout persistence. I was as persistent as it gits, till finally I overcame her inhibitions and she turned willin'. Then she bucked and twisted with the best of 'em. It was a sweet, wild ride, ole buddy."

"So who is she?"

Again he swiped his hand at me as he said, "Nah, I'm not gonna tell ya just yet. I want to see what comes of it first."

"You mean this could be serious?"

He eyed me with meaning. "Possible, ole buddy. So let's say I don't want to jinx it."

"You seeing her again tonight?"

From his position on the bed, he made what I interpreted as a shrug. "Not exactly set yet. I'll see her sometime today and set somethin' up then."

Afterwards, the police reckoned that whoever hit him, if under the influence of alcohol, might not have known what happened. Anyway, they determined it was an accident and that was that.

Enough about Lane. He was gone and there was nothing to be done about it. I mentioned it only because while my life was going on, I was still experiencing a great deal of turmoil over the loss of my best friend.

I had been a top ten-bull rider on the PBR circuit since its inception more than a decade earlier. Now at thirty-three, I was growing long in the tooth; the end of my riding days was definitely in sight to all but the intentionally blind. Because of my injuries, I was serving as one of three judges the night Cauy was killed. Two of us marked the scores; the third kept the time and broke all ties.

Turned out, I was quite good at judging bull rides, if I must say so myself. Knowing I would not be able to ride bulls for more than another year or two, three tops, I needed to explore other options. Judging was definitely one of the options. A viable one at that. Good judges were needed and everyone said I had what it took to be one. Besides, it was something that could keep me in the sport. Let's face it, no way was I going to hold down a "regular" job.

Judging, while satisfying, was not the same as riding. I can't describe the thrill, the rush, of riding a powerful raging, wildly bucking, fiercely twisting, tricky bull. Once you've done it, (I admit you have to be somewhat deranged to try it in the first place) you never want to do anything else. Wasn't I already yearning for the new season when I would return to the sport? But bull riding is a young man's game. The World Champions for the last few years have been men in their early to mid-twenties. Another sign I'm getting too old?

Events had already taken an inauspicious turn by the

time I arrived at the arena the night Cauy was killed. Around mid-afternoon, I'd received a call from my ex, inviting me to dinner at CJ's on King Street in Billings, a place where the steaks and ribs were flavor-singed over burning mesquite.

LeAnn had the dubious honor of turning herself into Mrs. Chance Boettecher eight years earlier, when we were both twenty-five. She divorced me five years later in Las Vegas after disputably fulfilling the Silver State's six-week residency requirement. If truth were told, I wasn't over her yet. Nothing else could explain some of my antics since she walked out. Along with pictures of my parents and Lane, I still carried hers in my wallet.

I could have contested the divorce on the grounds that she had not complied with Nevada's residency requirement. A person had to live six weeks in the state before claiming residency status. Of most importance, the six weeks must be uninterrupted. In her Bill of Divorce, LeAnn stated she'd become a Reno resident in early September of that year, claiming the time the PBR had conducted an event in that city. Then she'd spent time in Laughlin and Las Vegas before filing her suit against me. What she did not say, and where my grounds for challenging the proceedings would have rested, was that she'd left the state twice to attend other events with the PBR, one weekend in Nampa, Idaho, another in Portland, Oregon. The exact schedule changes every year but that was how it ran that year.

Even loving her as I did, I offered no challenge to the proceedings. What would have been the point? She wanted the divorce. In the long run, I couldn't stop her. She hadn't left me for another man, just grown tired of me, or rather tired of being married to me. She never said but I suspected that she grew tired of my good ole boy ways. We'd been a foursome, LeAnn and me, Lane and his current girlfriend, for he always had a current girlfriend, often several. On that score, Lane had been even more of a good ole boy than I ever was. Maybe LeAnn just plain got tired of us.

Partly because of the nature of our personalities, LeAnn's and mine, partly because we knew we had to work with each other and partly because underneath it all there seemed a lasting friendship between us—whatever—since the divorce our relationship had actually improved, and we'd become disgustingly, though genuinely, pleasant toward one another. Deep down, I knew we were never getting back together, but something equally buried within me had been holding out a smidgen of hope.

One thing I could truthfully say: I was never unfaithful to LeAnn when we were married. In fact, despite my reputation for cheating on my girlfriends, I was completely monogamous with both of my wives.

Come on now. You had to expect—or at least suspect— it. I mean, a guy like me?

I married my first wife a year out of high school. Not my high school sweetheart, though a girl I attended school with. We started dating the summer after graduation and married the following spring. We were too young, not as ready to settle down as our craving for steady gratification of our carnal natures led us to believe. Lasted three years, though. No children, fortunately. Haven't seen her since the day she left; I didn't have to go to court for that one either, letting her divorce me uncontested. She hadn't wanted anything from me, so why bother.

Truth was, I didn't have anything at the time anyway— except this insane desire to climb on the backs of two thousand pound bucking bulls. I was trying to break into the rodeo big time, saddle bronc riding in addition to bull riding. I wanted to be the All Round Champion, win it more times than Ty Murray. Turned out my career as a saddle bronc rider didn't last long. I was a much better bull rider. It was hard on Constance (that was my first wife's name), the traveling, the abstinence from sex. Wasn't sex the purpose we married in the first place?

You see, I was hurt a lot. Broken this, pulled that, strained everything—including marriage. Much of the time, it was too painful for me to perform. Sexually, that is. For despite the pain, I never had any trouble making my rides on the bulls. Stupid. You can't win hurt. But you're hurt all the time and you have to ride to win a paycheck. I think some people call it a Catch—22 after some book I never read. Heard there was a movie. Maybe I'll catch it someday.

Speaking of movies, I love that golfing picture with Kevin Costner where he was an obscure driving range pro who qualified for the US Open to impress some woman, only to blow up on the last hole of the tournament, taking an "immortal" twelve. In the movie, the woman had a telling line about cowboys. She said, "They're not as romantic when you're with one." Against everything connected with my entire way of life and upbringing, I have to admit she was right.

On the rodeo circuit, I was hurt too much to ride my wife, but not my bulls. My first ex took it for as long as she could, then split. Can't say as I blamed her. In her case, I was glad we didn't have children, though I'd always relished the notion of being a daddy.

Anyway, that evening, LeAnn had arrived at the restaurant ahead of me and was sipping a drink at a table in an all but deserted section. She was dressed in faded jeans and a blue western shirt, blue snaps instead of buttons, her ever present black Stetson perched over her stringy blond hair that fell to the middle of her back. Gorgeous as ever, athletic body, button nose, a firm lined face that showed off a pair of prominent cheekbones like a decorative picture frame. I couldn't have lusted for her more. But lust is not love, anyone will tell you, and I felt something more than lust for my ex. Call it respect.

For some reason, seeing her just then reminded me of our

wedding day. The only difference between the two occasions was her absence of make-up, the elegant white, floral jacquard wedding dress she'd worn and the white cowboy hat with its lacy hip-length veil that streamed down her back. We'd married in our hometown of Uvalde, Texas. Same ages, we had not gone to school together. She'd moved to town a couple years after my first ex and I divorced, hailing from Checotah, Oklahoma. We met at the annual Uvalde rodeo, always held shortly before Thanksgiving, and started dating soon afterwards. She was a world-class barrel racer, which she gave up after our marriage. At the time, she claimed she wanted to tour with me on the bull riding circuit. I believe the real reason she gave it up was because, deep down, she dreaded competition.

No question though, she loved bull riding. After our divorce, when I expected her to return to Uvalde, resume barrel racing or drift to parts elsewhere, she stayed with the tour, taking a support position with the arena announcers.

After our split she dated—bull riders, sports healers, a man on the music staff, a TV cameraman—but nothing serious came of any of it.

Before taking the seat across from her, I was tempted to give her a kiss, just a peck on the cheek, but I couldn't help noticing how she fidgeted with her hands. Controlling my impulse for once, I refrained and settled myself into the seat across from her, still visualizing in my mind the woman I'd married eight years earlier.

She flashed me a wan smile, let her sparkling green eyes dart away, then back again.

I smiled, said, "How ya doin', LeAnn?"

"Oh, fine. Good. Fine," she replied, then again, like a yo-yo, sending her gaze away before returning it to me.

"Well, which is it?"

"Huh?" The luscious but creased mouth accentuated the puzzled expression on her face.

"Fine or good?"

She blinked her eyes and shook her head. "I...I don't understand."

"I asked you how you were. You couldn't seem to make up your mind if you were fine or good."

"Oh," she said, tilting her head and pursing her lips impatiently. "Yes, I'm fine."

"Relax, LeAnn. I was only dinging with you. I see you're fine."

"I'm nervous, I guess." She laughed a cut-off laugh, eyes flitting around the room yet again.

"I'd have never guessed."

The smile that dressed her face like a slim gown was more strained than all the others that she'd sent me since my arrival.

The waiter stopped by, a short young man, barely out of high school, with an ingratiating smile, like one of those coastal waiters who, filled with his own pretentiousness, preferred to say, "Hi, my name's Kevin. I'll be your server tonight." Server, hell. Where I come from, he's a waiter and always will be.

LeAnn tossed off the last of her drink, bourbon and something, and seemed ready to order dinner. Whenever we dined out while we were married, she always knew exactly what she wanted after a cursory glance at the menu. A real cowboy's woman that way. (I would advise you not to say that to her face if you value any appendage connected to your person. Let me assure you, despite anything you might have heard to the contrary, the woman's movement *has* made significant inroads on the rodeo scene.)

That evening, distracted for some reason, she poured over the menu at considerable length, unable to decide what she wanted. In the end, we both ordered New York Strips, medium-well; I, feeling a need to catch up with LeAnn in the alcohol department, added a lite beer to my order. Before he left though, LeAnn clinked a fingernail against the side of her glass and said to the waiter, "I might as well have another one while you're at it."

LeAnn, her drink and food ordered, sighed and stared at the top of the table.

"What is it?" I said.

She looked up expectantly, said, "What?"

"LeAnn, I don't know if I've ever seen you like this before. And we were married five years. Why, you weren't this nervous when you told me you were leaving. Remember?"

She smiled, wanly again. "You're right. I've got something to tell you and I'm nervous about it." That said, she took a deep breath…and uttered not a word. She did look down, even sneaked a glance at me, and then peered across the room in the direction of the bar. Out of the corner of my eye, I spotted our waiter making his way toward us. He was carrying a tray with a beer and a glass with brown liquid in it. Whatever announcement LeAnn had to make would wait.

After the waiter left, she lifted her glass in a way that led me to believe she was going to offer a toast. Instead, without so much as a grunt, she pulled her drink to her lips and downed a big gulp.

"How many of those things have you had?"

She stared at me like a chastised child. "This is just my second," she insisted. "I arrived only a few minutes before you."

I nodded, and watched her take another drink from her glass, this one of only slightly less quantity than the first.

I tried to engage her in small talk, which she answered in monosyllables or as close to them as she could utter. Giving up, I let her imbibe her drink. Suddenly, she drained her glass and set it down on the table with a soft thud. Then she looked straight into my eyes and said, "I've got something I have to tell you."

# CHAPTER TWO

I'd expected a frosted glass for my beer, but the waiter had not brought one. It didn't matter, though, and I'd been taking short pulls straight from the bottle, each cold and wet going down. Working that night, I had to limit myself to the one. Can't have a tipsy judge at the PBR, now can we? For all my good-ole-boy ways, I seldom drank anything hard, only occasionally imbibing wine as well. I guess I was best qualified as a beer drinker. Lites, too. Had to stay in shape.

The waiter brought us our dinners. The steaks, broiled perfectly, sizzled on the plates. I sawed off a piece of smoking meat and settled it on my tongue as if it were delicate glassware. It melted in my mouth almost like ice cream. When I glanced at LeAnn, I noticed she was just sitting there, kind of spaced out. I chewed my first bite thoroughly and swallowed it before saying, "Aren't you going to eat?"

She looked down at her plate and said, "Oh," as if recognizing its presence for the first time. She picked up her knife and fork and slowly cut off a small piece of the beef. She placed it in her mouth with the absentmindedness of a medicated mental patient and began to chew.

I let her swallow the food before peering into her glistening eyes, and saying, "Lay it on me, LeAnn."

Imploringly, she looked straight at me and said, "I wanted you to hear it from me first, Chance."

I knew from the beginning there was a purpose to the invite. Like a guilt-ridden youngster needing to confess, her news had been something she was not all that fired up to share. From the first, I resolved not to push her, let her work around to telling me whatever it was in her own good time. I confess I'd grown curious as to what it was all about. I am human after all.

I continued staring at her. Her jaw muscles tightened and she pressed her lips together. For a moment, I though she was going to smile but then the corners of her mouth dipped down. I wondered if she was about to break into tears.

Finally, softly, she said, "I'm pregnant."

At her words, I felt a sudden sinking in the pit of my stomach. Everyone knows that feeling. Life hasn't been lived until we've experienced it; over the course, we get plenty of opportunities. My fork, hunkered down with another fat chunk of steaming red meat and already in flight toward my mouth, stopped mid-air. It was my turn to display a measure of agitation, like some melodramatic movie character.

I returned my fork to the side of my plate, still chunk laden, and reached for my half-full bottle of beer, which I fumbled clumsily in my attempt to pick up, though catching it deftly before spilling any of its precious contents. LeAnn had stunned me. Although she had practically whispered the words, they exploded like a bombshell in my ears. Up to that moment, I hadn't a clue why she had wanted to have dinner with me. I'd made a few mental guesses—she was going to tell me she was leaving the PBR, she was moving back to Checotah, she was seeing a bull rider seriously. But she was pregnant?!

I'd always wanted rug rats, a son to discourage taking up bull riding, a daughter to overprotect against the insatiable carnal nature of teenage boys and young men. In other words, I wanted the traditional family—to be not just husband but father (or rather dad), eventually, granddad. The bull riding circuit was a tough life for families. For years, I'd watched what it had done to the domesticity of many of my fellow cowboys, but I was not going to let that (i.e. reason and sense) stop me from destroying my own family.

As I've already mentioned, it was definitely best that Constance and I hadn't sprouted any new vines. But I regretted my failure with LeAnn, like a life wasted.

LeAnn, too, had been keen on children. During the blissful years of our marriage, we'd tried. Oh, how we'd tried. It didn't happen. We'd gone to doctors. Their prognosis? There wasn't a thing wrong with either one of us. Go figure. On several occasions, after the divorce, LeAnn had said she was relieved we hadn't had children because she didn't want to have to raise them by herself. I think that was just sour grapes. If we'd had children, there might never have been any divorce.

Had there been children and divorce followed anyway, I would have had to pay child support. Wouldn't have mattered to me. I was still disappointed at my childless plight. It wasn't just that it challenged my sense of masculinity, though I'm sure that was a part of it. I genuinely wanted them.

I lifted the beer to my lips but did not take a drink. Not taking my eyes off LeAnn, I watched her face relax slightly for an instant and then, like an ice sculpture, melt back into its former fretfulness. Just as I hadn't missed her trepidation at telling me her news, she hadn't missed mine at hearing it.

"I...I wanted you to hear it from me," she repeated, stabbing her fork into the dish to the side of her plate and extracting a trio of green beans that she wrestled into her mouth.

It had been difficult for LeAnn to speak those words. To her credit, she wanted to keep our relationship, ex-husband and ex-wife, a healthy one. She knew it pained me to learn of her pregnancy, but not as much as if I'd heard about it through the bull riding grapevine — good-hearted, light-hearted, filled with as little acrimony as grapevines go, but just the same, insidious. So, mustering all of her courage, she'd bitten the bullet, invited me out to dinner and told me herself. Without the father (fiancé?) present. I couldn't help but love her for that. A familial love.

"Congratulations," I spewed, with a smile I hoped said I meant it.

She smiled hesitantly and thanked me softly, before reaching for her water glass that she, too, fumbled, actually upsetting and spilling its contents across the table. With bull rider reactions, I jerked back, allowing the water to miss me and flow harmlessly onto the carpet next to my boots. The effort, however, sent a streak of pain racing through my recovering shoulder.

With lame wisdom, I said, "Shouldn't a pregnant mother abstain from alcoholic beverages?"

"I didn't spill the water because I'm drunk," she retorted testily. "I'm just not quite used to the idea myself yet. But I'll quit. In fact, this, these were my last." She paused, smiled wanly, held up her hand with three fingers showing, and said, "Scouts honor."

"You were never a girl scout," I reminded.

"I know," she said, and shrugged, adding, "but who's counting?"

Without bothering to call the waiter, we mopped up most of the water on the table with out napkins. I gave LeAnn my untouched water glass, assuring her that my beer would suffice, and we returned to our dinners. LeAnn ate only about a third of her steak, but I uttered not a word of reproach. Hadn't I made a poor selection for a pregnant woman? She did eat most of her potato.

I waited until I was all but finished my meal before venturing to ask *the* question. Believe me, I was dying to know *the* answer. "So," I said as lightheartedly as I could fake, "who's the father?"

Although I'm sure she was waiting for me to ask that

very thing, her fingers gripped her fork tighter, and her eyes darted away, fell to her plate. Without looking up, she said, "Roy...Royce Sirett."

Having spoken his name, she looked up with apprehension.

"Royce Sirett!" The incredulity on my face must have equaled that of my tone.

I could not believe my ears. Royce Sirett. A stock contractor. Not that there was anything wrong with stock contractors. Actually, they were great guys. Royce Sirett included. Smart and shrew, Royce had bulls in the PBR and the qualifying events; bulls, horses and calves in the PRCA; bulls, horses and calves back home on his Valentine, Nebraska, ranch waiting their turn for the show. He was big time, computerized.

Royce had been married to Wanda Webley Sirett for eight years until their high profile divorce four years earlier.

Wanda Webley Sirett. Now there was a wild ride. A dozen or so years Royce's junior, she'd managed to garner a third of his livestock when she left him, and five hundred thousand in cold hard cash. And she the fault for the break up of the marriage, though in her defense she didn't start cheating on Royce until the last year of their rancorous nuptials. Anyway, I believed her when she told me. Royce, though, was that kind of guy. Generous as a sugar daddy to his favorite mistress. Wanda spent money like that was the sole purpose for finding itself in her possession. No efficient little manager behind the scenes role for her. Wasn't that what computers and accountants were for? Why have them if she was expected to do it all?

Royce had sired a daughter with Wanda my first year on the circuit. They (or rather Wanda) named her Wanda Lou Sirett and called her Lulu. Wanda said, "If men can name boys after themselves, I can name this girl after me." Everyone in the PBR doted on Lulu. She was something special. Wanda refused to breastfeed the child, which was fine by everyone, because that meant we got our chance to bottle feed the little ewe. And Wanda used each and every one of us, not hesitating to just drop the child in our arms along with a bottle of warm formula and take off on a shopping binge. Unfortunately, the child fell a victim to infant crib syndrome the night after her first birthday. Both Royce and Wanda were devastated beyond imagination to anyone who has never lost a child. Royce was willing to try again, but Wanda refused, claiming, "Motherhood is not my thing. The appropriate tubes have been attended to."

Since the settlement, all kinds of rumors had circulated about Wanda and her spendthrift ways. I didn't know how true any of them were. They were just rumors, after all. To me it was somewhat telling that she hadn't sold any of her livestock, her only source of relieving any financial difficulty that might arise.

Well, she did have one other potential source — her body.

And what a body! Voluptuous doesn't begin to describe it. Soft and fleshy in all the right ways, she threw it around the bull riding circuit like it was salt to be scattered on icy sidewalks, sharing it with everyone, myself included, though, I reiterate, I did not partake until after I was divorced from LeAnn. In the sack, she was not just good; she was stupendous. She could do things to a man that would make him weep for joy, beg for more (as well as for mercy), turn him into Jell-O and every other tread-worn cliché relevant to the notion I'm trying to describe. Anyone who "experienced" her once wanted her again. Again, myself included. Yet, knowing how she was, no one, myself included, wanted to take up a serious relationship with Wanda. Which suited her to the proverbial T.

Which brings me back to Royce and....

.... "He's old enough to be your father."

"He is not. He's only forty-nine."

"If he's only forty-nine then why did we celebrate his fiftieth birthday last April?"

"Okay, he's fifty. So what? What's age got to do with it anyway? He's a young fifty and I'm an old thirty…three."

I smiled patronizingly. "You're not old," I blathered, though I meant every word of it. How could anyone want Wanda Webley Sirett when they've been married to LeAnn Hardesty Boettecher for five wonderful years? Well, four wonderful years and one something less so.

"Thanks," she said. "Royce doesn't think so either."

"How could he? You're what, eighteen, seventeen years younger than him?"

"Closer to sixteen," she corrected churlishly.

"Sixteen." I rolled my eyes. "I repeat. He's old enough to be your father."

Instead of denying my accusation again, as I expected, she just sat there, silent for a long moment, eyes gazing into the bar, the feistiness suddenly drained from her like energy from a battery. I sensed she wanted to say something, just needed a little prompting. I got headed off at the pass when the waiter chose that moment to check on how we were doing. After learning that everything was "Fine," and "We didn't need anything else at this time," he left for another part of the restaurant.

"So?"

She knew exactly what I was after and gave it to me, though it was not what I expected. "Actually, Royce said the same thing."

"That he was old enough to be your father?"

She nodded. "You're probably going to hear it from someone else, so I'll just go ahead and tell you myself."

She paused. Now she was sitting up straight, staring me in the eye.

"We've been dating for a little while." She eyed me pointedly. "I guess you heard about it, huh?"

I nodded. "I heard rumors," I admitted. "But I thought it was just casual."

"It was, at first," she agreed, nodding. "Anyway, we had a big fight."

"A fight?"

"Yeah. There was yelling and screaming."

"Royce? Doesn't seem the type. So laid back and all."

She nodded again. "Yes, that's him most of the time. But...." Her eyes glanced away, and then back to me. "...I infuriated him, I guess, when I kept insisting that he was not too old for me."

"He doesn't like to be disagreed with?"

"No. Nothing like that. He's a sweet ole bear. It was just this one time. This one subject."

"He was trying to dump you...and you're pregnant?"

"I wasn't pregnant when we had the fight," she said in a tone obviously meant to defend him, "at least, not that we knew."

"Which begs the question. How long have you been pregnant?"

"Oh, only a few weeks, give or take. Just learned the news yesterday. Which was why I wanted to let you know right away. Before you heard it from someone else."

"Yes," I said. "And again thank you for that. But after learning you were pregnant he decided to do the honorable thing and took you back."

"You haven't been listening to all the circuit gossip, have you?"

I know my face twisted in disgust. "No, never do. Why?"

"We kinda never broke up. Not really. We had a big argument but we patched it up. So, no, he's not doing the honorable thing after learning I was pregnant. He's...he's always been honorable."

"Oh, well how can anyone top that?"

"Now don't mock. I…I love him. You don't know what all he's doing for me."

"By marrying you? Listen, LeAnn, you don't need him. Or his money. You've got a good job. You can take care of yourself."

"That's true. But you're overlooking one thing I said."

"What's that?"

"I said I love him, Chance. I mean it. I love him."

The words hurt. Of course she hadn't meant to hurt me, I know. She was just trying to explain where she was with Royce. In her defense, she didn't know the torch I still carried for her. Cowboys were supposed to "love 'em and leave 'em." Believe me, I'd worked hard over the years to foster that selfsame image. But…LeAnn was different. We'd become friends since the divorce, but friends or no, I was still carrying a place in my heart for her. My second wife. So the words "I love him" spoken by LeAnn when referring to another man hurt terribly, like a woman digging long fingernails into my arm, only instead of the arm she was digging them into my heart.

"So, your little tiff blew over and everything is on the road to the altar. I take it."

The corners of her mouth dropped like the residue of a burst balloon. She looked down, but recovered and looked up again. "We haven't decided on that exactly."

"You're not going to get married? Just have the kid and live together?"

"Oh, we have. I mean…we'll probably get married. Just have to set the date, make the decision."

"Doesn't sound like the decision has been made to me."

"It has." She shrugged, was trying to keep the petulance out of her voice. "Just nothing definite about how we're going to go about it."

"What's there to go about? You get a marriage license, book a church...."

"Or wedding chapel."

"Huh?"

She was eyeing me smugly now. "We're thinking about Reno or Las Vegas. You know, where wedding chapels abound. So you see, Mr. Smarty Pants, we have thought about it. We're getting it worked out. But in our own time. Don't pressure me... us. We don't have to get everything settled when you think we ought to. Remember, I just learned I'm pregnant yesterday. Aren't we allowed a little time to get used to the idea, get everything worked out?"

I allowed as they were.

We left the restaurant together and stepped into a clear night, blinking stars spying down on us, the wind brisk, signing an early Montana fall.

"I need a ride," she said, "if you don't mind. Mine's in the shop."

LeAnn drove a fairly new Bronco. Cowboys (and cowgirls) drive only pickups and their relatives. Never cars. God forbid.

"Oil change and tune-up?"

She nodded, shot a glance up the street where a truck was changing gears noisily.

"How did you get here?"

Her expression clearly said, Can't you guess?

I nodded. *Royce.*

I drove her to the arena in my six-year-old Ranger short bed where John Henry killed Cauy Hall before twenty thousand people. Of course, at the time it happened, no one knew of Cauy's actual status. We just thought he'd been hurt bad, mauled — not killed. It was at The Snake Pit later that night we learned the truth.

# CHAPTER THREE

It was sometime after eleven when I sauntered into The Snake Pit, a rustic cowboy nightclub a few blocks from the Nile Arena in Billings. It was the first time since Lane's death that I had entered such a place, so I was feeling like a lost dog that had finally found its way home. I was on the make, I guess, feeling not friendless but, without my best friend, alone. If I hadn't known it before, with the news LeAnn had dropped on me earlier that evening, I knew I had lost her for good. Horny as a just released convict, I decided it was time to move on. It had been over six weeks since I had commingled with the opposite sex.

Buffalo Stampede, an aging local country band made up of four male musicians and a female lead singer, were belting out their rendition of the old Buck Owens' hit There Goes My Love, while a dozen or so couples two-stepped around the dusty dance floor. Rustic and cowboy-ish (I don't think there were two people in the place not trimmed with cowboy hats and needle nose boots), the place was crowded, even with all the people dancing I couldn't spot a vacant chair anywhere.

Then, as the last note sounded on the Owens' number, I heard someone abusing my name from somewhere off to the side.

I recognized the voice calling me and gave strong consideration to pretending the band and crowd noise had drowned it out. Since LeAnn and I had pointedly not spoken about her during dinner earlier, I had a guilty feeling that I owed her something.

I turned, smiled pleasantly and tossed a wave at Wanda Webley Sirett. Then, tilting my cowboy hat back on my head, I made for her table.

"Over here, Chance," Wanda twanged, beckoning me, a broad smile beaming off her fleshy but gorgeous heart-shaped face. "Got a chair waitin' just for you, darlin'."

She was standing, holding a glass of gold liquid that I could see carried the short side of its original contents. Knowing Wanda, I can assure you it wasn't ginger ale. Tequila straight up, though she had an occasional penchant for mescal — worm and all. She was decked out in an enticing outfit of black and gold, black hip-hugging jeans, that hugged and shaped and hugged some more, and a black suede leather halter top slanting two rows of parallel fringes that almost, but not quite, camouflaged the ponderous peaks protruding from her chest like ripe Texas Ruby Red grapefruit. The cowboy hat setting over puffy waves of black hair was black too. The gold? Gobs of expensive jewelry jangling off her ears, most of her fingers (including one thumb) and both of her wrists.

"Comin'," I cooed. Then, unable to resist, I tacked on my own "darlin'." So sue me. But it *is* the cowboy way.

I wove around a table crammed with bull riders. Ednei Machado and Adriano Alvarez, two veteran Brazilian bull riders, loitered with Jorge Garcia, from Mexico, Chad Michaelson, a second year man from Canada, Brian Farr, the lone veteran from Australia, and Justin Diver, a three year man from Iowa and the leader in the world standings. Each cowboy greeted me warmly as I passed.

When I was within range of Wanda's deliciously inviting presence, she took two mincing steps toward me, wrapped her long arms around my neck and plastered a very suggestive alcohol-infected kiss on my mouth. The mood I was in, I could certainly be suggested. Until, breaking from the kiss, I glanced upon the other people present at the table behind her. It was certain Wanda had blocked my view on purpose. Red Parhan and Cody Laws, bull riders both, about my own age and a couple of peas in a pod if there ever were any, were no problem for me. They sat with their arms draped around their most recent girlfriends, Tona Richards and Wynona Kopecki respectfully. The "Hi ya's" from the four were genuinely friendly.

Craig Kelton's presence was another story, though far from the worst of it. Craig, mid-forties, was tall and lean and dark — dark eyed, dark haired, dark complexioned, and Wanda's foreman, the man who really ran her operation. Shrewd and skilled at every aspect of his job, there wasn't another stock contractor, rodeo-connected, who wouldn't have hired him in a heartbeat if given the opportunity. But Wanda paid him well and offered him one perk none of the others could touch — sleeping privileges with the boss, something he took regular advantage of. Craig, a taciturn former bull dogger from the old school, was all right. He'd worked for her during both occasions I slept with her myself, knew it, but never held it against me. Least ways, not that he ever let on. We offered each other the slightest of nods in greeting.

There were two other people seated at the table whose presence one could say distressed me a tad: Royce Sirett and my ex — the real reason Wanda summoned me over in her over-bearing and boisterous way. It was vintage Wanda, the crooked smirk on her face an intentional give-a-way.

LeAnn was unabashedly snuggled up against the stock contractor whose brown eyes diverted in every direction but at me, though he refused to remove his pudgy arm from across LeAnn's well-rounded shoulders. Royce was barrel-chested with a round, well-fed face, and he displaced about one and a half of your typical bull riders. What set him off from the mold of classic stock contractors were his bushy eyebrows and his trim mustache that wrapped around his mouth like a halo, merging into the goatee that covered his chin like a patch of outdoor carpet and created a stark counterbalance to the thinning brown hair on the top of his head. If he comes off here as something of a buffoon, then know that I have allowed my personal feelings from my memory of the moment to creep in and, worse, I have failed to do the man justice. Truthfully, there was much to like about Royce Sirett, even beyond his solid financial foundation, so for LeAnn to team up with him actually made a great deal of sense. Still, the sight of the two of them sitting together so cozily filled me with more than a twinge of jealousy. LeAnn's green eyes, peering at me pointedly, were saturated with guilt, like a sponge with water, but she made no move to extricate herself from her snug quarters against her newfound knight in shinning armor. She did manage to cast a brief wistful smile at me, though; I though it better than all those wan ones she'd thrown me in the restaurant.

I was annoyed at the whole spectacle, though less at Royce and LeAnn than at Wanda for subjecting me to it. Fortunately, both the jealously and the annoyance soon passed. I mean, why spoil my first night back? Be happy. Party!

Except ole Wanda, sinking to the bottom of the cesspool of her natural self, couldn't just let it lie. She had to pick at it. "Thought you might be up for a perfectly sublime sight," she prattled with nasty humor and a matching smile. "*I* found it most shockin' when I walked in here and seen it. Why, I was so flabbergasted, caused me to take up drinkin'." She assuaged her "distress" by raising her glass to her lips and imbibing a healthy belt of its remaining quantity. "Why," Wanda clattered on after her gulp, "I've decided to throw these two lovebirds a little party. Tonight. Right here and now. I'm picking up the tab for the whole table. And you're included, Chance. I've saved a seat for you, special. Knew you wouldn't want to miss it. So just hobble over there, darlin', and sit your cute little ole ass right down. Order whatever you want. It's on me."

I couldn't help wondering exactly what Wanda knew about Royce and LeAnn. Had Royce told her of his impending paternal status? Or only that he and LeAnn were officially an item? I knew the state of his and Wanda's relationship as exes. Hell, everyone connected with the PBR knew what was what with that pair. Let me assure you, it was nowhere near the lofty plain LeAnn and I had managed to attain — and maintain. Actually, I felt a great self-satisfaction about the way LeAnn and I carried off our lives as divorced spouses.

Now Royce and Wanda *were* on speaking terms. If you could call Wanda's constant baiting of Royce speaking terms. Royce, being the kind of guy he was, wisely let it roll off and seldom retaliated. Usually, he'd just laugh at Wanda's spewing, saying, "Oh, Wanda you're so full of it."

Except once. By chance, I was present the time he didn't let it pass so easily. We had been celebrating at a honky-tonk just like The Snake Pit. It was after an event back east, Charlotte, North Carolina, if memory serves. It had been about a year after their divorce. LeAnn and I were still married at the time, though in our final year together. Wanda, as usual, had derived a little too much spirit from the spirits she'd been sipping. That night, she'd taken up with Casey Applegate, the winner of the weekend's event, and the two of them had been dominating the dance floor with their drunken gyrations. When the set ended, they slithered over to the table adjoining the one where LeAnn and I sat.

Royce was there with Denise Reichart, a nurse with the sports healing team, since gone on to a somewhat less hectic life. Royce always liked younger women and Denise was a little more than a year or two older than LeAnn and myself. That Royce was out with a woman younger than herself, I wish I could say was the thing that set Wanda off. In truth, I don't think it mattered. Wanda didn't need anything so trivial as an actual reason for the pastime of "Royce Baiting." Anyway, it was Royce and Denise's first date. Turned out to be their last as well. Thanks to good ole Wanda.

Wanda must have seen the two of them sitting together from the dance floor, hence, her beeline to their table at the conclusion of the set. There, she laid out one insult after another, as fast as her inebriated mind could conger them up. Not just at Denise, but at Royce and everyone sitting around them. Wanda believed in scattering her insults liberally. Naturally, she reserved her best sorties for Royce. Of course to her, they were all her best. After taking it for some time, Royce, his pride seemingly marred under the barrage of abuses, suddenly threw a full glass of beer in Wanda's face. No words. Pure action. Got to love him for that one. Wasn't he human? He hadn't really hurt her. In truth, I don't think it fazed Wanda one bit. Just put her where she loved to be — at the center of everything.

Casey, I could tell, was just inebriated enough to consider joining the fray. Greatly overmatched against Royce, and knowing it, he was not so inebriated as to prevent wisdom from prevailing over valor. Casey, though only thirty at the time to Royce's mid-forties, was like most bull riders, so the last thing you could call him was big and brawny. Although he was tall, he was much too lanky for fighting the likes of Royce Sirett, or too many other people for that matter. The exception might have been other lanky bull riders like himself, but we seldom get into scrapes with each other.

The irony was Denise refused to date Royce again after that. It wasn't because she was upset that he threw his beer all over his ex-wife. Or rather, it *was* because he threw his beer all over his ex-wife, but not because she was upset that he would do such a thing to a woman and, ergo, was thus capable of doing it to her if he got angry enough. No, it was because she concluded that if he could throw his beer all over his ex-wife because of a few drunken taunts, then he must still have feelings for her ("carrying baggage" was the phrase she actually used).

She wanted him to resolve those feelings before asking her out again.

Personally, I thought Royce's feelings for Wanda were long over, over when she took him for a third of his stock in the divorce settlement. He was willing to give her cash. He didn't care about money all that much. But his livestock, well that was something else. To guys like Royce — stock contractors — those animals were more than bread and butter. It's their life, their lifeblood, their raison d'etre. To part with one animal was to draw out the essence of their spirit like blood from a vein.

Wanda, bless her soul, held out, and softy that he was, Royce eventually gave in just to get rid of her. Biggest mistake he ever made. Instead of getting rid of her, he accomplished the exact opposite. Giving her part of his stock turned out to be the surest way of keeping her around.

Royce told me afterwards (and I believed him) that he really wasn't all that upset with Wanda for what she'd said that night in Denise's presence. He'd acted that way only because he thought Denise expected it of him, being a first date and all. Then he wagged his head morbidly and observed, "I couldn't have been more wrong, could I?"

Like a corporate "Yes-Man," I agreed with him.

There was an empty chair next to Craig; the one Wanda had purposefully "saved for me." I took it and ordered a beer from the waitress who came by a moment later.

The table next to us supported a couple of bull riders. I nodded to Casey Applegate, secretary of the PBR, and his latest girlfriend, Rebecca Something or Other — the brief tryst with Wanda a distant memory. Also present at the table was Casey's best friend, Kyle Nash, one of the three directors of the PBR, and his wife, Lucy. Casey and Kyle, like Lane and myself, had been best friends from high school, traveled the circuit together, sticking together like bugs in a glue bottle.

I leaned over to Casey and offered, "If I joined your table

would we have a quorum?" You see, I'm vice-president of the PBR, but more about that later.

Casey smiled at my witticism, said, "We'd have to dream up somethin' to put on the agenda other than partyin'. Besides, Daryl might not like it."

"Can't have the illustrious PBR president upset with us," I said. "Move to adjourn."

"Meeting adjourned," he quipped, at which we both laughed, and then I turned back to my table.

Wanda saw me and said, "Why, you and I ought to sit here and cuddle awhile together, don't you think, Chance darlin'?" That said, she turned an exaggerated grin on Royce and LeAnn, though I'm sure the effect was mainly for Royce's benefit.

"Anyone hear the latest on Cauy?" I asked, changing the subject and hoping to learn something encouraging in the process.

"Ain't heard nothin' yet," Red returned in a pure West Texas accent. "Just waitin'."

"He was out cold when they took him out," Cody added.

"He looked terrible," Tona threw in.

"I think he was out cold when he hit the ground," Wynona upped.

"Well, if no one at this table intends to climb off his pretty ass and make a simple phone call, I guess I'll have to be the one to take the bull by the horns so to speak. After all, poor ole Cauy might be layin' over in that hospital bed givin' up the ghost right this very moment." This piece of petty chastisement and tacky prognostication came from the wide full mouth of none other than our beloved Wanda Webley Sirett.

"I've got my cell phone," she prated, "but I'll have to go outside if I want to hear anything. Be right back." Without waiting for encouragement, she spun on her heels and made for the door.

Waiting for Wanda to return with the latest on Cauy, I settled into my seat; elbowed Craig in the ribs, who smiled pleasantly; nodded to Royce, who returned the sign; and mouthed a silent "Hi" to LeAnn, who winked back knowingly.

Then the waitress brought my beer and the band struck up their version of "Amarillo By Mornin'." I took a sip of my brew, tuned out the music and let my mind wander back to earlier that night at the arena when Cauy Hall tangled with John Henry before nearly twenty thousand deliriously screaming fans. I remembered the scene like it was a slow motion movie running in my brain. It was definitely one for the "wreck tape."

John Henry, a ton-plus of black and beige bovine with long thick dirty-white, filed-down horns, had been his usual cantankerous self in the chute. These animals are athletes, just like the men who dare to climb on their backs. For that matter, just like baseball players, swimmers or, and maybe this is the best analogy, just like thoroughbred racehorses. The average fan may not be aware of it but bulls have pride, determination, heart. Oh, and, also like athletes at every level, they have their off days. That's the only time bull riders, even the very best, ride the rankest ones.

But this was no off day for John Henry, one of the rankest of the rank. In fact, he'd had but one off day the whole year — the night, two months earlier, I rode him in Columbus, Georgia to a score of ninety-three. Despite that ride, he was well in the lead for Bull-of-the-Year honors. John Henry came to throw a bull rider that night.

Cauy was a middle-of-the-pack bull rider. Still, world-class. After all, there were only twenty or so ahead of him in the standings. Cauy had ridden Terminator for a ninety-four in Tampa Bay, Florida, a year earlier. In fact, he always scored in the nineties at least a dozen times during the season.

Twice while preparing to ride John Henry, Cauy had to redraw his rope because the darn brute bucked at the exact instant before Cauy had the rope tight in his hand. Both times, Cauy had to dismount and stand on the rails until the animal settled down. Only then could he sit back down and redraw the rope with the help of the other bull riders assisting him, before finally offering his nod to Lance Miles, the gate man.

Then, with Cauy perched precariously on his back, John Henry exploded out of the chute with a leap that, when he dropped, his hind end was a good ten feet off the ground. He was hoping the down draft he created would be enough to yank Cauy into the dirt like a lawn dart, burying him six inches deep. But he wasn't assuming it would be enough. Mid-air, he feinted as if he were going to the left, but when his front feet touched the ground he jerked back to the right with such power that any rider who wasn't ready for the move would have been flung off with enough centrifugal force to send him sailing into the side railing.

There are two basic bull riding styles: scrambling and make-it-look-easy. Any bull rider knows and uses both. It is the bull, and his quirks, that determine which will be employed for any particular ride. The more powerful or ragged the bull's gyrations, the more the rider will scramble. The more predictable the moves of the bull, the more the make-it-look-easy style will come into play. At every event, our fans receive multiple opportunities to observe both.

Cauy, at this point, was scrambling around on the back of that animal like a bumper car at a carnival ride. He'd studied John Henry's patterns, as all good bull riders do, and had anticipated the bull's early moves perfectly, and when John Henry offered up that powerful move early on, Cauy had kept his seat squarely in the middle of the big animal's back, his head down. Then, ignoring the feint, he "beat him around the corner," turned in sync with the spinning mass beneath him and, maintaining his perfect position, was ready for the next tactic the bull would throw at him.

But John Henry wasn't a rank bull by chance. He's the kind that as soon as one tactic fails, throws another at you before you can guess what it might be. Thus, he continued around in a spin to his right that, combined with the height he was getting in his jumps, meant a ride in the mid-nineties was in progress — if Cauy could stay on him for the duration. Believe me, eight seconds is the next thing to eternity in that situation.

Now, no bull rider rides all of his bulls. PBR level bulls are too smart, too powerful. A great bull rider having a great year will make about seventy percent of his rides. The average bull rider having a great year will ride about fifty percent of his bulls. Kind of where Cauy fit in. My best year, two years earlier, I rode nearly sixty-five percent of my bulls. Now with that in mind, I don't care who we want to talk about, the legendary Donnie Gay, Ty Murray in his prime, or Justin Diver, the year's leading rider, no one would have survived John Henry's next move. Breaking out of his spin, he turned back to the left, while at the same time leaping high. Then, with quickness you had to have been there to believe, he dropped his head and upper body in a move that mimicked the one he had made right out of the chute. This time, the drop was performed with twice the power of that opening effort. Cauy, now having been bounced around on John Henry's back for five long seconds, was not the same rider he'd been right out of the chute, nor was he in quite the same secure position as he'd been way back when the gate opened.

And that's all it takes on that kind of bull.

I've already said these bulls are smart. If one thing doesn't get you, they try something else. John Henry jerked down with such force that it broke Cauy's riding hand free from his bull rope and sent him flying through the air like a trapeze artist — only without the artistry. Cauy, with nothing to hold onto, was flung to the side, like a rocket shot off its launching pad. Except rockets are shot up. Cauy was shot down, taking a nasty headlong spill in the dirt.

Now let's put it in perspective. For bull riders, landing in the dirt is not even embarrassing. Just part of the dismount. If we ride a bull for eight seconds to receive a score, we don't even feel it when we hit the ground. Believe me, after a successful ride, that dirt brushes off real easy, and we're applauded with much appreciation by the fans.

John Henry, as soon as he touched the ground, though sans rider, quickly spun to his left. Once off, the bull rider should never lose sight of the bull. Cauy, having landed on his shoulder, rolled over onto his back. He gathered his feet beneath him and was preparing to scramble to the side rail of the arena with all the speed that fear and adrenaline could muster. John Henry, though, was still in his spin, coming around. It was in just this type of situation that Lane Lowick excelled. Seemingly always anticipating the perfect position no matter what, Lane, in that situation, would have been right where John Henry would have seen him as he came around. John Henry, then, would have charged the waiting bullfighter, leaving unharmed the bull rider struggling to save his hide. But Lane was not there, and John Henry, attracted by Cauy's movements just as he came around to face him, charged the hapless cowboy.

All three bullfighters present were caught, not out of position, but just at the moment, in less than ideal positions in relationship to Cauy and John Henry. Judd Blanchard, a fine bullfighter that I have never had any reservations riding in the arena with on any given day, threw his hat across John Henry's path. Either not seeing it or choosing to ignore it, John Henry paid the sailing sphere no mind. Instead, he lowered his head and charged straight at Cauy. Travis Nokes, another outstanding veteran bullfighter, was racing around from behind the bull in a late attempt to cover Cauy's body with his own, while Buddy

Bach, the bullfighter called up from the Challenger Tour circuit to replace Lane less than a month earlier, was between Judd and Travis on the opposite side of the action. Not out of position, I reiterate, but just away — too far away.

Meanwhile, Cauy, himself, vainly trying to scamper to his feet, was struck squarely in the head not by John Henry's forehead, which would have been hard enough by itself, but by his ugly left horn, loaded with all the punch a two thousand pound animal can pack into it.

I heard the sickening crack from where I was standing and knew it was not John Henry's horn that had broken off, though I looked around for a piece of flying fragment, just in case. As sure as my name's Chance Boettecher, I'm certain Cauy saw nothing but black after that — out like the proverbial light. At that time, I guessed he would be laid up in the hospital for days if not weeks with a severe concussion.

Too late, the bullfighters finally managed to divert John Henry's attention away from Cauy. Although distracted, John Henry's momentum carried him over Cauy's body that the bull then proceeded to maul, stepping on various body parts, catching a leg and an arm in the process. Not fun to be sure, I thought there was no permanent damage, even if bones were broken. Chasing after Buddy Bach, John Henry bounded away from his unconscious victim, and a moment later was swaggering through the open gate, on his way back to the warmth and comfort of his pen, where a bag of fresh grain awaited him as a reward for his night's work.

The sports healers carried Cauy out of the arena on a stretcher. The crowd, anxious for his well being, gave him a sick-stricken but heartfelt ovation that meant they hoped he would get well and return soon to the sport they, and he, loved. I remember thinking he would be back, but it definitely wouldn't be for a while.

I was aroused from my reverie when out of the corner

of my eye I spotted Wanda making her way to the table, her face ashen, her eyes zombie-like. I was not surprised. I knew Cauy was badly hurt. The report was going to be a dire one. But while Wanda's expression might have been "saying" how dire the report was going to be, I hadn't been "listening."

# CHAPTER FOUR

"How's he doin', Wanda darlin'?" Red asked.

Wanda's mouth sprang open like a trap door, but nothing came out. Totally un-Wanda-like. Craig jumped out of his seat and draped an arm across her round shoulders to steady her. She peered at him, then at Red, then at Cody, then at me, but I am not sure if she saw any of us.

"What's happened?" he asked.

"He's dead," she blurted, as tears sprung from her amethyst eyes.

"What?!" Most of us had cried it simultaneously.

"Poor Cauy is dead," she sputtered. "I spoke to Elissa Cross at the hospital. She told me he was dead when they put him on the stretcher. John Henry killed him instantly."

I slouched in my seat, stunned. Was it possible? Cauy was dead? We hadn't been the closest of friends but we had always been on good terms. I had helped pull his bull rope many times; he, mine. Now he was dead?

Bull riders know when they climb on the back of a raging bull the worst can happen. No frivolous words, we mean it when we say there is a risk to life and limb in bull riding. Death is not unheard of in our sport. Lane Frost, Brent Thurman, Glen Keeley, champions all, will be memorialized — and remembered — by the bull riding fraternity. We don't want to forget them.

Now another name was to be added to the macabre list — Cauy Hall. In time, we know there will be others. Bull riding is nothing like Russian roulette; the odds, much better. Most of the time, a bull mauls a rider pretty good without killing him. Been there, done that.

*It's not whether you're going to get hurt, but when and how bad.* Anyone hanging around the bull riding circuit for any length of time will hear that maxim ad nauseam. While I'm sick of hearing it, I'm not sick of taking it to heart.

Believe it or not, I've never considered death. That is at the hoofs or horns of a bull. I've been stepped on, butted, horned, fallen on, flung off, yanked down, bucked off, even bucked off in the chute, in other words, hurt, many times, usually not enough to keep me out of the next event, especially if I had more than a week to recover. Wasn't I recovering from one of my worst injuries ever? But death? Not an option. It wasn't going to happen to me. I never thought it *couldn't* happen to me, just that it *wouldn't* happen to me. I was going to escape that plight. I think a bull rider has to have that attitude to help make him fearless enough to get on the bull in the first place and then try to stay there for eight seconds. You can't be afraid a bull is going to kill you and get on its back. I've lived my entire bull riding life believing that I had a better chance of being killed in an automobile accident or an airplane crash than in a bull-riding arena.

Word of Cauy's death spread through The Snake Pit like the wave at a football game. The band caught the mood and stopped in the middle of a number. As vice-president, I was the highest-ranking member of the PBR board present, so when I saw everyone looking at me, and Casey and Kyle nodding in an expectant way, I felt obliged to make my way to the microphone on the stage. Personally, I thought I was the last one for the job.

Snaking my way around the tables, I had no idea what I was going to say when I got there. I slowly climbed the three steps to the stage, gaining some appreciation of what the condemned must feel like heading for the gallows. Avoiding eye contact with everyone, I treaded my way over to the microphone that awaited me like an executioner. To steady myself, I reached up and grabbed the metal pole, causing a loud screeching sound to reverb through the speaker system. Immediately, the band's bass player stepped over and said, "Don't touch the mike, man." I turned and looked at him. He smiled meekly. "Causes feedback."

I let go of the pole and the screeching sound stopped. I nodded and then turned back to the audience.

I have no idea what I said but somehow I got the awful news out. Later, a number of bull riders, including Casey and Kyle, came up to me and said I couldn't have said it better. One man told me that if a bull ever killed him, he wanted me to be the one to make the announcement.

The following Tuesday, Cauy was buried next to his parents in a small cemetery beside a white framed Catholic church in Okeene, Okalahoma, his home town. Jodi Hall, Cauy's sister, wept openly, consoled by her close friend, Lena Atkins. Jodi was a petite thing with freckled cheeks, short brown hair and gold-flecked brown eyes. Lena was darker-eyed, taller, fleshier, and absolutely gorgeous. Both women wore black. Neither Jodi nor Lena had official positions with the PBR, but they traveled with Cauy to all of the events. In addition to Jodi and Lena and a number of Cauy's boyhood friends, everyone remotely connected with the PBR attended the service — the bull riders, the bullfighters, the staff, the sports healers, the stock contractors — even Wanda Sirett, the unnaturally contrite owner of John Henry. Craig Kelton stood beside her, a supporting hand at her elbow.

The priest of Cauy's church and Tyler Kennelly, the leader of the Christian Cowboy Fellowship, officiated. Tyler gave a truly inspirational eulogy, though Cauy had not been a member of that wing of the PBR. We all, Tyler included, know that that's a personal thing, and we respect each other's faith journey completely.

The weekend after Cauy's funeral, a Challenger Tour event was held in Twin Falls, Idaho, while a main circuit event took place in Fort Worth, Texas. I was a judge in Fort Worth, so I was not present in Twin Falls when Jodi, herself, was found dead.

# CHAPTER FIVE

Challenger Tour events are the minor leagues of bull riding, yet more. A cowboy who earns enough money at these tour events can qualify for the World Championships at Las Vegas where, in seven days spread out over ten, he has a chance to win more than a quarter of a million dollars. Plus, the minor league tours provide an excellent door for younger, less experienced bull riders who want to make it to the main tour. Win in the minors and a cowboy can qualify for the majors. Even veteran riders use the Challenger Tour to garner extra money and assure themselves of a seeding at the World Championships.

Three years earlier, I had used the Challenger Tour for that very purpose. Injuries kept me off all tours until mid-July that year. After recovering and returning to the circuit, I wasn't riding well enough to qualify for one of the forty-five spots at Vegas, living off my buddy, Lane Lowick, the whole time. Two fifth places finishes on the main tour combined with back-to-back-to-back wins on the Challenger Tour in September sneaked me in there in forty-fourth position. I went on to place fourth in the average at the World Finals, including a go-round win, to take away a ton of money and salvage what had definitely been a disappointing year up to that point.

The lower-level tour not only plays an important role for the bull riders trying to make it to Vegas or into the main tour, but for everyone else connected with the sport of bull riding as well. Bullfighters gain experience there, too; when Lane was

killed in Laughlin, the PBR dipped into the Challenger Tour
to bring up Buddy Bach, who had honed his skills to the point
where he was more than ready for the big time when the call
came.

Then too, the stock contractors work their young animals
into the picture by testing them there, and the public address
announcers, the sports healers…but you get the picture.

Challenger Tour events do not take place in the same
cities where PBR events are held. Obviously, that would be self-
defeating. What Jodi Hall was doing in Twin Falls, Idaho at a
Challenger Tour event the week after her brother was killed by
John Henry was more than a little baffling.

Jodi was a couple years younger than her brother
Cauy, so, mid-twenties. A petite thing, I doubted she weighed
a hundred pounds. She had close-cropped black hair that she
combed back on the top and sides, jell-supported for shaping. I
don't remember ever seeing make-up on her narrow porcelain
face, or wearing anything except western work shirts and faded
blue jeans—Cauy's funeral the exception. I thought her look,
though somewhat masculine, gorgeous. Moreover, she was
sweet, about the sweetest person I ever ran into, always a smile
for everyone, nary an unkind word for a soul.

About a year or so after my divorce I found myself
enticed enough by her look and sweetness to ask her out. She
turned me down flat, but in a nice way. Disappointed, I asked
why. With a teasing smile, she said, "You're not my type,
Chance." When I asked her what her type was, she replied with
nothing more than a cryptic, "Just know you're not it."

The night her brother was killed, I remembered catching
a glimpse of her waiting outside the gate while the sports healers
tended to Cauy. Holding her hands and biting her thumbnail,
she stood there bouncing anxiously, like a child standing in a
long line for the restroom.

At Cauy's funeral, I saw her in a dress for the first

time that I could remember. A becoming black scoop-necked western cut thing that fell almost to her ankles and her black slouch boots. Sobbing quietly throughout the proceedings, she had been comforted by her close friend, Lena Atkins, who sat beside her in church and then at the gravesite service, holding her hand at both places.

I learned about her death early Sunday morning when Daryl Minnich phoned my motel room in Fort Worth. In addition to serving as president of the PBR, Daryl was a two-time world champion bull rider who, a month earlier, had announced his retirement from bull riding following the World Championships. He was currently sitting thirty-fifth in the standing and, at thirty-seven years of age, saw the handwriting on the wall. He'd said he would continue as president of the PBR as long as the fellows still had confidence in him. Believe me, Daryl has our confidence.

Daryl, like myself, is one of the founders of the PBR. He has been only our second president. He replaced the first one, Russ Ward, four years earlier after Russ took a mauling by the bull Cross Hairs at an event in Columbus, Ohio. (Yes, it made the "Wreck" tape.) Ross' injuries were so extensive that he has been confined to a wheelchair ever since. Despite a bleak medical prognosis, he has never given up the dream of returning to active competition. Although he did not want to relinquish his position as president, the bull riders felt they had no choice but to replace him with Daryl, PBR vice-president at the time. The PBR was still undergoing growing pains, and Russ, because he required so much medical attention, was missing too many meetings and failing to follow through on his duties. For a time, though brief, the circuit suffered as a result. In truth, our existence is still tenuous, though strengthening with every passing year. Each officer, director and rider has gone to great lengths to make sure nothing harms the great creation we've put together.

Although Daryl has done an outstanding job as president since assuming the post, Russ, who still serves on the board of directors, has been something of a thorn in his side. Daryl, who knows he has more than enough votes to override Russ' constant opposition, has handled it well.

One might wonder about yours truly in the role of vice-president. Good ole boy. Loose cannon. Unlike the presidency, a position of some stability, the vice-presidency of the PBR has seen over a half dozen occupants in its short history. It seems that whoever occupies the position contracts a severe case of dissatisfaction-itis. The ailment's primary symptom is a strong desire to depose the incumbent president—which makes for contentious annual meetings. Because when the vice-president runs for president, he has, except in the lone case of Daryl's replacement of the injured Ross, invariably been defeated—by a landslide. Despite the landslides, those elections, taken so seriously by the challenger and a small fraction of disgruntled riders, have been disruptive to the sense of harmony on the circuit.

Last year, in an attempt to eliminate the malady, a click of riders supportive of Daryl and the status quo decided they would bring a halt to the annual political shenanigans by electing someone as vice-president who, by nature, was absolutely devoid of any ambition to be president. They found him. You guessed it. Chance Boettecher. In fact, I was the one who brought up the idea in the first place (while in a somewhat inebriated condition I must tell you). Accordingly, it was a case of put up or shut up.

To my credit, I've tried to do my job. I've made all the meetings where I've supported Daryl's leadership at every turn; fulfilled the tasks, few though they've been, that he has assigned me; and developed no ambition to unseat him at any future election. With that solid record going for me, I'm a certain shoo-in for reelection.

I call myself a good ole boy, because...well, that's what I am. I party with the guys, I guzzle beer, I chase the fillies. Underneath that good ole boy façade, make no mistake about it, I'm a bull rider first. I mean it when I say I consider Chris Ledoux's Hooked On An Eight Second Ride to be my personal theme song.

Now, I'm a bull rider from the old school. That means get on the bull and ride him until he bucks you off. The younger set is going in for practicing, practicing, practicing, and conditioning, conditioning, conditioning, and eating right, sleeping right and watching their bad habits. They're right, I know. It's the only way to stay in top form when you mount the back of a two-thousand pound animal insane to get you off there anyway he can and then stomp the living be-Jesus out of you, and it's the only way to come back from injuries quickly. Long in the tooth as I am, old habits die hard. I watch my bad habits, all right, watch them as I practice and condition them.

Unlike me, most of the other members of the PBR board of directors are definitely solid family men. Casey Applegate, the other exception. In my opinion, despite his fling with Wanda, Casey rates as solid. Although he doesn't currently flit around with any particular significant other, he, like the others, is stable in every other way. And they all know who and what I am. So with only one loose cannon at the center of things, it works.

Daryl's call woke me from a sound sleep. I picked up the phone on what I guessed was somewhere around the fifth ring. I'd stayed late at The Cowboy Hangout, like The Snake Pit, another one of those post-event haunts, hoping to coax Lena Atkins back to my room for a little horizontal boogie. She'd wheeled into the Hangout alone, looking great in a red dressy western top with heart-shaped cutout sleeves. On the backside of her twenties, she was tall and willowy, with thick red locks that wrapped around a creamy oval face perfectly. When I finally got around to dropping the question, the half dozen beers I'd plied her with apparently weren't enough. Like her friend Jodi a couple years earlier, she turned me down flat, telling me she had to get up early the next morning to pick someone up at the airport. I was so disappointed I didn't bother to ask for a name. Turned out that while I was trying to ply Lena with my charms, including the physical one, her best friend was getting herself killed in Twin Falls.

"Chance, ole buddy," Daryl began in that dry Oklahoma drawl of his, "need you to drop by my motel room for an emergency meeting."

"What's up?" I babbled like a just-rustled toddler.

"Jodi Hall was killed last night in Twin Falls."

I almost said "Who?" But about the time my mouth assumed the O position the brain kicked in. "W…what? H… how?" I stammered.

"You'll get filled in the same time as everyone else. Can you be there?"

I said I could and after giving me his room number and a meeting time for one hour later, we rang off. Shaving, showering, dressing, I couldn't help wondering what was next. First Cauy, now his sister, Jodi.

Daryl and his wife, Courtney, were staying at a plush Doubletree not far from the Will Rogers Coliseum, site of the weekend event just concluded. The room had a warm décor, with large flower depicted watercolors hanging on papered walls, a king bed, an honor bar and twice the space of the room with its double bed I'd tried to lure Lena Atkins to the night before, all the place I could afford under my frivolous spendthrift ways. Trust me, if I'd succeeded in my quest, Lena and I would have had all the space we would have required.

I was the fifth of seven board members to arrive. Present in addition to Daryl and Courtney were Casey Applegate, our secretary, though it would be Courtney who would actually take the notes and type up the minutes. (Casey's a cowboy, don't forget, and cowboys don't do things like taking notes and typing up minutes.) Tyler Kennelly, the leader of the Christian Cowboy Fellowship, and Russ Ward, seated in his high-tech, motorized wheelchair, were also present. As you would expect, we were all dressed in jeans, western shirts and cowboy hats and boots.

While the cowboys in the room looked like cowboys, I wouldn't be doing Courtney justice if I didn't toss her a little special attention. She comported the cutest pug nose you'll ever see on the plains, gold-flecked brown eyes, a thatch of dirty-blond hair, dusky rose skin and, blessed by a London birth, the most lovable cockney accent you'll ever hear in cowboydom.

How did cockney and cowboy hook up? At a PBR event at Madison Square Garden in New York City. (Where else could it have been?) She had flown in "on holiday" and was persuaded by friends to attend "a bull riding to-do," where Daryl's suave "Howdy, darlin'" during the autograph session after the event intrigued her like nothing else she'd found in the country. Her accent (combined with her angles and curves) charmed him like a witch's hex. He realized he'd better act fast before she left the Garden and — worse — flew back to Great Britain (England was what he actually thought) and boldly asked her out on the spot. The rest is history.

Her only blemish, you might say, was a near-passionate dislike of Wanda Webley Sirett. She couldn't stand the woman and never hesitated to let everyone know it — especially Wanda, snubbing her every chance she got. Had something to do with Wanda's lifestyle, she said, always with a disapproving tone. Then, too, she didn't care for the men, or the kind of men, who pandered after Wanda. Hence, there was always a strain between Courtney and myself. My adventures with Wanda were no secret. Still, Daryl and I always got along fine.

"Good, Chance is here," Daryl noted, glancing up from his seat on the bed. "We can get started." Although just as spare of frame as the average bull rider, Daryl was taller, which makes smaller bulls more difficult for him to ride than for most of us. He had brown eyes, light hair and an even lighter complexion; for whatever reason, Daryl didn't get much sun.

As I entered the room, I offered a nod all around, and then grabbed a vacant chair near the door, while the others clambered for the remaining chairs or settled on the bed.

From his wheelchair, Russ Ward, his deep-throated Louisiana dialect well displayed, said, "Where's Jason and Kyle?"

"Jason flew home directly from the event," Daryl explained. "He won't be here."

An expression of disapproval registered on Russ' weather-lined face as if on a stern elderly maiden aunt.

Seeing it, Daryl said, "I'm sure had Jason known we would be holdin' a meeting this morning he would have been here."

"Then what about Kyle?" Russ solicited.

"His flight was due in twenty minutes ago," Daryl said. "I expect him any moment." He then shot a glance at his wife who was seated at a small table beneath a hanging lamp next to the window, pencil in hand, notebook spread before her. "With five of the seven board members present let me call the meeting to order."

"Is this a formal meeting with minutes and all," Russ queried.

"You guys will have to tell me," Daryl replied, eyeing first Russ, and then, as if going down a police line-up, each of the rest of us in turn, yours truly last. "Courtney will take notes but at the end if you think this should be considered an informal discussion, we can leave it at that."

"If we take any formal action, we'll have to call it a meetin'," Tyler stated in a high-pitched Texas twang.

"I guess that's right," Daryl said, "if we take any formal

action."

Just then, a knock sounded behind me. I glanced at Daryl who gave me a nod. I got up out of my seat and opened the door. Kyle Nash, looking haggard and drained, greeted me with a, "Hey, Chance," before pushing into the room.

"Good, Kyle's here," Daryl said. "Now we can get the latest update."

After a quick round of "Hi, ya's," Kyle took a standing position next to the table between Daryl and Courtney, facing the rest of us. He was in his early thirties, average height, slender built, just right for a bull rider. In general, there were no distinguishing characteristics with regard to Kyle. In fact, one might easily conclude, with considerable justification, that Kyle was rather dull, which, in a way, made him perfect for the PBR board of directors.

"Jodi Hall was killed last night," Kyle began, not bothering to hide his Dakota brail.

"How?" Russ interrupted.

"Let's let Kyle tell it without interruption," Daryl said. "Then we'll open it to questions."

He nodded to Kyle who resumed, "She was strangled...."

# CHAPTER SIX

"Then it *was* murder," Russ exclaimed. When Daryl looked at him pointedly, he raised one hand in a way reminiscent of the gesture an insincere tennis player makes when his ball clips the top of the net before trickling over for a cheap point.

"The police aren't sayin' much but they do admit that," Kyle stated. "It appears she was killed in her motel room, which was about five blocks from the arena."

"Good," Daryl said. When we all looked at him in wonderment, he quickly corrected, "I mean bad. I mean…what I meant was it's good she wasn't killed at the arena. That, at least, helps put it a step away from any connection with the PBR."

"Is that the only thing that's important to you?" This was from Courtney. "How callous, Daryl. A woman has been murdered." As if sending a message by Morse code, she was tapping her notebook with her pen, making a muffled sound.

"No, 'course not," he sputtered. "But we're here as the board of directors of the PBR. Of course…as an individual, I'm as appalled as anyone."

Although Daryl had put his foot in it, I knew what he meant. Everyone in the room, except Courtney knew. Usually, I was the one who said things like that, or thought them anyway. Over the years, I'd learned to keep my mouth shut, so, that way, everyone only *thought* I was a dense bull rider without me actually *proving* it.

Though I understood him perfectly, I wasn't about to

leap to his defense. I knew a no-win situation when I saw it. Courtney was right. He had come off callous. Daryl was actually a sensitive guy. With Cauy's death a week earlier, and now Jodi's, I think he was a little shell-shocked. If he were smart, he would shut up and leave it there. Turned out he was, for in the next instant, he'd closed his mouth and, again, nodded to Kyle to continue.

"It appears she was murdered before midnight the night before last."

"Oh, not last night then," Russ said, looking demonstrably at Daryl, "as we'd first heard."

"No, the night before," Kyle reiterated. "The maid didn't find her until she went to make up her room yesterday afternoon. The police expert...what do they call them?"

"Pathologists," Courtney supplied.

"Yeah, him," Kyle rejoined with a hangdog grin. "He said it happened sometime Friday."

"And she was strangled?" Daryl asked.

"That's what the police are sayin'," Kyle said.

"Anything else?" Daryl pushed.

"I did manage to get a detective to share the theory they're operatin' under." Kyle stopped, seemingly expecting to be interrupted. When no one did, he continued, "He said it could have been attempted rape. It seems they believe a man somehow got into her room and tried to assault her. She struggled. He got his hands around her neck, chokin' her in an attempt to stop her strugglin'. But he went too far and killed her. With her dead he must have given up the idea of rape and got out of there as fast as he could."

"Sicko," Courtney pronounced.

"Was she left...you know?" Tyler Kennelly muttered, an embarrassed mien conquering his face.

Kyle's expression said he didn't. When Tyler failed to catch the hint, Kyle put his voice to it. "What?"

"Why do they think attempted rape and not actual rape?" Tyler managed.

"I don't really know but from what the detective I spoke with said apparently she was mostly undressed, panties off, bra unhooked, that kind of thang. No penetration, though. They'll know for sure after the autopsy."

"So she was murdered in the commission of what could have been rape or attempted rape," Daryl summarized with just enough hint of relief in his voice for Courtney to fire him a dirty look.

"That's the theory they're operatin' under until they learn otherwise," Kyle agreed.

"That's it?" Daryl asked, studying Kyle closely.

"That's all I've got for now," Kyle replied with a nod.

"Good," Daryl said, and then turned to us. "Any questions?"

We were as silent as a plot of West Texas dirt on a windless day.

Finally, Casey Applegate said, "What should we do?"

"That's the question, of course," Daryl said.

"We've got to do something," Tyler put in.

"Why?" Daryl said, as if waiting for someone to offer that very notion. "Why do we have to do anything?"

"Because..." Tyler spoke again, but he couldn't finish his thought.

"I agree with Tyler," Courtney said. "We've got to do something."

Knowing he was already in Courtney's doghouse and likely to remain there for an event or two, Daryl must have felt he couldn't make it any worse by saying, "You stay out of this, Courtney. This is the official PBR board of directors. We're the ones who have to decide."

Courtney leaped to her feet, brown eyes narrowing, "Fine," she snapped, "if that's your attitude." She threw her pen on the notebook before her, snapped up her pocketbook and stormed out of the room, slamming the door behind her. The scent of expensive perfume waft over me like a gentle breeze as she passed by.

"Now who's gonna take notes?" Russ inquired.

"I don't think we need any notes," Daryl said. "Look, guys, if she wasn't killed at the arena and she had no official connection with the PBR, I don't see why we have to do anything."

"But she was one of our people," Tyler noted.

"She was the sister of a bull rider," Daryl corrected. "She was not and never has been an employee of the PBR. Everything is mere coincidence. Unfortunately, she was a victim of a random rape, or a rape attempt." Then gazing at the closed door, he added, "We're all sorry about it, but there's nothing for us to do except let the police handle it. Hopefully, they'll find the killer and that'll be the end of it."

The room was quiet for several moments until Russ Ward said, "While I agree with Daryl that nothing official should be done, we should have no real role in the thing, it might be best that we stay on top of it."

"Why?" Daryl demanded.

"From everything Kyle said," Russ countered, "it does appear that the PBR has nothing to do with it. But what if by some fluke we do?"

"What?" Daryl was incredulous.

"Hear me out," Russ said with a braking hand raised chest high. "What if by some slim chance it was a bull rider who did it?"

"Or some other Challenger Tour personnel," Casey inserted.

"Yeah," Russ agreed, stabbing a finger at Casey. "Not likely, I know. But if it turns out to be the case, we'll want to know, if possible, before all hell breaks loose. What do they call that?"

"Damage control," Tyler supplied.

"Yeah, damage control," Russ acquiesced with a nod. "So we can put our spin on it. Meanwhile, if it turns out to be someone not connected with the PBR at all, we'll know that to. What can it hurt?"

"Won't hurt," Daryl granted, sensing which direction the wind was blowing. "So what do we do?"

"Nothing official," Russ said. "Nothing we need to make any minutes over. But something unofficial."

"Again, like what?" Daryl asked.

"We appoint someone to stay in touch with the police in Twin Falls," Tyler suggested.

"Should be someone in this room," Casey added, "to keep it from spreading among the guys."

"Should be Kyle then," Russ said. "He's already made a contact with a detective."

"Not me," Kyle countered, shaking his head. "I'm on the bubble, guys. That's why I was in Twin Falls. I was hopin' to win enough money to assure myself of a spot at Vegas."

"Why didn't you come here?" Russ asked. "More money here than at Challenger Tour events."

"I've sort of lost my confidence," Kyle replied, hanging his head like a penitent child. "Didn't give myself a chance here."

I knew exactly where Kyle was coming from, and there was no shame in it. Over the course of a year, every bull rider, the best to the bottom, loses his confidence at some point or other. The year for each man boils down to how long before he gets it back.

"How did you do, buddy?" Casey asked.

"Came in third."

"Way to go," Casey said, and the two men gave each other a high five.

"Yeah, it helps. But over the next few weeks, I've got to stick it for every dollar I can. I won't have time to be callin' Twin Falls all the time." His face was pleading.

Daryl read the message, said, "We've all been where Kyle's at."

No truer words were ever spoken. Every bull rider "works" the whole year to make that top forty-five. Using every means at hand, we struggle to "play" in Vegas. Remember my experience from three years earlier? Kyle was doing exactly what I would have been doing under the same circumstances.

"We have to thank Kyle for flying down here to bring us up to date on what happened," Daryl continued. "So who then?"

There was a marked silence in the room. Several of the guys peered around at one another.

"In a way, we're all in Kyle's boat," Tyler said. "We're the old guys. The young ones are in the driver's seat. I don't think any of us is above twenty-fifth position."

"Chance was," Casey corrected, "'till he got hurt."

"Yes," Tyler agreed eagerly, narrowing his gaze to me. "Chance was until he got hurt. But you got hurt, Chance, and you're out through the World Championships. Ain't that right?"

Reluctantly, I nodded.

"So couldn't you do it?" Tyler asked.

"Me?" I was astounded.

It wasn't by accident I hadn't uttered a word throughout the entire proceedings. Sensing where things might be headed now, I just wanted out of that room. Jodie was dead. Someone had killed her. I, like Daryl, was saddened by that, genuinely saddened. She *was* a very sweet person. But let the police do their job. If it turned out to be some bull rider or other tour personnel, it would be terrible, but let the chips fall where they may. I wasn't worried because, in truth, I doubted it was one of us. Bull riders aren't like that. Oh, we can be rough with our women, even insensitive. But kill them? Not a chance! We find them too precious. If I turned out to be wrong, we'd handle it. With luck, meaning shrewd "damage control," the PBR and its minor leagues would survive. We had too good a product not to. We had the best bull riders and the best bulls in the world. If you don't believe it when we tell you the first time, we'll tell you again.

About Tyler Kennelly. Truly a good man. Everyone was looking for him to go into ministry when he retired from bull riding. Wasn't he already serving as the leader of the Christian Cowboy Fellowship within the PBR? While I'm not a member of the association, I support it with every bit of the fervor Patrick Henry mustered for liberty. Men like Tyler perpetuate a wonderful rodeo tradition—the praying cowboy. But what kind of judge of character can you expect from a guy like that? Tyler would see the best in everyone. Maybe even the Devil himself.

The others, to a man, were the height of accountability (read: responsible types). Keep in mind we're talking about cowboys here. Still, look at them. Except for Casey they were married men. (Well, Daryl was on the bubble on that score—at least for a week or two.) Anyway, I still say they were capable and accountable and responsible.

Now I would love to be seen in that vein. For all my confidence in the potential of the PBR to survive even the worst, I knew I was the least capable person in the room to help out if we got in trouble—any kind of trouble. Therefore, the most responsible and accountable and capable thing I could do was to jump in there before the damage got out of control.

"You don't want me," I assured them shaking my head.

"Yeah," Daryl agreed.

For a moment, I wasn't sure whether he was agreeing

with Tyler or me. It took only a few more words out of his mouth to learn where he wanted to hang his Stetson. First, I watched his face animate. Then, his misting gray eyes twinkled like a host of bright stars on the clearest of West Texas nights. Finally, he said, "Chance, you're perfect for the job."

# CHAPTER SEVEN

That damn Daryl (read: scoundrel). A blind man could see what *he* was up to. He was as sure as jellybeans are sweet I was the worst person in the entire PBR for the job. Wasn't he the one who brought the thing up in the first place? Now he wanted it buried. What better way to plant it halfway to China than by handing it over to good ole Chance Boettecher?

With five multicolored pairs of eyes gaping at me like spellbound children, I was decidedly uncomfortable. In a lame attempt at stalling, I asked what the job would entail. The lie I was told was "Nothing more than calling up the Twin Falls police from time to time and asking for the latest on Jodi's murder." Someone, trying to grease the path, said, "Kyle will give you the name and the number of his police contact. Won't you, Kyle?" Kyle dutifully assured me he would. "Got it right here," he claimed.

I tried to escape. "Come on, guys. You know me. I'm into partying, women. You know, good times, women."

It didn't fly. They shot down my pitiful objections with banalities like "This won't interfere with your carousin', Chance," or "You'll be settling down again," and "You'll find another LeAnn soon."

I'm pretty sure that last one came from Daryl. After all I'd done for him. I thought of running against him for PBR president at the year-end meeting. That would teach him. The ingrate. Trust me, I knew I would come to my senses long before then.

In the end I gave in. There was no real choice in the matter. They weren't going to take "No" for an answer.

Actually, I had them right where I wanted them. For I had my own plan on how I would do the job. I wouldn't. That's right. I just wouldn't do it. Whenever they asked me what was happening, I'd tell them there was nothing new in the case. How were they going to know? Check on me by calling Twin Falls themselves? Get real. Would serve them right for appointing Chance Boettecher to the job. If they wanted to replace me as vice-president for dereliction of duty, well I resolved to go quietly. So I took the card Kyle handed me with the police detective's name and telephone number and pretended to look at it before shoving it into my shirt pocket.

We'd settled the main issue, but before we could get out of the room, Russ Ward said, "Are we going to send flowers to the funeral?"

"I think we ought to, don't you?" Daryl said eagerly, recognizing he'd been offered the first step back into his wife's good graces (read: bedroom).

We quickly agreed and the "non-meeting" adjourned. On the way out several board members threw me encouraging barbs: "It's not going to amount to much, Chance," "They'll probably find the guy in the next few days and it'll all be over," "It's only a couple of phone calls."

Outside, Casey Applegate said, "We've missed you at the game, Chance."

Casey words were magical, wrestling me out of a kind of lingering stupor. I looked at him, smiled and said, "Look for me at the next one."

"Check with Red."

I nodded.

The "game" Casey had alluded to was the Thursday night poker game played the night before each event, the World Championships excepted. About a score of bull riders, bullfighters and other PBR personnel, guys only, (yes, we're chauvinists but what can you expect from cowboys) get together and play Texas Hold 'em and Dealers Choice under a set of strict rules. Thursday nights only, last hand at two A.M., no smoking, dollar ante, ten-dollar limit. Believe me, it can get pretty steep. No, we don't have twenty guys sitting around one table playing with one deck of cards. A maximum of seven play at any one time, the others watching until someone at the table drops out, first alternate filling in and so on. Red Parham organizes everything, Cody Laws supporting him. The game begins at seven-thirty sharp in a room Red arranges with the hotel or motel where he's staying.

There is one exception to the no-women-rule, or rather two exceptions — Red's and Cody's girlfriends. They can't play in the game, of course, but we gracious allow them to waitress for us — bring us beer, remove the empties, slip over to the ATMs to get us money. For that last one, we give them our cards and pin numbers without the slightest hesitation. Red has the system down pat, and it only breaks down when he and Cody are between girlfriends. Even then we manage.

Lane and I, next to Red and Cody, were the two most regular players in the game. Until Lane's death. Since then I hadn't been able to bring myself to play. Too many memories. But it was time to put the past behind me. I needed to let Lane go. I wasn't going to forget him. Ever. I knew if I had been the one killed, I would have expected him to mourn me for a reasonable time and then get back to life — and the game. Eight weeks was reasonable enough.

I left Daryl's room and returned to my own where I packed my things, checked out, got in the Ranger and trucked west on I-20 until I reached Abilene, Texas, where I turned south on U.S. 83.

Many bull riders go home between events, especially the married ones and those owning ranches, flying to the events

Friday morning and then going home again after the short-go either the next night or Sunday morning. They tend their herds and crops, visit with wives and children and practice bull riding on the mechanical bulls most of them have set up somewhere around their places. Usually, I just move on to the next city where the PBR is holding an event and wait. Wanderlust, I guess. Lane had it too. One reason we made such good traveling companions. Then again, the poker game was played on Thursdays—had to be in town for that. But whenever the schedule permitted, like during the two-month break we have following the World Finals, or whenever I'm just in the area like following the Fort Worth event, I try to drop in at the old homestead.

My parents died in a freak hotel fire while vacationing in Florida a decade earlier. An only child, I inherited a two-story white frame dwelling on a street in Uvalde, Texas, lined with live oak trees. Some of the trees are actually in the middle of the street; the town fathers, blessed with a brief spell of wisdom, had not cut them down. Except for the four or five times each year I drop in, my home mostly sits empty. I'll never sell the place because I intend to retire there when my bull riding—and rambling—days are over. Both Lane and LeAnn always liked it too.

My neighbors, Jim and Mary Holtz, fifth or sixth generation town residents, watch over it when I'm not around. Jim, a retired owner/operator of a western wear store, was a distant relative of Uvalde's most famous historical personage— John Nance Garner, former Vice-President not of the PBR but of the good old U.S. of A., under Franklin D. Roosevelt. Not to be outdone, Mary has historical relations of distinction as well. She claims kinship with the most successful bank robbers in our nation's history, the Newton brothers. Operating in the early decades of the Twentieth Century, they never killed anyone and, luckily for them, none of them got killed. In fact, all four bank robbing brothers lived to ripe old ages, a couple of them dying in nursing homes in Uvalde sometime in the last quarter of the century.

Jim has a large riding lawn mower, an eighteen horsepower job, or there about, and likes to mow lawns, his, mine and several others on the street. Won't let us pay him a dime for doing it. "I'm just playing in my sandbox," he insists.

I reciprocate. Each year, Uvalde conducts a big Fourth of July shindig. Mary and Jim host family members who drop in for the celebration. While they have a four-bedroom house of their own, they extend the invitation to not just their children and their families, but to their siblings and their families as well. My four-bedroom house with finished basement and two and one-half bathrooms comes in handy. Despite the absence of a PBR event over the Fourth, I'm never home at that time, riding bulls in a lucrative rodeo somewhere.

I spent only two nights at home, barely long enough to catch up on the local gossip with Jim and Mary, before heading out again. Had Lane been there, we would have waited until early Thursday morning and then driven straight through to Albuquerque, New Mexico, arriving half hung over but just in time for the poker game, probably with all of ten minutes to spare.

What if we had a breakdown? We don't have breakdowns, don't believe in them. We're cowboys, remember? We may not treat our women right all the time, but we treat our pickups like our forefathers treated their horses when they were the only means of transportation available. Like the cowboy of generations earlier who tended to his horse first before himself, we change the oil and filters and check hoses, belts and fluid levels at intervals so regular even the garage mechanics think they're ripping us off.

I drive to all events west of the Mississippi, fly to the ones east of that mighty river. With all that driving, I've never had a single breakdown. Like I said, don't believe in them.

Alone though, I wasn't about to make the trip non-stop. Late Wednesday morning, I headed out on US 90 for Del Rio, and then on to El Paso where I stopped for the night. I got off to another late start the next morning, pulling into Albuquerque and my motel there a little after six-thirty. I checked into my room, grabbed all the nourishment a fast food dive had to offer and then called Red Parham's cell number. I wanted to play in the poker game.

Red answered on the second ring. He told me the locale of the game was a meeting room at the Albuquerque Holiday Inn, not far from Tingley Coliseum, site of that weekend's PBR event.

Tona met me at the door. She was a blue-eyed model-shaped morsel, wearing a plaid shirt and faded jeans, her strawberry red hair straight to the middle of her back, freckles dancing on her high cheeks.

From the scuttlebutt I'd picked up, it sounded as if Red might make the ride with her. They'd been dating for six months, about triple Red's par, so it certainly seemed serious. Red had one failed nuptial behind him, no offspring. Tona, upper twenties like most of the women connected with the tour, had no notches on her belt to date. Because she seemed able to handle Red's cowboy ways, I thought them a good fit. Of course, what did I know? I was a two-time loser—and just idiot enough to go for a third at some point down the road.

"Hi, Chance," Tona said. "Been missin' ya."

"Been missin' you too, darlin'," I flirted. "Full house?"

"You make the seventh. Can sit right in."

I glided into the room where six cowboys were sitting around a large circular table, a scattering of vacant chairs ringed around them. Striped wallpaper and a matched series of desert pictures covered the walls of the room with typical motel blandness. The carpet was a tacky blue.

The players were finishing some wildcard game one of them had picked up since I'd last played. Jacks or better and seven-card stud are played in this game, but more as diversions from such stalwarts as Baseball, Low Hole Card Is Wild, High Spade In The Hole Splits The Pot, and a host of other strategy-less standbys. Of course, Texas Hold-em has caught on with this crowd too, and we play it about half of the time. The game starts as soon as four players take seats, though its been known for three guys to drop a few bucks playing blackjack until a fourth shows up to start the "real" game.

Casey Applegate won the hand, cheerfully greeted me as he raked in the pot. The others threw in their "Hey, Chance," "There's Chance," or just "Chance," with slightly less enthusiasm that I took as disappointment at losing the pot rather than a dread of my company. Remember, those were my friends, so it made them as happy to pick my pocket as anyone else's in their iniquitous game. Truth was, they were probably going to do just that. For while I loved to play, I wasn't very lucky, which is just a loser's way of saying I wasn't very good. Still, I had my nights — occasionally. Two or three times a year I got such a fabulous run of cards I walked away the night's big winner, four or five times the runner-up. Mostly I lost, though rarely big time, and combined with my winning nights there were probably a few years out of the dozen or so I'd played that I'd actually broken about even. Seemed to me most of the guys in the game lost most of the time. Only a few, Red, Cody and a couple of the others managed to win consistently enough to have been classified as good poker players.

The others at the table besides Casey, Red and Cody were Judd Banchard, Carlton Brazeau, the PBR's eminently qualified and experienced sports medicine physician, and Randy Marshall, one of the announcers. All wore needle nose boots, brown or black; jeans, variations of faded blue; western shirts in assorted colors; and cowboy hats, black, white, brown.

I pulled a wad of money, totaling about seventy-five dollars, out of my pocket and tossed it on the table, took the vacant chair.

"Beer?" Tona called, looking at me.

I nodded.

"Good to have you back in the game, Chance," Red said. "Understand why you've been gone." Red was a stocky, azure-eyed, ruddy-complexioned cowboy of average height, which made him about two inches taller than Tona.

"Yeah, Chance," Carlton Brazeau agreed, the expression on his puffy face sober. "We all miss Lane."

"That's for sure," piped Randy Marshall, a rock-jawed man with black wavy hair and a rich booming Arkansas drawl that any microphone could amplify to perfection. "What's the game, Cody?"

Cody Laws, a short, compact-built blue-eyed, light-haired cowboy, had the deal. "In honor of Lane," he called while shuffling the red backed Bicycles with his short stocky fingers, "Draw Poker, Deuces And One-Eyed Jacks Wild."

It was Lane's favorite game. He would call it about ninety percent of the time the deal came around to him, selecting Baseball the other ten percent if it hadn't been called in a while. Lane loved wildcard games. Guess they spoke in some way to who he was.

"Where's Wynona?" I asked Cody.

He twisted his frame as if experiencing a twinge of discomfort. "We're kinda on the outs," he drawled without looking at me.

It was obvious he didn't want to say anything more about it; I let it drop.

I had hardly lost five dollars in the first hand when a knock sounded on the door. Tona opened it to a threesome of poker regulars, Clete Fassel, a tall gangly stock contractor and good friend and contemporary of Royce Sirett; Wes

Nunnemaker, a five year bull rider; and Lance Miles, our ever popular gateman, i.e. the man who opens the gate to release the bull with the hopeful bull rider precariously parked on his back. Lance, forty-six, had been performing his simple but important role on the PRCA and PBR circuits for eighteen years, ever since his forced retirement from bronc riding. Never a world champion, he'd been a consistent top ten finisher until a back injury cut short his career.

I lost another fifteen bucks in two quick rounds of Texas Hold-em and then a couple of bucks more in a game of Low Spade In The Hole Splits The Pot. Tyson Roberts, a horseman (the guy who while on horseback chases after the bull if the ornery critter doesn't leave the arena on its own), wandered in. He, like most of the PBR, was a former rodeo cowboy, in his case, a calf roper, which was why he was such an excellent horseman.

Mike Dodd strolled in next, a lanky thirty-something cameraman for the cable network that televised our sport to the country. He had a strange arrangement with Denise Hilton, a TV commentator a couple years older than himself. Denise prepared an introduction to each show, interviewed the bull riders after their rides as well as other PBR personnel on what to look for in the bulls. Neither Mike nor Denise had been married, would date each other for a few months, then would date other people for a time, and then be found sharing each other's company again. The pattern had continued since Mike had joined the broadcast team three years earlier.

Next in was Chris Hart, the arena rookie music coordinator; short and stocky with sandy hair, prematurely balding, he was the only man connected with the PBR who didn't wear boots, preferring black sneakers to the trademark footwear. Then came Chad Michaelson, naturally blond hair and rosy cheeks, who stood seventh in the standings, not bad for a mid-twenties Canadian. Chad was different from the rest of us.

While he wore standard faded jeans and western shirts outside
the arena, inside, he was the flashiest thing to ever hit the circuit,
wearing his long hair in a braided ponytail, gaudy gold-glazed
pullover tops that might fit in at an African-American nightclub
in Philadelphia and the loudest chaps you'd ever expect to see
in a rodeo arena. But he was such an easy-going cowboy, we
rapidly came to accept his little showmanship eccentricities.

The next to last guy to put in an appearance was
Kyle Nash, who greeted Casey with a slap on the hand and
a "Winnin'?" When Casey wagged his head, Kyle guffawed
like a teenage boy told an off-colored joke, before finding a seat
where he could espy his friend's hand without difficulty.

"Wife let you out tonight, Kyle?" Tyson baited. It was
common knowledge, and a sore spot for Kyle, that Lucy kept
her husband on a short leash. Kyle's reply was a face of disgust,
but nothing verbal.

We were lastly joined by the Australian Brian Farr, who
was probably the worst poker player in the entire PBR. He knew
it but, with his well-known Australian nonchalance, played
anyway. To *his* fiscal health and *our* misgivings about missing
out on the easy pickings, he stood little chance of getting into
this game, having arrived too late that night.

Three hands later, I was raking in my first pot, which
made me almost even to that point when Chad Michaelson
said, "Did you guys hear about Jodi Hall?"

# CHAPTER EIGHT

For a long moment, no one said a word. Like wolves on the lookout for prey, eyes slipped furtively around the room. Casey, Kyle and I were a part of the pack exchanging pointed looks. The only thing I knew at the moment was I wasn't going to be the one to speak up. See no evil, hear no evil, speak no evil. I hadn't seen, only heard. I didn't think that qualified me to do anything more than sit there.

"Yeah," Randy Marshall exclaimed finally. "We heard."

"Too bad," Judd Blanchard added, as he picked up the cards and began to shuffle them. Nearly everyone in the room was nodding.

It was Wes Nunnemaker who pushed on the door. "I didn't hear," he claimed with his own cowboy accent. "What happened?"

"You haven't heard?" Lance Miles quizzed. "Where you been, boy?"

"I just got into town," Wes explained as if confessing to some wrongdoing. "Came straight here. What happened?"

I expected Casey to do the honors. Turned out it was Lance who accepted them when he declared, "She was killed in Twin Falls."

"Idaho?" Wes asked.

"Yeah," Lance confirmed.

"How did she die?" Wes pursued. "Auto wreck?"

Again there was a pause of notable silence. Lance's eyes

swept the table like a roaming butterfly, even lighting on mine for a second. "Er, no," he finally said. "She was strangled."

"Mur…murdered?" Wes sputtered with a gulp.

"Yeah, murdered," Lance said.

"Do they know who did it?" Wes continued.

"Not to my knowledge," Lance admitted.

"Probably that dyke friend of hers." This was from Red Parham as he tossed a pair of cards into the middle of the table, and then raised his hand and signaled the number two. He wanted two cards. Judd Blanchard had called Jacks Or Better To Open, Trips To Win. Red liked to bluff in this game; I doubted he even held a pair.

Mike Dodd, seated on a chair directly behind me, chuckled. "Yeah, you're probably right."

"Couldn't have been her," Chris Hart injected.

"Why not?" Red said. "You don't think dykes can have lovers' quarrels."

"It happened last weekend, right?" Chris posed.

"Yeah, so?" Red returned.

"Well, she was in Fort Worth," Chris insisted. "I saw her with Chance at the Hangout, Saturday night. Isn't that right, Chance?"

"What?" I said. I hadn't the faintest idea what Chris was blathering about. We were in the middle of a hand and I held four to a flush waiting for my draw. My focus was on Judd who was giving me the questioning eye, the one that asks, "How many cards do you want?" I flashed him my index finger and he tossed me one card, face down. My heart started beating wildly in my chest. I'd filled my flush. I wanted to play cards—win some money—not jabber all night about Jodi Hall, sweet kid that she was.

I was feeling somewhat guilty, too. I hadn't called the detective in Twin Falls. (Forgotten which shirt I'd put the damn card in.) I wasn't feeling guilty about not calling the detective. I was feeling guilty about not feeling guilty about not calling the detective.

I was taken off the hook when Randy said, "You're wrong, pretty boy. She was killed Friday night. Her body wasn't discovered until Saturday afternoon. Most of us didn't get the word till sometime Sunday. That's why we thought she was killed Saturday."

"So is anyone questioning Lena?" Chris asked.

That caught my attention. I looked at Chris, then Randy. Just then Cody Laws, seated on my right, said, "Check."

It was up to me to check or bet. I looked down at my pile of money, and then my cards. I had been momentarily distracted. Could I win this pot? What was the game? Jacks Or Better To Open. No, Jacks Or Better To Open, Trips To Win. I could win it. I bet ten dollars.

"How many cards did he draw?" Casey asked from across the table.

"One," Judd replied.

"Straight," Casey intoned, adding a knowing nod.

"He's bluffing," Carlton claimed.

"Chance doesn't bluff," Red stated mechanically.

"The hell he don't," Casey said, eyeing me pointedly. "Not often, but enough to make you think."

"And this is the perfect game to try it," Randy agreed.

"Yeah, I still say he's bluffing," Carlton repeated.

"Cost ten bucks to find out," I said, with a purposefully forced smile.

"No, it won't," Red said. We all looked at him. He was grinning all Cheshire-like. "Cause it's gonna cost him twenty. I raise ten."

I liked Red's action. If anyone liked to bluff it was Red. Even if he wasn't bluffing and had a better hand, he was at least giving me a chance to win a big pot. Everyone called. They pretty much had to. Under the rules of the game, if anyone dropped out at that point, they were out until someone had trips or better and won the pot. No one liked to be in that position. You stayed in even if you had nothing. This time, I had something. The bet came around to me.

"So is anyone questioning Lena?" Chris asked again.

"See your ten and raise ten more," I said.

"Awww, damn," Cody complained, joined an instant later by most of the others at the table.

"I'm sure the police have questioned her," Randy guessed.

"And ten more," Red oozed, gloating.

There were more "Awww's" and "damns" as the others saw what was going down.

Casey dropped out, saying, "One of 'em's got it."

There were two more raises, accompanied by two more dropouts, before Red finally called. I won. Red did have three sevens. He hadn't been bluffing after all — this time.

While I raked in my second pot in a row, Chris Hart said, "Does anyone know if Lena was in Fort Worth last Friday night?"

"I don't know," Wes said. "Maybe Chance knows. He was hittin' on her Saturday night."

"The dyke?" Chris asked, eyeing me with incredulity.

"Yeah," Wes exclaimed with a snicker. "Did you see her Friday night, too?"

"Huh?" I was eyeing my winnings. Way ahead. If you think I wanted to scarf them up and bolt out of there, you are sadly mistaken. I came to play, expected to lose, but now I would be playing, for probably the next few hours or so, with other people's money. Why not have some fun. That was the way Lane and I always approached that very situation — rare though it was for either of us — and it was exactly what I intended to do until two in the A.M.

Except, like a nagging cold, the conversation about

Jodi Hall wouldn't go away. It just hung in there like a punch drunk fighter too beaten up to fall down. For some inexplicable reason, this passel of cowboys wanted to keep picking at it, like an itching scab. Somehow I figured into this thing but I truly couldn't figure out how. Why was my name constantly cropping up?

The next dealer was Randy Marshall. He called "No Peeking," the poorest excuse of a game in the annals of gambling. That's my opinion and I'm sticking to it.

"How many cards?" Red asked.

"Oh," Randy mused, rubbing his chin with the fingers of one hand. "Let's make it interesting. Seven cards. Ante up, boys."

I threw in my dollar, wincing in the process. Since the game was a no-brainer, I allowed my focus to drift to the conversation in progress.

"What's all this about?" I said, peering alternately at Chris and Randy.

Randy, while dealing out the cards one by one face down, was the one who spoke. "We want to know if you were hitting on Lena Atkins last Friday night in Fort Worth?"

"Lena Atkins?"

"Yeah," Red put in, "Lena Atkins. Jodi's significant other."

"What?" I said, truly baffled. "What do you mean Jodi's significant other?"

"Just what I said," Red said. "Haven't you been listenin'?"

"Hell no, he hasn't been listening," Randy complained. "He's been winning the last two pots."

"You were hittin' on her Saturday night, remember?" Red resumed. He was like a hunter chasing after a deer he knows he's wounded but hasn't brought down. "We want to know if you were chasin' her skinny dyke ass Friday night. In other words, was she around?"

"Your turn, Chance." This was from Casey.

"My turn for what?"

"To turn your cards over."

"Oh." I looked at my cards, said, "Did we bet?"

"Everyone checked."

That suited me. "What have I got to beat?"

"A pair of sevens."

I turned over the deuce of clubs, the trey of diamonds, the king of clubs, the ten of spades, the second red trey, the spade queen, and the five of hearts. As far as I was concerned, I'd gotten lucky. I was out of that hand. I wouldn't have to give away any more of my "other people's money" on that game. Maybe this would be my night after all.

Out of the hand, I focused on the conversation I'd allowed myself to get drawn into. "What's going on?" I said, looking at Red.

Red glanced up. "Didn't you know about Jodi Hall?"

"I know she was murdered in Twin Falls last weekend. What else?"

"She wasn't turned on by cowboys."

"Preferred cowgirls, if you know what I mean," Cody Laws clarified.

"You mean…?" I said.

Red and Cody nodded simultaneously. "That's exactly what we mean," Red said.

"I hadn't heard," I confessed.

"We gathered that when we spotted you hitting on Lena Atkins last weekend at the Hangout," Chris remarked with a gleeful laugh.

"I guess that's why she turned me down," I said with a shrug. Did I ever hate admitting that to this crowd. I did it because I'd learned the wisdom of something my mother had imparted to me a long time ago: Crow was best eaten warm.

"But did you see her Friday night?" Randy asked.

I shook my head. "Nah. Only Saturday."

"I bet the cops will want to talk to you," Randy warned.

"Me? Why me?"

"She'll probably tell them she spent most of Saturday night with you," Randy explained. "They'll want you to vouch for that."

"But I wasn't with Lena Friday night. In fact, I don't remember seeing her Friday night at all. If Jodi was killed Friday night, how do I come off vouching for Lena? Makes no sense to me."

"You help her some," Randy suggested with a shrug. "It would have been pretty hard for her to have killed Jodi Friday night, then fly down to Fort Worth and let you hit on her Saturday night."

I shot a look at Kyle Nash. He was still seated behind Casey Applegate. Only he wasn't watching his friend's cards, was staring down at his hands, intertwining his fingers nervously. "Not that hard," I muttered, barely above a whisper.

Kyle must have heard me, for he glanced up, eyes honing in on me like a viper trying to mesmerize a rat. I'm sure he guessed I was remembering how he'd managed to fly into Fort Worth Sunday morning after competing in the Twin Falls Challenger Tour event the night before. Although he stared at me for a long moment, he said nothing, then returned his gaze to his still twiddling hands. His edginess had me wondering.

I remembered, too, that Lena Atkins had been somewhat edgy Saturday night. Not greatly so, just some. Still, was her edginess because of the absence of what I had just learned was her lover—her sexual preference a bombshell to me—or something else? Maybe I had misread her emotional state in the first place. Maybe it wasn't edginess I'd seen in Lena the previous Saturday night. Guilt? Remorse? Pain?

Then, too, maybe what I'd really noticed was fatigue. To fly to Twin Falls sometime Friday, murder Jodi, fly back to Fort Worth Saturday morning or afternoon to attend the event, and then hangout at the nightclub until all hours of the night, all in an attempt to make it look as if she'd never left Fort Worth in the first place, would have been exhausting.

As I tossed my ante into the center of the table for the next hand, I wondered if the police had questioned Lena, or if they'd even been aware of Jodi's sexual preference.

# CHAPTER NINE

Turned out I was the night's big winner. Took away over eight hundred dollars of "others people's money."

Two nights later, Saturday, I marked down a twenty-three and a half for the effort Pugnacious, a four-year old spotted Brahma-mixed, put out, and a twenty-three for the ride, and did my share to help Tyler Kennelly to a ninety-two and a half, and a victory in the event by half a point over Chad Michaelson.

I know youth will be served, but that night, maybe I gave one to the old guy. Earlier, I had judged Chad's ride in the short-go, an outstanding display of world-class bull riding on Prime Destruction, Bull of the Year two years ago. Prime Destruction hadn't lost a step when Chad rode him "like a yard dog" as one colorful TV commentator, a retired world champion bull rider, liked to say. Prime Destruction was truly in his prime that night. He broke from the gate and turned away from Chad's hand, the more difficult direction for the bull rider. Bucking and spinning without quit for the full eight seconds, he'd tried every which way from Sunday to throw the rider off his back. However, Chad, ponytail flapping as if blown by a western wind, had kept his seat and, with flair, spurred him like a man possessed for the last four seconds or so.

Now before the animal rights people get too uptight, let me hasten to point out that spurring hurts a bull about as much as a ladybug landing on a man's arm. The rowels on the spurs are short and dull, barely tickling their thick hides. Spurring gives the rider extra points, however, because he puts himself at

greater risk of being tossed off in the process. I'd marked Chad
a twenty-three, Prime Destruction the same number. When I
judged Tyler's ride, I thought he merited a twenty-three, also.
I gave Pugnacious a twenty-three and a half, a half point more
than I gave Prime Destruction. The difference? Nothing more
than one judge's opinion of which girl is prettier. (Yeah, I stole
that one, too. It's something else that retired bull rider/color
commentator liked to say.)

Pugnacious, big and powerful and fast, had come to put
on a show that night. He'd broken from the gate and turned to
his right, into Tyler's hand. Yes, that's better for the rider, but
in this case it was totally unexpected. In the past, Pugnacious
had always followed a predictable pattern, which didn't make
him easy to ride. He would break from the gate, and then turn
to the left. I could justify the extra half point on the basis of the
change of pattern alone, but there was more. He spun faster
and bucked higher than I'd ever seen him do before. Actually,
if he kept up that kind of bucking for a full season, he just might
take away Bull of the Year honors one day. I know Clete Fassel
would have liked it, since he owned the animal. But Tyler did
his part, too. Spurring and scrambling at every turn, he'd make
it look easy.

Rich Nobels, the other judge, a two-time PRCA World
Champion who retired as a bull rider a decade earlier, gave
Pugnacious a twenty-three. He, too, thought the bull had put on
quite a show. And he'd given a twenty-three to Tyler, same as
myself, resulting in a half point difference between our scores.
Chad would not complain. None of the bull riders ever did.
They understood. Over the long season it all evened out. Maybe
I can be second-guessed, but I'll sleep okay.

Chad's second place finish that night leaped him from
seventh position all the way up into second place in the World
Championship standings behind Justin Diver, who held a
commanding lead in the race for that title and the million dollar

bonus it carried for winning it. Justin, after an unbelievable first half of the season, winning five events besides placing in the top six in four others, had cooled off considerably in the second half. Adding insult to injury, he'd gotten bucked off in the money round that night at Albuquerque, finishing tenth, well behind Tyler and Chad. With Chad coming on, it might turn out to be a horserace for the world title after all.

John Henry? That bull seemed to be growing meaner and meaner with each event. Killing Cauy Hall was a freak accident. His penchant for more and more violence in the arena was anything but, which had begun before the Cauy Hall episode.

In truth, it was nothing new. We had seen bulls like him before. Lots of them. As a two or three year old they aren't so bad. As they age, though, they develop a lust for going after bull riders (and bullfighters and anyone else who gets in their way) as if possessed of a license to kill. Several great bulls, Bodacious to name one, had to be retired early because of their extremely violent natures.

John Henry, ranked as he was, was usually saved for the short-go. To lower his profile, Wanda had withdrawn him the previous weekend at Fort Worth because he'd killed Cauy in Billings the weekend before. Back for Albuquerque, Jason Moss, in third position in the short-go, had drawn him. Jason was bucked off two jumps out of the chute, just as John Henry entered a spin to his left. Coming around, the bull spotted Jason scrambling to his feet and bolted for him. Jason, seeing the position he was in, started for the rail. He was fast; the bull, faster. Ignoring the bullfighters trying to draw his attention, John Henry charged Jason, catching him "a shot in the shorts" that pushed him along faster toward the rail. Too fast. Jason couldn't keep his feet and like a baseball player sliding headfirst into a base, sprawled facedown in the dirt. Then John Henry lowered his rock-like head and butted Jason in the back.

Running right over him, the enraged animal stepped on Jason's right thigh with a hind hoof. Only then were the bullfighters able to cover the downed bull rider with their bodies. Lance Miles, the gateman, swinging the escape chute gate wide open, caught John Henry's attention. Distracted from his murderous intention, the bull pranced proudly out of the arena, his night's work, from his perspective, a rousing success.

Jason managed to gain his feet with the aid of the sports healers and, after taking several guarded steps, found he was able to move on his own. The crowd gave him a stirring ovation as he limped unharmed out of the arena. I say "unharmed" because the limp and the bruises…well, that's all they were—a limp and a few bruises. He would be able to ride in the next event. Any cowboy who can make his next ride is "unharmed" by bull riding standards.

I received numerous accolades for my job that night when I walked into The Bucking Bull, a visibility-challenged post-event honky-tonk. Kyle Nash greeted me first, offering a rousing, "Hey, Chance." He'd come in fifth, which would decidedly solidify his chances for making it to Vegas for the World Championships. He was obviously regaining his confidence. For the record, I didn't give him a thing; he'd earned it himself.

Then several bull riders that included Adriano Alvarez, Chad Michaelson and Brian Farr, seated at a table not far from the door, called me over. Also at the table, were Craig Kelton, sans Wanda, Red Parham, Tona to his right, and his ever present sidekick, Cody Laws, Wynona to his right (I guessed they'd made up and were an item again). Wynona was a cutie, with big doe eyes, chestnut hair and a pug nose. Although she loved cowboy boots, she never wore anything but low flats when around Cody. That way she managed to keep the top of her head on a par with his whenever he wore his cowboy boots, which was all the time.

"Great job tonight, Chance," Red sounded, echoed in turn by the others.

Even Brian, who'd scored an eighty-four on his second bull and missed the short-go by two points, in that distinctive Aussie accent of his, said, "You got that bull of mine right, Chance. He didn't buck worth a wallaby's damn."

He was right. Often, and all the bull riders know this, it's the luck of the draw. A bull rider doesn't want to just ride his bull, he wants to score enough points to get into the short-go where he has a chance to win money and points. Each event consists of a Friday night go-round in which all forty-five bull riders compete. Then on Saturday night, there is a second go-round, in which, again, all forty-five bull riders compete. Only the top scoring fifteen riders on two bulls go on to the short-go round, the money round, where the top six finishers win cold hard cash. At the end of the season, in October, the top forty-five bull riders go to Las Vegas for the World Finals.

In a nutshell, bull riders want to get to the money round at every event. If a rider, like Brian, that weekend, gets bucked off in one of the rounds, he has to make a high score, usually eighty-six or better, on the lone bull he does ride, in order to make it to the short-go. That's because bull riding is so demanding, there are seldom fifteen bull riders who ride two bulls to make it to the short round. It happens, but only twice that I can recall, meaning you can make it to the short-go on one bull where a successful ride can put you in the money, usually around fifth or sixth place. It begins with drawing at least one bull in the first two rounds that will buck hard and high enough to let you get to the short-go in the first place. That's where the luck of the draw comes in.

Brian Farr, after getting bucked off the night before, drew poorly on Saturday, the non-ranked Vindicator, who can buck well enough to allow a rider to score in the high eighties if he's on, but who wasn't that night, causing Brian's score to suffer as a result. Brian knew it, and Rich and I knew it. Too bad, but next weekend, he'd get another chance.

After bantering with the guys a few moments, I moved on, meandering through the crowd in search of a table with an empty chair. Just as the band struck up a hot rendition of Faded Love, I espied a lone seat among a huddle of familiar faces off to my left. Royce Sirett had his arm draped comfortably across my second ex's shoulders. LeAnn was glowing like a child with rosy cheeks, which I contributed to her impending motherhood. At the table, too, were Travis Nokes, his arm wrapped around the shoulders of his wife, Marie, and Judd Blanchard with his arm covering some local gal who was introduced to me as Karen.

Judd was one of the guys who'd had a fling with Wanda. This was back when he'd been happily married. Anyway, he'd told me he and his wife had been happy and I believed him. He'd said he'd become somewhat complacent in the marriage, and Wanda had caught him at just the right (read: wrong) time. By the way, his wife also carried the moniker "Wanda." I understood how Judd, though still in love with his wife, could be tempted. After all, he was just a man, and a cowboy at that. Where women are concerned, cowboys have no chance. Don't forget, we have an image to live down to. With something packaged like Wanda, there's nothing easier in the world.

Following the affair, which lasted somewhere between a week and ten days when Wanda (Webley Sirett) tired of him, Judd swallowed his pride and crawled back to his true Wanda, who, still loving the crazy bullfighter, took him back. We heard she made him perform some strange penance that the two of them never divulged but giggled over like a pair of sixth graders whenever the subject came up. Needless to say, there was no love lost between Wanda and Wanda (Webley Sirett). Still, the marriage seemed to run its course and Judd and his wife divorced a couple of years later, fortunately no children to get harmed in the process.

There was an empty chair, two in fact, though not together, at the table. I took the one between LeAnn and Judd, and then ordered a beer from the cute waitress, who'd appeared as if from behind a curtain despite the fact there was no curtain. I looked at LeAnn's glass, then her, "Hope that's a coke."

She stuck out her tongue playfully, and then smiled, before saying, "Root Beer, if it's all the same to you."

I could tell she was pleased I'd taken enough interest in her unborn child to hope she wasn't imbibing anything alcoholic.

"Chance, you sure look like some lost puppy," Travis said.

"Lost puppy?"

"Yeah, you're running around here without your other half."

"My other half?"

"Yeah, your old buddy, Lane."

I bristled, turned away. I saw LeAnn, her jaw opened wide in horror. She couldn't believe what Travis had spewed either. I looked at Royce. His eyes darted away, back. His lips pursed as if he were about to offer something sympathetic. When he said nothing, I gave my ex a look that said it was all right, turned first to Travis, then to Judd, and said, "What do you fellows think of the job Buddy's doing?"

"Great job," Judd put in before Travis could shove his foot deeper into his mouth.

Travis, realizing his faux pas, echoed Judd's comment, with his own, "Great job."

"Great job," Judd repeated, and then gulped his beer.

"But he ain't gonna be no Lane," Travis added, with a distinct lowering of his head for emphasis.

I knew he was trying to atone for his bungle.

"I mean," Travis continued, "we've already had one death since he's been here."

"But that wasn't Buddy's fault," Marie piped in, slapping her husband's arm with an open hand.

"Course not, darlin'," Travis said. "That ain't what I meant neither."

"We know you didn't," Judd said, tossing me an imploring look.

I winked at him. I liked these guys. Travis hadn't meant to fall into it. His heart was in the right place, just a case of too much beer and trying too hard. Well, that and insensitivity and not thinking. Hey, he's a cowboy and that's the cowboy way. To help bail him out, I said, "In truth, Lane might not have saved Cauy."

Everyone's gaze fixed on me, incredulity gushing from multi-colored eyes like oil from a new well. To them, it was as if I had spoken heresy.

"What I mean is," I began to explain, "Lane might have been in perfect position. Probably would have." Everyone nodded. "He might have tossed his hat at exactly the right moment, at exactly the right place, and that damned ole bull might have ignored him and the hat and still caught Cauy the way he did."

"Course," Judd hastily concurred.

"But he would have been in the best position to try for the save," Travis interjected.

"But Buddy's doin' an outstandin' job," Judd said. "I'm not afraid to be in the arena with him."

"Me neither," mimicked Travis.

The waitress brought my beer, smiled sweetly as she set it before me. I picked up the bottle, took my first sip and watched Wanda Sirett as she wandered through the crowd, slowly making her way straight for our table.

# CHAPTER TEN

It was obvious Wanda was inebriated; at least two sheets to the wind. (I think it was the staggering that gave it away.) It was a dead solid certain she was going after Royce.

I shot a glance at the big man. He stroked his goatee while his face cringed. I'm certain he wanted to shrivel up like a dried leaf and slip through the floorboards, anything to avoid the coming inundation. LeAnn's features tightened at the sight of Royce's ex meandering toward them. She did her best to disguise it, but I could sense she'd reacted to Royce's reaction. Then they both smiled. Their expressions contained about as much sincerity as one would expect from an evil genius about to destroy the hero who is trying to stop him from taking over the world. (I'd just watched an old James Bond movie before I wrote that.)

Wanda saw the insincerity. It didn't stop her. She was about to have as much fun as she'd probably had since before the night she'd learned her bull had killed Cauy Hall.

I hadn't seen her since Cauy's funeral. In the tight aqua-colored pantsuit that accented her bust and the rest of her figure like (I can't believe I'm going to write this) a Bond girl, no one could have missed her. Wanda loved to make a spectacle of herself wherever she was. She liked to pace the narrow walkway behind the chutes during events, baiting the other stock contractors and taunting the cowboys both before and after their rides. Maybe, after Cauy's death, she decided to keep a low profile for a time because she was the owner of John

Henry. It would be nice to know she possessed some degree of sensitivity. It would be nicer if it were true.

Travis must have been missing her, too, because spotting her approaching, he said, "Well, if it ain't ole Wanda. Where you been keepin' yourself, darlin'? Ain't seen you in awhile."

"Watch that old stuff, Travis honey," she said, eyeing Marie. "I don't like to be referred to as old." As if to accent her point, she reached out, grabbed his white felt hat and pushed it down over his eyes.

Travis corrected the position of his Stetson, pushing it farther back on his head than where it had sat before. "I wasn't calling you old...."

"I know you weren't," Wanda agreed pointedly, "just watch your damn language around a lady."

Wanda eased herself into the other vacant seat, grabbed the arm of a passing waitress, ordered a trio of tequila shooters and then smiled at us with all the warmth of a starving hyena. "Well, ain't we all just a fabulous bunch of exes."

"Speak for yourself, Wanda," snapped Marie, leaning in closer to Travis and hooking her arm through his.

The smile Wanda flashed her was most condescending. "You're right, Marie dear. I should have said exes and almost exes."

"Almost doesn't count except in horseshoes," Karen returned smugly. At that, I spotted Judd clinching his date's shoulder as if cautioning her.

"Don't forget hand grenades, dear," Wanda jibed, equally smug. "They're explosive, don't forget."

"Just like you, Wanda," Royce shot in, in an attempt at biting sarcasm, something very un-Royce-like.

"Why of course just like me, Royce darlin'," Wanda agreed sardonically. "What the hell you think we're talkin' about here?" Then she laughed outlandishly.

Marie rolled her eyes, said, "Come on, Travis. Let's

dance," and tugged on his arm.

"But the band ain't playin' yet, darlin'," Travis noted.

"Will be soon enough," Marie assured with a glance at Wanda that said no music was better than the serenade playing at that table, and she continued to pull on Travis' arm until he slid off his chair and followed her, reaching back to grab hold of the neck of his near-empty bottle of beer.

I couldn't miss the venom with which LeAnn was eyeing Wanda. You know the old expression: If looks could kill.... But she held her tongue, which surprised me. Very un-LeAnn-like. I'd never known LeAnn to restrain herself when it came to insulting Wanda, and that included before she ever started dating Royce. In fact, as far back as when we were together, LeAnn never hesitated to utter disparaging remarks about Wanda every chance she got. In her defense, she never said anything behind Wanda's back that she wouldn't say to her face. LeAnn was that kind of girl, nothing two-faced about her.

Wanda could have cared less. In fact, I don't think she was completely happy unless she had all the women traveling the PBR circuit carping about her. Behind her back or to her face, it didn't matter. I think she saw it as jealousy on their part, something she took as flattery. In truth, it all flowed out of her boorish behavior. Was she insecure? Did she have low self-esteem? Maybe. Probably. I don't know. Whatever, she was Wanda being Wanda.

So why was LeAnn so taciturn tonight? Must have had to do with Royce. Maybe he'd gotten her to promise to hold her tongue. Maybe he hoped the two of them would treat Wanda like adults are supposed to treat heckling children. If LeAnn didn't bait Wanda, or humor her, or whatever, Wanda would get bored and stop baiting him, tormenting him and — mercy of mercies — go away.

On the other hand, I had to wonder if for some depraved

reason Royce liked having Wanda around, as if in a sense they were still together. Was that why he'd caved during the divorce proceedings and surrendered a third of his livestock to her, including John Henry?

However, with LeAnn on the scene, the picture had decidedly changed. Like from black and white to color. Now, he wanted to get rid of Wanda. She was superfluous to the new Royce. Then again, maybe I was reading too much into LeAnn's silence in the face of the enemy.

But Wanda, being Wanda, wasn't about to go quietly. In the next instant, she batted her green painted eyelids provocatively, and said, "But we don't want any little explosions going off around us, now do we, Roycey?"

Roycey! Never heard her call him that before.

Royce rolled his eyes; apparently, this was a new one for him, too. LeAnn looked away in disgust. Lips moving, I knew she was cursing under her breath.

The waitress brought Wanda her drinks along with a dish of limes and a shaker of salt, all of which she took without so much as a thank you. She downed the first shooter straight, set her glass on the table and then sucked on a lime while ignoring the salt.

Then, eyeing Royce pointedly, she coaxed, "Do we Roycey, dear?"

Royce twiddled his half empty beer bottle and stared passed her. Wanda reached out and tapped the back of his hand, which he jerked away as if she'd touched it with a lighted match. Wanda smirked at his reaction. "Come on now. Answer Mommy," she wheedled as if talking to a baby.

That was the last straw for LeAnn. She slammed her fist down on the table and slid to the edge of her chair. "That's enough, Wanda! Why don't you take your silly baby talk and get out of here? You sure as hell know what you can do with it."

Was I ever proud of my ex. I knew she couldn't remain silent forever. I could almost feel her other hand tighten in Royce's.

Wanda, bless her heart, didn't flinch, wasn't the least intimidated, never was. In fact, I don't ever remember seeing her flustered, not once.

Anyway, she just laughed, fixed her gaze on LeAnn, and said, "I heard the wonderful news that you're going to be a mama, LeAnn." Then she turned her eyes to Royce. "And that of all things, Roycey here is going to be a father. Can you believe it?" Without pause, she continued, "Do you know yet if it's going to be a boy or a girl? I bet it's a girl. I don't think Royce is capable of producing boys. Then I guess I don't really know what all Royce is capable of. He can be so full of these little surprises. I mean, getting ready to play house and all has to rank right up there."

LeAnn looked at Royce who was shaking his head. Then, surprising, she looked at me. I couldn't fathom in the least what that meant.

The band came out and the members picked up their instruments, tuned them and prepared to strike up their first number of the set.

Judd Blanchard nudged his date out of her seat while saying, "I've had enough of this. Let's dance, darlin'." The girl nodded her assent and together they made their way toward the dance floor.

After Judd and his date left, Royce looked at Wanda through slits of eyes. "What is it you want?" he demanded.

"Why nothin', Roycey dear. I just want everything to turn out fine for you and LeAnn. I want you to have your little family and live happily ever after if that's what you want."

"I'll see that we do, Wanda," Royce replied gruffly. "Does that suit you?"

"Now don't you feel bad that you're talking to me in

that tone of voice?" Wanda chirped liked an innocent bird. "But I'll take that to mean we see eye to eye." She downed the second of her shooters.

"Eye to eye about what?" LeAnn wanted to know. She looked at Wanda and then at Royce.

"Oh, nothing for you to worry your pretty little head over, LeAnn dear," Wanda assured, picking up her third shooter. "Just go on and enjoy marriage and motherhood. Roycey is going to take care of you very nicely. Just like he's always taken care of me."

Having completed her ex-husband's humiliation to her perverse satisfaction, Wanda downed the third shooter, sucked on a lime for a moment and then rose as if to leave. But Wanda was not through, for she wiggled the index finger of a hand in Royce and LeAnn's direction and said, "Now let's have no more fighting from you two lovebirds." Flashing a mischievous air, she said, "That's right. I heard all about it."

Royce and LeAnn stared at each other, wisely held their tongues. It was obvious Wanda had learned of the tiff between Royce and LeAnn, the same one LeAnn had describe to me when she told me she was pregnant.

Prattling on, Wanda said, "Course everyone loves making up after a good fight. Though I've found drinkin' helps, too. I'll send over a round for the table. My treat." Then leaving her empty glasses on the table as if we could not possibly live without some residue of her presence, she sashayed away, calling back, "Bye all," as she went.

"What was that all about, Royce?" LeAnn demanded.

Royce gulped his beer, trickles of brew dripping off his goatee.

"Royce!"

"Damn if I know," Royce snapped. "You know how she is."

LeAnn saw he wasn't going to say anything more. She

roughly extracted her hand from his grip, leaped from her seat in a way that made it clear she was in a huff and, mumbling something about "bathroom," charged off.

Hard to believe. Not LeAnn running off in a huff. Nothing unusual there. She must have done that a dozen times during our courtship. But Royce, why, he was the easiest guy in the world to get to spill the beans. Sometimes you didn't even have to prod him. He was one of those guys that would come up to you, ask you a question and, without giving you a chance to reply, start answering the question himself. He'd tell you anything and everything. One year, he bragged about how much money he had to pay the IRS. Oh, he said it in that whining, complaining way that we all use when speaking of taxes, but we knew he was just bragging, letting us know how much money he'd made the previous year. Still, we all loved and relished the guy. There wasn't an easier going soul connected with the PBR tour.

But it was because he *was* her ex, that I put him on my list of suspects, when a week later in Atlantic City, New Jersey, Wanda Webley Sirett turned up strangled.

# CHAPTER ELEVEN

Fortunately, Wanda was killed Saturday night and not Friday. Believe me, I know how callous that sounds. Of course, it was unfortunate for Wanda whichever night. I'm one of those people who believe in little other than God, country and the PBR. No, make that God, the PBR and country. I do love this wonderful land, still tingle at the playing of the Star Spangled Banner before each event, but when it comes right down to it, it's God and the PBR, one and two. Now, I'm not all that religious, not even a part of the Christian Cowboy Fellowship led by Tyler Kennelly. I'm a believer. I'll never deny that, just not much of a practitioner.

Had Wanda been killed on Friday night, it would have put some kind of damper on Saturday night. Who would've had his heart in what he was doing? Certainly not the cowboys who have to be one hundred percent focused every time they climb on the back of a two thousand pound bull. Could we then expect the support personnel to provide complete attention to what he or she was doing?

Like a mysterious virus, the news would have gotten out; the Atlantic City media would have turned it into a circus. What would that have meant for Saturday night's attendance? With it all, visions of disaster danced in my head. Maybe worse...cancellation.

Let's return to my callousness. It's there, can't be denied. But let's put it in perspective. I loved Wanda Sirett. No, not in the romantic sense, though there was that brief period right after we slept together the first time. That, however, was long over. She was...Wanda. A beloved character. Why, she had more entertainment value than a houseful of stand-up comedians, more than most movies produced in Hollywood.

Take the weekend in San Jose, California a year and a half ago, when she and Royce got into it. I sat at the table with others throughout Wanda's entire chiding of her ex. A number of people seated around us got disgusted and pulled out early. I loved every biting word of it. Neither Royce nor Wanda ever suggested, by word or look or deed that what was happening was something private and that I should go. They would never have dreamed of it. They knew I was there and, like toddlers in a sandbox being observed by adults, they expected me to watch them "play."

I made love to her a couple of times, and loved that, too. The first time I slept with Wanda was three years earlier, on a Friday night after the first go-round, Colorado Springs, Colorado. It was great. For her, too, so she said, and I believed her. Anyway, the next night at The Rampage, after the event, when I expected Wanda to sit and dance with me, looking to a reprise of our previous night's escapade in what just might be a budding of a serious romance, she waltzed in and out with Horace Moody, the night's third place finisher, now retired to his Missouri ranch. First and second went to a pair of early twenties cowboys. That left them out, leaving Horace the oldest money earner that night. Wanda didn't fool with them if they were under thirty years of age, or twenty-nine, or twenty-eight. Definitely twenty-seven. Anyway, watching my budding romance wither on the vine, I was angry and jealous—and wanted to kill her dead—but like everyone, I soon got over it and forgave her.

LeAnn, when we were married, loved to rag on Wanda. Yes, but in a way she loved her, too. That was how we all saw her. I know, because I heard it over and over again, and I believed it, every time.

Who would want to kill her? No one. Everyone. Everyone at one time or another. Myself included.

Except that my being the one who discovered Wanda's lifeless body only encourage the police to put me on *their* suspects' list.

Saturday night in Atlantic City, after Chad Michaelson, continuing a streak of hot riding, finished the last ride of the night, a ride that closed the gap on Justin Diver for the World Championship to just over a thousand points, a rather urgent nature call had me scampering out of the arena for the nearest men's room, the one near the walkway back to the pens where the bulls were kept. I took care of business and made my way over to the announcers' stand where I turned in my judge's paraphernalia to LeAnn. I then got caught up in a conversation with Daryl Minnich that lasted until the place had pretty well cleared out. The arena personnel had even dimmed some of the lights to signify it was time for any stragglers to make tracks. Our conversation was lengthy because Daryl had wanted to let me know that the bull riders were saying I was doing such a good job as a judge that if I wanted the position permanently, it was mine. That would mean retiring from bull riding. Needless to say, I wasn't sure I was ready to move in that direction and told him so. The prognosis of my injury was favorable, so Carlton had said, and, of course, I believed him.

Daryl informed me the PBR would have to fill the position for the next season soon, but I had until after the World Finals Championships to make a decision. With the same judges working each of the events, the bull riders received more consistent scoring. It wasn't perfect, and fill-in judges were needed from time to time throughout the year, but, on the whole, the bull riders were satisfied with the system.

I was filling in for Jake Forsyte, a former bull rider and all around great cowboy, who'd retired six years before and become a judge at thirty-four. A ranked bull name Stampede's Delight had put Jake on the ground, and then stepped on his hip twice while making for the escape chute. Stampede's Delight caught him where the ball of the femur meets the socket in the pelvis. Crushed it into seven pieces. He'll limp for the rest of his life. In fact, Daryl was telling me during our lengthy exchange that Jake was going to have to give up his judging position because he was experiencing a slow disintegration of his joint area, which meant he would probably have to spend most of his time in a wheelchair. He would be able to walk some, Daryl said, but it would amount to little more than a few steps from his living room to the bathroom and back.

"Will the PBR find him another position?" I wanted to know. Naturally, I was dubious about taking another man's job. Jake needed to eat, too.

"You know us, Chance," Daryl said. "We take care of our own. Believe it or not, Jake has bookkeeping skills. Don't know where he got 'em, but there's always a place for a guy like that in the organization."

I told him I would think about it, evaluate the progress of my recovery and let him know before I left Las Vegas following the World Finals. That satisfied him and together we made our way toward the exit at the back of the arena. By that time, only a few arena personnel lingered, most of them in the office area. The bulls had been removed, loaded onto the trucks that would carry them to the airport from where they would be flown west to Phoenix, Arizona, for the next event. (PBR bulls travel first class.)

Although the lighting consisted of little more than the faint overhead emergency lights, Daryl and I had no problem finding our way past the holding pens where the bulls were kept while awaiting their turn in the arena. Somehow, probably because of the dimness of the place, my eyes caught a single reflective sparkle that drew my attention to the back of the very last pen, the one that had held Wanda Sirett's bull, John Henry, that night.

Earlier, John Henry had bucked off Kyle Nash in the short-go. Had Kyle ridden the animal for eight measly seconds, he most likely would have won the event. Since no one except yours truly had accomplished that feat all season, why would Kyle be the one to break the string? Anyway, when John Henry bucked him off, I was relieved of the necessity of having to jot down a score.

Like a robot programmed to kill, John Henry, after throwing Kyle, came out of a spin seemingly searching for the bull rider. Kyle, though, had been lucky. Although bucked off, he'd managed to land on his feet, and before John Henry had a chance to maul him, Kyle was climbing the rail with the agility of a monkey. Not taking any chances, he didn't stop until he was safely on the other side, actually diving over the top of the rail to delighted guffaws from the crowd.

However, John Henry was still in his rage. Spotting Buddy Bach near the escape chute, he pawed the ground with his right front hoof, lowered his head and made a dash directly at the bullfighter. Buddy, like Kyle, played it safe and scrambled up the side rail before John Henry could get close. The bull, ever the optimist, took a swipe at his legs with his horns, but missed. Then he peered around for more potential victims. Finding none, he let out a snort that drew laughter from the crowd. Tyson Roberts, swinging his rope and edging his big chestnut mare forward cautiously, managed to maneuver the big fellow toward the escape chute where he proceeded to saunter through the open gate and back to his pen.

Watching him go, I remembered thinking that John Henry might be getting too dangerous. If he kept up his shenanigans, the riders would raise a clamor that would lead to his elimination from the PBR. It wasn't that the riders were becoming timid. They're cowboys, expecting a certain degree of wildness and meanness in a bull—but there are limits. And John Henry was butting heads with those limits.

With my attention drawn to John Henry's now empty pen, I grabbed Daryl's arm. "Wait a minute," I said.

"What's the matter?"

I took a step back and pointed to where the light was reflecting off of something in the straw at the back of the pen.

"I don't know," I said, "but look at that."

"Let's check it out."

"You read my mind."

We hurried over to John Henry's vacant pen where we easily found what was reflecting the light—a black rhinestone studded jacket that I had seen Wanda Sirett wearing earlier that evening. My attention had been drawn to it when John Henry was being loaded into the chute for Kyle's ride. She had been standing directly behind the chute as if directing the entire operation. Of course, no one paid a lick of attention to anything she said. She didn't know what she was doing. Why, Royce always said she could turn any ten-minute job into twice that just by saying, "Hello." It was true. To her credit, she had good people working for her, people who did know their jobs and performed them with pride and skill—Wanda or no Wanda—and she paid those people well, for which they were loyal to her.

Most of them, Craig Kelton for example, took a perverse pride in working for the most outrageous stock contractor in the PBR. Craig knew many of the other stockmen, Royce Sirett included, would take him on in a heartbeat. Why for spite, Royce might even pay him more money just to lure him away from Wanda. Craig, though, preferred Wanda.

Of course, in his case, it had to do with that extra perk none of the other stock contractors could offer him. It was no secret that she let him into her bed on some kind of a regular basis. Under her terms, of course, which was totally acceptable to Craig, something of a rake himself.

Craig had been married once, he'd told me. I have to take his word for it because he was divorced long before he hooked up with the PBR. After that experience, he vowed he would never sidle up to an altar again. Not directly, but through innuendo and other means, he let it be known that his arrangement with Wanda suited him just fine. Now there wasn't going to be any arrangement with the boss. She was dead.

I guess I ought to point out that Wanda was still wearing the rhinestone jacket as she lay sprawled on her back in the straw, one leg bent at an awkward angle, the other straight out before her. Her clothes were only slightly ruffled, suggesting there had not been much of a struggle. One arm rested across her chest, the other flung in the straw, a few inches shy of where John Henry had dropped a cow pie. I took a kind of familiar pleasure in breathing in the pie's fresh putrid aroma. Didn't bother me in the least; cowboys are used to that smell from their infancy.

"Is she...?" Daryl asked.

"I'm sure she is," I replied.

We knew we had to notify the police. I did not possess a cell phone, had never owned one. Lane had one once, for about a week, but he lost the damn thing when drunk (Lane, not the phone). Daryl, after claiming he always gave his to Courtney before a round, volunteered to find a pay phone and make the call. Reluctantly, I agreed to remain with the body until he returned.

I had seen enough movies and television shows to know I wasn't supposed to touch anything. I didn't—but I didn't need to touch her to know she was dead. The eyes told part of the story. Wide open and bulged, their bluish tint was dull in the dim light. They were assisted by the purple and black bruises, which, like a necklace, ran around her neck, itself twisted awkwardly to one side. Her swollen tongue threw in a supporting role as it hung perversely out of her mouth. As a rank amateur pathologist, even I could see she'd been strangled.

Wanda's head was turned at a slight angle, an angle that projected the line of her sightless eyes directly at me. I was horrified by the dead sheen they cast and had to divert my gaze. Although only for a moment, for something drew my focus back. We all, to one degree or another, are drawn to the macabre, and, in truth, I'm no different. Staring down at her, I thought how her expression, while leaving her still recognizable, was so un-Wanda-like. Wanda could smile with breathtaking beauty and mischief, and she could let you know she was disenchanted with you with a multiplicity of looks, each of which was familiar to anyone who knew her, even briefly, and could she ever smirk with the best of them. Those, as well as a number of others, were the Wanda-like expressions I remembered. This one, this un-Wanda-like countenance, was one of stark terror. I think that was what made me turn away at first. I could only imagine if her terror flowed from the thought that she was about to die, or that someone would actually dare to kill her. No, the terror that lingered on her mien as she lay still on the straw in that pen was not characteristic of Wanda. You see, I'd never known her terrified of anything. Certainly, nothing as common as insults and ridicule ever fazed her, except that she could *mock* a horrified face after hearing them, of course. I guess death, staring you in the face, would be enough to terrify anyone…well, most of us anyway.

My sense of the ghoulish momentarily satisfied, I peered around. John Henry's pen was off to the side from the main path leading from the bucking chutes to the loading ramp at the rear of the building. It was the next thing to secluded. Wanda's killer, with perfect timing, could have strangled her in John Henry's pen and not been seen. It had to have taken place when there would have been little activity on the walkway.

I'd seen Wanda watching Kyle, the next to the last man

up in the short-go, climb on John Henry's back in the bucking chute. That meant she was probably killed after the conclusion of the event. At that time, most of the bull riders would have been in the locker room, showering and changing. Daryl and I were probably in conversation near the announcers' stand. Most of the stock contractors and their wranglers would have been back at the loading dock, loading the bulls onto trucks. The crowd would have been climbing the steps of the aisles heading for the main concourse and the exits. Accordingly, there would have been few people in the area. Still, it had to have been a high-risk proposition. Someone, anyone, could have walked down that pathway at anytime. How planned could this murder have been?

Daryl returned, claiming the police were on their way. He was trailed by Carl Earp, a wiry, tobacco-chewing, weather-beaten wrangler who tended the bulls and their pens, kept the animals fed, forked in clean straw and removed their pies. He loved his job, loved being a part of the PBR. A rodeo cowboy in his younger days, he was sixty-plus with the body of a forty-five year old, except when he complained of aches and pains, which was all the time.

"What we got here?" Carl asked before shifting the Red Man lump from one side of his mouth to the other.

"It's Wanda Sirett," I said, casting a glance at Daryl and wondering exactly what he'd told the wrangler.

"What's wrong with her?" Carl questioned with his deep Kansas drawl.

"She's dead."

"Dead!" he echoed, showing instant agitation. "Wh… what happened?

"Looks like she's been murdered."

"You sure John Henry didn't fall on her or kick her?" Daryl asked hopefully.

I pointed out the marks on her neck.

He sighed wearily, muttered a "Damn," that wasn't all the way under his breath.

"She still warm?" Carl asked.

I thought that was a good point. Despite the admonitions from the entertainment world, I decided to check her pulse. Doing so would cover two bases. One, to determine if she might be alive, though I was certain she wasn't, and two, to check for residual body heat. Maybe, the police would be interested.

I stooped down and clasped the wrist that lay on the straw. Her skin felt neither warm nor cold. In fact, it felt somewhat natural under the conditions, clammy, like skin gets on a hot muggy day. There was no pulse that I could discern, but since I wasn't skilled at checking for that bodily function, maybe I had missed a faint one.

"Well?" Daryl asked verbally, Carl with a look.

I divulged my analysis, such as it was. Since they weren't about to touch her themselves, neither man questioned it. In the next moment, the cops showed up and things started getting dicey.

# CHAPTER TWELVE

Markus Washington, an Atlantic City veteran detective, stormed onto the scene like a bull with a purpose. He was mid-forties, six foot three, two hundred and thirty pounds of rock hard Afro-American muscle with a stony expression and eyes colder than Wanda's. At that moment, I was never gladder that I'd discovered Wanda's body in the presence of someone else. For had I discovered her by myself, I knew that Detective Washington's continuous accusatory stare would have had me squirming to confess to the crime just to make him stop looking at me that way. But what more impeccable witness could I find than the president of the PBR? Check our backgrounds. Sure, mine might stink just enough to make a cop a tad suspicious. Especially, if he learned about my trips to the bedroom with Wanda, but Daryl would come out smelling like the proverbial rose, sweetening my scent by association.

As it turned out, my trips to the bedroom did come out and Daryl's association did not help a twit. But I'm getting ahead of myself.

Detective Washington was dressed just as you would expect, a ruffled gray-striped suit, white shirt, solid blue tie loose at the neck, scuffed black shoes. He looked around, gaze passing over Wanda's body as if it weren't there, settling on me. Then he drew a filtered cigarette out of his smudged shirt pocket and lit it with a cheap yellow plastic lighter. I spotted a big gold ring on his finger, glistening diamond in the center. Aren't we all creatures of contrast?

"Can't we get more light in here?" he grumbled, blowing a haze of smoke into the air.

"I'll take care of it," Carl volunteered, and tore off in a way that had me wondering if he would return. Smart cowboys knew when to make themselves scarce.

A second detective had accompanied Washington, also African-American, a decade younger, an inch or two shorter, a few pounds lighter, similarly dressed, also a smoker. Detective Cletus Bookman. He quickly examined the body, nodded solemnly at Washington.

"So tell me, gentlemen," Washington said, "what happened here?"

We told him how we'd discovered the body and as much as we could about what we remembered immediately before and after. He asked if anyone had touched the corpse, and I confessed I had. The look he gave me clearly said, *Don't you watch television?* At least, he didn't actually say it.

He asked if we knew anyone who might have wanted to kill the woman whose corpse lay in the straw. Daryl and I looked at each other. Which road to take? I took the jesting one; the one I should have least traveled.

Turning on my best Texas charm, I began, "Well, officer...."

"Detective," he corrected.

"Detective. Wanda was.... You know."

"I don't know. Suppose you tell me."

A few drops of sweat chose that moment to bead up on the back of my neck like hot grease in a skillet. Out of the corner of my eye, I spotted Detective Bookman cordoning off a wide area with yellow crime scene tape. "Wanda was something else," I mumbled. At that, Detective Washington's expression took on a hue of total exasperation. I tried again. "She was the kind of woman who everyone loved and...."

"Yes," he prompted, his dark eyes narrowing.

I looked at Daryl. He was no help. Just stared back at me blankly. He must have been wondering what I was searching for. So I said it. "...and everyone wanted to kill." Trust me, I could sense my weak jest had done exactly what it deserved to do — BOMB.

Detective Washington sucked on his cigarette, blew out a thick stream of smoke. "Everyone?" His tone said he was taking me literally.

"Not really," I corrected, feeling a drop of sweat loosen and then trail, cold, down my back. "I mean not really kill. I mean she was one of those...people (I almost said women) who have a way of making you want to strang..., you know."

The look he shot me said I didn't want to go there again.

Then inspiration struck and I said, "Not really kill her. Just pull your hair out."

Detective Washington made a face. "We need to know who had a motive to kill her."

That's when I thought of Royce, but it was Royce we were talking about here — good ole boy stock contractor. So I said I didn't know of anyone. Daryl told Detective Washington he couldn't think of anyone either.

The pathologist arrived. A tall, leggy, redheaded woman, mid-thirties, plain faced, all business, a smoker, too. She didn't fool me though. Why, with a bit of make-up, hair styling, maybe a smile every now and then, she could easily have been attractive enough for the PBR. If you like your women big. Not fat, mind you, just pleasantly plump. Even though bull riders are usually small or wiry or both, some of them like a woman who can dominate them. Not my taste. But I've heard cowboys boasting with those very words. Of course, they were drunk, or nearly so, at the time. That didn't stop me from believing them, however. Takes all kinds, I reasoned.

She donned a pair of latex gloves as the main overhead

lights spilled on, brilliantly lighting the scene as she set to her grim task. She stooped down beside Wanda's motionless body and checked her pulse, and then lifted her hair away from her neck for a better look. A moment later, she turned to Detective Washington and confirmed that, subject to an autopsy, Wanda had been strangled. To Detective Washington's question of "When?" all she would say was "Not long. Still plenty of body heat. Probably less than ninety minutes. Let you know better in a few hours."

Detective Washington nodded, looked alternately from me to Daryl and back to me again. I wondered why he was so interested in me, but then my mind jolted when something the pathologist had said struck me like a boulder to the head. Less than ninety minutes? That meant the murder couldn't have occurred more than fifteen or twenty minutes before Daryl and I walked through the area, while we were talking to one another as a matter of fact. Had I heard anything? A scream? The sound of a scuffle? I couldn't recall. If pushed, I would have to say no. From where we carried on the most of our conversation, the distance from Wanda's body was considerable. But ninety minutes? I couldn't get over it. Did that mean Wanda was killed by someone she knew? Was taken by surprise? Not surprise like a cat jumping on you when you open a door, but surprise that the person who stood before her would even consider such a thing. I concluded that was exactly what it meant. Only someone she knew could have killed Wanda. Who else would want to kill her? A serial killer was out of the question. The PBR was not the right venue. Only bull riding maniacs came to PBR events. Serial killers stalked nearly empty streets, didn't they?

It was later that I remembered Jodi Hall.

"All right," Detective Washington said, squashing his cigarette on the arena floor. "Let's eliminated you two."

I was relieved until I discovered what eliminating us actually meant. It meant a grilling, and for the next fifteen minutes did we ever get it. I reviewed with him my story of having last seen Wanda alive when she paced behind the chutes while Kyle Nash was in the process of mounting John Henry.

Daryl chimed in to say he didn't remember seeing Wanda behind the chutes at all, but admitted he was more interested in whether Kyle rode John Henry, since he sat in sixth position at that point and was anxious about finishing in the money.

Washington took my starting point as his and quizzed us from there. Where were we at all times, what did we see and hear and when did we see and hear it.

Washington then had us repeat it all again, everything we'd already told him. I guessed he was looking for inconsistencies or slip-ups. In the end, he was satisfied, I think. Actually, I was only guessing from when he finally said, "Okay, that's it for now." He paused a moment and then turned to Daryl, saying, "You're the president of this bull riding thing, the association?"

Daryl nodded, added the superfluous, "Yes."

"We've got one hell of a problem here, cowboy," Washington resumed. "None of you people live in Atlantic City. Every one of you is out of here in the morning. By this time tomorrow, you're all gonna be on the other side of the country. Including, in all likelihood, the killer of this woman here." Washington turned and thumbed to where Wanda lay on the straw in John Henry's pen, and then turned back to Daryl. "How we gonna let that happen? How we gonna make this investigation work?"

"I don't know, off'cer...Detective," Daryl replied meekly. "What do you suggest?"

"I need someone. Someone connected with your association...."

"The PBR," Daryl corrected.

Washington gave him a look. "Yeah. PBR," he repeated with attitude. "As I was saying, I need someone to work with us. Someone who knows everyone, can get to everyone, can get me to them."

Ole Daryl didn't miss a beat with that one. Blasting out of the chute spurring, the ingrate's face glowed like a light bulb. Smiling like an eight-year-old boy on Christmas morning looking at his presents under the tree, he said, "He's right here. Chance, here, is our liaison with the police. He's our vice-president, too. Anything you want, he'll get it for you. He'll give you the names of everyone, tell you where they're staying. Anything you need."

Don't think my mouth didn't drop a foot with that dribble. How was I to know where everyone was staying? I did know where some of the cowboys, and cowgirls, were bunked down, of course, but nothing like what Daryl was implying. That didn't stop him, though. "He's your man, off'cer...Detective," he said.

# CHAPTER THIRTEEN

Detective Markus Washington stared at me with an expression that clearly said as far as he was concerned the PBR had pretty much scraped the bottom of the barrel to come up with its liaison. Victim was how I saw it. Naturally, I kept that to myself. He had dismissed Daryl, who scampered out of there faster than a bull anxious to leave an arena. A moment later, Carl Earp returned.

Washington questioned Carl, though seemingly just going through the motions. In the brief grilling, Carl told Washington that for well over an hour, from sometime before the event concluded until a few minutes before Daryl flagged him down, he'd been back and forth from the pens inside to the loading docks outside, goading ornery bulls onto trucks that would cart them to the airport. Carl said he'd just seen the last truck off, the one carrying John Henry and several others, and was making his way back inside to clean the stalls when Daryl came along and brought him back to where I was waiting beside Wanda's body.

Washington asked him if he'd seen "the victim outside at anytime during the loading of her bulls?"

"She was out earlier," Carl claimed through tobacco stained teeth, "when we loaded Kryptonite and Purgatory, two others of her bulls. But after they was on the truck, she went back inside. I'd gone inside to bring out a bull when I seen her behind the buckin' chutes as they was loadin' John Henry. I didn't see her again till, you know." He nodded toward the corpse in the pen.

"What time was it you saw her outside during the loading of the two bulls?"

Carl shook his head. "Not sure." Then he added, "I don't keep close track of time. I know it was before the event ended."

"And you're saying she was definitely not present when that last bull...what was its name?" He turned to look at me.

"John Henry," Carl and I mouthed simultaneously.

"Yeah, John Henry," Washington echoed. "She was not present when you were loading John Henry?"

"That's right," Carl said with a nod.

"And she usually is?"

"Always."

"Didn't that strike you as unusual?"

"Course it did."

"And...?"

"And what?"

"You didn't do anything about it?"

"What was I to do? I can't go runnin' down every stock contractor who ain't there to supervise the loadin' of his bulls. 'Sides, they just gits in the way. 'Specially her. All stock contractors want to do is admire their animals and act important. I knows how to load bulls. Been doin' it for nigh on twenty-five years. Whenever they holler orders at us, ones doin' the work, we just ignores 'em and goes on loadin' the danged critters the way we was doin' it, anyway. Haven't failed to git 'em on a damn truck yet."

Washington's mouth crinkled up ever the slightest at Carl's region-laden diatribe. He asked for the names of all the stock contractors and the other men loading the bulls that night. Carl rattled off the ones he could remember, after which Washington let him go, which was only right. Carl had no more killed Wanda than I had.

After Carl left, Washington turned to me. With pointed expression, I might add. I knew how he felt. Well, join the club, Detective Washington. I didn't want to be there either.

The good detective apparently accepted his situation with some degree of resignation, for he let the neutral expression return to his face as he said, "Was she married?"

"Divorced," I supplied.

"Her ex around?"

I explained the situation leaving out the part of Royce and my ex turning themselves into an item.

"Did she have a boyfriend?"

I paused before answering in the negative.

"Why the hesitation?"

You try to explain Wanda. Personally, I didn't know where to begin. But I knew I couldn't get out of it, so I did my best. "It wasn't hesitation," I said. "It was the definition of boyfriend."

"Yes?"

"Wanda was that type of woman."

The expression on Washington's face was pure question.

"She liked men. Everyone was her boyfriend." Then I corrected that to mean only those thirty and over — with a few exceptions every now and then.

"From what you're saying," Washington said, "she didn't take up with any man on any long term basis."

"That's right," I confirmed.

He mused over that for a few moments before lighting his next cigarette. Then he said, "Who has she been seeing lately?"

I gave him a few names (those I knew) covering the last few months. There was almost a different one for each weekend. I included Craig Kelton's name, of course, wondering to myself if Carl had seen him during the loading of Wanda's bulls. He hadn't mentioned him. Detective Washington had asked only for stock contractors. Craig was not a stock contractor. In Carl's mind, therefore, Craig probably hadn't counted.

I didn't know how far to go with helping Detectives Washington and Bookman. I wanted Wanda's murderer uncovered, of course, but I didn't want to be a stoolie, a term I remembered from watching old Bogart and Cagney movies when I was growing up. The killer could very well turn out to be a friend of mine, or maybe only a casual acquaintance. Either way, I didn't like being in the middle.

Wanda, too, was a friend, of sorts. A sexual partner on two beautiful occasions when the feminine attributes were most appreciated. Now she was dead. Didn't I owe her something? Yes, I decided. I owed her an obligation to help in anyway I could.

But it was Royce who worried me most. Had he killed Wanda? Actually, I had already rejected him for the role because, well, like Wanda was Wanda, Royce was Royce. He wasn't the killer type. He was easy going, too easy going, and too much the big lug who would do anything for you. Besides, he was about to sire a family. What kind of father would he be to LeAnn and his child if it turned out he'd murdered his ex-wife and had to parent from behind prison walls?

Then I remembered Jodi Hall and brightened, for Royce couldn't have killed her, which made it a safe bet he hadn't killed Wanda. I distinctly recalled Royce had been in Fort Worth the entire weekend when Jodi was killed. Jodi was strangled, same as Wanda. That meant the murderer had to be someone who had been in both Twin Falls and Atlantic City. That left Royce out. I told Washington what I knew.

"Why didn't you mention this before?" he demanded, eyes narrowing as if wanting to convict me of something.

"It just came to me. Must have slipped my mind for a moment."

He glared at me before saying, "Strangled, huh?"

I nodded.

He looked thoughtful for a moment. Then he said, "You're implying, I take it, that because the one killing took place at a so-called Challenger event, the other one here, and both victims were strangled, all we have to do is find out who was at both places and we'll have our killer?"

"I doubt if it will be that simple...."

"That makes two of us."

"But doesn't it mean something?"

He glared at me in that expressionless way he did so well. "Maybe," he conceded. Then, gazing at me beneath raised eyebrows, he said, "Do you know the names of those who were at both events?"

I had to say I knew a couple but I didn't know them all. He flashed a look of annoyance. "Still," he said, "it might narrow the field. Gives us a place to start and a theory to go with it. But," and here he looked at me pointedly, "I still want to speak to the ex-husband."

Had he just said Royce was a suspect? Sure sounded that way to me.

# CHAPTER FOURTEEN

I rode in the back of the unmarked police cruiser; Bookman, smoking, drove; Washington, smoking, grabbed shotgun. The night was pleasantly warm, moonless. Small clouds, wisped off the ocean by the strong breeze, intermingled with the star-laced sky. It was after midnight and we were on our way from the Convention Center, site of the PBR event and Wanda's murder, to a Trump resort. Over the weekend, I'd bumped into LeAnn, and in one of the voids that inevitably occurs when two people in an awkward situation try to make small talk, she'd mentioned where she and Royce were staying.

Bookman pulled up in front of a huge hotel, parked, got out. Washington exited the vehicle on his side, flashed his badge at the approaching valet, stopping him dead in his tracks. "Police business," he said. I didn't know Royce and LeAnn's room number so he flashed his badge a second time at the front desk.

Royce opened the door to his eighteenth floor ocean view suite dressed in a maroon striped robe tied loosely around his chubby gut. He was back into suites. When he and Wanda were married, they always stayed in luxury suites, everywhere. Wanda wouldn't have it any other way. For a long time after the divorce, Royce seemed satisfied with little more than a clean room. Now, with LeAnn, he'd apparently stepped it up again. No big deal. He could afford it.

By his mussed hair and groggy manner, it was apparent

we'd awakened him from some level of hibernation. Before we'd said a word, he asked us to keep our voices down because, the "little woman" was asleep in the bedroom. I wondered (to me it seemed natural) if they'd shared each other before dropping off.

He spotted me behind and between the two broad-shouldered detectives, said, "Chance? What's this all about?"

"May we come in?" Washington asked, moving forward at the same time.

"Guess so," Royce replied, stepping back and turning away. Then hastily facing us again, he repeated his, "What's this all about?"

Displaying his badge like before, Washington told him who he was, nodded toward his partner, added, "This is Detective Bookman. Your wife has been killed."

"Killed! Wanda?" He shot an open-mouth glance at the bedroom door, and then quickly back to Washington.

Washington said nothing, just watched. Royce turned away again, seemed to look for something. He spied a glass two-thirds full of what I surmised to be straight bourbon on the coffee table in front of a loveseat so luxurious it seemed capable of sucking Royce right into it and keeping him forever. Royce must have poured the drink earlier, sampled it until LeAnn made it clear it was time for bedroom rodeo, and then wisely left the drink unfinished. (I guess I answered my own nosy question.)

Royce picked up the drink, downed a swallow. Then, still holding the glass, he turned back to Washington. "You said killed. You don't mean...?" He looked at me, back to Washington.

"Yes, Mr. Sirett?" Washington toyed.

"Murdered?"

"Yes, Mr. Sirett. That's exactly what I mean."

"How? Where?"

"She was strangled. Her body was found in an empty pen at the arena." Washington extracted a cigarette from his shirt pocket. "Mind if I smoke?" he asked, and without waiting for a reply, said, "Thank you," and lit up.

"Strangled," Royce repeated meekly as he, still holding his drink, flopped on the loveseat. Then, mechanically, he stroked his goatee with his free hand before looking up at Washington and saying, "It *is* a non-smoking room."

Detective Washington issued an unaffected wave as he drew on his cigarette, and then blew a shield of smoke out into the already stale room air. A moment later, Detective Bookman followed suit, and it wasn't long before the room was a dense cloud of smoke.

"Why are you here, Chance?" Royce asked. Then letting a flash of anger sweep over his mien, he said, "You didn't...?"

I thought he was about to leap off the sofa. Had he doubled a fist of his free hand? I thought I'd better head him off at the pass. "Kill her, Royce?" I said. "Of course, I didn't kill her. But I did find her body. That is Daryl and I did."

He relaxed, slumped in his seat, took another swallow of his drink. The glass was now two-thirds empty. Royce wasn't sipping. "So why are you here?" he asked after lowering his glass from his large lips.

I thought it was time to blame someone else. "Daryl appointed me liaison with the police."

"What the hell's that?"

"He's to help us anyway he can," Washington shot in. He'd apparently decided it was time to assume command of the situation. He'd given Royce his chance to soak in the information about Wanda and was now ready to launch his inquisition.

Before he could say another word, however, Royce turned his look pointedly on the detective. "Ex-wife," he said.

"Beg your pardon," Washington said.

"You said earlier she was my wife. Ain't so. She's my

ex-wife."

Washington nodded, muttered, "Fine."

Somehow I had the impression that all along Washington had known what he was doing, was always thinking. He saw, as I did, that Royce Sirett, deep down, still looked on Wanda as his wife.

Royce emptied his glass. Then he said, "You fellows want a drink?"

"Duty," Washington intoned, echoed in the next instant by Bookman. Then everyone looked at me. I shook my head. Royce shrugged and took another sip from his glass.

"Mr. Sirett, how long have you been divorced from your ex-wife?" Washington began.

"Four years, give or take," Royce said, still clutching his glass.

"Did you want to kill her?"

"Every damn day," Royce fired back without thinking. Although Washington smirked and Bookman dittoed that action, Royce wasn't being flippant.

"Did you see your ex-wife tonight?" Washington continued.

"Sure. Three or four times, in fact."

"When and where?"

Royce paused before replying, thinking, and then said, "I seen her before the second go-round."

"Go-round?"

I explained the term to Washington. When I finished, he nodded for Royce to continue.

"She was behind the chutes admirin' her stock."

"Was she with anyone?"

"Craig Kelton was there." He paused, looked at a questioning Washington. Supplying the answer, he said, "Her foreman."

"Anyone else?"

Royce thought again, shook his head, said, "Don't remember no one else."

"Did you speak to her?"

"Not then."

"When?"

"Later, following the short-go."

I had included an explanation of the short-go to Washington during the explanation of the second go-round, which had included an explanation of the first go-round as well.

"Was that the last time you saw her?"

Nodding, Royce said, "Yeah."

"What was the conversation about?"

"Same thing as always," Royce said.

"What's that?"

"I offered to buy John Henry from her."

"It was John Henry's pen where her body was discovered."

"Oh," was all Royce could say to that.

"So you weren't serious."

"'Bout what?"

"Buying this John Henry bull."

"Damn straight I was," he exclaimed, wide-eyed. "I want nothing more than to get John Henry back in my stable."

"You had the bull before?"

Royce's face displayed a generous proportion of disgust. "Had to give him to her in that damn divorce settlement."

"So you've been trying to buy him back ever since."

"It's our little ritual I guess you'd call it. I ask her to sell John Henry back to me. She says 'No way, Jose.' I laugh and move on. That way, you see, I don't have to talk to her 'bout nothin' else. Keeps everything civil. Don't know what we'd do if she actually did agree to sell him to me."

"But you really do want the bull back?" That seemed to

be important to Detective Washington.

"I said it, didn't I?"

"Was there anyone else around when you had this conversation about buying the bull?"

Royce paused again to muse over his answer. "Well," he drawled, "there were people milling around, the usual ones I guess." He brightened. "I remember Carl Earp. But he's always around. He was helping to load the bulls. That's his job."

"Anyone else you can remember? Specifically."

"Like I said, the usual cowboys." That drew a look of exasperation from Washington.

Then Royce brightened again. "There was one guy who strolled through there who was out of place."

Washington waited. His expression, if not his mouth, clearly said, "Who?"

"Kyle Nash was there."

"Who's he?"

"A bull rider."

"Treasurer of the PBR," I added.

"Why wouldn't it be appropriate for him to be there?" Washington wanted to know.

"Well," Royce stuttered, "It's not that it wouldn't be appropriate. It's just that the bull riders return to the locker room after their rides. They don't usually come to the pen area behind the chutes. They know the fellers, like Carl, are back loadin' stock. Unlike the stock contractors, they usually try to stay out of the way."

"Any idea why he was there?"

"You'll have to ask him."

"I will. You see anyone else who normally didn't belong there at that time?"

Royce thought for a moment. Then shaking his head, said, "Can't remember none."

"Then I'd like a better handle on who was there,"

Washington said. "You were there, your wi...your ex-wife was there, Carl Earp was there, this," he looked down at his notes, "Kyle Nash was there. Who else?"

"Well," Royce stroked his goatee, rubbed his abundant chin, "the usual people."

"I want to know who they were."

"What's going on?"

LeAnn had stepped to the doorway of the bedroom. She had on a shiny pink bathrobe, very dressy, over what I assumed was some kind of bed wear; LeAnn had never liked to sleep in the nude, though, on occasion, I found it erotic. Her thick hair was mussed, and she'd washed the make-up off of her face. Seeing her standing there, I thought her gorgeous and wished I were still married to her — at least for the night.

Royce set the empty glass on the coffee table. Then he stood, staggered a step before saying, "Somethin' terrible has happened, Hon."

When LeAnn waited, he continued in a low voice, "Wanda has been killed."

LeAnn's mouth fell open. "Killed? How?"

"Murdered."

"Murdered?"

"She was strangled. They found her in John Henry's pen. Can you believe it?" Royce was babbling now. "Can you believe anyone would do such a thing?"

LeAnn stepped toward Royce and he put his arm around her shoulders. Together they sat on the loveseat where she took his other hand in both of hers.

"This is terrible," she said. Then looking first at one detective and then the other, she said, "Are you policemen?"

Washington acknowledged they were.

LeAnn then looked at me. "What are you doing here, Chance?" Then her eyes widened, and she put one hand to her mouth, "You don't mean...?"

I wanted to laugh. "That's exactly what Royce thought," I said. "Does that fall into the 'Great minds think alike' category?" But since I was the only one who saw my humor just then, I let the grin on my face dissolve like granules of sugar in hot liquid.

"Mr. Boettecher is helping us make contact with the rodeo people we need to speak with," Washington volunteered.

LeAnn returned a knowing nod. Was that a note of relief on her face?

"Maybe you can help us, Mrs. Sirett…." Neither Royce nor LeAnn (nor I, for that matter) made any effort to correct the detective's misconception. "We're trying to figure out what people were in the pen area before and after the woman was killed."

"I saw Wanda several times tonight," LeAnn exclaimed, shoving aside a clump of hair that had fallen demurely across her face.

"When did you see her, please?" Apparently, Washington could be polite when he wanted to be. "The last time."

LeAnn struck a thoughtful pose. "Let's see. It had to have been shortly after the last go-round. I found Royce…" here she stole a glance at the stock contractor who was staring down at their rejoined hands, and then returned her gaze to Washington, "…coming back after the loading of the last of the bulls. I also saw Wanda come back. I think Craig was with her, but I'm not sure. Yes, he was there, I remember. She said something to him but I didn't hear it." She looked at Royce again. "You asked me to get you a beer. As I was leaving, I heard you…." She looked at Washington and smiled. "He and Wanda have this little ritual. Makes me think they still have a thing for each other."

"I don't have no thing for Wanda," Royce snapped.

LeAnn patted his hand. "I know, Hon. I'm not the least threatened." She looked at Washington. "Anyway, he asked her, as he always does, if she's ready to sell him John Henry.

She gave him her 'No way, Jose' reply."

"Who else was milling around back there, if you can remember?" Washington asked.

"I've already told him I seen Kyle Nash," Royce shot in.

"Yes, Kyle was there, wasn't he?" LeAnn agreed as if suddenly remembering. "Let's see, who else? Oh, Carl Earp, of course, but he's always there. It's his job."

"He has Carl, too," Royce said.

"Carl too, huh." LeAnn nodded. "Then, let's see…."

"I know," Royce interrupted. "Clete Fassel was there. And a couple other stock contractors."

"But wouldn't they have been outside on the loading dock, Hon?"

"Yes," Royce agreed. "Most of the time. But they would have been in and out. I think that's what the detective wants to know." He turned his gaze to Washington. "Am I right?"

"Anyone who would have been in the area whether inside or out, whether working or passing through."

"So let's see," Royce said, gathering enthusiasm for his task. "There would have been the boys on the trucks."

"But they would have stayed on the trucks," LeAnn noted.

"But they all have to take a leak," Royce put in, though with a hint of irritation. "So they would have gone inside from time to time."

LeAnn gave Royce a look, then said, "I guess that's right."

"So Shorty Maul would have been one," Royce volunteered. "Ross Curry, another."

"Wouldn't Jesse Cantu have been there, too?" LeAnn suggested.

"And Carl, who we've already mentioned," Royce said. "That along with the stock contractors would have been 'bout it."

LeAnn nodded her agreement. These were essentially the same names that Carl Earp had given Washington earlier.

"Anybody else who normally would not have been in the area?" Washington asked.

They both looked thoughtful and then agreed they couldn't remember seeing anyone else.

Washington asked Royce where he and LeAnn were going from Atlantic City.

Royce said they were flying directly to Phoenix to tend to the bulls before the next event. "The men are good," he stated, "but you still have to watch everything like a hawk."

Washington handed each of them his card and asked them to call back with their telephone number when they got to Phoenix in case he needed to ask them any more questions. Royce said they would, and then asked the detective if he wanted their cell phone numbers. I think Washington was a little surprised that a cowboy stock contractor would possess such an instrument. Little did he know there was a new kind of cowboy to go with the times.

Outside, clouds were rolling in off the ocean. Earlier, the night air had felt warm; now, it was turning cold. In the car, Bookman asked his partner where they were going next.

Washington turned in his seat and peered at me sitting in the back. "Know where we can find this Kyle Nash?"

# CHAPTER FIFTEEN

It took some doing (I called someone who called someone who called someone) but I finally located Kyle Nash and his wife, Lucy, in the other Trump casino. It was a few minutes after three in the A.M. when Washington knocked on the bull rider's gold-trimmed cream-colored door, Bookman and myself in tow.

Kyle was an interesting specimen. Not for his somewhat delegate features, pale complexion and thin sandy hair. So, what made him interesting? He had a small round mouth that didn't appear to move when he spoke. He probably would have made a great ventriloquist had he chosen to take it up instead of bull riding.

But he was a bull rider. And a damn good one at that. Never World Champ, he'd finished in the top ten eight times in the last decade. No easy trick.

Lucy was a wonderful woman, but make no bones about it, she wore the pants of that happy duo, made *all* the family—and otherwise—decisions. Probably told Kyle to run for the PBR Board of Directors, or at least gave her consent. Not very cowboy to my demented way of thinking, but if it works, I say more power to them.

Since it was so late, we had called ahead. They were both waiting when we knocked on the door. Kyle answered in garb and mood you would have expected—mussed and grouchy. He was about my height and weight so Washington and Bookman towered over him, too. Lucy was Kyle's height though a few pounds lighter, as was the shade of the short hair that curved around her clean oval jaws. She had a natural way of standing straight and tall, her small breast erect and dominating, that her body seemed to cry out for a uniform — military, police, Gestapo. She wore a pair of dark maroon men's pajamas under a green kimono-style housecoat. In some strange way, neither Washington nor Bookman towered over her. I can't explain that and don't want to try. And I found it interesting that neither detective smoked a single cigarette during the entire interview.

The oceanfront room they inhabited for the weekend was large but not a suite. It consisted of a single king-sized bed flanked by black marble-topped nightstands, two tweed chairs around a circular all-purpose table next to the window and a large flat-screen television set resting inside a fancy opened-door entertainment center.

"What's this all about, Chance?" Lucy demanded in a hard-bitten Mississippi accent. She'd taken spiked glances at Washington and Bookman before turning to me.

I looked from Lucy to Kyle and then back to Lucy. "Wanda Sirett was strangled tonight."

Instinctively, Lucy reached for her throat, took a step back. Like LeAnn, her mouth gaped silently open, blue eyes clouded over. With the wind clearly knocked out of her sails, she plopped on the end of the ruffled bed, where, in the next instant, her husband joined her, laying an arm across her sharp shoulders. The two detectives and yours truly remained standing.

"These men are Atlantic City detectives. They need to question Kyle."

"Question Kyle?" Lucy regained the spark in her eyes and was flashing daggers between the two men. "Whatever for?" She continued to hold her neck with one hand.

"Mr. Nash," Washington began, fixing his gaze on the

bull rider. "We understand you happened to be milling around the area where the victim was killed. Mind telling me why?"

"I…." Kyle seemed befuddled. He looked at Washington, then Lucy, then Bookman, and then me. Turning back to Washington, he said, "I don't know when you mean. I seen Wanda tonight. Several times, in fact. When do you mean?"

"Oh, sorry," Washington muttered, smiling sheepishly. "Guess you do need that centered a bit."

I saw Washington's game, his cleverness in action. Had Kyle jumped right in and begun speaking of the time when he happened to be around the pens, something would have been tale telling, wouldn't it? But Kyle's confusion seemed genuine. At least I believed it.

Washington directed Kyle to the time he was seen behind the chutes after the conclusion of the event. Kyle, nodding, said, "Yes, I was back there at that time. I'd finished my ride — such as it was — and wanted to see Clete Fassel to tell him we were gonna buy Pugnacious. That's a bull he'd offered to sell us when we told him we were interested in startin' our own breedin' stock."

"Your wife wasn't with you?" The question from Washington made it clear he'd picked up on the dynamics of the couple's relationship.

"I was working my way down the stands," Lucy answered in a tone that clearly registered a want of wisdom on her husband's part for not waiting for her.

"Yeah," Kyle agreed, "she caught up, but I wanted to let him know we'd decided to buy the bull before he sold him to anyone else." He looked guiltily at his wife. "So, I was in kind of a hurry."

Like a surge of electricity running through a thin cord, I had a momentary infusion of envy, only wishing I were doing something for my own future. Obviously, Kyle and Lucy were looking down the road to the day after Kyle rode his last bull.

He was a year or so younger than me — thirty-one or two. He'd been injured pretty severely three years before (one of the years he'd failed to finish in the top ten) when a bull, Violator I think it was, kicked him in the abdomen and ruptured his spleen. He'd lost six or seven months tour time for that. Anyway, he, or more likely, Lucy, was planning ahead.

So what kind of post-bull riding life did I have to look forward to? Guess I needed a woman of Lucy's caliber to put me on the straight and narrow. What a thought!

"Did you see him and convey that decision?" Washington asked.

"Yes, I seen him," he replied with a nod that was exactly the kind he always gave when seated on the back of a bull and was signing the gateman to release the two of them into the arena for his ride. When Washington just looked at him, he added, "Told him to."

"Did you see Wanda Sirett on your way either to see Mr. Fassel or on the way back?"

"I seen her…both times."

When he failed to elaborate, Washington nodded, said, "Tell me about seeing her on the way back."

"What do you want to know?"

Washington displayed none of his earlier exasperation. Instead, his face remained impassive as he said, "Was she with anyone?"

"I seen her with Royce Sirett."

"Tell me what you saw, please."

"They were talkin'. When they seen me comin', they broke up and went different ways."

"Who saw you, Royce or Wanda?"

"Was Royce. He was the one facin' me. Wanda had her back to me. Royce seen me, must have mentioned it to Wanda because she turned, looked at me, then without a word to anyone, she started walkin' away."

"In any particular direction?"

"Let's see." He looked pensive for a moment. "Started towards the pens. She glanced at me, then without a word started towards the pens."

"How about Royce? Did you notice which way he went?"

"He started towards the arena, actually the back of the chutes. I remember he tossed me a wave, then turned towards the chutes. Remember, too, thinkin' it was funny because all of his bulls were gone from there."

"And this was on your way back from speaking with (he looked at his notes) Fassel?"

"Yeah, had to be. I was followin' Royce towards the arena."

"Tell me about seeing her on your way to see Fassel."

"What do you...oh. Who I seen her with?"

Washington smiled formally and nodded.

"She was alone except for Craig Kelton...."

"Her foreman," Washington filled in.

"Yeah, her foreman. They were talkin'. That one was rather heated. I was closer to them than I was when I seen her with Royce and heard her say, 'I'll decide when we do it. I always have and that is one thing that is not going to change.'"

"She used those words 'I'll decide when we do it. I always have and that is one thing that is not going to change,'" Washington repeated. "You heard those words?"

Kyle nodded. "Yes, sir. Those very words."

"What did you take that to mean?"

Kyle snickered, shot a repentant glance at Lucy. "Why, that Wanda would decide if she and Craig would have sex together, I guess."

"How did this Craig take it?"

"He didn't appear all that pleased."

"Did you hear either of them say anything else?"

"Nah," he said, wagging his head. "That was about it. They seen me and stopped talkin'. I walked past. Just as I was about to step out onto the loadin' dock, I heard Royce Sirett and turned around. I seen Wanda and Craig but now Royce and LeAnn (he shot a glance at me) were there, too."

Washington was silent, obviously musing.

In the void, Lucy said, "Will that be all?" She was looking at Washington through slit eyes.

Washington turned his gaze to her, said nothing. He continued to stare at her until she looked away. Then, returning to Kyle, he said, "A few weeks back, you attended a bull riding rodeo in Twin Falls, Idaho, didn't you, Mr. Nash?"

"Yes," Kyle said, diverting his look to Lucy, back to Washington.

"What does that have to do with anything?" Lucy demanded.

"I don't know," Washington admitted. "Maybe nothing."

"So what's the point?" Lucy pursued.

Washington ignored her. Instead, maintaining his focus on Kyle, he said, "Was your wife with you in Twin Falls?"

"No," Kyle said, and again looked at Lucy.

"I was visiting my parents in Tupelo for a few days," Lucy claimed defiantly. "Any crime in that?"

Washington eyeballed Lucy for another long moment, and then asked Kyle his and Lucy's destination upon leaving Atlantic City. He was told Phoenix.

We left Kyle and Lucy's room around half past three. By four-thirty we knew Craig Kelton had left Atlantic City with Wanda's bulls on an eleven-twenty flight for Phoenix. Washington was not happy, no less disappointed when he learned Clete Fassel had also flown (literally) the coop.

I could see Washington hated to do it, but circumstances were forcing him to call it a night. He couldn't interview everyone.

Most of the bull riders had not traversed the pen area; the public address announcers had been in the arena doing their jobs, as were the cameramen and so on. Still, I sensed he would have liked nothing better than to have taken everyone downtown and pumped them dry, rubber hosed them if necessary, until they confessed — all of them. But I was ready for some sleep and told him so. After a last cold stare, he let me go.

# CHAPTER SIXTEEN

I was staying at the Acey-Deucey Motel, a cheap place away from the boardwalk. Traveling alone, I had to cut expenses even more than when Lane and I'd traveled together. Either that or win more at the Thursday night poker games.

It seemed I'd hardly fallen asleep when the telephone chirped annoyingly on the stand next to my bed. I had fallen asleep sometime after five; a glance at the small motel radio clock told me it was now a few minutes after nine.

"This better be good," I snapped into the phone.

"Sorry, Chance," Daryl said, "guess you haven't gotten much shuteye." We really didn't talk like that much. Usually saved it to bait greenhorns.

I told him how little. He was sympathetic, but his consolation did not stop him from informing me of a board meeting set for his room at eleven. Following a pregnant silence, I told him I would be there but only if he called back at ten-fifteen to wake me up again. He blithely agreed and we rang off.

I was the last to show. Only ten minutes late. Everyone was there except Russ Ward who never attended events east of the Mississippi. I knew he would want to know everything that went on, however, and hardly had the meeting been called to order when Daryl said, "Russ, of course, is home this weekend, but I called him this morning and filled him in on what happened and that we're meeting about it. I'll be calling him as soon as we're finished to bring him up to speed."

Why so many board members still in town? Isn't it obvious? The action — gambling and shows. The people tending the bulls have to leave for equally obvious reasons, same with certain dedicated stock contractors. But everyone who can usually reserves a day or two after an event strictly for fun and games. Our weekend is Sunday and Monday. There are a few cities that practically everyone deserts the night the event ends. Not even a decent cowboy club to celebrate in. Fortunately, there aren't many of those. Of course, Atlantic City is not one of them.

Daryl had sprung for a luxury suite at Harrah's, ocean view. What else? He'd confiscated enough chairs from other rooms so that he remained the only one standing. Courtney sat at a table, pencil and pad ready. She was dressed in jeans and a long sleeved plaid shirt, wet hair wrapped in a towel so thick and huge it made those at the Acey-Deucey Motel seem like washcloths. As I took a seat, I wondered if she had forgiven Daryl for his insensitivity at the previous meeting.

Following the obligatory "Now that Chance has arrived, we can begin," Daryl said, "Chance, I know you didn't get much sleep last night, but can you bring us up to date where things stand with the police?"

"They didn't find the murderer, did they?" Kyle Nash asked.

I wagged my head. "No. Don't know if they have any real leads."

"You couldn't tell if that detective was on to anyone by his questioning?" Daryl asked.

"Not me," I admitted.

"So who besides me did he wake up in the middle of the night?" Kyle asked peevishly.

I recapped the entire evening for them. Took nearly half and hour. Every time I would begin, I would have to go back further and further in the story because those who had received only a sketchy tracing of events from Daryl and Kyle before I arrived wanted more details.

"So how do the detectives plan to interrogate Craig and Clete?" Tyler Kennelly wanted to know.

I confessed I had no idea.

"Anyway," Daryl intoned, "with Chance's update, we have to decide what we're gonna do."

"Why do we have to do something?" Kyle asked.

"Yeah," Casey Applegate agreed, nodding at his buddy. "We didn't do anything with Jodie Hall. Why do we have to do anything now?"

Daryl glanced at Courtney, and then scanned us. "Jodi Hall was one thing. Wanda's another."

"What's the difference?" Jason Moss asked.

"Jodi had no official connection with the PBR," Daryl reminded. "Wanda was an official stock contractor with us. Big difference, I would say." He shot another glance at Courtney who was vigorously taking notes.

I sensed that Courtney had given Daryl his marching orders, and as long as he marched, she'd vowed to maintain her silence, take notes and let the official board make its official decisions.

"I guess there is a technical difference," Jason acknowledged with a glance at Courtney. "But I don't see how that means we have to do somethin'."

"I think we do," Daryl urged.

"Okay, what?" Casey asked.

"First," Daryl began, "I think we have to send flowers to the funeral...."

"Goes without sayin'," Tyler interrupted.

"Right," Daryl agreed. "Then we have to issue a formal press release." He stopped and looked around.

"That says what?" Kyle asked.

"Well," Daryl muttered sheepishly, "that's kind of what

I was hopin' you guys could tell me. What should we say?"

"I don't know," Kyle said.

"It should say how sadden we are at Wanda's untimely death," Courtney suggested.

"Yes," Daryl agreed. "And we are."

"Of course, we are," Casey said, shooting a look at Courtney.

"Damn straight," Jason said, "I mean she was a character."

"Could be a bitch at times," Kyle reminded.

"Yes, she could," Jason agreed, "but she was a character just the same."

"And we all loved her," Casey said.

*Someone didn't*, I thought.

"Well, we can't say that in the press release," Daryl said.

"No, guess not," Jason agreed.

"So what else do we say," Daryl pursued.

"We say we're sadden by her death," Courtney put in, "and that we are going to cooperate with the police…."

"Cooperate to the fullest," Tyler added.

"Cooperate to the fullest with the police," Courtney modified, "in the investigation. And that we hope the culprit is brought to justice as soon as possible."

"Yes, Courtney. Good," Daryl said.

"Should we say anything about the PBR goin' on?" Kyle asked.

"Well," Daryl said, looking around, "seems to me something along those lines ought to be in there."

"Because Wanda would have wanted it that way," Casey amended.

"Yeah," Daryl agreed, pointing a finger at Casey. "And she would have, wouldn't she?"

"I would if it was me got killed," Casey said.

"Me, too," Jason avowed. "I mean I love the PBR. If a bull kills me, a murderer or I just go out in a fiery crash of some sort, I want the PBR to go on, get bigger and bigger."

"Way to go, Jason," Kyle commended.

"And for the fans," Jason stuck in. "We're gonna continue the tour for the fans."

"Yeah. Want that, too," Daryl agreed.

"I pretty much have the idea," Courtney said. "I can write up something that includes everything that's been said."

"So what do we do with it?" Casey asked.

"First we have to pass it," Daryl said. "Let's do that. All in favor?"

All were in favor.

"So what's next?" Casey asked.

"Whenever I'm interviewed by the press, or TV...." Daryl began.

"The media," Courtney corrected.

"Yeah, them," Daryl said, and grinned. "Whenever I'm interviewed by the media, I'll mention how we passed this resolution and give them the gist of it."

"Shouldn't it say that everyone connected with the PBR is mandated to cooperate with the police?" This was from Tyler.

"Good point," Daryl said. Then he turned to Courtney and said, "Add that, will you, Hon?"

Hon nodded.

"So we're sorry about Wanda's death," Kyle reiterated. "We're goin' to continued the PBR tour, and we're gonna cooperate with the police. What else?"

Silence burst forth in the room, like a star exploding in space.

Daryl wagged his head from cowboy to cowboy, included Courtney. Suddenly, his face brightened like a Christmas light. "Chance is what."

# CHAPTER SEVENTEEN

Heads swung in "Guess Whose?" direction. Paired, plural-shaded, patsy-seeking eyes reamed in on me. Hadn't I dutifully proffered my report from the previous night's activities as a junior G-man, mumbled my perfunctory "Aye" when Daryl presented his motion for official sanctification, uttered nary a peep when he added the mandate for police cooperation without a formal vote? I thought I was fulfilling my raison d'etre quite nicely. So why was everyone suddenly out to get me?

And those guys were supposed to be my friends?

Daryl had gone on to say, "Chance is already our unofficial liaison with the police." He peered around nodding. "With the Twin Falls police, anyway, in the Jodi Hall…thing. We'll make him our official liaison with the Atlantic City police. Make everything official. What do you think?"

Oh, I had a thought, all right! Don't you think I didn't! I even considered it inspirational. I would resign as vice-president of the PBR—and as liaison (unofficial, official, whatever) to the Twin Falls police. On the spot. And bolt from the room.

Before I could get my thoughts voiced, Casey, grinning like the village idiot, said, "Always wanted to play detective, Chance? Now's your chance." Then he laughed.

*No! I never wanted to play detective.* I smiled. Wanly, I was sure. At least, that was my intention. How it actually came off, I haven't the foggiest.

Swinging my gaze at all of the smug, satisfied faces

staring at me, I noticed that two were not quite as pleased as the others. Courtney's expression couldn't have been more sober. I couldn't help sensing that, in her opinion, selecting me as the police liaison was a horrible joke, a way of burying the matter about as deep as possible while misleading the public into believing that we were doing something meaningful. Was Daryl going to hear about it later? For that matter, had he heard about it the last time?

If that *was* her thinking, I agreed with her completely. I was a joke in the role. A terrible one at that. Official Liaison With The Police. I was a bull rider, for heaven's sake. Apparently, I was also a pretty good judge of bull rides. In no way, shape or form was I a detective. Of course, I knew, and everyone else in the room did too, that I wasn't really being asked to "play detective." But to my feeble way of thinking, the role of liaison did possess some elements of Sherlock Holmes. The Atlantic City police could not track the PBR around the country. The detectives had other cases that required them to remain in Atlantic City. Someone, therefore, was going to have to do some investigating. Not detecting. Detecting is different from investigating. Detectives detect. Journalists, for example, investigate. I would be like a journalist, just keeping my eyes and ears open, maybe ask a pertinent question here and there, from time to time. Nah, not me. No matter how it added up, I wasn't the right cowboy. I wasn't even going through the motions with the Jodi Hall murder, just faking it.

Then the Devil sat on my shoulder and whispered in my ear. (Had to have happened that way. Nothing else could possibly explain it.) And what he said was something like, 'Go ahead. Take the job. And if you find you ask no questions here and there, from time to time, well, you can fake it in Wanda's murder just like you're doing in Jodi Hall's." Unbelievable. But that was all it took. Anyway, with that evil notion tearing down what I thought was a strong wall of brilliant inspiration, I held my tongue—and kept my seat.

The other face in the room that wasn't smiling belonged to Kyle Nash. Curiosity piqued the cat. Why was Kyle so sullen at my undertaking this role? Could he possibly have something to hide? If so, how did he think I might possibly uncover it?

"So what do you really think, Chance?" Daryl asked, still grinning. The ass.

*RESIGN, RESIGN, RESIGN. RESIGN EVERYTHING*, I thought. (An angel on my other shoulder whispering?) But for some reason, (Vanity? The Devil?) the only thing I could say was, "Liaison?" In saying it the way I did, I hoped I was conveying the message that I did not think I was being called upon to be a detective—or, for that matter, an investigator.

"Yeah," Daryl fired back. "Exactly what you're doing now. Staying in touch with the police. Keeping us apprised of what's happening. Only this time, we're going to make it official. Pass a motion. What do you think?"

I thought for a moment. No thoughts came into my head. Where had RESIGN gone? The assembly was staring at me with blank, waiting faces, like expectant children on the first day of school. I had to say something. The only thing that came to mind was, "Pass your motion."

They did. Without further discussion. Although I did not officially abstain, I didn't vote either.

As soon as the deed was done, Kyle drawled through barely moving lips, "When and how often is he going to report?"

"What do you guys think?" Daryl asked, peering around.

Kyle divulged his thinking. "I believe it ought to be on some kind of a regular basis."

A couple of the bull riders looked askance at that.

Jason came to my rescue, or at least opened the door. "I don't want to be meetin' all the time if we don't have to. Too many meetin's will quickly become a pain in the ass."

"I just think we ought to stay informed," Kyle pressed. Casey Applegate nodded in agreement.

"What do you think, Chance?" Daryl asked.

If I were really going to play investigator, I wanted to do it right. (Was I really thinking that? If so, the Devil truly is a wily creature.) I didn't want to have to tell everything I learned, as I learned it. Maybe I should keep some things to myself. For all I knew, with excessive reporting, I might be disclosing to the killer just how close the police were to him. Yes, I'd formed the notion that Kyle not *was* but *could be* involved. The killer was probably someone who was in both Twin Falls and Atlantic City. And that fit Kyle. He was in Twin Falls when Jodi Hall was killed, and he was near the scene where Wanda Sirett met her end. That meant I had to put him on my list of suspects. At the top? Was I turning into a detective…investigator, after all? Anyway, it seemed to me I had to keep my options open.

Brilliantly, (if I must say so myself) an idea sprang to mind. "I don't see why we should be meeting all the time, if I don't have anything to present."

Courtney grunted in disgust. In her mind, I was sure, she was saying Hell would freeze over before Chance Boettecher would call a special meeting to bring the board up to date. Still, there were the regular meetings. When was the next one? After Vegas?

"I think I hear you, Chance," Daryl said, ignoring his wife's body language. "When you have something to tell us, you'll let me know and I'll call another emergency meeting."

"Is that what this is?" Jason Moss deadpanned.

"Couldn't you tell?" Casey shot back. "No one asked you for a treasurer's report."

"We're in great shape," Jason assured, raising an arm and pointing his index finger at the ceiling.

"Better be," Daryl quipped.

"That's why finding Wanda and Jodi's killer is so important," Courtney asserted, adding, when we all looked at her, "To keep it that way."

"Yes," Daryl agreed, "but to find the killer, too, Hon. Don't forget that."

"*I* hadn't," she said, almost nastily, eyeing me coldly. "Unfortunately, I'm probably the only one in here who hasn't."

"Now, Hon, don't be like that," Daryl whined. "I mean it when I say we all want the killer found. That's why we appointed Chance."

"Fine," she said, tossing her pen on the pad before her and enfolding her arms beneath her ample breasts. "Is this meeting over?"

Daryl ran his gaze around the room one more time. "I think so. Anything else, guys? No? Meeting adjourned."

# CHAPTER EIGHTEEN

The phone was chirping on the nightstand as I walked into my room. Washington.

"Can you drop around headquarters?"

I wasn't planning to leave Atlantic City until the following day. "When?"

"As soon as you can get here. I can send a car for you if you'd like."

Innocently, I took him up on his gracious offer, and twenty minutes later, after a rather scenic ride through the more bleak sections of Atlantic City in the backseat of a conspicuously marked police vehicle, I found myself seated in a nondescript interrogation room at Atlantic City Police Headquarters where the walls were painted bureaucratic green, the metal table battleship gray, the chairs, though padded, armless. Like a small island in an ocean, a black cassette tape recorder rested alone on top of the table, its cord plugged into an outlet in the wall. Curious, I looked over and noticed that a cassette had been inserted into the player.

Before I had rung off from my motel room, I had asked Washington how long he thought it would take. "Not long," he'd lied.

They grilled me for five hours solid. The constantly restructured cloud of cigarette smoke the least of the tortures.

The look on Washington's face when he walked into the room clearly said I deserved lethal injection on the spot. He took the seat across from me and lit a cigarette. A moment later, Bookman entered the room and, without a word, walked around and stood in a corner behind me, lit a cigarette. To a nonsmoking cowboy, the scent of a barnyard filled with cow dung is a whole lot sweeter than a room filled with cigarette smoke.

To my astonishment, Washington reached over and pressed the record button on the tape player.

"You didn't tell me everything last night, did you, Boettecher?"

"I didn't?" I returned innocently.

"That's right," he said, dishing out a smile that reminded me of a cobra about to strike, minus the probing tongue, of course.

With ever increasing perplexity, I said, "What did I fail to tell you?"

"Oh, just a little matter that LeAnn Sirett isn't LeAnn Sirett at all, but one LeAnn Boetecher."

Now I understood. Both what he meant and that I was in big trouble. Under the circumstances was I entitled to a lawyer? Did I need one? Did I want one? What for? I was innocent, wasn't I? I didn't kill Wanda. But all I could think to say, stupidly, was, "I never said she was LeAnn Sirett."

You know that old joke in which someone holding a gun and pointing it at a muscled three hundred pound six foot six giant of a man is admonished by a bystander not to shoot the giant because doing so will only make him angry? Well, in a sense, that's exactly what I'd just done. Washington was three hundred pounds of pure muscle just then, and I was holding a bee bee gun—at best, a pellet gun. With my last words, I had only awakened the giant's wrath.

Washington leaned over and stuck his nose in my face. "Now you listen to me, cowboy," he blustered, "you don't know it, but from what I learned this morning, you've put yourself at the top of my list of suspects for the murder of Wanda Sirett."

"What!"

"You heard me."

"How could I have killed her? I wasn't anywhere near the scene of the murder."

Here I was supposed to be the PBR's liaison, and I was a suspect. Would Courtney be satisfied? Would Kyle take some measure of satisfaction when he learned? Certainly, the real killer would, once he, or she, heard the news.

Washington backed away, sat up straight. From there he smiled, not like a cobra this time, but no one, seeing his look, would have called it friendly. "You weren't? Well, that's not how it looks to me. Seems to me you had not one but two opportunities to kill her last night."

"What?"

"Tell me what you did after you finished your stint as a judge last night."

"I told you. Daryl and I…."

"No," he interrupted, shaking his head, this time with his eyes closed.

"No?"

"No." He stopped shaking his head, opened his eyes. "That's not what you did."

"I didn't?"

"No. But I want you to tell me. Tell me everything. And I mean everything."

I stared at him blankly.

"Think," he charged me. "Think back over everything you did. Leave out nothing. Now begin. This time at the beginning."

"When's the beginning?" Believe it or not, I was sincere in my asking.

Washington sucked on his cigarette, took it away from his mouth, and, after blowing a stream of smoke that mushroomed in a dense cloud directly over my head, said, "The last bull rider has finished his turn or ride or whatever you call it. Start from right there. What did you do?"

I thought for a moment, my gaze passing over Washington's right shoulder to the blank wall beyond. I knew how it felt. My mind couldn't have been blanker.

Finally I was able to pick something to focus on. "Chad Michaelson was the last rider up," I said.

Washington nodded. What *had* I done? Daryl and I talked. I turned in my judging equipment. That was in reverse order. One way to approach it. So I kept going back. Back to Chad's ride. Then I remembered. I brightened and said, "I had to go to the bathroom."

I saw a slight relaxation of Washington's dark eyes. He was certain he was on to something. Did he think he had me? In his mind was I as good as convicted? How did New Jersey dispose of its convicted murderers?

"I had to go to the bathroom as soon as Chad's ride was through. Did he ride...? Who was it? Haymaker? That was the bull. And he did. I gave the bull a twenty-three; Chad, a twenty-two. For a total score of forty-five. Half of the ninety he received to win the event. I marked my score and then hurried to the bathroom."

"You remember where you went to the bathroom?" Washington's tone made it clear that he already knew the answer to that question.

But so did I. After all, I was the one who went, wasn't I? "Yes. At the men's room behind the chutes."

"Behind the chutes?" He flashed a look at Bookman.

"Yes. There behind the chutes."

"Where else are they?"

"Where are other men's rooms?"

"No!" he barked. "Think about where the men's room you used is in relationship to other places in the arena."

I thought. The light bulb turned on, and along with

it a feeling of hopelessness swept over me like an ocean tide. "They're near the walkway leading back to the pens."

"Yes," Washington affirmed, pointing his cigarette at me, "and you say you hurried to the men's room. My source said you were running."

"Running?" I echoed.

"Running," Washington reechoed.

Had I? Maybe. I thought for a moment, and then said, "Now that I think about it, I remember I had to go bad."

There was a pause in the questioning. I think Washington expected me to just continue talking, confess how I had not actually gone to the bathroom, but diverted myself to the holding pens where I found Wanda and heinously placed my wicked hands around her fragile neck and squeezed the life out of her, letting her limp carcass collapse in the straw where John Henry had previously resided.

Washington must have tired of waiting for the confession, because in the next moment, he said, "Who did you see in the men's room?"

"In the men's room?"

Washington nodded, eyed me narrowly.

Again I had to think. Took a long moment. There had been no one in the men's room when I used it. I told him that.

"So, we don't know if you really were in the men's room or not, do we?"

"I guess not," I admitted meekly.

"What do you make of that?"

"Me?"

"Yeah. Mean anything to you?"

"I still had to go."

That did not make Washington happy.

Before he could say anything, I added, "I hadn't had to go during the break between the second go-round and the short-go. Then, about halfway through the short-go, I noticed I had to. Came upon me suddenly. As the short-go continued, I started feeling a growing urgency. So when Chad finished his ride, I hurried out. I thought I had merely walked fast. I don't remember running."

"You having prostate troubles?"

In my early thirties, I didn't even know what "prostate troubles" were. I don't remember drinking all that much either before or during the event. Sometimes it happens. Sensing any response I gave just then would sound smart to Washington, I held my silence.

"So no one saw you in the men's room."

"I wasn't trying to draw attention to myself."

"No. You weren't, were you?"

His response sure made me wish I could take back my words. Even I thought they made me sound guilty.

Hoping to extricate myself from the morass I was making, I said, "From the men's room I made my way over to the announcers' stand where I turned in my equipment to LeAnn."

Washington chewed on the inside of his mouth for a moment. Then he said, "Did you see Wanda Sirett?"

"On my way to the men's room?"

He nodded, adding, "Or after you came out?"

I shook my head. "I wasn't looking for her either time."

"Could she have been there?"

After a moment's reflection, I admitted it was possible.

"So you trying to tell me you never went down that walkway back to the pens where the bulls are kept?"

I nodded, dumbly, said, "That's right. I didn't go back there until later. With Daryl."

Washington again paused, blew smoke out of his mouth. Finally, he said, "Why didn't you tell me LeAnn Whatever was your ex?"

"I didn't see how it mattered."

"Didn't see how it mattered?" The look he issued was pure dubious.

"No," I said, in a pleading tone. "If neither LeAnn, nor Royce, nor I killed Wanda, how would it matter?"

"Why couldn't any one of the three of you have killed her?"

"Because…." I started, and ended there. I knew I didn't kill her. LeAnn wouldn't kill her worst enemy, and Wanda certainly wasn't that. Royce? Well, Royce wouldn't have killed her either. But how many murderers wouldn't have killed their victims?

"Right," Washington said. "Because…."

"I didn't think, still don't, either Royce or LeAnn killed Wanda."

"So you withheld pertinent information."

"I didn't know I was withholding anything. I never gave it a thought."

"So tell us what you know about Royce and LeAnn's relationship."

I told him what I knew.

"She's pregnant, you say?"

"That's what she told me."

Washington shrugged. "Pregnancy makes some women do some pretty crazy things."

"I don't remember seeing her until after the short-go. She would have been in the announcers' box until then. It would only have been after I turned in my stuff that she would have been able to go to the pen area."

"Which is what she did."

I thought for a moment. "Yes," I agreed. "She said that, didn't she?"

Washington nodded. "And she spoke with the victim."

"With Royce right there," I reminded.

"So she and Royce said. How do you know they weren't

in collusion?"

"I don't believe that. I mean, why?"

"That's our question." Without giving me a chance to say anything, he continued, "Why would Royce and LeAnn want Wanda dead?"

"I thought I was the suspect." Now why did I say that? Did I say it to lure Washington away from considering LeAnn further? Was I that noble? Had never been before.

"Yes, you are, Boettecher. Which brings me to another point. There was a time you were alone with Wanda Sirett last night, wasn't there?"

"When?"

"When your friend Daryl went off to find help after the two of you found her lying in a pen."

"But…Wanda was already dead."

"So you say. Seems we have only your word for that, don't we?" He sucked in a drag from his cigarette, blew it out, saying, "Maybe she'd just fainted. My pathologist said there was plenty of body heat left in her. Said, too, her hyoid bone was fractured. Case you don't know, that's the small U shaped bone here in the upper neck." He pointed to his own neck area. "Now you can strangle a person and not break or even damage that bone. That it was shows someone with strong hands killed her. Someone like a bull rider. The way I figure it, you saw her lying there. Saw this as your opportunity. Sent the other man, Daryl, to get help. Killed her after he left."

"I didn't. I…I mean, why would I?"

"Good question. Let's talk about your motives for killing this woman."

"Wh…what? My motives?"

He held up a hand as if stopping traffic in a school zone. "Humor me. Did you have a motive for killing Wanda Sirett?"

"No."

"You say 'No,' just like that? Last night you said everyone

wanted to kill her. Didn't that include you?"

Feeling emboldened, I laughed. "Not for real. I think I said that, too, didn't I? Wanda could make you want to tear your hair out was all I meant. You know, drive you crazy. But I never wanted to kill her for real. Never had the thought."

"When did she make you want to tear your hair out?"

I smiled. "'Bout three years ago."

"Want to tell me about it?"

"No."

It was his turn to smile. "Let me rephrase that. Tell me about it."

I told him.

"And you haven't…wanted her since?"

"I slept with her once after that," I confessed. Since I didn't know if he already knew that, I figured I might as well tell him. Besides, I had nothing to fear. I didn't kill Wanda.

That widened his almond eyes. "You did?" He looked at Bookman. He hadn't known. "Tell us about *that*."

"It was a little more than a year after the first time. Guess that makes it about twenty months ago or so. A Friday night in Portland, Oregon. I went into a restaurant around noon. She was there. We ate together, talked and then she suggested we go back to her place and kill some time before going to the arena. Who was I to argue?"

"And she didn't make you want to turn the two of you into an item?"

"Not in the least. I'd learned my lesson. I mean I was on my guard with her. Once bitten, twice shy." (As my mother liked to say.) "I knew what she was, knew what I meant to her, which was a big fat zero, knew we weren't going anywhere as an item, as you say. So, I just took maximum advantage of the situation and let it go at that."

"And there's been no contact since?"

"Not of that nature. Oh, we kissed each other from time

to time at a celebration after an event. Talked suggestively. Danced with each other. But that's it."

"Had she offered herself to you, would you have taken advantage of it?"

"Hell, yes. But the initiative had to come from her. And only if I wasn't in any relationship at the time." Then I wanted to get the record absolutely straight. "Or married, anyway."

"Are there any other reasons you might have had to kill her?"

"Such as?"

He pursed his lips thoughtfully. "Such as jealousy. Maybe, despite her past rejection, you wouldn't have been all that happy if she were to take up with other men."

I waved a dismissive hand. "She never took up with a man romantically. Only for the night."

"But if she had, would that have made you jealous?"

"I wish she would have," I said, meaning it. *Might have led to less troubles on the tour.* "And if she had, I would have felt good for her. I loved her, you see. Not in the romantic sense. But as a friend. We all loved her."

"Someone didn't," Washington pointedly reminded.

"Had to be a reason," I stated proudly.

"And jealousy could be it," he said, jabbing a finger in my direction.

"Had to be something else."

"And we're looking for it. But you're not helping."

"Me?"

"You."

I was about to say something, but he waved me off. "I repeat, you're at the top of my list right now. But I don't have all the holes filled in. That means I have to explore every possibility. Understand?"

I owned that I did.

"So, any thoughts?"

"'Bout what?"

Washington blessed me with another one of his venomous looks. "About other possibilities. Like why your buddy Royce and your ex would want Wanda Sirett dead."

I hadn't realized we'd returned there. "I don't think they killed her," I said limply.

The grilling continued. Relentlessly, hour after wearisome hour. From there on there were few new questions from Washington, just the same ones over and over again, in different forms, in different orders. A bull rider, I had no stamina for this kind of thing. After all, I was used to working for eight whole seconds; sixteen tops on Saturday night if I was lucky enough to make the short-go. Accordingly, I knew I couldn't act tough in that situation, being a hundred and fifty pounds to Washington's considerably more. But there was one thing I could do. I could be pigheaded. So I stood my ground, and told him everything I knew, over and over again.

# CHAPTER NINETEEN

The grilling finally ended. With a little daylight left, believe it or not. Then again, it *was* Sunday. Washington probably hoped to spend some time with his family, though he'd never mentioned having one. At least, I wasn't under arrest.

Before releasing me, he asked for my immediate plans, when I intended to leave Atlantic City, where I planned to go next. I told him I would be leaving for Phoenix on Tuesday where I would remain through the next event. I had to promise him I would call and let him know where I was staying and the telephone number for my room. To everything I said, he just glared at me, as if certain I was lying. He already knew I didn't carry a cell phone.

After a rather boring Monday in Atlantic City, I exited my plane in Albuquerque on Tuesday, got my pickup out of long-term parking and pointed myself west. I hadn't exactly filled Washington in on all the details regarding my plans. I'd led him to believe I was flying directly to Phoenix. But my wheels were in Albuquerque. Can't get around without wheels, now can I? As I said before, west of the Mississippi, I drive to all PBR events.

Not divulging my exact plans to Washington was just my way of acting tough — in the only form open to me. It was no big thing but it was something. Did you really expect me to "act tough" with him? Out of the question. Since the conclusion of the events in this story, but before taking pen in hand (actually computer keyboard), I read a number of detective stories to familiarize myself with the genre. I wasn't much of a reader in my formative years, didn't seem very cowboy to me. I did read a few things in my not completely wasted youth. *Tom Sawyer*, *Treasure Island*, an abridged version of *Robinson Crusoe*, and a few other worthy tomes, before telling myself I'd read (past tense) everything worth reading. My mother did try to encourage me to read more, but I had other interest at the time. Anyway, before trying to describe what you're reading here, I thought I ought to learn something of the ways detectives operate. The literary kind anyway.

I confess I enjoyed Dashiell Hammett's *The Maltese Falcon* with Sam Spade, Philip Marlow in Raymond Chandler's *The Big Sleep*, Ross Macdonald's Lew Archer in a number of works. I learned these were different generations of the venerable hard-boiled detective. The heroes of those tales were tough and salty, with physiques to match, happy to give a hard right to someone's rock-solid jaw or take the punch themselves. Anything to solve the mystery.

Now I'm of average height, one hundred and fifty pounds, and except for a few playground tussles in my childhood, the kind where the combatants more wrestle than actually fight, I have never hit another person in my life. And while a number of bulls have knocked me silly, no man has ever laid a hand on me, though more than a few women have slapped my face, but I don't count those. How was I going to act tough with a man like Washington? Sure, Sam Spade wouldn't have hesitated, same for Marlow and Archer. Each, in his own way, would have told the cop to put up or shut up — with attitude no less. Each would have dared Washington to arrest him, dared him to try the third degree. But I wasn't them, or any semblance thereof, and couldn't be if I tried. So you'll have to forgive me for not throwing my lack of weight around.

That didn't mean I couldn't play it "tough" with Washington in some other way. My way. I figured I was doing a Sam Spade by deceiving Washington both about where I was going when I left Atlantic City and when I would be arriving in Phoenix. It wasn't much of a deception, though, since I was intent upon turning up in Phoenix before the end of the week. Actually, only a day later than I'd told him, the time it took to drive from Albuquerque. But I must confess executing that little deception gave me great personal satisfaction. As far as I was concerned, it couldn't have happened to a nicer guy.

The ride west along I-40 accomplished one other thing. It brought me to the conclusion that I had no choice but to actually look into Wanda Sirett's murder. Not actually play detective, but...look into it. I was a suspect. At this point, Washington's only. So if I didn't find the real killer, Washington was going to keep climbing on my back. He would treat me as if I were his ride to the money round.

On reflection, I could see his point. I, seemingly, had a motive, jealousy. And the opportunity, the time I spent alone with Wanda while Daryl went searching for help. But she was already dead when Daryl and I found her, and I hadn't killed her. That much I knew with certainty. Would Washington actually try to railroad me onto New Jersey's death row? It wasn't a tactic unknown to police forces everywhere, if you can believe some of the things you read. So to get Washington into the short-go, I had to uncover something, another theory, another suspect, another piece of evidence. I didn't have to solve the crime, I reasoned, just come up with another bull to get rode.

Resolution made, I found my thoughts drifting elsewhere, which was strange. Wouldn't you think that, with a murder having shaken my world, and having decided I would need to conduct some kind of investigation into that murder, my thoughts would dwell on suspects, motives, avenues of approach, etc.? Well, they didn't. Instead, clipping along at seventy-five miles an hour, I considered my future.

Kyle Nash was not the only bull rider contemplating

going into stock contracting. Could be a smart move — for him. But for a few years now, I'd been thinking there were getting to be too many breeders in the business, making it difficult, too difficult, for the little guy. There were a handful of big operators and a couple dozen small ones. Whenever a small guy bred a prime bull, the big boys would swoop in and offer him a ton of money for the animal. The little guy always sold — the money too good to pass up. Only someone with a big enough bankroll to immediately make himself a big operator stood any real chance of making it. Big that is. Remaining small, the little guy could still eek out an existence — if he came up with a good bull every other year or so. In considering my own aptitude for stock contracting, I knew I could only start out small and go down from there.

With stock contracting out, I gave thought to Daryl's offer, judging full time. Why not? I was good at it. I could look forward to the remaining bulls in the pen and the upcoming bull riders and judge the quality of the immediate ride I was observing while taking into consideration the possibilities of what was coming up. Sounds complicated? It is and it isn't. To be sure, not everyone can do it. It takes a certain knack. To my surprise, and that of everyone complimenting me for the job I was doing, I seemed to have it.

But (isn't there always a "but") I was still a bull rider. And I loved it. You have to experience it. There's the adrenalin rush and sensual awareness you feel while mounting a two thousand pound wild animal bent on mauling you to his heart's content first chance he gets. And that's just in the chute. There is still what follows. If there's dread during the mounting phase, there's nothing but holy terror during the ride itself. With that snorting, sniveling, jumping, bucking, twisting monster determined on displacing you from its back, it's enough to scare the be-Jesus out of the insane. So why do we do it? The money? Sure, but that's secondary. After a bull rider completes a successful ride, watch him. He's pumped. He's elated. He tosses his hat across the arena. He high-fives the bullfighters. He takes an adrenalin-hyped walk along the rail and slaps hands with the guys hanging over to congratulate him. The crowd cheers wildly. It's a high like you wouldn't believe. I didn't know if I was ready to let that go. I knew, once healed, I could still ride bulls, for a time at least, so the thrill that comes from riding one of those suckers, the ranker the better, was still possible for me, if I wanted it.

More "but." But I needed a future. Something. And I was being handed a golden opportunity. Judging could be just the thing. Fit me like a rifle on a gun rack. Once I had the position, it would be mine for as long as I could walk into an arena. Why, in a few decades, I would probably be considered a legend. As a judge, if not as a bull rider. Whatever, my future would be secure. And I couldn't lose sight of the fact that, as a bull rider, I was never immune from a mauling. Maybe one so bad I wouldn't be able to walk, much less judge. It's happened before. There are bull riders who are now quadriplegic. Russ Ward, a case in point. Did I believe I was immune? No way. I knew it could happen to me. John Henry. Need I say more?

If only Lane were here. No, in truth, he wouldn't have done me much good. I knew exactly what he would have said: "Ride 'em till you can't ride 'em no more, ole buddy, and let the future take care of itself." Lane never gave a lick for the future. Riding bulls, or in his case, fighting bulls, was everything. So judging, for him, would have been nothing but a cop out. Like a childless widower, I was all alone on this one. Still, I had a little time. No need to act in haste.

I pulled into the Five Star Motel, a one star dive on the edge of town that Lane and I always used when we came to Phoenix. After checking-in, I called Washington to give him my room telephone number.

"Where the hell you been, Boettecher? You didn't fly to

Phoenix like you told me you were going to."

"Change of plan."

"Change of plan? That all you got to say to me? Change of plan." I hope you can read the suspicion in the words he used. Let me assure you, his tone reeked of it. And without a pause to suck air, he stormed on, "And just what was the cause of this change of plan?"

"My pickup. I forgot I left my pickup in Albuquerque. Had to get it. My only means of travel." Yes, I was messing with him.

He wasn't fooled, though, and after a short pause, said, "How long you going to be where you at?"

"I don't know. Just got in. Might catch a nap."

"Good. Stay there till I get back to you." Without waiting for a reply, he hung up.

It was almost five in the afternoon. I grabbed a shower and then crawled into bed. I had hardly settled in when a rude pounding sounded on the door.

I threw back the covers and, though garbed in nothing more than a pair of print boxers, strolled over to the door.

A tall male Latino, neatly dressed in a blue seersucker suit, covered the doorway. "You Boettecher," he grunted.

I affirmed my identity.

"Gutierrez, Phoenix PD."

The light bulb turned on. "Washington sent you, didn't he?"

He smiled with all the sincerity of a drooling wolf. "You got it. Wanted me to look you over, keep track while you're in Phoenix." He sneered. "Don't guess I have to tell you why."

I pursed my mouth in what I hoped was a picture of contempt. His eyeballing finished, he didn't stay long. Before leaving, though, he asked me to point out my pickup, which, compliantly, I did. He wrote down the Texas license plate number, handed me his card and then drove off in a blue unmarked car.

I gave a cursory glance at the card. It read Detective Raul Gutierrez, listed an office address and telephone number. I tossed the card on my dresser where it landed backside up, crawled back into bed and, more tired than I thought, slept through the night.

Next morning, I downed a hearty breakfast at a small local restaurant within walking distance and then drove over to the arena where I spotted Red Parham and Cody Laws milling around the pens. Seeing them together made me wistful for the days Lane and I were inseparable.

"We're starting a half hour later tomorrow night," Red told me when I came over.

"No problem," I said, knowing full well he was referring to the poker game.

"Gonna make it?" Cody asked.

"Always ready to parlay my winnings into bigger things."

Both cowboys laughed good-naturedly, fully assuring me I'd seen the last of anything resembling a winning night for a long time.

I ambled around the pen area until I spotted Craig Kelton talking with Carl Earp. They were draped over the upper rail of John Henry's pen, a boot on the lower. Both men turned as I approached, nodded.

Craig turned back to Carl and said, "If you'll take care of that, Carl, I'd be appreciative."

"I'll git right on it," Carl said and, with another nod to me, tramped off.

"Heard you was somethin' with the police," Craig said, motioning for me to join him on the rail.

I draped both of my arms over the top rail where Carl had stood moments earlier, still warm from his time there, and placed a worn boot on the bottom one. Then I allowed as I was the PBR's liaison.

"Thought you might be lookin' for me."

"Something, eh?" I said.

"Got that right. Who'd a thought anyone would kill Wanda."

Was that a tear I spotted at the edge of an eye?

"Got somethin' in mah eye," he said, wiping it away.

"Did an Atlantic City detective get hold of you?"

"Washin'ton?"

I nodded.

He stared at John Henry in the pen. The bull was resting on his straw, peering regally over his kingdom. "Yeah, he caught up to me yesterday."

"Telephone?"

His expression reflected his disgust. "Damn Phoenix cops picked me up and hauled me downtown. Only thing they didn't do was handcuff me. I had to talk into a speakerphone to Washin'ton while the Phoenix guys listened in. They cam corded me so they could see what I looked like while givin' my answers. All went back to Atlantic City while I was doin' it." His mien spoke his amazement at the capabilities of it. "Treated me like a damn suspect."

*I knew the feeling.*

He shook his head. "Man, I loved that woman. I'd never kill her. No matter what she done. I mean I knew me and her would never hook up or nothin'. And in truth, it wasn't really a romantic thang. How I felt about her, I mean. But…we had somethin'. Somethin' no one else would understand. Now, I got to git myself 'nother job."

I assured him that wouldn't be hard.

He agreed but said it wouldn't be the same, never as much fun.

I wanted to ask him about the perks Wanda handed out to him, though I said, "I guess he asked you what you and

Wanda were quarreling about the night she was killed."

He nodded, "I told him there had been no quarrel."

"Wanda was heard telling you, 'I'll decide when we do it. I always have and that is one thing that's not going to change.'"

"That didn't have nothin' to do with me."

"What was it about then?"

"It was about business, the bulls."

"Which was it? The business or the bulls?"

"Bull business," he said testily. "It was all bull business. She was sayin' she would decide what bulls would be entered on what circuits."

"You told Washington that?"

"Course."

Moving on, I said, "Did Washington ask you anything about Twin Falls?"

Kelton's brow ruffled noticeably. "Twin Falls? No. Why?"

What did I want to know? Although I'd gotten off to a good start with Craig, I could see this detec...investigator thing wasn't going to be easy. Where to go from here? When all else was failing, I decided a different tack might serve. Like the plunge-right-in approach.

"Why were you in Twin Falls for the Challenger event?"

He looked at me as if I'd asked him the dumbest question in the book.

"Why was I in Twin Falls?"

I nodded.

"Cause that's where Wanda said we were goin'. Why else?"

"What was her rationale for going there?"

Craig wagged his head. "What's the matter with you, Chance. Don't you remember?"

It was my turn to wag my head. "Remember what?"

"John Henry had just killed Cauy the weekend before. Everyone, myself included, agreed it was best to take him out of the PBR for a week or so. You know, case the crowd wouldn't like him there. Wanda decided to take all of her bulls out at the PBR level. We were playin' it safe, I guess. Anyway, Wanda decided to go to Twin Falls to watch some of her younger stock. We seen three of her bulls in action that weekend."

Of course, and I knew it. Just wasn't thinking. What good is a detec…investigator who can't remember the obvious?

And it made sense. The politically correct thing to do would have been to let John Henry lay low for a spell, but the bull wasn't guilty of anything. We call those bulls smart and, for animals, there is a measure of truth to it, but they can't think; they don't experience guilt; they just do what they're programmed to do. John Henry was programmed to buck and kick and stomp the breath out of anything that got in his way. And he was good at it. That's why he was a star in the PBR. No one wanted him to kill a bull rider. But it happens, part of the sport, part of what makes the sport "extreme." Some fans come to see the bulls maul someone—bull rider, bullfighter, judge, they don't care. And I guess a few demented minds even come to see someone get killed. Fortunately, the times that happens are few and far between. Most people just come to see a great show. That happens all the time.

"Did you see Jodi Hall in Twin Falls?"

He jerked his head in my direction. "Jodi Hall?"

"Yes. You know she was murdered in Twin Falls?"

"Yeah. Strangled."

"Just like Wanda."

For some reason, my reminder seemed to rile him. He removed his foot from the rail and turned to face me square. We already know my height and weight. Never a bull rider, Craig had me by two inches and thirty pounds. For a brief moment there, I wondered if he was going to maul me — or strangle me.

"I don't like your implication, Chance. 'Sides, who the hell do you think you are? Where do you get off askin' me this crap? Bein' liaison or whatever don't make you a cop."

I took what I was sure was my last shot. "You're not answering the question, Craig. You got something to hide?"

He squeezed his fist. "I don't have nothin' to hide. Just don't see why I have to answer to you."

"You want Wanda's murderer found, don't you?"

"Damn it, Chance. That ain't fair. Course I want Wanda's murderer found. When he is, I want to be the one to pull the switch or push the plunger to inject him, which is how they do it now, I guess. But that don't give you no rights." He pursed his lips together tightly, turned away. Then immediately turning back to me, he said, "All right. I'll tell you. I seen Jodi, sure. She was around. Spoke to her from time to time, never much. I even found her somewhat attractive. But what can I say. She's a dyke, or was one anyway. Since she wasn't interested in men, what did I care? Is that all, Mister Grand Inquisitor?"

Whether I had more questions or not was irrelevant. Craig had had enough. Issuing me an expression of disgust, he turned and walked away. Watching him go, I sensed we'd parted on what no one would call the best of terms. I had to wonder if I was acting foolish; playing detective could cost me a lot of friends.

Then I remembered there was someone else Washington had wanted to question. Clete Fassel.

# CHAPTER TWENTY

Finding Clete wasn't hard. He was standing next to a pen of his bulls. When he saw me approaching, he smiled broadly and greeted me cordially.

"Don't mean to interrupt," I said.

"Oh, no interruption," Clete iterated. "Just admirin' ole Igniter."

I made it a mutual admiration society for a few moments, and looked on the five year old black and white Brahma sitting in his pen, calmly chewing his cud. After a few moments of "admirin'", I said, "I'd like to speak to you for a minute, Clete, if I may."

"Sure, sure," Clete said. "What can I do for you, Chance?"

He was smiling knowingly, and, in that instant, I understood where he thought this conversation was headed. With Kyle's pending purchase of Pugnacious fresh on his mind, he must have believed all the other aging bull riders would be after him to sell them bulls. If so, he was about to be as disappointed as a city child expecting a pony for Christmas.

"Did you get a call from a Detective Washington from Atlantic City?"

Clete's brow ruffled in a manner similar to the one I'd watched come over Craig Kelton's a few minutes earlier.

"Yeah," he said. "I did."

"When did he call you?"

"Day 'fore last."

"Did he talk to you from police headquarters?"

"I guess he was at police headquarters. He didn't say."

"I mean, did he have you taken into Phoenix police headquarters? Talk to you on a speakerphone?"

"No. He got a hold of me here."

"At the arena?"

"Yeah, the arena."

"What did he ask you?"

He scratched his lean cheek a moment. "Should I really be telling you this, Chance?"

"Daryl and the board have named me liaison with both the Twin Falls police and the Atlantic City police...."

"Twin Falls? Why you liaison with them?"

"Because of Jodi Hall."

"Jodi Hall? Oh, yeah, she was killed, wasn't she? Wasn't thinkin' 'bout her. Didn't really know her."

"Did Washington ask you if you were in Twin Falls?"

"Yeah, he asked."

"What did you tell him?"

"Told him I was there."

"Why did you go there? Thought you only went to PBR events."

"Why?" he echoed, setting his big cowboy hat back on his head. "Cause I wanted to see how a young bull of mine was doin'. Thinkin' 'bout bringin' him up. He could be rank in a year or two. Might put him in the first go-round in Vegas and see how he does. Was only there Friday night. Flew back here Saturday mornin'. Spoke to you that night, remember?"

I did. He'd caught me near the announcers' stand as I was turning in my clipboard. He'd asked me how I'd thought a bull of his bucked that night. Rapacious. I'd told him he seemed as rank as ever.

Clete's pointing out when I'd seen him that weekend piqued my interest. Jodi Hall was killed Friday night, not

Saturday. Could Clete have had anything to do with that? If so, Why? For the time being, though, I had to leave it there. Just then, I wanted to know what he'd told Washington in connection with Wanda's murder. It took some prodding, but I finally got him to reveal that he'd told Washington he'd seen Royce, LeAnn, Craig and Kyle in the pen area shortly after the go-round that night. But not me. At least, now, I had a witness to the fact that I hadn't been there. Then, maybe that didn't count for anything. In Washington's book, that is. He still had me alone with Wanda at what to him was a critical time.

Since Clete had nothing more to tell me that I didn't already know, I left him and drifted back to the area behind the chutes where I spotted Royce standing next to John Henry's pen. The stall smelled of fresh straw and grain and bull manure. The bull was standing in his pen, munching on a mouthful of grain and staring contently out toward the arena. He then looked at me in such a way that I had to wonder if he were daydreaming about his next mauling, as if to say he wished I were going to be his victim.

Royce turned at my approach, nodded and said, "Got to decide what I'm gonna do."

"How's that?"

"I'm Wanda's 'xecutor."

"You are?"

"Yeah." He laughed sheepishly. "She never changed her will after the divorce. Truth be told, neither have I." Then he tilted his black cowboy hat back on his round head and rested his burly forearms on top of the rail. "Well, in a way it makes sense. We had no kids. Wanda had no brothers and sisters. Her parents gone. There wasn't no one."

"LeAnn mind you doing it?"

"LeAnn?" His look reflected bewilderment. "Why would she mind?"

"So what are you going to do?"

"Have sale, I guess."

"You going to buy John Henry?"

"I'll try to, course. I expect the biddin' on him will git right pricey. But whoever gits him will be gittin' a great bull."

I had to agree, and as if to prove it we both turned and gazed upon the magnificent animal, just then in the process of rising to his feet for the purpose of evacuating; that is, taking a dump. I chatted with Royce for a few more minutes and then left the arena and returned to my motel.

The cowboys slowly filtered into town, so that by Thursday morning there were more than enough for the weekly poker game set for that evening. After winning in Albuquerque, I was anxious to give back some of my money (read: all of it). I'd missed the Atlantic City game because I had flown in and hadn't arrived until Friday afternoon.

Before the card game, however, there was something important to take care of. That morning, I drove to Tucson, Arizona, for Wanda's funeral. It was as good a day to get buried as any. The sky was blue, temperatures in the low seventies and a blustery wind blowing puffball clouds along overhead like racecars.

We'd caught a break. Wanda was from the area. Born and raised in Arizona, she was to be laid to rest between her child and her parents in a large cemetery in the heart of the city. (She had met Royce in, where else? Las Vegas.) The PBR turned out en masse. All of the officers and board members were there along with all the stock contractors and an overwhelming majority of the bull riders. Royce and Clete, along with Daryl, myself, Casey and Kyle served as pallbearers. LeAnn, accompanying Royce, was present, too. The expectant couple committed no body contact at any time during both the church and graveside services, out of respect for Royce and Wanda's dissolved union, I guessed. As far as I could tell there were no police, Phoenix or Tucson, in attendance. But who knew? After all, there were a number of people present I didn't know, extended family, former neighbors, former elementary, middle and high school "best" friends. Pre-Royce "sex-friends?" The subdued eleven A.M. service went off without a hitch and, pedal to the metal, I was streaking back to Phoenix by one in the P.M. Of course, I had stayed for the meal after the funeral. We all have to eat, don't we?

Late afternoon, I returned to my room where, bored, I decided to play liaison and give the Twin Falls PD a call in order to catch up on the latest in the Jodi Hall murder. I entertained myself for a good ten minutes rummaging through the pockets of all of my shirts in search of the card with the Twin Falls policeman's name and telephone number, before finally digging it out. The shirt and, ergo, the card had been washed once, maybe twice, in the interim. Fortunately, the name and number, though faded, were still legible. Card in hand, I picked up the telephone and dialed.

Detective Malcolm Rollins was in his office and took my call after no more than a few minutes of keeping me on hold. A silent one, at that. How refreshing to be kept on hold without a note of music or that incessant "Your call is important to us. Please hold and someone will be with you shortly," or a combination of the two. I guess the Twin Falls police budget didn't allow for such frivolities. Suited me.

"Yeah. What can I do for you?" Rollins asked in a tone of undisguised disinterest when he came on the line.

I've said it once and I'll say it again: You can't judge how people look by talking with them on the telephone. Sometimes we think we can, but we're right so seldom the few times we pull it off only proves the rule. Rollins' voice had him sounding short, bald, close to retirement. From it, too, I would have guessed he had on a ruffled suit, ala Washington, wore suspenders to hold his pants up over his rather sizable potbelly and left his wrinkled coat draped over the back of his chair.

While I was probably right about the coat in particular and the dress in general, I was probably wrong about everything else.

"Are you the officer handling the Jodi Hall murder?" I inquired.

"Yeah, who you?" He was all ears now, as if expecting to hear a hot tip that would break the case wide open. Maybe a confession.

I told him who I was and described my role as liaison for the PBR.

"So why does the PBR need a liaison?" Now, disappointed, his voice had returned to its previously bored state.

"Jodi had no official connection with the PBR, but because she was the sister of one of the bull riders, and traveled to most of the events, we're concerned. Naturally."

"Naturally, huh." I could see him chewing the inside of what I guessed was a rather puffy cheek. "I don't see nothing natural about it. Seems unnatural to me."

"I was just wondering where the case stood. Do you have any suspects?"

"Tell me. Where were you the night she was killed? That whole weekend, in fact."

"I was in Fort Worth."

"Whole weekend?"

"Yes."

"Doing what?"

I explained how I was a judge and had stood in the arena for both nights of the event.

"Ever been to Twin Falls?"

"Yes, couple years ago."

"Why?"

"I was coming back from an injury. Used the Challenger Tour event to get back in shape."

Silence. I could see him nodding, thinking.

"Why did they select you for this liaison thing?"

"I'm injured…."

"Again? All you cowboys do is get injured?"

I was in a mood. Had it been a good one, I would have given him Bull Rider Platitude Numero Uno: It's not whether you're going to get injured. It's when and how bad. But I didn't. Like I said, I was in a mood. What I did say was, "Yes, again. Which means I'm out of the World Finals in Vegas. So they figured I had the time."

"Okay. Guess I can eliminate you as my latest suspect. That means we've got no leads or suspects at this time. Whoever killed her left nothing for us to go on."

"Like what?"

"Like fingerprints in the room, an eyewitness, a blood or semen type. Get what I'm saying?"

I allowed as I did. "You still think it was some rapist…."

"Would be rapist," he volunteered. "She wasn't raped. Looks like the beginning of a rape, but, apparently, whoever it was who tried, killed her before he could do her. Get what I'm saying."

"So it was a rape gone bad."

"Seems so." There was a pause. Then he said, "What else you want to know?"

I wondered if Rollins was aware of Jodi's true sexual persuasion, whether he had interviewed Lena Atkins, whether I should ask. I remembered I had a poker game to go to, decided he was the detective and ought to know how to do his job without input from me, thanked him for his time and hung up.

# CHAPTER TWENTY-ONE

The room where Red held the poker game was the same one he'd used for the last three or four years, Phoenix Holiday Inn. I was early, anxious to get into the game, but, also, I wanted to be ready to question anyone who might seem appropriate. At the time, I had no idea what would meet the qualification for "appropriate," but I figured I'd recognize it when I stepped into it. In the end, I didn't ask a single question of an investigative character.

Tona, dressed to kill in tight black jeans and a sexy plaid top, greeted me at the door with a warm smile, soon contriving a reason to swipe the air with her left hand so I wouldn't miss the gaudy diamond ring on her third finger. I heartily congratulated her and Red, the latter throwing me a nonchalant wave. Then I noted the sour expression on Cody's face. Apparently, he'd had other thoughts regarding his friend's forthcoming nuptials. Wynona Kopecki was there, too, the spat with Cody all patched up.

I asked Tona if she'd succeeded in getting Red to set a date. "No," she replied, with a meaningful glance at the prospective bridegroom, who, meaningfully, refused to look her way, "but we're looking at sometime between the end of the Finals and Christmas."

I took a seat at the table and started sipping the beer Wynona set before me. The game started when Wes Nunnemaker and Brian Farr (were we ever drooling) stomped in, followed a few minutes later by Casey Applegate. It wasn't long before the room was packed with bull riders, bullfighters, stock contractors and other PBR personnel, all regulars. Casey had such a run of bad luck that, after an hour of constant losing, he folded his few remaining bills and bowed out of the game, leaving in a sulk. Can't say as I blamed him. He'd drawn a jacks over nines full house and lost to queens over fours, and then drew a king high heart flush, losing to an Ace high spade one. Naturally, with those kinds of hands, he'd bet heavily, losing heavily. But, holding those cards, I would have done the same thing. In fact, I did. I was the one with both winning hands against him. Unbelievably, I was having another lucky night.

Mike Dodd replaced Casey and won a big pot at Low Hole Card Is Wild. His five sevens beat four tens and worse. Luckily for me, he won mostly Red's (four tens) and Cody's (worse) money with that hand. We played Texas Hold 'em for a while and then returned to Dealer's Choice.

I found myself concentrating so much on the game, in other words, on my cards and how to play them, I forgot to think about interrogating anyone about Wanda's murder, surreptitiously or otherwise. No one present seemed to be right (or ripe) for "grilling." Except for Clete Fassel who wandered in, an unlit and illegal Cuban cigar dangling from his mouth, a half hour or so after the game commenced. Everyone else I was interested in — Craig Kelton, Royce Sirett, Kyle Nash, even Carl Earp — were conspicuous by their absence. Didn't expect Carl in the game anyway. He never played. But the others, like Clete, were pretty regular. Still, their absence was only conspicuous to me. I was sure no one else in the room proffered them a thought. At least, that they mentioned. But that was the way it always was with the poker games. Whoever showed, showed. No one missed the ones who weren't there; they would turn up down the road. Wasn't I a case in point?

The night, however, was not a complete waste — from the investigative point of view. It was Cody Laws, maybe hoping to distract me into a losing streak, who got the ball rolling.

"Say, Chance," he began in the middle of dealing a hand of Jacks Or Better To Open, Trips To Win, "Clete, here, was tellin' me you were our rep to the police in connection with Wanda's murder. That right?"

I looked at Clete who was eyeing me back, expressionless.

"Wasn't that a great sendoff for Wanda?" Wes piped in.

A chorus of hearty agreement showered the room like a spring rain.

"I thought the Reverend said it beautifully," Mike said. "About her free spirit being a vessel for the Holy Spirit."

"Think he knew how she really was?" Judd Blanchard, the seventh player at the table, asked.

"Course he knew," Mike said. "That's why it all tied together so well."

"You say so," Judd returned.

"So is it true?" Cody pursued with a glance in my direction.

This time, no one interrupted and I found myself staring at a choir of faces. "The board named me what they call liaison to the police," I said.

"Why you?" Mike asked.

"Cause I'm injured and out of the Finals."

"So that's why you're askin' everyone a boatload of questions."

This was from Judd. He hadn't raised his voice at the end as if to ask a question. Made it a statement. Despite the words used, the tone was not hostile.

I decided the sociable thing to do was to treat it as a question. "Yeah," I said, picking up a card as if trying to concentrate on my hand. Wasn't much to concentrate on—a pair of red tens, a spade jack, a club trey and a heart deuce.

Couldn't open.

"We doin' this to protect the PBR?" Wes asked.

I nodded.

"If the press makes a big deal of it, no telling what harm could follow," Mike suggested.

"Could send us back to the PRCA," Wes said.

"Don't knock the PRCA," Red chimed in. "They're great. Always have been."

Red was one of a handful of PBR cowboys who rode on both circuits. Although the PBR was his first choice, he was also trying to qualify for the NFR, the PRCA championships, also held in Las Vegas, during the front half of December. At that time, he sat just on or just off the bubble—either fifteenth or sixteenth.

"I know, partner," Wes said, chastised. "But the money's so much better with the PBR. Got to protect that."

"Who besides Clete you been questionin', Chance?" Judd pushed, maintaining his tempered tone.

"Somethin' I didn't 'preciate all that much, neither," Clete said.

I shrugged, stared at my cards. "Just a few people like Clete who knew Wanda or saw her shortly before she was killed."

"We all saw her shortly before she was killed," Mike said.

"So you goin' to question everyone, Chance?" Wes asked in a timbre that suggested he would have considered it an honor for me to interrogate him. Did he want me to consider him a suspect, too?

"Who do they think killed her, Chance?" Cody asked, just picking up his cards.

I shook my head. "Haven't the faintest."

"I think it was Craig," Wes drawled.

"Why him?" Red asked.

"Cause of what was goin' on 'tween him and Wanda," Wes replied with enthusiasm. "You know."

"*Because* of what was going on between Wanda and him," Mike said, "I don't think it was him."

"Maybe she was tryin' to cut him off, or somethin'," Wes suggested.

"She wasn't cutting him off," Mike said.

"How do you know?" Wes snapped.

"Cause it was Wanda. She liked it too much. And she liked it with Craig. Besides, meant she didn't have to give him a pay raise."

"Had to give it to him more often, is that it?" Wes said with a stupid grin. "That her way of givin' him a raise?"

After the guffaws faded, Red said, "You got any guesses?"

I shot a glance at him, just long enough to catch him peering intently at me.

"Me? Where would I get a guess from?"

"Well, you *are* questionin' people," Cody shot in. "Who you questionin' again?"

I put on my best poker face. "Bet you can figure it out."

"By either you or the police?"

I nodded.

"Yeah, let's make it a game," Brian exclaimed, tossing three cards into the center of the table and signaling Cody for the same number to replace those he'd discarded. He'd opened and we'd bet around without anyone raising. "We'll guess who's been questioned. Chance will tell us if we're right. Okay with you, Chance?"

I offered the slightest sign of assent I could think of at the time.

Royce, LeAnn and Craig were quickly eliminated, as were Daryl and myself. It took a few minutes before they got Carl, agreeing they should have mentioned him sooner. They never did name Kyle, nor did I volunteer him. It took three hands before I won the pot (Trip nines), and the guessing game seemed to have died down as the disappointed onlookers watched longingly while I raked in my winnings.

But then the conversation took a different tack, a surprising one. Judd Blanchard suddenly said, "Have they found out who killed Jodi Hall yet?"

I did not deem it prudent to mention what little I knew about the subject, but my ears were as perked up as those of a startled jackrabbit.

"The dyke?" said Brian Farr, who then laughed.

"Hey, she might have been a dyke, but she was a real sweet kid," Wes defended. "Wouldn't harm a fly."

"Yeah, she was a real sweet kid," Brian agreed with a toss of his head, "who wouldn't harm a fly on a bull's ass, but she was still a dyke."

"You think Cauy was the same way?" Randy Marshall wondered aloud.

That drew pointed looks, and a silence that swept over the room like a plague.

Red Parham broke it. "What did you say?" he demanded.

Randy shrugged and tried to look like a just-chastened boy. "I don't know for sure, but I saw him, or thought I saw him one time."

"What the hell you mean?" Red pushed, continuing his demanding tone. He was almost livid. Cowboys don't appreciate either their manhood or the manhood of other cowboys challenged in any way. Were there homosexual on the PBR tour? Officially: *No way, Jose.* Unofficially: *No way, Jose, but who really knows*? All I knew was that if there were, unlike the rest of society, they were so deep in the closet no one knew which doorknob to jiggle. Until now. Was Randy opening a Pandora's box?

Red, while picking up the cards to deal the next hand, said, "I mean it, Randy. What do you mean by you thought you seen him?"

"We were in Laughlin and I was walking down the street. I passed a woman that I swore looked just like Cauy. You know, in the face. About his height, too."

"You sure it was him?" someone asked from behind me.

"He was all painted up. You know, something like a whore would do. Lots of rouge, lipstick, eye shadow…. I mean, no real woman would have that much makeup on. I remember thinking that at the time."

"What color hair?" Cody asked.

"Blond, reddish blond."

"What was he, er, she, wearing, a dress?" Red asked.

"Yeah. Which was strange. Cause all the other girls around were wearing jeans. Shirts and jeans. It was because there was this one girl dressed so much like a girl in the midst of all these girls dressed like guys that drew my attention. And she, or he, if it was Cauy, was with some guy. Holding hands. I swear it looked like him."

"But you ain't sayin' it was him," Red concluded.

"Can't go that far. Just looked like him."

"When was this?" Cody asked.

"Last year."

"Not this year?"

"No. Last year."

"Hell, that don't mean nothin'," Red said. "Just means it couldn't have been him."

"Why you say that?" Randy enjoined.

"Cause no queer can keep being queer for that long and not get found out," Red replied smugly.

"That's a load of bull," Randy said.

"How would you know?" Red asked, and then added,

while laughing, "You weren't the guy holdin' his or her hand were you?"

"Nah, I wasn't the guy holding his hand. But you don't know what you're talking about."

"I have to agree with Randy," Judd put in. "Up until a few years ago, queers stayed in the closet their entire lives. They was good at keepin' quiet. Only been in the last twenty-five years or so you hear so much about 'em."

"What I want to know," Red inquired, peering at Randy, "is did you say anythin' to Cauy?"

"When?"

"Afterward."

"I did. I told him what I saw."

"What'd he say?"

"All he said was 'Where'd you get a crazy notion like that?' then he laughed and walked away, shaking his head."

"Now isn't that interestin', " Judd said.

Although I found it so myself, the perfectly hidden full house I was developing sapped any further interest in the subject on my part, and, mercifully, the conversation moved on to other subjects.

For the second time in a row that I'd played, I was the big winner.

"You learned how to play this game, Chance?" Cody asked as we gathered up our money.

I looked at him, saw he meant nothing by it. Smiling wanly, I said, "Guess I'm learning all kinds of new things."

Before everyone filtered out, Red said, "Remember, cowboys, no game next week. First weekend of Finals. We all want to do our best."

"Damn straight," Wes agreed, "too much at stake."

"So get plenty of sleep," Red extolled.

"With or without someone helpin' us to get all that sleep?" Cody queried, glancing at Wynona.

"That's up to you," Red returned, "but in light of some of the conversation run out here tonight, I guess I better remind you that real cowboys sleep with cowgirls."

"Or anywise somethin' of the female persuasion," declared Mike.

"Do cows and mares count?" Judd wondered.

"Yeah. And how 'bout sheep and goats?" added Wes. "I mean if they're of the female persuasion."

The laughter continued as we filed out the door, everyone tossing back one more round of congratulations to Tona for inducing Red to turn her honest.

# CHAPTER TWENTY-TWO

Next morning, the telephone jangled angrily from the nightstand. Daryl. Becoming the story of my life. When he realized he'd awakened me from a sound slumber, he said, "Why sleepin' so late, Chance? Day's awastin'."

I wasn't up for platitudes at...what? I looked for the clock. There wasn't any. I found my watch. It read ten-fifteen, or something close.

"What's up, Daryl?" I asked, rubbing some of the sleep out of my eyes.

"Seen the papers?"

I wasn't much into news. Never had been. Traveling the PBR circuit had me hopping from one city to another, on average, every other week. The local news, local sports, local obituaries, even the local weather, were Greek to me. With the Republicans opposing everything the Democrats proposed and vice-versa, national news was entertainment only for masochists. With the never-ending War on Terror, the Palestinians hostile to the Israelis and vice-versa, international news was no less painful. Even when at home in Uvalde, the two months between the Finals and the first event of the new year, I seldom bothered with the newspaper, local or otherwise. Besides, my wonderful neighbors soon had he me up to snuff with the really important stuff — divorces, car wrecks, sex crimes.

Having just been wrenched out of a truly satisfying snooze following my unprecedented second consecutive winning poker night, I was feeling somewhat surly. With attitude, I said, "I was asleep, Daryl. Remember?"

"The PBR is in grave danger. We have to control the spin of this thing, if you know what I mean."

I grunted.

"We're holding a press conference at eleven. Want all the board members there. You know, to show support. Get a copy of the paper and read it before the press conference."

"Where?"

"You can get a paper anywhere."

"Not the paper," I said. I wanted to add, "idiot," tactfully refrained. "The press conference."

"Out front of the arena."

I showered, shaved and dressed, and then bought a Phoenix Gazette from the rusty box outside the motel office. I read the pertinent article on the first page of the second section, The Entertainment Section, while downing pancakes and sausage at the Mickey Dee across the street.

PBR TO OPEN HERE UNDER CLOUD, the headline read.

*Atlantic City Murder Still Unsolved* the subhead claimed.

Phoenix. With established stars like Red Parham, Tyler Kennelly and Kyle Nash on hand, challenged by newcomers, Chad Michaelson, and current number one bull rider, Justin Diver, the PBR opens tonight at the American West Arena. But under a dark—and deadly—cloud. For murder has found its way into the PBR.

Last Saturday, Wanda Sirett, a PBR stock contractor and owner of the famed killer bull, John Henry, was discovered strangled in the pen area behind the bucking chutes at the Convention Center in Atlantic City, New Jersey. In addition to John Henry, the forty-two year stock contractor owned the bull Instigator as well as other popular stock used for PBR events. She was the wife of Royce Sirett, a long time PBR and PRCA rodeo fixture.

Detective Marcus Washington of the Atlantic City Police Department, in a telephone interview, said, "We are conducting an ongoing investigation. While we're still in the early stages, what we've learned strongly suggests someone linked with the PBR is responsible for this ghastly crime."

Also reached by telephone last night, Daryl Minnich, president of the PBR, said, "We are all appalled. No one ever dreamed that such a thing could happen in the PBR." Minnich indicated he would hold a press conference outside the arena this morning at eleven A.M., during which he would make an important announcement.

One stock contractor, Clete Fassel, said, "We all mourn the loss of our dear friend, Wanda. She was a beautiful person. I only hope the culprit is brought to justice before the week is out." When asked if he knew why she was killed, he said, "It doesn't make any sense at all. Wanda didn't have an enemy in the world."

The cowboys have been drifting into town throughout the week, but interrupted their preparations for tonight's event to attend funeral services for the popular Ms. Sirett, yesterday, in her hometown of Tucson, Arizona.

The murder casts some doubt on the future of the PBR. The circuit, founded little over a decade and half ago, has grown in popularity every year throughout the country. The increased fan base has meant increased purses for the bull riders. Now, those purses may very well be in jeopardy.

To prevent that, everyone connected with the PBR agrees the murderer has to be brought to justice. To that end, Detective Washington said, "Our investigation will have to be conducted with a long arm. But thankfully, we have obtained the cooperation of the police departments in all the upcoming cities where the PBR holds events. We definitely expect to catch the culprit."

The PBR was already reeling from the tragic death of

bull rider, Cauy Hall, a few weeks earlier, killed by the bull, John Henry, which, ironically, had been owned by the murdered Wanda Sirett.

The arena doors (the article concluded) will open an hour and a half before the eight P.M. starting time for what is expected to be a sold out weekend.

At least, Washington hadn't pointed a finger at Chance Boettecher, his prime suspect.

After putting the newspaper down, I found myself surprised in three ways. Wanda was forty-two, though she'd claimed she wasn't a day over thirty-eight. No question, she'd lived hard, but through it all, she'd managed to keep her looks. Some people are just lucky that way, I guess.

That there was no mention of Jodi Hall's murder was the second surprise. I wondered how the reporter had missed it. For this omission, however, the PBR had to count itself lucky.

The final surprise had to do with Daryl. Now, what big announcement did he have in store?

I was the last board member to put in my mug at the press conference. I arrived right on the minute but still drew peevish miens from Daryl and Courtney, who was present along with the other board members' wives. Lucy Nash made a big production of adjusting Kyle's buffalo nickel bolo while whispering in his ear, probably instructions to standup straight and look sober but not grim.

Not only had representatives of the local press, television and radio turned out, but also one national network had sent in its A-team. Surveying the scene before me, I couldn't help thinking that Daryl was right—the kind of publicity unfolding for our beloved PBR was going to be very damaging. Permanently so, if not contained. And I had no control over it.

The only way to save our collective hide was to find Wanda's killer. No other solution. The future of the PBR was definitely at stake.

With his entire board lined up behind him like contestants in a beauty contest, Daryl stepped to the wooden podium where a cluster of microphones resembling a spray of silver roses awaited him. I have to give him credit. He handled it perfectly, at least at first. Reiterating the points made in our motion at the meeting the previous Sunday, he made it clear that everyone connected with the PBR was shocked and saddened at what had happened in Atlantic City. He said, "We're cooperating fully with the police both in Atlantic City and in Phoenix to bring Wanda's murderer to justice."

Knowing full well everything that was coming, I tuned Daryl out and studied the crowd. The newsprint people were scribbling copiously, while the other media folks fidgeted with recording equipment; video for TV, audio for radio. Then my gaze was drawn to a man who, like a clown at a funeral, seemed disjointed from everything going on around him. Early thirties, he was tall with dark hair, dressed in burgundy slacks and a yellow dress shirt. He had no visible notepad or pen, no recording machine. None of the media people paid any attention to him (I almost wrote "took note of him"). I was wondering at the purpose for his presence when, suddenly, I heard my name mentioned.

"At this time, I'd like to call on Chance Boettecher," Daryl said, turning and nodding in my direction before returning his look to the audience standing before the podium. "Chance, as you know is a top-ten bull rider, and has been so for years. Lately, he's been injured and filling in as a judge, doing an outstanding job. He's also our vice-president where he's also doing a great job. At this time, I want to announce that the board has officially appointed him our liaison to the police in connection with Wanda's death. He's only been in his position a short time, but I'd like him to give you an update of where things stand. Chance."

Had I known Daryl was going to pass the buck to me

like that, I would have prepared properly, meaning, I would never have shown up in the first place. You can take that to the bank, but it was too late. I was there and Daryl had already put me on the spot. Maybe he hadn't told me what he was planning because he understood my options (and character) quite well. Or maybe Courtney was behind it. I could sense her hand in this unwarranted duplicity, telling her hubby exactly how to handle me — and receiving smug satisfaction watching it go down.

Feeling as if I were walking to a firing squad, I made my way to the podium. With a couple steps to go, Daryl leaned in and whispered, "Keep it brief, Chance."

I nodded and stepped to the microphones.

Staring at that ocean of hostile faces was daunting. It's one thing to peer over a mass of people when you're calm and collected and thinking you don't have to do or say anything, but definitely another to stand before them with perspiration (sweat to cowboys) beading up under your arms, etc.; especially when you have nothing prepared, yet knowing full well they would be hanging on your every word.

I have never been as afraid to climb on the back of a one-ton bull as I was at that moment. Given my choices of tackling that host of reporters or climbing on John Henry's back, I'd have chosen the bull in a heartbeat, even with my injuries. What was I afraid of? Simple. That something I said would cause embarrassment or harm to the PBR. With my emotions running a little out of kilter, I needed a few moments to gain my running feet. So, after a few "Ers and uhs" that included some sentence containing "my, er, sadness at the tragic loss of a dear friend of the PBR, Wanda Sirett," I got down to business.

BS-ing, that is. I said, "Just last Sunday, I was appointed as liaison to the police by the PBR board. In Atlantic City, I met with Detectives Washington and Bookman of the Atlantic City police. I helped arrange interviews with various people… witnesses, potential witnesses, to the crime. When I arrived in

Phoenix, I was met by a representative of the police, er, here, so we've touched base. As Detective Washington said in the article in the newspaper, the investigation is going to have to take place in the cities where the PBR holds events. To accomplish that, we are all going to cooperate. My job is to see that the board stays abreast of the status of the police investigation and to help the police reach the people they want to question. I think that's all I have at this time. Except, as Daryl said, we hope the police catch whoever did it as soon as possible. Thank you."

Believing my task completed, I started to step away from the podium. Immediately, a din of shouts from the people (everyone of them, I was sure) on the other side of the podium arrested me.

"Mr. Boettecher, weren't you the one who discovered the body?" This came from an attractive woman I'd seen on national TV from time to time on the rare occasions that I happened to catch the news on the network she worked for. She was dressed in a blue business suit, hair and makeup perfect. She was shorter than I thought she'd be from watching her.

I glanced at Daryl who merely nodded back. I leaned into the microphones and said, "Yes, I discovered the body, but Daryl was with me at the time."

"How did that make you feel?" she followed.

*What? Excuse me! What a stupid question. And they let people like her on national television?* I knew how I wanted to reply to that. Instead, I said, "Like everyone else, I was shocked. Couldn't believe it."

"Have the police told you whom they suspect?" asked a younger, less gorgeous reporter. Local station, I surmised.

No, I didn't say they suspected me. Instead, I said, "To my knowledge, the police have interviewed everyone who was in the vicinity of where Wanda was found around the time of her death. I don't know who, if anyone, they suspect." I'd given passing thought to playing it cute and saying "whom" like the reporter had; in the end, I decided it would be disgraceful for a cowboy to ever utter such a word out loud.

"Did the police say whether anyone they questioned was a suspect?" asked a man from the print media, the Phoenix Gazette I thought.

"I think, right now, everyone is a suspect, but the answer to the question is no."

"Are you a suspect, Chance?" the same questioner followed up.

"I guess I am," I confessed awkwardly.

The questioning continued for another twenty minutes. I couldn't believe how many versions of the same questions could be offered. And it didn't let up even after I'd exhausted all the ways of saying "I don't know any more than what I've already said." For the inexperienced, reporters truly can turn themselves into people to be dreaded and avoided—take it from someone who has been there.

Finally, Daryl came to my rescue, thanked everyone for coming out and announced that the press conference was over. So that was his big announcement? That I was the PBR's liaison with the police. I never felt more like a sacrificed sacrificial lamb in all my life.

# CHAPTER TWENTY-THREE

That night, I blew my first score since becoming a fill-in judge. Ty Hudson, an Arizona native and the first bull rider up, drew Tatanka, a sand colored Braham goliath I'd never seen before. We, judges and cowboys, had no idea what to expect. Certainly not a ranked effort. But Tatanka was unbelievable. He broke from the gate and immediately executed a powerful turn to his left, away from the bull rider's hand. Any unprepared bull rider would have bucked off right there. Hardly had Tatanka spun around once when he broke out of the spin and leaped high in the air before dropping the front half of his body downward with unbelievable force. I have no idea how Ty stayed on. Then Tatanka changed directions, spinning back to his right. Ty had no choice but to throw caution to the wind. He gambled that the animal would not come out of the spin until the eight second whistle. Luck held. Tatanka stayed in that spin, not turning back until the whistle sounded when he finally broke Ty's hold on his bull rope and sent him sprawling into the dirt on his back. Had the animal seen him, Ty would have made an easy target for a mauling. Fortunately, Tatanka's attention was drawn to the escape chute where Lance Miles was in the process of opening the gate. Tatanka bounded through, thoughts of warm straw and a tasty snack dancing in his big hard head.

Before marking a score I had to check with Rocky Walls, the timekeeper, to see if Ty had actually made the whistle. Rocky gave the thumbs up sign and the crowd let out a deafening roar.

I marked down twenty-two for the ride, twenty-three for the bull. Hindsight, good old Mr. Twenty-twenty, revealed clearly that I was too low. I should have given Ty a tweny-three for the ride and the bull a twenty-three. Doubled, that would have come to ninety-two, the more accurate mark for what I'd just seen. When the score of eighty-nine flashed overhead, the crowd jeered at a level that almost equaled their earlier cheer. They were absolutely justified. They were booing the judges— Rich Nobels, my fellow scoring judge, and me. Rich gave Ty a twenty-two; the bull, a twenty-two. You see where the eighty-nine came from. So, we both had blown it.

In reality, Rich and I were casualties of bad timing. Had Ty ridden Tatanka near the end of the go-round, he would have gotten his ninety-two, a ninety-one, at least. But when the first guy out of the chutes draws the rankest bull in the pen and rides him, yard-dog fashion, the judges invariably mark the man and the ride lower than it deserves. There's a perfectly good reason for this inequity. We have to leave room for another sensational ride. If we don't, we might find ourselves having to give someone a ninety-eight or ninety-nine, and theoretically a hundred, when the proper score should be mid-nineties. One judge told former World Champion, Tuff Hedeman, he would have marked his ride on Bodacious, who was only ridden four times in his entire career, higher if the ride he'd made on that bull had not come so early in the go-round.

What Ty's ride and our faulty scoring meant was that for the rest of the evening we had to consistently dole out paltry eighty-twos and threes for bull rides deserving of eighty-sixes, sevens and eights. So while it doesn't happen often, it happens. The bull riders understand, but not the crowd. And, in Phoenix that night, they were on us the whole time.

Helping to mar the night further, a small solid black Mexican bull named Pistola Pete, a fast spinner, stepped on a rookie bull rider's chest, breaking three of his ribs in the process, and then, before exiting the arena, butted Judd Blanchard with his head, catching the bullfighter in the hip and sending him to the sports healers.

One of those nights. At least, Judd was back after the intermission. Those bullfighters are tough.

It was as intermission was ending and I was returning to my place in the arena that Randy Marshall caught my attention. Per usual, I was standing on the announcers' side of the arena and only had to stride over a few steps to where he was leaning over the railing. He was pointing toward a row of seats near the chutes—prime seats. "Chance," he said, excitedly, "that's him."

Him? Naturally, I asked Randy what he meant.

"The guy I was telling you about last night. The guy I saw Cauy Hall holding hands with in Laughlin, last year."

"You're sure now it was Cauy you saw?"

His shoulders sagged and his look was sheepish. "I can't say a hundred percent. But that's the other guy." He was pointing again. "No doubt in my mind. That's him."

I took a look in the direction he was pointing. "The heavyset guy with the white cowboy hat?"

"No, the guy to his right. Next to Lena Atkins."

I spotted Lena. A pleasant surprise—even if I had unearthed some disappointing news about her. I hadn't seen her since the night before I learned Jodi Hall had been killed in Twin Falls. She'd dropped completely out of sight. But here she was, looking good in black laminated jeans, and a cheetah printed halter-top. Then, when I saw who was sitting beside her, my mouth caved in disbelief. It was the man from the press conference that morning who had seemed so out of place. Only now he was dressed for the occasion in jeans, striped shirt and a black cowboy hat. Questions railed though my brain, the same ones from the morning only with a basketful of others. Who was he? What was he doing here? Why had he been at the press conference? Was he the man Randy presumed held Cauy Hall's hand a year ago in Laughlin? Was it Cauy's hand he'd been holding? Had Cauy been dressed up like a woman? If so, did this man know who and what he was?

Those were questions to be asked by a detective. But wasn't I playing detective? Well, not playing, for this was serious business. My concern for the health and the future of the PBR had not diminished a twit since Daryl's press conference. Seeing that Wanda's murder, and by extension, Jodi Hall's, was solved so the PBR could thrive and grow was paramount. But even I thought the salvation of the PBR was secondary to the notion of bringing the culprit of these crimes to justice. Murder should not be condoned by individuals or society, and murderers should get their due. Sentimental, I know, but still a treasured value nonetheless.

Then, without my mentioning it further (or out loud), I was certain one of my questions was answered--the second one, the purpose of his presence. Don Rhodes, Randy's sidekick, chose that moment to make an announcement over the PA.

"Folks," he began, "you'll want to be on hand tomorrow night when the PBR pays tribute to a dear friend and a great bull rider, Cauy Hall, tragically killed a few weeks back doing what he loved best — riding bulls. So be sure and be here. It'll be a great tribute and we'll throw in some equally great bull riding to boot."

If he had been the man holding Cauy Hall's hand in Laughlin the year before, if it was, in fact, Cauy's hand he'd held, the presence of the man sitting next to Lena made sense. He was here for the tribute to Cauy.

# CHAPTER TWENTY-FOUR

The go-round ended a little after ten, to a host of brutal catcalls directed squarely at the judges by the unforgiving fans. To our credit, Rich and I had managed to keep Ty in the lead, which was only right since his ride was the best of the night.

Bull riding fans are the best sports fans in the world. They are loyal and knowledgeable. They cheer every cowboy who makes a good ride, whether a favorite or not. They agonize over every wild get-off and mauled bull rider until they know the cowboy's status, and then, walking or carried, send him off with an appreciative ovation. Despite their wonderful qualities, they are human beings, the fallible kind, and I love each and every one of them.

Following the conclusion of the round, I spotted Lena and her companion leave their seats and start up the aisle for the main concourse. I hustled over to the announcers' stand and waited until LeAnn spotted me. She stepped over to the rail and I handed her my clipboard and scores. My eyes gravitated (naturally, I want to think) to her abdomen, which appeared as flat and hard as before; but, of course, it was too soon for her to be showing.

"Tough night," she commented.

I agreed but changed the subject. "Royce, picking you up?"

"He's my main ride now," she said, letting a coquettish grin sweep across her face.

"What happened to your Bronco?"

"Oh," she said, eyes darting to the stands, back at me, "Royce and I like to ride together."

"Of course." No! It couldn't be. Not true love. Royce must really have something after all. I didn't think a nuclear explosion could separate LeAnn from that Bronco of hers.

Randy called LeAnn away so I checked Lena's progress. She and the object of my interest were following the mob, moving slowing, a third of the way up the aisle. I was about to chase after them like the straggling runt of a litter of pups, when I found myself peering into a pair of alert dark eyes belonging to one of Phoenix's finest, Detective Raul Gutierrez. Even his attire screamed "Cop." Although pressed, the suit surrounding his husky frame was pale blue, and the tie covering his white shirt was the flag—red, white and blue.

"Judge Boettecher," he said, trying to infuse mockery into his bland tone.

"Yes," I said frowning, shooting another glance in Lena's direction. She was halted in the aisle.

"Didn't make yourself many friends tonight." Gutierrez was gloating like a gambler who'd just cleaned up on a long shot.

"The cowboys understand what happened."

"What did happen?" His mien suddenly changed, and I sensed he really wanted to know.

Settling on the short version, I explained it to him, all the while keeping one eye glued on Lena and her companion, the pair continuing their slow climb up the aisle. If I could get rid of Gutierrez quickly, I still had a chance of catching them before they reached the concourse. Unfortunately, Gutierrez hadn't finished humoring himself at my expense.

"So you kept the scores in line, one bull rider with another, at the expense of not giving high scores."

I nodded, said, "That's right."

"Which are popular?"

"Yeah," I said, nodding again.

"But now you are not so popular."

"I can stand the heat," I claimed with no little self-satisfaction, and I meant it. Another nail in the coffin settling my future as a PBR judge? While I had not enjoyed the booing, the crowd hadn't gotten to me. Rich and I knew what we were doing, and we did it. No real training. But then there isn't any formal training for a bull riding judge, not even a one-day seminar, just years of keen observation. The first score locked us in but locked in we stayed and made it right for the cowboys, if not for the fans.

Gutierrez eyed me pointedly. "Maybe you can," he said, "but then you haven't experienced the temperature turned all the way up."

I gave him my best stupid grin as I said, "Are we talking about the same thing?"

He wrinkled up his mouth and said, "Perhaps. Perhaps not."

"What can I do for you, Detective? I've got somewhere to go, if you don't mind."

He arched his brows. "Where to in such a hurry?"

"Is that really your business?" Now where did that come from?

His jaw set tight, his eyes squinted. Then he relaxed, smiled and said, "Never mind. Just thought you might be wanting to help the police catch a murderer is all."

"What do you mean by that?"

"I hear you're asking questions." When I didn't respond, he added, "Washington in Atlantic City won't like that."

I wanted to give him that sarcastic, "Riiigghhttt!" so popular sometime back, but I didn't see any point in provoking him further. Lena was getting away, albeit slowly.

He noticed that I kept glancing in a particular direction, turned and looked for himself. "Looking for someone?"

"Just want to say 'Hi' to some friends."

I started to walk away but Gutierrez caught my arm. "Remember," he said, "don't leave town without letting me know."

I climbed over the rail and proceeded up the aisle. Lena and her companion had just topped onto the concourse where they spilled into the crowd and slipped out of my sight. I'd taken an aisle several sections over from the one they'd used and knew I would have to hurry to have any chance of catching them. I had one thing going for me though. If they planned to exit through the main entrance, they would have to come in my direction. However, if they were parked in a lot on the west side of the arena, they would actually walk away from me, and, in the crowd, I would never find them.

Because my aisle was nearly empty, I was able to take the steps two at a time and soon reached the concourse where I looked first in one direction and then the other. Neither Lena nor the man were anywhere in sight.

Here the throng was as thick as spawning salmon swimming upstream. Only, laughing and chattering, the crowd was "swimming" in both directions. One teenage girl, holding hands with a short pimpled boy about her age, spotted me and pointed. I smiled. That effort earned me the point of a pink tongue from the young lady's mouth, followed by a boisterous laugh, joined in by her date.

I didn't take offense.

I continued searching the crowd but spotted nary a glimpse of Lena or the man with her. Fine detective I was turning out to be. In all the mystery novels, weren't the people to be questioned always present when needed — at home, at the office, at a bar — perfectly available for the detective to question? I know it's a plot device to keep the story moving, but plot devices are not real life. Still, I had one consolation. The next night, Saturday night, the PBR was holding a memorial tribute to Cauy. If what I was surmising were true, Lena and her friend would be there. I could hope.

With no other option, I joined the crowd moving toward the far exit where I figured Lena and her friend were probably headed. If they came in my direction, I would have seen them. Since I hadn't, I assumed they'd gone the other way. I was behind them, way behind.

Inching along, I thought about the two murders. For some reason, I began to doubt the Twin Falls police's premise that Jodi's death was a result of a rape attempt gone awry. After letting it slip my mind at first, I'd told Washington about what happened to her. What did that say? Something about my gut feeling? That maybe there was a connection between her death and Wanda's in some way other than in just the similarity of the method by which they were killed? If so, didn't that support the conclusion that the same person killed both women? Probably a man? It was the only way it all made sense — if the two murders were connected. But what did that tell me? Only that the killer had to have been someone who'd been in both cities when the two killings took place. I was amazed that Craig, Kyle and even Clete fit the bill. Each of them probably had a motive for killing Wanda at some time or other (like we all did), though I had no idea what.

Suddenly, I was struck by another question. Was there anyone else who was in Twin Falls at the time of Jodi's killing and also in Atlantic City for Wanda's? I'd have to give it some more consideration.

Anyway, because I was so in the dark about motives and connections, I had no idea what to ask Lena's friend if and when I caught up with him. That is if he would talk to me in the first place. When it came right down to it, I was hoping he would shed some light on Jodi's murder or offer some connection between Jodi and Wanda. A lot to hope for. One thing I was certain he could do, if for no other reason than to stifle the poker game scuttlebutt initiated by Randy Marshall, was verify Cauy's sexual inclination.

The odds were he knew nothing helpful. Why, he might not have known Jodi at all. Whatever he knew, he would probably refuse to answer my questions or worse—lie.

I reached the exit and stepped out into the cool October air. Cigarette smoke (mingled with the scent of a not so legal substance) drifted toward me from one side. Must have been a dozen people puffing away. One woman in a brown cowboy hat whined, "Can you believe the low scores? On television they're always higher." A tall man standing beside her responded, "You don't see much of the first go-round on television. This might be typical for a first night. Bet tomorrow the scores will be higher."

*You'll win that bet.*

I passed through the smoky cloud to the top of the stairway. Overhead, the stars twinkled like a billion tiny Christmas lights. Off in the distance, Phoenix glittered as if in competition with the heavens. I had time for only a fleeting glance at the sky and skyline, for just then I got lucky—or half-lucky. Driving by in her red Jeep Cherokee went Lena Atkins, alone, window down.

"LENA!" I called.

She turned at the sound of her name. Seeing me, she smiled and waved. I hailed her and started running down the steps, three at a time. A perplexed look alighted her face at the sight of me scurrying toward her, but she stopped the vehicle long enough for me to run between it and a yellow Mustang behind her and jump in.

"Thanks for picking me up," I said, pulling the door closed with a solid thud.

"Happy to, Chance. Where to?"

"Mind driving me around to the other side of the arena? My pickup is there."

"Glad to. What happened? You forgot what side of the building you were parked on?"

"I guess I thought south was west or vice versa." We laughed good-naturedly.

Then Lena said, "What's up, Chance?"

I tried to act innocent, failed. I mulled over the best tactic to take. Maybe straight on would do it. Hadn't it worked before? "Did the Twin Falls police ever question you?"

She tilted her head back knowingly. "I heard you were some kind of something with the cops. So what are you, a detective now, along with being a low scoring judge?"

"Now...."

She covered her mouth with the back of her hand to stifle the giggling. "I've traveled the circuit enough to know what happen, Chance. You guys did a great job. Just too bad about that first bull."

I thanked her for understanding.

"So did the police call you?"

"No. Why would they?"

I couldn't believe my ears. I thought I was asking something perfunctory, designed to open the door. "Because...?" I thought that word combined with a little upturn in my voice would say it all.

"Because what?"

"Lena. Let's not play games, okay? I've heard all about you and Jodi."

"Just what have you heard?"

"You know what I've heard. About your sexual preference."

She held her head at an angle. "So you've heard something. Big deal."

"It's not a big deal with me except as it applies to these murders."

"So what is your involvement exactly?"

"I'm supposed to be the liaison to the police."

"What does that mean?"

I blinked. Then inspiration struck. "Whatever it is I'm the same thing in connection with Jodi's death."

"Jodi's?"

I nodded. "Only in her case, I'm unofficial."

"Jodi's murder was unofficial, huh?"

"Not to me."

"But isn't that just the way it always is? Jodi was the sweetest thing around. Her murder is…unofficial. Wanda was a bitch. So in her case, everyone cares about justice."

I muttered something about unfairness.

"So what kind of fishing expedition you on, Chance?"

"I really don't know, Lena. But I want those murders solved."

She nodded her head knowingly. "The PBR's survival depends on it. The newspaper hinted at that."

"That's a part of it, of course."

"And you're going to be the one to save it."

I decided a quip might save me. "It's a dirty job but somebody's got to do it."

That got a smile, a wan one. I told her it seemed to the board that I held the highest qualification for the job — the only one out of the Finals due to injury. Then I added, "But I knew Wanda well. Loved her in the way we all loved her…."

"Loved/hated you mean," she interrupted in a tone that clearly spelled her contempt.

"Exactly."

"She could be so exasperating at times," she continued, wagging her head.

"That's for damn sure. But I want her murder solved."

She snapped a look in my direction. "You don't care about Jodi's, though," she baited.

"I didn't know Jodi well," I confessed. Then I eyed her

pointedly. "I only heard things about her after she was murdered. You know what I'm referring to because I was hitting on you the night after she was killed." That drew another smile on her face, this one pleasant. "I did that because I thought you might possibly be interested in me. Only afterward did the things I heard about you and Jodi make me realize I'd made a complete ass of myself."

"But such a nice ass, Chance. Believe me, I wasn't laughing at you. I knew you didn't know."

"I've learned how sweet a person Jodi was. And whatever she was, she was Cauy's sister and Cauy was my friend. And he was a bull rider. A damn good one. I respected him. So for his sake, if nothing else, I want Jodi's murder solved, too."

"Do you believe Jodi was the victim of a rape attempt?"

I stared out the windshield. "In truth, I don't have the vaguest notion. But, for some reason I can't explain, I believe the two murders might very well be connected. It seems to me Jodi could have been killed because of what it was she flew to Twin Falls to do."

"Jodi hardly knew Wanda. They were like night and day. You know what Wanda was. Jodi was the exact opposite, sweet, wouldn't hurt a fly. And Wanda and Jodi didn't exactly travel in the same circles. I know the PBR is supposed to be like one big family. But there's family and there's family. Know what I mean?"

I nodded. "I don't know the connection, Lena. But that's what we've got to find out."

"We?"

"The police. Me. I'm the board's liaison, remember? But also you. If you'll help me."

She looked away, was silent a long moment.

I took her silence as consent and said, "So tell me why didn't you go to Twin Falls with Jodi?"

A trickle from her near eye started a slow cascade down her cheek. She wiped it away with the sleeve of her shirt.

I felt a pang of pity for Lena. Couldn't believe my own response. I'd felt sadness, hurt and sadness, when LeAnn told me she was leaving, even more when she actually walked out the door. I was devastated when I learned Lane had been killed. Going back further, I remembered the tears I'd shed when my parents were killed. This was the first time I could ever recall feeling someone else's pain, and a lesbian's to boot.

"I didn't go because Jodi insisted I stay in Fort Worth."

"Did she tell you why she was going?"

"Just that she was going to see someone. That's all."

"Man, woman?"

"She wouldn't say. Was very secretive about it. She said, 'I don't want to get your hopes up before I know whether I can pull this off.'"

"So she went to Twin Falls to see someone."

"That's what she said."

"No hint of what it was about?"

She paused ever so briefly. "Except that she said we'd probably be picking up some money."

"Picking up some money?"

"That's what she said."

Then it struck me. "We. She said, 'We?'"

Lena nodded.

"She didn't expect to pick up money in Twin Falls then?"

"Apparently not."

"Any clue as to how much?"

"I sensed it would be a fair amount."

"What did she say to make you think that?"

Lena cocked her head pensively. "Let's see. She said, 'I'm not going to tell you what it's all about because I don't want to involve you. But if it goes the way I expect, we'll have a little money to play around with.' That's what she said. Close to her exact words."

"What day did she leave Fort Worth?"

"Thursday. In the morning."

"Did she call you from Twin Falls?"

"She called me that evening from her room to let me know she'd arrived. Said she expected to catch up with me on Sunday. Course she…." Another tear slid down her cheek; again, she wiped it away. "Sorry," she said.

I let her compose herself for a moment, before saying, "Why haven't you been to the police about this?"

She sneered, added a derisive grunt for good measure. "What good would that do? To them she was a rape victim gone sour. What I would tell them wouldn't open their closed little minds. Just the opposite, in fact. If they're like most redneck cops, once they learn the truth about Jodi, they'll probably lose interest in the case. At least this way, they're still working on it. Or so I've heard. Besides, what have I said? Nothing. No names of who she was going to see, whether they were PBR or someone else. Nothing about what she was going to talk to the person about, whether it was legal or not…."

"Did Jodi engage in illegal activity to your knowledge?" When a door opens, Chance Boettecher, cowboy detective, believes in barging right in.

She laughed without humor as she said, "Now wasn't our relationship still considered illegal in some states?"

"I'm not talking about that."

"Of course you're not. But couldn't answering that implicate me in illegal activity?" She issued another forced laugh. "Actually, there's no reason not to tell you. We were on the up and up. Jodi never committed a nefarious act in her life."

"Nefarious?"

"Don't know what that means?"

"Actually, I do. I'm just not used to hearing people use such a word in everyday conversation."

"Well, welcome to Phi Beta Kappa."

"You?"

"Me." She admitted proudly with an exaggerated nod. "Course I wasn't Ivy League. UT."

"University of Texas?"

She nodded. "Though it's genuine."

"What major?"

"Art history."

"Impressive."

"Not really. We're a dime a dozen. Phi Beta Kappa or no."

"And interested in bull riding, too."

Laughing, this time with a hint of gusto, she said, "It takes all kinds."

We had been inching through the parking lot, the traffic directed by off duty policemen. We reached a point where she could cut over to a lane that would take us to the other side of the building where my pickup patiently awaited. In truth, I could have walked back through the building faster, but I was enjoying Lena's company, even if I hadn't learned anything I thought could help the police solve a murder—Jodi's or Wanda's.

Lena pulled into an empty space next to my pickup, put the Cherokee in park, engine running. She looked at me expectantly, waiting for me to say goodnight.

"Lena," I said, "I also need to ask you about the man you were with tonight."

Her mouth opened in mild surprise. "Ray Bridges? What do you want to know about him?"

"Where's he from?"

"From Laughlin. Why?"

"Were he and Cauy…?"

"I don't divulge anyone's sexual preference," she interrupted, "without their okay. To get that information, you'll have to ask him yourself."

"Where is he now?"

"I don't know where he's staying. He didn't say."

"Will he be here tomorrow night?"

"Definitely. He wouldn't miss it."

"Think he'll speak with me?"

"Sure. I'm not saying he'll answer your questions, but he'll definitely talk to you. He's really a nice guy, Chance. You'll like him."

# CHAPTER TWENTY-FIVE

That night, I had a dream that had me awake and sweating at four A.M. In my dream, I was riding John Henry in the short-go. I was still injured and wore no shirt so that my taped shoulder was fully exposed. For some reason, there were no bullfighters in the arena to protect me. John Henry was bucking and twisting furiously, like a hurricane and tornado combined into one apocalyptic beast. No way I would have ridden him had I been awake. But in my dream, I rode him the full eight seconds and was looking to get off. Suddenly, he leaped out of his right turning spin and started back to his left, a move I did not anticipate. I was off balance at the exact instant he bucked and was flipped completely over, like a gymnast performing a summersault. In mid air, I saw that if I did not revolve far enough I was going to land on the back of my neck, and John Henry, coming around in his spin, would have me squarely in his sights. Next thing, I was on the ground, watching him as he came straight toward me. An instant later, he was nearly on me, a seemingly deranged grin on his face. Just as the bull was about to slam into me, I woke up, cold, my t-shirt soaked, beads of wetness running down my chest and back.

Happy to have survived John Henry's little middle of the night frolic, I was standing in the shower, daybreak a gray slit in the eastern sky, the hot water pricking my skin like darts.

With the previous night's scoring debacle and my nightmare burning in my mind as if branded there, I stepped into Phoenix's American West Arena with more than a little trepidation for the second go-round. Fortunately, the first bull, Bushwhacker, bushwhacked Jorge Garcia, bucking him off less than three seconds out of the chute, relieving Rich and myself of another opportunity to embarrass ourselves. It wasn't until Kryptonite, having an off night, let the fourth cowboy up, Tyler Kennelly, ride him to a mediocre eighty-six that we had to make any decision at all. The people in the stands, still in a mood from the previous night, issued a few lame boos, but Rich and I were in the clear.

I'd taken a moment before Bushwhacker did his thing to survey the crowd. I caught sight of Detective Gutierrez seated in the section next to where I stood. He was dressed casually in jeans and a short sleeve shirt, though sans cowboy boots and cowboy hat. Nibbling on nachos, he seemed to be enjoying himself, though I assumed his real purpose for being there was to keep an eye on me.

But it wasn't Gutierrez I was looking for. I was hoping to spot Lena and Ray. I expected to find them comfortably ensconced in the same seats as the night before. They weren't there but did turn up in the front row of an adjacent section. Lena spun her perky head at that most opportune moment, indicated the man to her left and then smiled and nodded. I like-signed back and went to work.

Tyler Kennelly came from sixth position going into the short-go to win the event with an outstanding ninety-three point effort on Mr. Wonderful, who bucked and twisted and changed directions the entire eight seconds Tyler had contracted to ride him. Tyler, his concentration at one hundred and ten percent, was with Mr. Wonderful all the way, maintaining perfect balance, making adjustments exactly when necessary, getting around the corners just in time, all without once overriding the animal.

Ty Hudson, after his ride on Igniter the night before, had ridden an inspired Pugnacious to an eighty-nine in the second go-round and was in first place going into the short-go. He'd drawn John Henry and got yanked into the arena dirt three seconds into the ride, thereby having to settle for fourth. Two other riders besides Tyler rode all three of their bulls to take second and third.

One of those riders was Justin Diver, whose third place finish extended his lead in the race for World Champion over Chad Michaelson, though not enough to put the outcome completely out of the question.

The crowd, the ninety-three point score to cheer, was much kinder to the judges than the night before. They ignored us.

I turned in my clipboard to motherhood-radiating LeAnn. For once, I found myself stumped for something to say. Groping, I tried joking with her. "So, are you going to name the baby after me?"

"Hold your breath for that, Chance. You'll be doing the kid a favor." (Yes, she smiled to show she had fed back what I had spooned.)

I made my way over to where Lena and her friend, Ray, were patiently waiting for me. Although the crowd around them was filtering out, they had remained in their seats conversing quietly. Just before the halftime program commemorating Cauy's career as a bull rider, I had slipped over to Lena, who quickly introduced me to Ray Bridges, and arranged for the two of them to remain in place after the event with the understanding that I would join them as soon as possible.

Halftime had been memorable. A short film of Cauy's life was shown that included some of his most spectacular rides, a ninety-two on Wipeout four years earlier, a ninety-three and a half on Rambunctious twenty months previously as well as the ninety-four on Terminator earlier that year. Then Daryl delivered a rehearsed speech, brief but eloquent, and presented a plaque to Cauy's nearest surviving relative, a maiden aunt who lived and taught high school French in Hartford, Connecticut. Finally, all the cowboys, myself included, passed out decals displaying Cauy's name and number to every fan in the arena. I thought it a wonderful tribute to an outstanding bull rider.

During the celebration, I'd taken the opportunity to observe Ray Bridges. His reactions ran the gambit—pride for Cauy's accomplishments, applause for his sensational rides, laughter at the humorous anecdotes, tears when Daryl mentioned how much "Cauy will be missed." But if he harbored any notion that he should be the one standing on the dais receiving the plaque instead of Cauy's aunt, he never betrayed it.

I climbed over the rail and inched my way down the aisle. At my approach, they both rose, Ray extending a hand that I shook.

"Where would you like to talk?" I asked.

He turned to Lena, who said, "Don't look at me. I don't see that I'm a party to your party."

Returning his gaze in my direction, he said, "Doesn't matter as long as it's private."

"That leaves out The Outlaw Den."

"What's that?"

I saw Lena roll her eyes. She knew the place.

"It's a cowboy watering hole several blocks from here," I explained, "where most of the PBR gather to celebrate the night's event."

He tilted his head slightly, grinned painfully and said, "I guess I'd rather not."

He suggested a Denny's on the northern end of the city not far from his motel. He gave me the Interstate exit number, and I agreed to meet him there.

Lena said her car was parked next to mine, so I walked with her out of the west door while Ray left through the main entrance. The place was mostly deserted by then. While only a few people mingled along the concourse, one of them was none other than my Phoenix watchdog, Detective Raul Gutierrez.

He was leaning against a wall just inside the door from where he motioned with his head for me to come over. I excused myself from Lena who waited by the opposite wall.

"A few less boos tonight," he said, grinning.

"We were luckier," I said.

He nodded and then said, "When are you leaving town?"

"Tomorrow," I replied.

He nodded again. "Where you going?"

"Vegas."

"Directly?"

I shrugged. "Got nowhere else to go right now."

"Driving?"

"Yeah."

He nodded. "Know what time you'll be leaving?"

I shrugged again. "Probably late afternoon."

He looked surprised. "Why so late?"

"It'll take me that long to sleep off the hangover."

He smiled knowingly, glanced at Lena, "Call me before you go. You got my card."

I shrugged yet again. "I guess," I said, remembering I'd already tossed it.

"See ya," he said, bouncing off the wall and walking down the concourse toward the main entrance.

"Who was that?" Lena asked when I rejoined her.

"That was one of Phoenix's finest," I said. "Detective Gutierrez."

"About the murders?"

I nodded, not telling her I didn't think he was too interested in Jodi's death at this time.

"Why is he talking to you?" She swiped her hand, said, "Oh, that's right. You're that liaison thing."

"That and, believe it or not, Lena dear, yours truly is a

suspect for Wanda's murder."

"What?" Her mouth was open.

I nodded. "Apparently, I'm at the top of their list."

"That's nonsense."

"They don't think so."

"So that's why you're really working on this, to clear your name."

I took her arm and guided her out the door. "I'm not worried about the police suspecting me. I just want the murders solved. For Wanda and Jodi's sakes first, the PBR second, me third. You can believe that if you want or think something else. Doesn't matter to me."

"Now don't get all huffy with me, Chance Boettecher. I'm on your side remember? Which is why I wanted to talk with you."

I looked at her.

"I think Ray will tell you everything he knows, though I don't think he knows much."

"I guess I just want some insight into a few things about Cauy and Jodi."

"He'll do what he can."

We arrived at Lena's pickup. I asked her if she was going by The Outlaw Den. She shook her head, said, "I'm not ready to return to that scene yet."

"Where you headed next?" I asked.

"Las Vegas. I want to see the Finals." She looked beyond me. "Then I'll decide what I want to do, where I'll go."

I thanked her for smoothing the way with Ray. She climbed into her truck, flashed me a pensive smile and drove off.

I crawled into my own pickup, inched my way out of the parking lot behind the last of the arena traffic and made for the north side of town.

Lena was right about one thing — Ray Bridges was a nice guy.

# CHAPTER TWENTY-SIX

He'd arrived at the Denny's before me and was seated in a wide booth in the nonsmoking section, downing a banana split that looked so delicious I considered ordering one for myself. He had long wavy hair, brown, like his eyes, and a complexion that ran slightly to the ruddy side. His voice was as masculine as that of most men I knew, his mannerisms normal. If you think I was looking for telltale signs of his sexual inclination, well...I was. After all, this was the first man I knew to be a homosexual in whose presence I'd ever been. Was I waiting for him to act effeminate? Yes. Was I listening for the stereotypical lisp portrayed by actors while portraying gay men on television and in the movies? Yes, again.

He displayed none of those attributes. Until then, I couldn't believe I couldn't detect a homosexual. That meant Cauy Hall could very well have been one, and if so, then maybe other bull riders were also homosexuals. If Cauy Hall was a homosexual and I couldn't detect it, then, clearly, I had been mingling with other homosexuals all my life without knowing it.

Ray Bridges came out of the closet right off the bat. I sat down and when the young waitress (they were all looking younger and younger lately) stopped over, I ordered a banana split for myself. While waiting, Ray pulled up the sleeve of a practically new PBR sweatshirt and revealed a tattoo on his forearm of the Marine Corp insignia with the letters USMC beneath it.

Spotting the insignia and the lettering, I said, "You were in the service?"

The smile that spread over his face was as impish as that of a boy who'd just played a prank and got away with it. "They didn't ask and I didn't tell," he revealed, and laughed joyfully. I joined him in the laugh, actually enjoying the quip.

Then, still smiling, he said, "Lena told me she refused to tell you I was a homosexual. Just know, I have no such inhibitions whatsoever."

"Cauy, too?"

His gaze lowered to his dish where he scooped a spoonful of ice cream, let the chocolate drip over the sides of his spoon until it stopped. Then, while raising the dessert to his mouth, he said, "He was."

My stomach turned. Until then, I still harbored the notion that Cauy was straight. That no bull riders were gay. Cowboys were men. Men's men. The sinking feeling soon passed, especially when the waitress returned with my banana split, and I found myself playing catch up with Ray.

While I was regaining my equilibrium, Ray said, "I guess you remember me from the news conference."

I owned that I did.

"I was curious what you would say about Jodi's murder. Guess you didn't want to play that one up."

I admitted he was right, but then I said, "But we really do want Jodi's murder solved, too. After all, we all knew her."

"I'm going to tell you everything I know. Truth is, because I didn't really know Cauy all that well, it isn't much. But I want Jodi's killer found." He stared intently at me as he added, "Also, the other woman's. Lena tells me you think the two murders are tied together. She told me you're more interested in the other woman's...."

His expression suggested a question.

"Wanda Sirett," I supplied.

"Yes. You're more interested in the Sirett woman's killer; I'm more interested in Jodi's, for Cauy's sake. You believe the killer of each could be one and the same person. That's why I'm willing to help in anyway I can."

"You say you didn't know Cauy all that well?"

"Not really. I met him in Laughlin during an event there."

"This year?"

He wagged his head. "Year before."

I signed for him to continue and he said, "I live in Laughlin, a blackjack dealer at Harrah's. I'm a recent convert to bull riding. Can't you tell?" He thrust out his chest so that a bull rider displayed on his sweatshirt, puffed up like a balloon. "I picked this up at the Laughlin Shoot-Out the first night. This year. After I met Cauy last year, I started watching bull riding on TV, even caught the World Finals. Liked it right away. Then I decided I would turn out when you guys came to Laughlin this year."

"So you didn't meet Cauy at the event last year."

He wagged his head. "No. Not at the Shoot-Out, if that's what you mean. He came into the casino the Thursday night before the event and plopped down at my table. I'm talking about last year, of course. Played a few hands. Lost them all. But then he looked at me. It was an open door invitation." He smiled. "Invited, I walked through. We had a quick fling, then parted when he left town for the next stop on the tour. When he returned this year, Thursday again, he looked me up. Although we really hadn't hit it off that well the year before, I said, 'What the heck.' After all, I wasn't going with anyone. We agreed to dinner that night."

"Where did you go?"

"You mean for dinner?"

"I guess what I want to know is where do two gay men go on a date in Laughlin, Nevada?"

He smiled pleasantly. "Anywhere anyone else goes."

"But Cauy…."

"Lena told me you already knew about Cauy's cross-dressing."

Of course! I had completely forgotten. "So he dressed…."

"He liked dressing up like a woman. Not my thing. But…to each his own." He pointed across the table at me. "Doesn't mean he played the submissive woman. He was just the opposite, in fact. But he liked dresses. Told me he did it all the time. Often saw his bull rider friends out and about. Said they never recognized him."

"Well, he was wrong once."

"Not really. I was with him that night. Later, he told me what happened when he ran into the guy who spotted him. Confronted, he simply played it cool, acted as if it couldn't have possibly been him. It was only after Jodi's murder that the man remembered what happened."

"You heard about that?"

"It's all over the PBR. Lena told me. Said she picked it up from someone who heard it at a poker game."

I winced, remembering all the glib talk during the poker game two nights earlier. Regaining my composure, I said, "Do you know of other bull riders who are gay?"

He finished his banana split, scraped the last of the juice from the bottom of the dish with his spoon. "How would that help?"

"I don't know. Might. Might not."

"Actually, I don't really need to make an issue of it," he said with a wag of his head. "Cauy hinted there were. Didn't tell me for sure, though. So I can't help you there."

"Reading between the lines, it seems you and Cauy weren't an item very long."

"Very perceptive. Remember I said that despite cross-dressing, Cauy wasn't submissive. Well, neither am I. We weren't compatible. Truth is, we just had those two weekends a year apart."

"Then why were you here tonight?"

He straightened up, looked at me as if I'd just insulted him. "Hey, I knew the man. Intimately. He was the first bull rider, gay or otherwise, I'd ever met. Despite our incompatibility, I still considered him a friend. A damn good one at that. He'd been killed doing something he loved. I wanted to be a part of the commemoration."

I asked him how well he knew Jodi.

"Sweet, lovable kid. I met her last year. Again, this year with Lena. Wouldn't hurt a fly."

"So where did you and Cauy go this year?"

"On our date?"

I nodded.

"The Branding Iron. Steak place. It's quite good." He let out a little chuckle.

"What's so funny?"

"I'm laughing because I suddenly remembered how tickled Cauy was with himself that night. He'd spotted some of your people there. Course they didn't recognize him."

"So he was pleased about what he was pulling off?"

"That's part of it. Cauy recognized this couple. A man and a woman together. Pointed them out to me and said, 'Isn't that interesting? Wouldn't be surprised if there wasn't a little fireworks in the ole PBR when this gets out.'"

"Did he say what he meant?"

Ray shook his head. "No, only something to the effect that someone was going to be surprised to learn his wife was out with his best friend. I wasn't really interested, wasn't a PBR insider, and didn't know the people, so I didn't prompt him any more. Man and a woman. Not my thing so to speak. Besides, I believe in live and let live."

I couldn't think of anything else to ask Ray Bridges, so I finished my ice cream, scraping out the last of the melted run-off from the various sauces. I paid the check and we left. On the parking lot, we shook hands and I thanked him for his time.

During the drive back to my motel, I thought about what I'd learned from my little tête-à-tête with Ray Bridges. Didn't seem like much. That we had homosexual bull riders in the PBR. That Cauy Hall cavorted in women's garb right under my nose without my knowing it.

Where had I eaten dinner the evening Cauy and Ray were in the Branding Iron? And with whom? (It's all right for me to write that word, just not speak it.) Regardless of where and with whom one thing was certain — it wasn't at the Branding Iron. Although I'd driven by the restaurant a number of times during my annual trips to Laughlin, I had never dined there. It wasn't a PBR in-place.

What did all that have to do with the murder of Wanda Sirett? Jodi was a lesbian, was murdered. Wanda, though the opposite as far as her sexual interest went, was also murdered. Moreover, Jodi and Wanda hardly knew each another. I doubted either had spoken five words to the other in their lives. Nothing was adding up. Was I on the wrong track? I had to consider that maybe I was mistaken about the two murders being connected.

# CHAPTER TWENTY-SEVEN

I called Washington in Atlantic City to garner his thoughts on the matter and get the latest take on Wanda's killing.

"What you want?" he demanded, once he learned I was his caller. "Not playing detective are you?"

I chose to ignore his question and asked him my own. He paused a moment as if weighing what he would tell me. Then he said, "Want to know if I think they're connected, huh? I gave it some thought, called Twin Falls. In the end, I don't think so. I'm working on the premise they are isolated crimes. Twin Falls thinks the bull rider's sister was the victim of a rape attempt gone sour. They can find nothing to tie the crime to any of you PBR people. It seems all the bull riders and the like have alibis. I have to assume the Twin Falls people know what they're doing. Unfortunately, that leaves me with you for the Sirett murder."

I reminded him that Jodi Hall was a lesbian.

"So what?" he said. "Why would a rapist care? She resisted, maybe told him she didn't like men. That could have been the trigger that set him off, the reason he killed her. Or maybe it made him even more determined to get what he wanted."

"But he didn't get what he wanted," I said.

"He got infuriated. Went too far. Killed her. Once he saw she was dead, he ran out without taking what he came for."

I had to agree it made sense. Especially since there was

nothing tying anyone with the PBR to a motive for killing her.

Hardly had I hung up the telephone when Daryl called wanting an update. "Some of the guys are getting antsy about the press."

"How so?" I asked.

"You know. If some reporter decides to do an article on the killings in the PBR, it could get pretty bad for us."

"Who's worried?"

"Oh, Kyle for one…actually a number of the guys. I mean, aren't you?"

"I think we'll be all right in the end." To my astonishment, I found I actually meant it.

"Well, good. At least someone thinks everything is going to turn out honky-dory. Got anything to tell me?"

Since I'd just gotten off the telephone with Washington, I did have something. Daryl was especially pleased the authorities believed Jodi Hall's death had nothing to do with the PBR, said he would pass it along.

Twenty minutes later, I was on my way to Uvalde. My passive aggressiveness had set in again and, contrary to what I'd led him to believe the night before, I didn't bother informing Gutierrez of my departure or of my intended destination. While the novelty was wearing off somewhat, like a boy (or a man) who's played with a new toy for a time, it still felt satisfying.

I spent a relaxing day at home catching up with my neighbors, before heading out for Las Vegas. Two hard days driving had me pulling into the gambling Mecca Thursday afternoon. Although I had fallen to fourteenth in the standings, I was still entitled to five thousand dollars bonus money for finishing in the top forty-five. I decided to use that wealth to treat myself to a room in the host resort — Caesar's Palace. It's a grand facility on the Strip, with vibrant carpet beneath an ocean of bright lights, everything within the sound of jingling slot machines and rattling money buckets.

I dropped off my carrying case in my eighteenth floor room and then drove over to the Thomas and Mack Arena at the edge of the UNLV campus where the PBR World Finals would be held starting the next night.

The first person I ran into was Craig Kelton coming out the door as I was going in. He frowned when he spotted me, and I sensed he would have avoided me altogether if he could have done so.

"Here to bid on John Henry?" he asked.

"Huh?" was the brilliant retort that escaped my mouth like the first puff of steam from a kettle.

"Didn't you know?"

I shook my head.

"Yeah," he said, "Royce is auctioning all of Wanda's bulls today. Doin' it hisself."

"He is?"

"Starts at four."

I glanced at my watch. Three thirty-five. Curious as to what the wrangler was going to do after Wanda's stock was auctioned, I asked.

He shrugged. "I've been offered jobs by Royce and Clete. But I got some nibbles from a few others, too. Some of the smaller outfits."

"Made up your mind which one?"

He issued me a shrewd look. "Think I'll see where John Henry lands first."

I told him that made sense, and then asked him a question about Wanda's spending habits.

"I got nothin' to say to you 'bout that, Chance."

"Wanda was a big spender."

"So?"

"So, was everything all right there?"

"How do you mean?"

I sensed Craig knew exactly what I meant. "Her bills

and…the like."

He didn't answer at first, just stared at me through moist brown eyes. Then he hunched his shoulders and said, "Far as I know everythin' was copasetic."

I decided to test a previous touched-on front. "You told me before that what you and Wanda were arguing about the night she was killed was bull business." He stared at me without comment. "But it could be interpreted to mean she was going to cut off your bedroom perks."

He wagged his head in disgust. "She threatened me with that all the time. Never amounted to nothin'. She was always drinkin' when she said it. Now damn it, Chance. I don't want to talk to you no more 'bout it. What went on 'tween me and Wanda was our business. Haven't you ever heard of privacy? 'Sides, you think I'd kill her just for cuttin' me off? That's crazy."

"Been known to happen."

His expletive was an eloquent reply to my unenlightening maxim.

I started to ask him another question, but he interrupted me by saying, "Ask someone 'sides me your damn questions," and stalked off.

I was more than a little baffled by Craig's uncooperative attitude. Why wouldn't he answer my questions? If he was innocent, they shouldn't have posed the least threat to him.

Inside, I bumped into an international pack of bull riders that included Chad Michaelson, Ty Hudson, Brazilian Ednei Machado, Aussie, Brian Farr, and Mexican, Jorge Garcia. We kibitzed until nearly four when we all drifted down to the pen area to watch Royce auction off John Henry and the rest of Wanda's stock. A sizeable crowd had accumulated to participate in (or at least witness) the event. Over a din of murmuring and laughter, I spotted Kyle and Lucy Nash standing next to a pen fidgeting with what had to be the auction bill. They peered alternately into the pen at some animal, and then down at the list. I was sure John Henry was out of their price range, but some of the lesser animals might be tempting seed stock for a pair of budding stock contractors.

The thought that Kyle might have killed Wanda because she wouldn't sell him any of her bulls gusted through my mind like a desert wind. An auction would offer him a chance at some of the animals. Too far fetched, I concluded. There were plenty of stock contractors ready to sell animals from their inventory to any and all comers. Seeding a herd would have been easy without the necessity of killing someone. All it really took was money.

Kyle spotted me, proffered a weak nod and then quickly returned to the business of examining stock. It was clear he didn't wish my company.

The other officers and board members of the PBR were also present for the big to-do. Too, all the stock contractors were there. Clete and Royce, the largest, would keep each other honest. LeAnn stood next to Royce, sober faced, though she tossed me a wan smile when she saw me.

Craig Kelton, of course, had shown up. Curious as to his new employer? I would have liked to ask him a few more questions but felt I needed to rebuild my rapport with him before trying.

There were a number of people present I didn't know. Potential stock contractors from around the country, arena personnel, UNLV students, people who had been wandering around, tourists.

Me? Well, I wasn't the least tempted to bid on Wanda's stock, hadn't changed my mind about becoming a stock contractor. I guess I was there for the spectacle's entertainment value.

Promptly at four, Royce stepped onto a small stool that put him a head above everyone else. LeAnn held a clipboard in one hand and a pen in the other. From behind him, John Henry chose that moment to let out a challenging snort. Royce turned and gave the animal a look and then turned to us with a roguish grin on his face.

"Think he's tellin' us who he wants to buck for, Royce?" Clete yelled between hands shaped like a megaphone.

"Wouldn't be surprised," Royce called back, stroking his goatee.

The crowd tittered appreciatively.

"All right, folks," Royce, turning serious, drawled in his best Nebraska brogue. "We're here to auction Wanda Sirett's stock of prime buckin' bulls. I'm the duly appointed 'xecutor of her will...."

"How'd that happen, Royce?" Red Parham interrupted, Tona standing beside him with her arm hooked in his. "Weren't you two divorced?"

"Damn it, Red, you know very well we were. Wanda never changed her will after the divorce. So I'm it."

"Did you change your will, Royce?" Cody Laws called, an arm draped across Wynona's shoulders. That brought a burst of laughter from the PBR folks, searching looks at my ex, a deep blush to her complexion.

"What's the big hurry, Royce?" Russ Ward queried from his wheelchair.

Royce looked at Russ. "Fair question. The truth is, folks, Wanda had a lot of debts. We think we might have just enough assets to cover the bills. That is if you good people bid these animals to what they ought to bring. But if we don't get them bills paid fast, the interest is gonna eat more and more of the estate, and we won't have enough. 'Kay?" He peered around for a moment. "Before we begin," he resumed, looking first down and then up, "I want it known, in the interest of fairness, that I'll be biddin' on some of the stock."

"'S that legal, Royce?" Red wondered good-naturedly.

"Course it is," Royce returned testily. "Lawyer said I didn't lose my rights to buy at an auction cause I'm 'xecutor. Just that in the interest of fairness, I'm lettin' you know my intentions."

"Then we all know where John Henry's goin', don't we?"

That caused another ripple of laughter from the crowd.

"Don't be so sure," Royce said in a tone that definitely said, "Damn straight."

Clete pushed him, made him pay ninety thousand dollars for the star, but in the end, Royce bought John Henry. When Royce asked if the bidding was all done and announced himself the high bidder, I happened to glance over at Craig Kelton for his reaction and found him giving the amateur auctioneer a thumbs up.

Clete got Kryptonite for seventy-five thousand. (Royce pushed *him* on that one.) Kyle and Lucy picked up one of Wanda's younger bulls, though paying almost twenty thousand for the animal. Everyone said afterwards they'd made a wise choice, paid a fair price.

"That get Wanda out of debt?" Cody Laws cried when the last animal had fallen under the hammer.

"We'll have to see," Royce responded.

The crowd dispersed around me. I stayed where I was, thinking. Did Wanda's debts have anything to do with her murder? How far in debt was she and how did she get there? How could I find out?

Of course! Plain as the ole nose on the ole face. Royce. Now that he was Wanda's executor, he knew the status of everything. Had as much as said so. Moreover, because he'd been married to her, he knew her ways and would have insight into the type of debt she'd run up.

The auction lasted hardly half an hour, and a few minutes after its conclusion, I caught LeAnn on the main concourse coming out of the ladies room. We greeted each other warmly after which I said, "Like to take you and Royce to dinner."

She tilted her head to one side, eyed me suspiciously and then grinned. "Doesn't sound like the Chance Boettecher I know."

"I want to pump Royce for some information about Wanda."

"You're taking this liaison thing seriously," she commented. She started walking along the concourse in the direction of the main entrance.

"Nah," I rejoined, falling into step beside her, "just trying to put two and two together a little. Can you believe the police suspect me?"

"You? Why you?"

I shrugged. "My wonderful personality?"

She grunted, said, "Don't think Royce will be interested."

"Royce won't be interested in what?" It was from the man himself. He'd stepped out of an office we'd just passed and caught LeAnn's last comment. He was smiling pleasantly, obviously not the least threatened that his fiancée was walking with her ex.

"Oh, honey," LeAnn exclaimed. "Chance wants to take us to dinner. Wants to pump you about Wanda."

"He does?" he returned, his smile turning mischievous, his look to me. "And just what does the PBR liaison to the police want to know?"

"Mainly about Wanda's debts."

He shrugged and pressed his mouth into an expression that clearly said I've-got-nothin'-to-hide-about-that-so-why-not. "Well, LeAnn darlin', it ain't often we get to eat out at Chance Boettecher's expense. Why don't we take advantage of it?"

"Only if he takes us to some place expensive," she

popped in.

I took them to Caesar's Palace. Wasn't my idea. I would have opted for LeAnn's costly proviso, but Royce wanted the prime rib at Caesar's, said he'd been dying for it all day.

I met them at the dinner line a little after seven. LeAnn had changed into a black cocktail dress and matching plumps that said she was at home in the big city as well as on the ranch. I complimented her profusely. Royce wore a gray western suit, white shirt and a diamond-studded bolo. I was decked out in brown western dress slacks and a new cowboy dress shirt I'd picked up after leaving the arena.

While we waited in line for our turn to be seated, Royce, grinning from ear to ear, said, "We got the word this mornin', before the sale. LeAnn's gonna have a boy."

"Congratulations," I said to an embarrassed LeAnn and a proudly beaming Royce. Despite the fact the child was not to be my son, I meant it. I was happy for them.

"You're the first to know," Royce claimed.

"Other than my sister," LeAnn amended.

"Leona? Where is she now?"

LeAnn returned an expression that said she was shocked that I would remember her sister's name. She had a point. Other than the wedding, I had met her sister exactly one other time. We'd stopped in for a brief visit following the Reno event during the third year of our marriage. It wasn't the best of times. LeAnn explained afterwards how she and her sister had engaged in a fairly brutal case of sibling rivalry. Leona, the younger by but a single year, always did her best to show-up her "big" sister at every turn. Leona Markley was three inches taller and twenty pounds heavier than LeAnn, had been since LeAnn was in the ninth grade; Leona, the eighth. I don't remember LeAnn calling her sister on more than three occasions the whole time we were married, though they did exchange Christmas and birthday cards.

"She's still in the same old place," she said, an expression of censure draping over her face like a theater curtain.

I snickered, wondering if I could even find that place again. It was tough enough when I had written directions. Leona lived smack dab in the middle of a large twisting subdivision east of Reno with her husband, John, a plumber, and their two children, a pair of prepubescent girls whose names I didn't remember ever being told, though I probably was.

"You two any closer than you were?"

LeAnn shrugged, looked away. That said it all.

We had to wait half an hour before being seated. We ordered drinks, Royce and myself, Mexican beers; LeAnn, a Dr. Pepper. She'd apparently sworn off alcohol as she'd vowed. We were finishing off our prime rib dinners (all three of us ordered our meat cooked medium) when Royce opened the door to my purpose for the dinner. "So, Chance, what can I tell you?" he asked.

I shoved the last bite of meat into my mouth and chewed on it hurriedly until it was ready to be dropped down my gullet, and then said, "You mentioned today that Wanda had money problems," I began. "Can you tell me more about that?"

"This detective thang got you thinking about a new line of work after your bull ridin' days, Chance? We all think you're doin' a great job as a judge. Like to see you lock that up for yourself."

I emphasized I was not into becoming a detective, relating how my role as liaison with the police had actually gotten me into trouble. I added I was definitely considering the judge position seriously. I was pitching but, from the doubt on the face peering back at me, he wasn't catching.

In the end, Royce couldn't tell me much that offered me anything resembling a lead to follow up on. He did elaborate on Wanda's debts, however. "Wanda spent money faster than John Henry could buck off cowboys," he said, wagging his head sadly. "Naturally, she was heavily in debt. After our divorce, she refused to curb her spending. Damn shame. Married to me, she spent like the stuff was water. We've all seen it. Person who didn't have much when they were young, when they git a little something, they don't know how to handle it. And when she divorced me she kept at it. You seen how she was, Chance."

"Got worse if you asked me," LeAnn enjoined dryly.

"So who gets her money?" I queried.

"As I said at the auction, till I git done payin' all her bills, won't be nothin' left."

"Did you know this?"

"Know what?" His expression suggested he was baffled.

"That she was in such financial straits."

He stroked his goatee once, twice. "I suspected it. I seen how she was, how she spent. Had a good idea what she was takin' in from what I was doin'. I mean you seen how she picked up tabs, Chance. And how about how she dressed? She didn't care 'bout whether it was the best or not, just whether it was the most expensive. Did you know she bought a new Cadillac every damn year?"

I shook my head.

"Had this image she felt she had to keep up?" Royce added.

"What kind of debt did she have?"

"The ranch she owned in Arizona was mortgaged to the hilt. By sellin' it we should clear enough to pay it off, but won't be nothin' left afterwards." He shook his head sadly.

"What about the bulls?"

He smiled wanly. "They was free and clear, but she owed feed and vet and transportation bills. On top of that she owed clothin' stores and jewelry stores. Moreover, she owed for her cars and trucks and her credit cards. Would you believe she owed over a hundred grand on her credit cards?"

"What about the help?"

He nodded. "Yeah, she owed them too. Though only to Craig at the time of her death."

That caught my attention. I remembered he'd told me everything with Wanda on the money front was "copasetic." "How much to him?"

"'Bout four months worth. A tad over sixteen grand."

"She hadn't paid Craig for four months?"

"Nah, it didn't work that way according to him. She'd miss five hundred here, a thousand there, sometimes smaller amounts. Over a couple years he said. But totals 'bout four months worth."

"What about the others?"

"Apparently, she kept up with the others pretty well. Had only fallen behind with them a time or two. And like I said was all caught up at her death. Course, Craig didn't really mind her gittin' behind to him. He had other compensation, you know." His look was meaningful.

I nodded.

"Guess he called that the interest on the debt." Then he snickered.

To my sad discredit, I mimicked him. LeAnn, to her credit, turned away in disgust.

"So, did you get enough today to pay her debts?" I asked.

Royce screwed up his mouth as if he'd just sucked a lemon. "Yes," he said.

"No," LeAnn countered.

"Huh?"

The look Royce gave LeAnn clearly said, "Cut me some slack." Then he turned to me, and explained, "If I forego my fee as 'xecutor, I can pay her debts. If I take my fee, we'll come up short." He sighed heavily. "I've already decided to skip the fee. The debts 'll be paid. Guess I owe Wanda that."

"You don't owe her a damn thing." LeAnn's bitterness was like a mushroom cloud following an atomic blast.

"Now, Hon, we've been all through that and it's settled." Turning to me, he added, "Handlin' a person's estate, 'specially one like Wanda's, ain't no picnic. Even though I don't need the money, if it was there, I would take it."

"At least you got John Henry back," I consoled.

He tilted his head, straightened it. "Yeah, I guess. Though Clete got Kryptonite."

"Craig going with you?"

He nodded. "Said he would if I got John Henry. Told him I wasn't going to be responsible for what Wanda owed him though."

"Which isn't a problem because you got enough money to pay him from the sale, right?"

He nodded. "He'll git his money. I mean I told him before the sale he would git it if the stock brought enough, but I wasn't gonna be responsible if they didn't — even if he did come with me."

Royce then suggested we order a little dessert but changed his mind when LeAnn gave him a look.

Although I didn't learn much that put me on a track to a killer, at least, I got off cheap for trying.

# CHAPTER TWENTY-EIGHT

The next night, and for Saturday and Sunday as well, I dedicated myself to judging bull rides. The first weekend of the PBR World Finals saw lots of great rides and wrecks, but few changes in the world standings—none at the top. Justin Diver and Chad Michaelson rode two of their three bulls for similar mid-eighties scores. They were in a two-horse race for the World title and the million-dollar bonus that winning carried. However, it was Cody Laws and Red Parham who were putting on the show. Both friends rode all three of their bulls, each recording a go-round win while placing in the top five the other nights. They were one-two in the event standings, Cody a couple of points ahead. Kyle Nash captured the other go-round win with a ninety-one-point ride on a bull named Hysteria. He rode well enough the other nights to land himself fifth overall. It seemed as if he'd regained his confidence and was going to take home a ton of money.

Sunday evening following the go-round, I decided to take in a show. I'd never seen any of the big ones, those for which the city was famous. I headed for the Mirage where I knew a long running act was taking place, only to learn it was sold out, had been for months. Too discouraged to try another casino, I dropped around to the B-lounge where an old rock and roll icon wailed away on a bluesy number he'd made famous a decade before I was born. The few vacant seats in the place spoke volumes for his continued popularity.

From the center of the room, I caught an arm beckoning

in my direction. I peered around to make sure I was the intended quarry, and when I saw no one standing nearby, snaked my way through the crowd toward the empty seat next to the owner of the flapping appendage. It was attached to a woman beneath a green cowboy hat who, because of the dim lights, I hadn't recognized from a distance. As I gained ground, I saw it belonged to Elissa Cross, the registered nurse who worked with the sports healers and was an invaluable member of the team.

Elissa was about my age, a lone offspring of a rodeo family, had worked with sports healing since the day she'd graduated from nursing school, summa cum laude I was told. She was a brown eyed, dirty blond from the bottle like most of the breed, tall and graceful, with features that taken individually were too this or too that but somehow came together to offer up a product somewhere between very attractive and gorgeous depending on your point of view. She had a wonderful bedside manner, except when she had to be tough, which was seldom — the cowboys learned quickly to shut up and listen when she spoke.

On that score, I'm most definitely writing from experience. Her first year with the PBR was my second. At the second event that year, in Guthrie, Oklahoma, an old eliminator bull, Hard Rock, threw me in the short-go. I'd ridden the beast for seven and a half seconds before a spin to the left set-up by a feint to the right (don't ever think these dumb animals don't have smarts) had me strung out on the end of my arm. The force caused my hand to pop out of my bull rope, and I was flung through the air like a piece of space debris, landing hard on my back in the arena dirt. Stunned, I tried to get to my feet but, like a tripped up drunk, fell back and lay there.

The sports healers raced over, carefully gathered me on a stretcher and carried me out of the arena to a round of appreciative applause. By the time they hauled me back to the first aid room where Elissa awaited, I was feeling no pain and thought I'd recovered. The sports healers, having deposited me with the nurse, returned to the arena to await the next casualty. Thinking all that was wrong with me was a little roughing up, I decided to return to the chute area to watch the last few cowboys ride their bulls, maybe even help them with their bull ropes.

Elissa had different ideas. In her wonderful bedside tone she told me to stay put. She'd watched my fall on the monitor and sensed I might have done more damage than just have taken a little bruising.

Thinking I knew it all, I ignored her entreaty (in the nice tone don't forget) and tried to rise. The streak of pain that ran down my leg was excruciating.

"LIE DOWN!" she ordered (in that other tone now).

I lay back down. Because I had not listened the first time, I missed the next three events of the circuit. Because she barked at me like she did, and I did (finally) obey, I missed *only* three events. The doctor told me that had I continued to rise off that table contra to Elissa's strict admonition, I would most likely have lost the entire season and would have had to spend six months in traction to boot. Needless to say, I never resisted Elissa after that.

Going further, shortly after my breakup with LeAnn, I hit on her. She was unattached at the time, but she was well aware of my emotional state, more than I was. Her medical training I guess. She turned me down. Not flat—exactly— but.... She said she knew it was LeAnn who was forcing the breakup and that I wasn't over her. (Wasn't that insightful?) She said she wasn't interested in a man who was interested in another woman. By the time I was over LeAnn (at least to the point where I was ready to look for a relationship, even casual, with another woman), Elissa was involved with another man— Lance Miles, the gateman, for two years. Everyone said they were a perfect couple.

So why was she sitting in a Las Vegas casino's B-lounge,

Lance-less? I took the vacant seat, ordered a beer from the waitress who appeared nearly simultaneously and asked her that very question.

"Lance and I broke up," she informed me.

"When did this happen?"

"During the drive to Las Vegas." Then, following a short pause, she added, "It's been coming on for some time."

"Who's the culprit?"

She laughed. "Both of us."

"Well, is it too soon?"

She looked at me, knew exactly what I meant. She looked away and didn't say another word until the rock icon finished his set.

I woke the next morning in Elissa's king-size bed. Caesar's Palace, one floor up from mine, same view. We grappled through a reprise of our previous night's horizontal boogie, soaked each other in a long sultry shower and then set off for the casino's buffet breakfast, holding hands. That quickly we were an item. I knew because we discussed it while drying off following the shower and came to an understanding. Or should that be "understanding."

Since it was Monday and the next go-round of the World Finals didn't kickoff until Thursday evening, neither Elissa nor I had anything much to do. After a light breakfast, we meandered through a few casinos, losing a few dollars at Blackjack, a few more in the slots. Soon tiring of the gambling scene, we wandered over to the Thomas and Mack, drawn there like a newborn calf to its mother's utters. We spotted a few cowboys hanging out, like us, with little to do. We chatted briefly with everyone we saw, and then moseyed over to the pen area to take in the sights and scents of the bulls, lounging comfortably like pampered potentates in their straw-filled stalls.

John Henry was resting quietly with his back to the crowd while Royce and LeAnn entertained a small mob of admirers.

(Of John Henry, not Royce and LeAnn.) LeAnn smiled at me. Then I watched with amusement as Royce's gaze fell first on me and then shifted to Elissa. About that time, a funny expression fell over his face. Then he collapsed. Just fell to the concrete floor like a sack of feed. LeAnn gasped and then dropped to her knees beside him.

"ROYCE! ROYCE!" she called, panic in her voice.

Elissa slipped her hand out of mine and dashed toward the stricken stock contractor. "Out of the way," she commanded. The onlookers backed off as if she'd pulled a gun on them. She knelt down beside Royce and pushed his eyelids up with her fingers, and then clasped his wrist. In the next moment, she said, "I want six men to bring him to first aid."

"Is he...?" This was from LeAnn.

"He's fainted," Elissa announced as she led the way.

The first aid room was not far away. I grabbed Royce about the middle and with five others was following Elissa along the concourse. Royce was heavy, even for six of us. Dead weight. Two of my confederates grunted when we hefted him. I wanted to issue a like sound but held it in. Old-fashioned cowboy, I guess.

Elissa, meanwhile, was rummaging through her pocketbook as we walked, pulled out a ring of keys. She unlocked the door, flipped on the light and pointed to the leather-topped table while grabbing the receiver from the nearby wall telephone. The place smelled of antiseptic, just as you would expect.

"I want an ambulance at the Thomas and Mack," she said into the telephone mouthpiece, giving her name and position. "That's right. First aid."

She hung up, turned to LeAnn, said, "They're on their way."

Just then, Royce stirred. With soft moans, he raised a hand to his head, mumbled, "What happened?"

"You fainted, Royce," Elissa said, again taking his wrist and watching the second hand on her watch.

LeAnn stepped over and took his other hand. "How are you feeling now?" she asked.

"Woozy."

"Don't try to get up," Elissa directed. "An ambulance is on the way."

"Ambulance?"

"Yes, an ambulance. Now don't be a big baby. I've already ordered it so you're going to the hospital. You need to be checked out."

"Don't want no hospital."

"Maybe you ought to go," LeAnn said plaintively. "Hopefully, it's nothing. They'll run some tests." She looked at Elissa who nodded her confirmation.

"I want to be here for the Finals," Royce whined.

"It's only Monday," Elissa said, throwing in a light laugh. "I'm sure you won't miss a thing. Just let them check you out."

"Craig can handle everything until you get back," LeAnn said.

Royce lay back on the table and closed his eyes, resigned to his fate.

After helping to place Royce on the table, I had backed away and was resting an arm over a gray filing cabinet that set in the corner away from, but on the same wall as, the door. I stood there admiring Elissa. The consummate professional, in control, she was handling the situation like a military commander who actually knew what he (in this case, she) was doing. Who wouldn't admire her? Emotions stirred within me that I hadn't felt since my early days with LeAnn.

After Royce had been shipped off to the hospital, Elissa said she wanted to see Hoover Dam, claimed she'd never been there. Naturally, I took her. On the drive back following the tour, I complimented her on how she'd handled the incident with Royce. She thanked me, adding, "I'm sure it's just the pressure he's under. His ex getting murdered, handling her estate, buying John Henry, LeAnn, becoming a daddy. Only that..." And she laughed.

"What?"

"Nothing," she said, quickly sobering, swiping the air with a hand. She turned her gaze to the sun-scorched rocks on the passenger side of the pickup where she held it for a good five miles. When she spoke next, she said, "How do you feel about your ex marrying Royce?"

I shrugged before saying, "Same as her marrying anyone, I guess. Royce is a great guy. I think he'll be good to her. He's just older."

"Older or old?"

"Older. I don't think he's too old for her, if that's what you mean."

She smiled. "You over her?"

I didn't answer right at first, but then I said, "I loved her. But that's over and I'm reconciled to it. I'm ready to move on."

"I sensed that. You've been pretty wild since you and LeAnn split. You and Lane were a pair, that's for sure."

What was she implying? That Lane's death was good for me? Although I was dying to know the answer to that question, I wasn't about to ask it—if I wanted to form a meaningful relationship with the woman. Still, bottom line, Lane was the best friend I ever had in my life. There were no circumstances in which I would be happy he was dead.

"Are you up for a fight?"

"Bit soon, don't you think?" she replied casually. Then she eyed me coyly. "Right now, we don't need a fight to put us in the mood."

Back in Vegas, we ate at a little Mexican restaurant on a side street near the Strip, and then tried to get tickets for a popular show. Sold out. We did manage to squeeze into one featuring a famous part Indian crooner, a show I'd vowed I would never attend. It wasn't that I had anything against the crooner, I'd made the vow during my first trip to Sin City when in a contrary mood (meaning I didn't have the money for a ticket) and felt too contrary afterwards to forget my silly vow. But Elissa said she'd like to see him, so the vow fell by the wayside — where, like clothing in a well-organized bureau drawer, it always belonged. I enjoyed the show. Go figure.

We returned to Caesar's Palace where we ran into LeAnn at the elevators. When I asked about Royce, she said he was fine. "He's in the room now taking it easy."

"Did the test reveal anything?" Elissa asked.

"Heart's fine," she said. "But his blood pressure was elevated. That plus the stress he's been under probably took its toll."

Elissa nodded.

The elevator arrived and the three of us got on. On the way up, LeAnn said, "So, what's with you two?"

I looked at Elissa, she at me.

"Thought you and Lance were going to go the distance," LeAnn commented, eyeing Elissa. "Seems kind of sudden."

"We'd been going downhill for six months or more," Elissa divulged. "We kept it quiet so no one knew. It only seemed sudden to everyone else. Not to us."

LeAnn nodded like an approving schoolteacher as she said, "Well, congratulations then. You two could be a good fit."

The elevator arrived at Elissa's floor where she and I got off, leaving LeAnn to ride on alone. I don't think she minded. I wish I could say I detected a tear in the corner of one of LeAnn's eyes, a sadness in her mien. Didn't happen. I think she was genuinely happy for me.

# CHAPTER TWENTY-NINE

The next morning, I was just stepping out of the shower when a knock sounded at the door.

"For you, Chance," I heard Elissa call.

We were in my room. Elissa and I had showered together in hers. She'd dressed there and then accompanied me to mine so I could do the same. I'd already stuffed my shirt into my pants, hooked the belt and was just slipping my boots over my stocking feet.

Two men, LVPD detectives (it was written all over them), were standing in the middle of the room. Elissa had taken a seat in one of the two chairs the hotel provided for the room.

"You Chance Boettecher?" one of the men asked. Of medium height, he had a pale pudgy face and a nose to match, wore a sloppy suit, gray (what else?). The other man was younger, slightly taller, not quite as pale, square jawed, neatly dressed—a rookie detective, I surmised.

"Yes," I said.

"Why didn't you check in?"

"Check in?" Did I miss it? Was I wrong about these two being LVPD? It was just a guess, after all. Were they hotel detectives instead? But I had checked in, so I told them so.

"Not the hotel," he returned with a look and tone that clearly implied I was mentally challenged. "LVPD."

I was smugly satisfied that I'd been right after all.

"LVPD?"

"The police. Detective Washington of Atlantic City PD

asked us to keep an eye on you. You should have made contact with us the day you got here. That was last week."

"No one said I was to check in with the police."

"You were supposed to let Detective Gutierrez in Phoenix know when you were leaving."

The scowl on his face and his surly tone said that the next thing out of my mouth would convict me of any crime he subsequently decided to accuse me of.

"I told Detective Gutierrez I was leaving on Sunday. I left on Sunday. Besides, I'm not under arrest. I thought I could come and go as I pleased."

"Now that attitude will only get you on our bad side." Although he'd spoken in the plural, he'd made no motion that could have been taken to include the other man. I wondered if he resented his younger partner, couldn't wait until retirement so that he wouldn't have to break in any more snot nosed kids.

I thought about how I'd arrived in town the previous Thursday. Why were they just getting around to me? I decided to play innocent. I didn't ask.

"Washington tells me you're still his number one boy."

I hunched my shoulders.

"You got a problem with that?" said Detective.... He'd yet to tell me his name. Whether he was going to or not, I didn't care. It was just a bullying job.

When I didn't say anything, he announced he would be keeping me under surveillance. He said I was to call him and tell him when I planned on leaving town. Then he turned his cold gray eyes on Elissa, took a hard look at her before motioning his partner to follow him out.

The door had hardly closed when another knock sounded. It was the younger of the two detectives. He held out a pair of cards that I took. The one read Detective Harold Marks, LVPD; the other, Detective Roger Hornblower, also LVPD. The younger man tapped the second card with his index finger and indicated that was himself, then left. There were phone numbers on the cards and a police headquarters address only a few blocks away.

I laid the cards on the dresser and finished dressing.

"You're a suspect? The prime one at that?" Elissa asked, amazement in her voice.

"It's a crock," I said. "I think Washington wants the real killer to think I'm the prime suspect so he'll get careless." I said it but, in a way, I knew it, too, was a crock.  In truth, beyond my motive and opportunity for killing Wanda, I didn't think Washington had clue one. Then again, neither had I.

Elissa and I wandered down to the lobby. From a chair strategically facing the elevators sprang a pint-sized twenty-something woman wearing jeans, a white t-shirt with colorful lettering that supported a walk for some worthy cause that had taken place a year earlier and black sneakers. She made for me like a dart headed toward a target and said, "Chance Boettecher?" After I nodded, she added, "May I ask you a few questions?"

"Who are you?" Elissa asked for me.

"My name is Jamie Clarke. I'm a reporter with the Post."

*Uh oh. Trouble.* Not so much for me this time as for the PBR. What could I do? My mind raced. The last thing I wanted to do was answer a reporter's questions. But if I failed to cooperate, what kind of signal was I sending? I remembered how well I'd handled the questioning during the press conference Daryl had called in Phoenix. I'd winged it then, maybe I could wing it now.

"What's it all about?" I asked, hooking Elissa's arm and making for the exit.

Jamie Clarke fell in step beside me. "Mind if I tape our conversation?" she asked.

I looked around at the people, considered the noise.

"Not the most opportune of settings, wouldn't you say? Let's forego taping for now. Maybe down the road."

"Can we go somewhere then?"

"We haven't had breakfast. Let us get something in our stomachs. You can interview me while we eat. Join us, of course." I was the height of politeness, hoping to win the PBR some brownie points.

We walked down the Strip until we came upon an inexpensive eatery where I ordered a big breakfast of eggs, pancakes and bacon; Elissa, juice and toast; Jamie  Clarke, coffee.

"I'm doing a story on the recent tragedies afflicting the PBR and what the PBR is doing about it," the reporter said after we'd placed our orders. "What is the latest on the murders?" She'd drawn a notebook from her purse and appeared ready to dote on my every word.

"Murders?" I asked innocently.

"Yes," she returned, nonplussed. "The stock contractor in Atlantic City but also the young woman in Twin Falls—Jodi Hall."

"Jodi Hall?"

"Yes, and her brother Cauy Hall. He was killed by a bull at an event."

I nodded. "You want to tie them all together?"

"Yes. In a story. Of course, the death of the brother has nothing to do with the murder of his sister. After all, a bull killed him. But the other two deaths could be related, don't you think?"

Was I being setup? Did she know I was a suspect? Was I growing paranoid? "When will the story appear?"

"It's timely now. I'm shooting for Monday, following the Sunday Finals. Think you'll have the murderer by then?"

"Me?"

"I mean the police. You're just the liaison to the police,

I understand."

"Right. Liaison. Nothing more. I don't know much. Have you spoken with the police?"

She nodded. Our breakfasts arrived. Jamie Clarke took a sip of her coffee before jumping back in. "I've spoken with Washington in Atlantic City, Rawlins in Twin Falls and Hornblower here. Beyond how, when and where the victims were killed, they didn't tell me much. The cases are open and they are investigating. Not much in the way of leads."

"I don't know that I have anything more to tell you." And I didn't. By the time we finished breakfast, I'd told Jamie Clarke exactly zero. Of course, I'd BS-ed her to the best of my ability, relating how everyone was cooperating with the police and that it was only a matter of time before the culprit was brought to justice. Needless to say, I did not volunteer my suspect status. Later, Elissa complimented me on how well I'd handled the reporter.

Although I, too, thought I'd handled Jamie Clarke like putty in the hands of a sculpture, something about her left me ill at ease. For all her youth, she was hungry — and on the prowl. She wanted a story and she was going to write one. Still, how many people read the Las Vegas newspapers? The out-of-towner comes to gamble, not read. Surely, the damage could be contained. Especially if the police could find Wanda's killer before sundown Sunday. Fat chance! Washington was in Atlantic City. Although he was the one who had to do it, I didn't think he was all that motivated to accomplish the feat by sometime Sunday. The Las Vegas people certainly weren't up to it. It wasn't even their case. Something told me the PBR was on the brink — and on its own.

# CHAPTER THIRTY

That evening, Elissa and I dined in one of the resort restaurants, and then traipsed over to the B-lounge where an ensemble of some sort was on break. We spotted Denise Hilton and Mike Dodd at a table next to a pair of empty chairs. It appeared their relationship was in one of its on-again periods.

We decided the empty chairs at their table needed filling and filled them. "We think we'll crash your party," I said, assisting Elissa with one of the chairs without waiting for permission from Denise and Mike. I knew we were welcomed, and the smiles and insistence that we join them that practically exploded from the couple like an artillery shell confirmed it.

Denise was as tall as most of the bull riders, who tended to be on the short side themselves, which meant the top of her head came to my eyes. She had long chestnut hair, naturally attractive features and a wide trademark smile that lit up her face like a flashbulb when she flashed it. I'd always enjoyed being interviewed by her after I'd made a good ride. It was something I would definitely miss if I retired from bull riding to take up judging permanently.

"We heard about you two," Denise said, smiling. Turning to Elissa, she added, "Sorry to hear about you and Lance, though. But, apparently, it had run its course."

Elissa assured her it had and we were soon guzzling beer and chatting away while the band returned and began its next set.

At a break in the conversation, I asked Denise if she'd

ever heard of a Jamie Clarke.

She struck a thoughtful pose for a moment before saying, "No, why?"

"She's a reporter with the Post and…?" I stopped because Denise's eyes bulged like a walleyed fish. "What?" I asked.

"The Post?"

"Yeah. I assume the Las Vegas Post."

"What Las Vegas Post?" Then she answered her own question. "Chance, there is no Las Vegas Post."

"There isn't?"

"No. But there is a Washington Post."

A queasy feeling sloshed around in my stomach like beer cans in a chest of melting ice. "You mean…."

She nodded. "And now that I've thought about it, I have heard of a Jamie Clarke with The Washington Post. She's deadly, Chance. What's going on?"

I told her.

"Oh, Chance, she'll crucify the PBR. Take you down too. What are we going to do?"

I wagged my head. I hadn't the faintest idea. The Washington Post. Along with The New York Times, one of the most poured over newspapers in the…world? An exposé about our recent troubles through such a forum could doom the PBR. Daryl and the rest of the board were certainly justified in worrying about public reaction over Wanda's murder. Throw in Jodi's and the problem was multiplied. If the bull riding crowd were turned off by the murders, they would stay away in droves. The television contract would disappear like a morning mist. Because neither the police nor I had anything of substance to tell Jamie Clarke about the murderer, I sensed we were not going to come off looking very pretty in any article she wrote. Our public image was in jeopardy. Is that an understatement or what?

There was one solution: find the killer. That would save

the PBR even if I went down.

At least there would be no article in the paper for the next few days. Jamie Clarke would hold off until the completion of the World Finals on Sunday so as to include anything colorful she might glean from the rest of the event. That gave us a window of opportunity — though a narrow one. No doubt about it, the future of the PBR was in deep doo-doo. If only someone (I had little confidence it would be the police) would uncover Wanda's killer by Sunday....

The band, following another break, returned and struck up a danceable tune that had Elissa tapping her toe against the side of my boot under the table. The code, Morse or otherwise, couldn't have been clearer. She looked at me expectantly. The truth was, from thinking about the fate of my beloved PBR (as well as my own), I wasn't in the mood for dancing. Besides, the number was too fast. I might have been more willing had the band been playing something more amenable to a two-step. So when Elissa asked me pointblank if I wanted to dance, I begged off. However, Mike was game and, leaping into the void, said he would stomp on her toes if she liked. Elissa flashed a look at me and then accepted Mike's invitation.

Hardly had they made it to the dance floor, when Denise said, "You finally over LeAnn, Chance?"

Did everyone know I'd been carrying the torch for LeAnn for all the time since our marriage broke off?

When I told her I thought so, she said, "That might be the only positive thing to come out of Lane's tragic death."

Were she and Elissa sharing notes? Or just reading each other's minds? Still, I wanted her take on the subject and asked her what she meant.

"I read somewhere that change changes us, Chance. Sudden change can change us suddenly. You and Lane were close. The best of friends. During the time after you and LeAnn split up, you and Lane were a pair of real cowboys. And I don't mean that as a compliment. But because of what was going on, flitting from one girl to the next like a bee gathering nectar, you couldn't get over LeAnn. Then when Lane got killed, something happened. You changed. For the better. I think you're steadier now and it shows up in the job you're doing as a judge." She nodded toward the dance floor. "Elissa thinks so too. She's solid. She wouldn't have climbed onboard so fast after breaking up with Lance if she didn't."

Was I steadier? Elissa had implied as much. Was it a good thing? A good thing to come out of Lane's death? Maybe. I realized the allusion to a positive benefit flowing out of Lane's death did not offend me. Was I growing comfortable with the idea?

Then she shocked me. For the next thing to quake out of her mouth was, "I bet I know when the baby was conceived." Hastily, she added, "LeAnn's coming blessed event."

I nodded, knowing full well what she'd been referring to.

"Is it all right if I talk about it?"

I said sure. And to my surprise, I discovered it was. "When?"

"Saturday morning in Laughlin," she claimed smugly. "Timing seems about right."

"How do you pinpoint it down to then?"

"Because of the big fight she and Royce had the night before."

"They had a fight so the baby was conceived when they made up?"

"Course. Isn't that what always happens?" Her face lit up in a prurient grin. "Like I said, the timing is about right."

"So tell me what happened." I was as curious as a busybody.

"It was after midnight, Saturday morning. LeAnn had the room next to me…."

"You weren't with Mike?"

She looked at me with pursed lips. "No, nor with anyone else either. I was all alone in the next room."

"Sorry. Go on."

"Come to think of it, I hadn't seen Royce with LeAnn all weekend. I was staying in a small motel on the edge of town—the Happy Rest or something like that. As I said, LeAnn had the room next to mine. Maybe that's why I don't think I'd seen Royce much. Wasn't exactly his style, was it? Anyway, LeAnn came and went alone. Driving that gas-hog or whatever of hers. Then early Saturday morning, I heard the two of them arguing. I thought that peculiar because that's not like Royce. I don't think he ever raised his voice to Wanda a single time during their marriage. LeAnn brings that out?"

I wagged my head. "No," I said, "she isn't like that at all."

And she wasn't. LeAnn had never been the type to engage in or provoke inflamed quarrels. Over the course of our marriage, we had our differences, of course, but they never ended in shouting matches. Not once. Like the time LeAnn wanted to visit her sister. I hadn't wanted to go. I'd strained my riding arm and had stayed away from a number of events waiting for it to heal. We were in Reno and LeAnn thought it an appropriate time to drive down to her sister's place. A mere hour or so away. But I reminded her that we'd been there the year before, and things hadn't gone all that well. Even LeAnn admitted that. I let her know I was anxious to return to the circuit and wanted to get to Bakersfield, California, site of the next event. I wasn't going to ride, merely observe—a bull rider can learn much about the bulls by watching others ride them, which way they tend to spin coming out of the chute, how hard and how high they buck, judge how powerful they are. LeAnn was not happy with the decision but she went along with it, though moping during the entire drive to Bakersfield.

Still, there hadn't been any big argument about it. Then again, maybe it hadn't been all that important to her.

The argument with Royce must have been over something important. Like maybe age difference?

"Course I was never around Royce and Wanda all the time to know if he ever raised his voice to *her*," Denise was saying. "Anyway, though I couldn't understand what it was about, they're arguing loud enough I could hear them through the walls. I was about to knock on their door and tell them to tone it down when suddenly the shouting stopped."

"You're thinking that's when the baby was conceived?"

She shook her head. "No. Had to be later."

"Why?"

"Because they left. Drove off somewhere."

"After midnight?"

She nodded.

I asked how she knew it was LeAnn and Royce who left.

"Heard the door open and close." Then she took a thoughtful pose. "You know," she continued, "they must have driven separately. I distinctly remember hearing two engines start up and two vehicles drive off."

"Maybe the second car was people from a different room."

She shrugged. "Maybe."

"How long were they gone?"

"Don't know for sure. Actually, I didn't hear them come back."

"Then how do you know they did?"

"Cause I saw them come out of LeAnn's room the next day. Actually, the same day. Sometime after noon. They got in Royce's pickup and drove off. Saw them through my window. I wasn't being nosy or anything. I'd pulled my drapes back sometime before and was just sitting there. Happened to see them."

"So how do you figure the child was conceived that night?"

"They didn't wake me up with any more shouting after they got back, and…" here she leaned over toward me and grinned lecherously, "…they were holding hands when they came out of the room. All lovers makeup after a fight. Right? Now, LeAnn is pregnant. Sure looks like one and one makes three to me."

I had to agree.

Elissa and Mike returned from the dance floor and the four of us talked and danced (yes, I hoofed it, too) for another couple of hours before deciding to turn in.

Back in her room, Elissa asked me what Denise and I had been discussing while she and Mike were dancing. I could see Elissa was already keeping pretty close tabs on me. I didn't mind. Deserved it, in fact. I didn't see Elissa as either the possessive or insecure type. I knew I no longer craved the life of a rake, but Elissa would need some time for me to prove it. Despite Denise's newfound confidence in me, she (Elissa) had justification for keeping those tabs on me. After all, I did have something of a reputation. My brand-new steadiness had to take permanently, didn't it?

When I told her the gist of the conversation, she said, "I doubt if the baby was conceived that night."

"What does that mean?" I pumped, staring at her.

She rolled her eyes. "Oh, nothing."

"Nothing? You say you doubt the baby could have been conceived that night but then won't say why? That doesn't make a bit of sense. How would you know anything about it?"

She gave me a pained look. "I know. Anything more I would say would be a violation of professional ethics. Can we leave it at that?"

"What do you know?"

She stonewalled it. I couldn't get another word out of her. It seemed professional ethics were blocking the way.

Personally, I couldn't see how it really mattered. Why I was so curious about when LeAnn's baby was conceived was not so baffling. After all, LeAnn had been my wife. We had not had children, another reason I believed my curiosity was piqued. Perfectly normal as far as I was concerned.

However, I didn't see this as an issue worth fighting over just so Elissa and I would have an excuse to makeup afterwards — as wonderful as that would have been. So I dropped the subject and we had a wonderful encounter anyway before dropping off to sleep. Sleeping with a wonderful intelligent woman (a looker to boot), I found myself gazing at a not so distant horizon where I visualized an altar waiting. I just hoped I wouldn't blow it.

# CHAPTER THIRTY-ONE

Over the next two days, Elissa and I continued to get to know each other. Quite well, I might add. We visited tourist attractions, took in shows (the ones we could scrounge tickets for) and enjoyed each other morning and night. (I don't have to spell that out. You know exactly what I mean.)

Thursday morning was sunny and calm, temperatures in the low sixties. Perfect. Except for an article in the newspaper that I read at breakfast with Elissa before she had to run off to the Thomas and Mack.

The article had not been written by Jamie Clarke, and it was not in The Washington Post. Like the paper in Phoenix, this one, in a Las Vegas daily, spotted the dark cloud hanging over the PBR. It mentioned all the recent deaths, which meant it included Jodi's. It did not explain that Jodi had no connection with the PBR other than as a sister of a bull rider killed in the arena, but that would have made no difference to the vultures of the press. Of course, their way, the story was more newsworthy, more sensational.

At least, when Daryl spotted me in the lobby of the hotel and asked me if I'd read it, I was able to reply in the affirmative.

"Shouldn't have too great an impact," he said.

Then I told him about Jamie Clarke of The Washington Post and what Denise had said about how the reporter liked to crucify her victims.

"Damn," he said. "She interviewed me. I didn't know

she was with The Washington Post. I thought she was with some local rag. We are in deep trouble, partner," he said. "Any ideas on how to handle it?"

Now that was a shocker in itself. Daryl asking my thoughts on something so important. Well, I was the vice-president of the PBR, wasn't I? Guess that meant something. Shaking out of the reverie his unexpected solicitation had momentarily caused me, I said that from now on we should make no comments to the press other than that we wanted the killer found as quickly as possible and to put on the best PBR Final we could.

He nodded as if I'd spoken the wisdom of the ages and then asked if I was staying in touch with the police about the murders. I told him I had spoken with people in Phoenix and Las Vegas as well as Atlantic City and Twin Falls.

"Good, good," he murmured, and then mentioned he was meeting Courtney for a late breakfast and left.

Daryl was the first cowboy up that night. He'd drawn G-man, a black freckled bull out of Clete Fassel's pen. G-man broke from the gate and turned to his left. Daryl got around the corner and threw a spur to the animal's thick side. His score would have been in the high eighties if G-man had kept spinning as he was prone to do, but he broke out of the spin and bucked down the arena several times before turning into a right hand spin, flattening out in the process. It was a crowd-pleasing ride but not one for a high score. Between Rich Nobels and myself, Daryl garnered an eighty-three. At least, he'd ridden his first bull of the final weekend, the one the bull riders like to get out of the way.

Over the next four nights, there would be a bull for each of the forty-five bull riders in the event. The top fifteen after seven bulls (don't forget the three from the previous weekend) would compete in the short-go on Sunday to determine the World Finals Event Champion. That's different from the PBR World Champion, which is won by the top bull rider from throughout the year. So there was a World Finals Event Champion to be crowned on Sunday as well as the PBR World Champion. Of course, the World Finals Event could determine the year's PBR World Champion, though it did not look as if that was going to happen this year.

Going into the final weekend, Justin Diver, only twenty-one years old, had a substantial lead for the PBR World Championship over the Canadian, Chad Michaelson, in second place, with Wes Nunnemaker, a distant third (read: he was out of it). If Justin bucked off every one of his remaining bulls and Chad rode all of his, Chad would win the title. If Justin rode just one bull over the final four days, or Chad bucked off the same number, Justin would be PBR World Champion — winner of the one million dollar bonus to boot.

Wes' chances were even more remote. Both Justin and Chad had to come down off all of their bulls, and he had to ride everyone of his for a score of ninety-two or better. Not going to happen. Personally, I considered it a lock for Justin. Still, everyone connected with the sport expected the final weekend to be exciting.

The most interesting ride that night, for me, was Kyle Nash on Exterminator. Kyle had made it to the Finals by virtue of his success since Twin Falls. Having regained his confidence, he'd ridden two out of the three bulls he'd drawn the opening weekend and sat in fifth place for the event. Now, he rode his night's draw for a go-round leading ninety-one.

But that was not what was interesting. It was what happened after his eight seconds on the back of the animal. Exterminator had bucked high and hard, had thrown in some fast spins in both directions that had Kyle strung out on the end of his arm with less than half a tick to go. Had Kyle been required to ride Exterminator for eight and a quarter seconds, he would not have made the whistle. Since eight seconds was all he'd contracted for, he got the score. We as judges are not to take into consideration anything that happens after eight seconds. In other words, we do not base our score on the quality, style or the difficulty of the get-off. Often the get-off "ain't pretty." Kyle's was one of the ugliest I'd ever seen. Strung out on the end of his arm, his hand broke free of his bull rope right at the whistle, and the centrifugal force that Exterminator had built up flung Kyle up and away with a thrust impossible to measure.

And that's when the interesting part started. As Kyle was airborne, Exterminator, still coming around from his last spin, bucked his rear high in the air just as Kyle was sailing over that particular portion of his anatomy. The rising rump caught Kyle's descending one with as perfect a timing as you could ask for, and the blow sent Kyle spinning head over heels in a flip that carried him a good dozen feet above the arena dirt. As perfect as the timing for the contact between bull and bull rider had been, that was how imperfect Kyle's spin worked out for him. Tumbling around in the air, he completed one and a half revolutions, his head the first part of his anatomy to make contact with the ground. Fortunately, I didn't hear any sound of a bone (neck) snapping, just the collective gasp from the crowd, and I was in the best position to hear anything. Kyle had been thrown in my direction, such that he landed not ten feet from where I was standing and then rolled onto his side.

My first inclination was to run to him, and I took several steps in his direction, which placed me but a couple of feet from where he lay.

"Don't touch him," I heard Carlton Brazeau yell. I looked up and nodded, and then stepped out of the way, though not far.

I heard a soft moan and knew Kyle was alive. He picked up one arm as if to rub his forehead, stopped, let the arm drop to his side.

"Kyle, can you hear me?" Carlton asked the injured cowboy.

Another moan served as a response.

"What's your name?" Carlton asked.

Moan.

"What did he say?" Carlton asked, looking at Rod Hartley, one of the sports healers who'd come bearing a stretcher.

"I think he said Momma," Rod said.

Carlton nodded and pointed to the stretcher, said, "We'll need that."

The healers carefully lifted Kyle onto the stretcher, protecting his neck throughout the process. They carried him out of the arena (concerned applause from the crowd resonating throughout the cavernous place) to the first aid room where I knew Elissa awaited him.

Then I blew my next score. If only Hardtack had thrown Ty Hudson. I knew Hardtack's reputation. He was a bull every bull rider should ride. Seldom did anyone score greater than an eighty-four on him. Luck of the draw. But he had the outing of his life—if you can believe all the flack I took afterwards. I felt I even gave Ty the benefit of the doubt. When the score appeared on the giant screen above the arena, the crowd booed with disapproval. When I saw the replay, I knew I'd blown it.

Hardtack had come bursting out of the chute and immediately turned to his left, the opposite of his usual pattern. He had a determination about him that night that he usually lacked. Perhaps he'd heard things—like he was going to a hamburger factory after the weekend. It wasn't just his false direction, he bucked higher than he'd ever bucked before, and the downdrafts were accomplished with a force I didn't think he had in him.

Complicating matters was Ty. He rode the animal with a flash and daring that was inspirational. He spurred, flung his free arm around with perfect balance and style. The ride deserved a score in the upper eighties or low nineties.

Which was why I heard it later. Several cowboys and a

veteran PRCA judge came up to me during the first break and asked me for my rationale for the low score. I had a hard time explaining. Hemming and hawing was the best I could do.

So why wasn't the score what it should have been? A partial answer: I gave the ride a score equivalent to an eighty-three. In other words, had Rich Nobels' numbers matched mine, the ride would have garnered Ty that total. As it was, my low score pulled him down to an eighty-six. Had my pencil jotted down more appropriate figures, Ty would have gotten an eighty-nine or so.

So what happened? The complete answer: I wasn't watching. Oh, my eyes were peering in the right direction. But they weren't seeing. They were focused inward. You see, I was thinking. When Carlton Brazeau asked Kyle Nash what his name was, because of where I was standing, I heard something different from Kyle than what Rod told Carlton he'd heard. I hadn't heard "Momma." But I was willing to bet that what I heard was what Kyle had said.

People who are partially deaf don't actually hear as well as they think they do. I was at a reception for the PBR in Anaheim, California, a few years back where I got caught in a soliloquy by an ear, nose and throat specialist. He prided himself a bull riding aficionado, was one of a large number of patrons who had separated themselves from a sizable gratuity that benefited The Rider Relief Fund, which helps cover medical expenses for injured bull riders. The good doctor had gone on and on about how people who are partially deaf subconsciously read the lips of the people they are in dialogue with, thinking they are "hearing" them. But my hearing is twenty-twenty, and I know what I heard.

Lying on his side in the arena dirt, Kyle had been facing me directly. Carlton had been standing over him looking down at his ear. I, and I alone, could see—and read—Kyle's barely moving mouth.

# CHAPTER THIRTY-TWO

I regained my concentration and did a pretty good job of judging the rest of the night, despite spotting Jamie Clarke in the crowd, watching the action with all the enthusiasm of a high school bull rider forced to sit in English class reading one of Shakespeare's plays.

By virtue of his ninety-one on Exterminator, Kyle finished first in the go-round. Surprisingly, a few other bull riding geezers took second, third and fourth respectively; Tyler Kennelly had scored a ninety on Killer Too, Cody Laws had racked up an eighty-nine and a half with a wild ride on Dreamkatcher, and Red Parham had eked out an eighty-nine on Catch-Me-If-You-Can. I was sure the PBR youth movement was yet to be served, but there were three more nights of bull riding to go.

In that vein, Justin Diver was thrown from his bull, T For Two, in a ride everyone attributed to nerves, while Chad Michaelson clung to his slim chances of taking the PBR World Champion title home to Canada with an eighty-five on Captive. Wes Nunnemaker was out of it. He'd ridden his draw, Hercules, for only an eighty-seven. No PBR World Championship for him this year.

I turned in my equipment to LeAnn, asking her in the process how Royce was doing. She swiped the air with her hand and claimed he was fine. Over the previous couple of days, I'd seen him around, talking and smiling like his usual self. That night, I watched him standing at his favorite position on a rail behind the chutes, barking orders at Craig Kelton and the others handling his bulls, wrangling with other stock contractors about the best way to breed bucking bulls, razzing the bull riders who got bucked off his animals, maintaining his bull had an off-day to any cowboy who rode one for the required eight seconds. He seemed to be having a great time.

And yet, like an intricate plot, it all seemed somehow contrived. He was a little too jovial, the smile a little too wide, as if he wanted everyone to think there wasn't a thing wrong with Royce Sirett—and never would be.

In case you might be wondering, I could not read Royce's lips, subconsciously or otherwise. So if you're asking how I knew what he was saying to everyone, the answer was simple—it was his usual blather during an event. Until my injury, I'd been a part of it and knew it all by heart. Now, as a judge, I had to stand on the fringe, out of the camaraderie. Was I missing it? Definitely. Enough for me to decline the permanent judge's position I'd been offered? I needed to think about it some more. Act in haste, repent in leisure, my mother always said.

I slipped back to the first aid room where I expected to find Elissa bandaging some cowboy or counting her supplies, but the place was empty. I stepped out onto the concourse, looked both ways, saw no sign of her. I went back in the room and hopped up on the patient's table to wait. Peering around, I noticed a neat wooden desk, a rolling stool shoved into the area reserved for the feet. A counter ran down the length of one whole side of the room, empty except for a lone barf pan near the middle, like an oasis in the desert. There were cabinets above the counter, some locked with medicine bottles and other dangerous looking containers, others with gauze and bandages and splints and the like. There was a file cabinet in one corner.

A file cabinet? Did the PBR cart that thing around to every event on the circuit? If it contained what I thought it did,

I reasoned we had no choice.

Suddenly, the germ of an idea wiggled itself into a corrupt corner of my brain. I hopped off the table and checked the concourse again. The coast was clear. (Yes, I really thought that.) I hurried over to the file cabinet, grabbed the handle of the top drawer and pulled. The distance it moved before running into the locking mechanism could be measured in milli-somethings, same with the next drawer down. I uttered an expletive under my breath, rich with color. I tried the other two drawers in succession and found them similarly secured. I was in the process of hopping back up on the table when Elissa walked into the room.

"I just returned from the hospital," she said.

"Kyle?"

She nodded.

"How's he doing?"

"He'll be all right. Has a concussion. They're going to keep him tonight for observation. Just to be safe. But he should be ready for tomorrow night."

"What room is he in?"

"Three twenty-seven."

"Lucy with him?"

She nodded. "But she's going back to the hotel in a little while she said."

"I want to speak to Kyle," I mentioned, half to myself.

Elissa's face turned tragic. "Not now, I hope. I'm tired and would like to get to bed early…if you don't mind."

I put on what I hoped was my best lascivious smile, said, "Not in the least," took her hand and led her to the parking lot where we got into my pickup and drove to Caesar's Palace.

My performance was spectacular that night—a score well in the nineties, if I must say so myself. I was spectacular because I really had my mind elsewhere yet managed to elicit some very interesting noises from my bed partner. My distraction was not her fault. She was fabulous. Nor was I in the early stages of tiring of her. In truth, I sincerely wanted to make the budding relationship work. So my distraction had nothing to do with her, but was the product of thoughts of what I was planning after she fell asleep. For the earlier corrupt germ was mushrooming in its corner of my brain like a full blown nuclear cloud.

The performance completed, Elissa rolled onto her side, my arm draped around her waist. Soon, her breathing grew slow and sonorous. I gave her a few minutes more to fall deeper into her sleep, and then I turned over and slid slowly out of the bed. I grabbed my clothes and Elissa's pocketbook and sidled into the bathroom where I dressed as rapidly as I could. Then I crossed the line. I lifted Elissa's keys out of her pocketbook. Needless to say, I was as quiet as the proverbial church mouse as I crept out of the room.

It was after midnight when I pulled into the parking lot of the Las Vegas hospital. Heading down the corridor, an antiseptic smell pungent to my nose, I received a few wary stares from the hospital staff. I made my way along confidently and arrived at the elevators unchallenged. I knew exactly where the elevators were located; this was not my first time in that facility. In fact, I'd probably been in the place on average once for each of the previous ten years, twice because I'd been a patient (the first time for having been knocked out, again because of a separated shoulder), the other times visiting injured cowboys. Maybe, I went unchallenged because the nurses recognized me and knew me to be harmless, relatively speaking that is.

I wasn't exactly harmless that night. Oh, I had no thoughts of murder or mayhem, or any other form of bodily harm to my fellow humankind, but I wanted an answer to a question, an answer only Kyle Nash could supply.

I found him in the room where Elissa said he would be, lying in a raised bed with his head turned away from me, hair a little unkempt, but otherwise showing no sign that anything was wrong. Too much a veteran of this scene, I had no expectation of finding him with his head wrapped in bandages like in some hokey television show. Luckily, a nurse had just finished taking his vitals, which left him awake, if groggy. Just the way I wanted him.

"Kyle," I said, and watched his head turn toward me.

He smiled when he saw me. "Chance," he murmured, lips vibrating only slightly, "Great to see you. Glad you came by. They don't want me fallin' into a deep sleep. Concussion, you know." I said I did and he continued, "Want to ride tomorrow night. Heard I won the go-round." I confirmed his news. "The money will buy us another bull. Might win the whole damn thing."

"You got a shot," I agreed. "Kyle, listen. I need to ask you a few questions."

"Sure, Chance. Anything."

"Tell me about Wanda."

"Wanda?" he echoed, his eyes narrowing. "What about her?"

"You mentioned her tonight. Why?"

"I mentioned her?"

"Yes. You were lying in the arena after your spectacular dismount." He smiled wanly. "You said her name when Carlton was talking to you. Remember?"

He rolled his head to one side and then back. "Don't remember that, Chance. You sure?"

"I'm sure," I said, and I was. He had distinctly mouth the word "Wanda" while lying in the arena dirt. Even if his mouth hardly moved, it had moved enough.

"Now why...?"

"That's what I want to know."

He looked away as he said, "I can't tell you a thing, Chance."

"I think you can, Kyle. Did you see Wanda in Twin Falls?"

"Twin Falls!" He shot a look straight at me, his eyes fully opened now. He was on his guard.

"This is no time to play coy. Did you see Wanda in Twin Falls?"

He lowered his eyes, turned his head away again.

"I'm taking that as a yes, Kyle."

He continued to look away. Then I saw tears running down his face and he muttered something I couldn't hear. I asked him to repeat it.

"It was only that one time. The first and only time I ever cheated on Lucy. But, Chance, she was just so sexy when she came on to me. How could I resist?"

I was getting somewhere. Kyle was talking. That was a start. But I had to handle him just right. "You couldn't, Kyle," I patronized. "You couldn't. No one could. So don't beat yourself up about it." I wasn't lying to him. That's how powerful Wanda was. When she came on to you, no man could resist her. I knew.

"I can't forgive myself."

"Kyle, I need to know when you saw her in Twin Falls."

"I stayed away from her after that, Chance. I swear it."

"I know you did," I said, not knowing any such thing. Of course, there was Lucy. Possessive as a miser, she played Kyle close to the vest when she was around. So why hadn't she been in Twin Falls with Kyle? I remembered she'd told Washington she'd gone to visit her parents. Lucy had told me one time they lived on a farm outside of Tupelo, Mississippi. Now why did she pick that particular weekend to go home? He told me soon enough. First though, I wanted to know when he'd seen Wanda in Twin Falls. I pressed him.

"Friday afternoon," he said. "Lucy had gone home to

talk to her father about puttin' up any bulls we might buy until we could handle them ourselves. I seen Wanda at the arena in the afternoon when I was lookin' over some of the stock that we might try to buy. She came on so strong. She was a randy thing, Chance. She took whatever was available, and I happened to be available. Asked me where Lucy was in that phony but cute way she had. When I told her, she let me know in no uncertain term, she was ready to play Mrs. Nash for awhile."

I nodded. "So what happened?"

"She said we had to hurry. We did it in the ladies room there in the arena. Near the pens. Since there weren't any other women around we thought that safest. Though at one point, Wanda giggled and asked if I wanted to take a chance and do it in the men's room. That's what she said. She was something, Chance."

I agreed with him.

"And could she be loud."

I remembered that part, too. One of the wonderful things of mounting Wanda under those circumstances was her vocals. They were inspiring, drove you to want to ride her with your best style, scrambling and spurring right out of the gate. I felt I could easily score in the mid-nineties both times I rode her. Wanda was definitely no one to make it look easy.

"What was her big hurry?"

"She said she had to meet someone."

"Did she say who?"

He wagged his head ever so slightly. "No."

"Was it Craig?"

"Could've been. She didn't say. Listen, Chance, you're not going to say nothin' to Lucy, are you?"

I assured him I wouldn't utter a peep. A nurse popped in to take his vitals again, a ploy to keep him awake. She was surprised to find me there but relaxed when Kyle said it was all right. I thought I'd learned everything he could tell me, so I wished him a speedy recovery and left.

Hindsight is always crystal clear. I should have returned to the warm bed and the wonderful woman waiting for me at Caesar's Palace. Although I was finished with Kyle for the time being, my nocturnal prowling wasn't complete.

# CHAPTER THIRTY-THREE

All the way to the Thomas and Mack, I felt an ocean of guilt. Maybe that should be a desert of guilt. After all, I was in Las Vegas. My guilt had nothing to do with my interrogation of Kyle in the hospital. Catching him in a vulnerable state didn't bother me in the least. Injured, without Lucy around, I actually felt a detective's pride. (If they feel such.) In recognizing that *then* was probably the best time to question him, I'd found out exactly what I wanted to know. I hadn't guessed that Kyle had partaken of a Friday afternoon fling with Wanda when they were in Twin Falls together, but I had suspected that their paths had crossed for some purpose. Was a one-time fling reason enough for Kyle to kill Wanda? To keep her from blabbing about it to anyone, especially Lucy? Of course. A child could tell you people have committed murder for far less. If he had killed her because of a fling he didn't want exposed to the light of day, wouldn't it have been a big mistake to confess that fling to me? Then again, he had been somewhat out of it. Maybe, he did not know exactly what he was saying. True, he was feeling guilty about something, and the guilt was a burden, a burden that was crushing him like a great weight, a burden he needed to get off his chest. Telling me served to expunge the transgression like liquid cleaner wiping away grime on a kitchen counter.

Now, riding along in my truck, *I* was the one feeling the weight of guilt. Guilt—not for what I'd done, but for what I was about to do. I was about to betray Elissa. That I had honorable motives did not lessen the burden. While my guilt, like Kyle's, was burdensome, it was not debilitating. I reasoned if I could get what I needed and creep back into her bed without her knowing I'd ever left, well…it wouldn't excuse it, but only I would know.

I tried telling myself it was Elissa's own fault. I hadn't taken up with her because I thought she could tell me something that would help me uncover Wanda's killer. Twice in my presence, though, she'd hinted at something. What it was, I had no clue. I believed it was something she'd learned in her capacity as a PBR sports healer. My guess was she did not suspect the relevancy of what she knew. Then again, maybe this was a wild goose chase. Still, I had to be sure. Guilt or no guilt.

I pulled into the parking lot of the Thomas and Mack. It was nearly two A.M. and nothing moved anywhere. There were no other vehicles parked on that side of the arena. I found the outside door near the pen area locked as I expected. Elissa had nearly a dozen keys on her ring, four times what I carried. I have a key for my house in Uvalde, another for my truck, a third for the room wherever I'm staying. That's it. Don't need any more.

It was the third to last key that opened the door to the place. Suspecting that a night watchman lurked somewhere on the premises, I eased myself in quietly and then peered along the corridor in both directions. I saw and heard nothing. I walked to the first aid room where it took the sixth key on Elissa's ring to open the door. It was then I realized I was not much of a detective. What kind of snoop shows up for a night job without a flashlight? The room was dark, except for the dim corridor light that leaked through the cracks around the door. Without a flashlight, I had no choice but to turn the overhead room light on.

When I flipped the switch, the room burst with so much light I had to squint for a few moments until my eyes adjusted. I glanced around, noted that everything was pretty much as it had been left earlier. I stepped over to the filing cabinet and pulled the metal handle of the top drawer. Still locked. I didn't bother with the others this time, just stared down at Elissa's keys that were still in my hand. I figured it had to be the smallest key on the ring, the one that looked like a file cabinet key. I inserted it in the lock and gave it a turn. The distinct ka-chunk of the cabinet unlocking gave me a "hitting-the-jackpot" feeling. (We were in Las Vegas, weren't we?)

I put the keys in my pocket and pressed the pewter-colored lever on the top drawer to the side and pulled. Although heavy, it slid out easily. Full of files. In alphabetical order. There were files for each of the bull riders, staff personnel, stock contractors and even their help. I was surprised how complete the records were. I proceeded to close one drawer and open the next one until I got to the bottom one. After checking to see how thorough the PBR was about medical records for the people connected with it, I went back through the drawers until I came to those files that interested me in particular, the reason for my nocturnal sojourn in the first place. There was more than one, and I needed time to peruse them all.

Since I was there, I figured what the heck, so the first file of interest was my own, located about a third of the way back from the front of the top drawer. I skimmed through it. Although some of the handwriting was illegible, probably Carton Brazeau's scrawl, it seemed to be complete. It contained one little surprise, however. I had a three-inch scar across my upper back on the left side. I didn't know that, couldn't remember how I got it. Of course, the only thing that made any sense was that some bull must have ripped me there with a horn, probably sometime when I got knocked out, which had happened five times in my career—about once every third year. I don't remember a thing about any of them. I was out cold after all.

I closed the file and put it back in its place. Then I drew

out LeAnn's, which was right behind my own. She'd passed all of her annual physicals with flying colors, was in great shape, excellent blood pressure, blood count, blood sugar level. At first, I thought it strange for what I did not find. There was nothing about her pregnancy. Of course, when I thought about it, I concluded why would there be? She was seeing an obstetrician for that condition, not the sports healers. While I was certain some notation would find its way into the file in due course, at this point, her pregnancy wouldn't have any relevance for the PBR medical staff.

I returned the file to its proper place in the drawer, and then rummaged through those of the other people I was interested in. In most of them, I found nothing to pique my interest. I did find the mention of back and buttock scars in a number of the files of some of the bull riders and wondered if these men, too, were unaware of the blotches on their bodies.

There was one file that made my novel career of breaking and entering worthwhile. Although it, too, contained much in the same illegible hand that dominated most of the files, it contained one word — very legible because it was printed — that seemed of some importance. It didn't explain everything, like who killed Wanda Sirett and Jodi Hall and why. Actually, I hadn't thought it would, but I'd come for some piece of the puzzle and thought maybe I'd found one. I still had to figure out exactly how and where it fit in, if it did. In truth, it might have nothing to do with the recent tragic events on the PBR circuit. The new question for me was what was I going to do with it?

I was standing there, file in hand, musing that very point, when suddenly the door burst open, and a burly man wearing a gray security uniform seemed to think he had a right to know what I was doing there.

# CHAPTER THIRTY-FOUR

All in all, the Las Vegas city jail wasn't that bad a place. Not that I'm an expert on jails. I knew it wasn't the Ritz. Not that I'm any expert on the Ritz either. The place had the obligatory derelict stench about it, of course, along with the customary unsympathetic personnel. I was thrown into a cell surrounded by — what else — derelicts.

I deserved everything that was happening to me, didn't I? After all, I had been caught red-handed in the commission of a felony — burglary if you want to be technical about it, which was exactly the LVPD's interpretation.

I used my one phone call to wake up...I had no idea. Had Lane been alive it would have been a no-brainer. He would have had a good laugh at my expense, never letting me live it down, but, in the end, he would have been there for me. I thought about calling Elissa, rejecting her as very iffy under the circumstances. As it was, I considered myself in considerable Dutch with her even if she took the time to hear me out. Next, LeAnn came to mind for the job, but I ruled her out on the grounds of motherhood.

In the end, I settled on Daryl. At first, he didn't believe my story, thought I was drunk, refused to bite on the so-called joke and then relented, putting in a sleepy-eyed appearance around four A.M. There was nothing he could do. It wasn't that he was useless. It was just that we had to wait until ten o'clock in the morning when the judge would set my bail. Accordingly, Daryl went back to Caesar's Palace and a warm bed with

Courtney.

Lying sleepless in my cell awaiting my court appearance, I couldn't help thinking. Questions, related and unrelated, swirled around in my head like a tornado in full fury. My little talk with Kyle raised an interesting hypothesis, and not just about Kyle's possible motive for killing Wanda. Had Lucy discovered the affair between Wanda and her husband and killed Wanda in revenge? Did she have the opportunity? Thinking back, I remembered she had said she had been in the stands at Atlantic City when Kyle was looking for Clete Fassel in the pen area, that she hadn't caught up with Kyle. Had she actually gotten ahead of him?

Then there was Craig Kelton. Had Wanda "cut him off" sometime before she was killed? For reducing his "wages" so to speak. Why would she do that? Because she'd found she liked sleeping with Kyle Nash? Not likely. But Craig, horny in Twin Falls, ran into Jodi. Hit on her. She rejected him as she would have rejected any man. He killed her while trying to rape her and then killed Wanda in Atlantic City after she'd made it clear she would determine whether she would resume granting him his special privileges. Would Craig have killed Wanda because she wouldn't sleep with him? From beginning to end, I believed the whole scenario ludicrous.

Yet I thought Craig had another motive for killing Wanda. One that made more sense. Money. The real thing. Not his other "wages." He hadn't been exactly forthcoming when I'd asked him about Wanda's financial condition. According to Royce, Wanda owed him four months worth of salary. Sixteen thousand dollars. Maybe not much for some people, but a considerable sum for a working cowboy. Did he need it at that time? Maybe he saw, that with the way things were going, he would have to kill her if he ever expected to collect.

While I was at it, I wondered if Jodi Hall's murder had anything to do with rape. Could there have been some other reason?

Then there was Royce. And Clete. And…. Anyway, it went on like that throughout what remained of the night, one hypothesis after the next coming to mind, each baffling in turn.

Daryl showed up in court at ten-thirty--a disgusted but silent Courtney in tow — five minutes before my case was called. He always had a sense of timing.

My bond hearing was held before the Honorable Howard Stem, a tall lanky dark haired man in his early forties. After hearing the particulars and noting that I was from out of state, Judge Stem (seemingly reluctantly) set a bond of five thousand dollars. Daryl lent me the five hundred I needed to pay a bondsman, and by high noon, I was, as they say, back on the street.

It was another perfect desert day, sixty-eight degrees, windless and cloudless. We were standing next to Daryl's pickup, a year old loaded Ram, in the municipal parking lot, when he said, "What were you doing breaking into the first aid room at the Thomas and Mack?"

Without going into details, I stated (rather convincingly, I might add) that I was working for Detective Washington back in Atlantic City.

"He has a lead, does he?" Daryl inquired, the edges of his thin eager mouth turning up in anticipation.

"I think so. Though I don't know what it is."

"Or who it is?" he asked, eyeing me knowingly.

I wagged my head. "No. I don't know."

"Whose file were you holding when they caught you?"

"I was looking through a number of files. Including my own." Then, for Daryl's sake (so I told myself), I lied. "Don't remember which one they caught me with."

His face bespoke disappointment. Then he smiled, stuck out his hand, said, "Well, see you tonight, Chance."

That's when Courtney stuck in her two cents worth. With smug glibness, she said, "Aren't you forgetting something, Daryl?"

"What's that?" he asked innocently.

Like a woman scorned coldly wielding her fury, she looked at me. Then she peered at her husband and with her smugness having blossomed into full bloom, said, "You have to tell him you'll have to bring it up to the board whether he can judge the rest of the event."

"Oh, yeah," Daryl said, his gaze dropping to the parking lot macadam before settling on me. "Listen Chance, in the light of what has happened, I think it only right that I bring the matter before the board to decide if it's in everyone's best interest that you judge the rest of the event."

I nodded, had expected it, in fact. It was another thing I had thought about while waiting in my cell. I was ready.

"It's not that I don't want you," he prattled. Then he slapped me on the shoulder, and said, "Hey, you're a doin' a great job. It's just that what with the murders and all, well...."

"We've got the PBR's reputation to consider," I finished.

His face brightened like that of a small boy told he's going to the PBR World Finals. "Yeah, we've got the PBR's reputation to protect. We all want the PBR to succeed and grow."

I nodded.

"So I'll call the meeting for four in the lounge at the Thomas and Mack."

"You want me to stay away?" I asked. Believe it or not, I hoped he would say that was a good idea.

"Nah. Not at all," he replied with a swipe at the air, the skin on his forehead rolling. "Definitely want you there. You tell your side. I want to be perfectly fair. You be there, Chance. Okay?"

I nodded.

Daryl and Courtney got into the pickup. Daryl fired up the engine, and then wound down the window. "You got a ride back?"

I replied in the negative. He motioned for me to get in. I slipped around to the other side and opened the door. Courtney slid over next to her husband, unabashedly making sure she was far enough away from me so that not even the threads of our clothes could commingle. We were silent the entire ride back to Caesar's Palace where Daryl said, "Remember, Chance, four o'clock."

I said I would be there.

I went straight up to my room where I called Detective Rollins in Twin Falls. Something Washington had mentioned concerning the condition of Wanda's body had me wondering if the same was true in Jodi's case.

When he came on the line, I reintroduced myself and said, "I would like to ask you a question."

"Get on with it," he said, oozing boredom.

"Was Jodi Hall's hyoid bone broken or damaged?"

"Yes. Crushed, in fact."

"Which makes it a man killed her."

"Most likely. Though it could have been a woman."

"How so?"

He replied that since Jodi was not very big, plenty of women would have had the strength to strangle her and break her hyoid bone in the process. "Still," he concluded, "because of the attempted rape, it was most likely a man who killed her."

I thanked him and rang off. I showered and dropped into bed, not waking until three-thirty when I hurriedly dressed and beat it over to the Thomas and Mack.

I walked into the fair-sized room on the main concourse where the meeting to determine my fate was to be held. It was a room the board used whenever we had a reason during the World Finals event. The plush carpet was a print blue; the leather chairs, wine-colored; the mahogany table, stained dark. To a man, the members of the board were already assembled, the ongoing conversations dying like a doldrums wind when I entered. Amazingly, I found myself totally devoid of any nervous anticipation. I was pretty certain what the outcome would be — my ouster as judge.

I have never considered myself a candidate for Russ Ward's vote as board member of the year. He knew what was what and didn't appreciate it. Had he been in Atlantic City when I was being railroaded as liaison to the police, I think he would have objected, vehemently.

To my complete surprise, he came to my defense, as only he was capable. Of course, it had nothing to do with me.

"It has to do with the integrity of the World Finals," he asserted. "If we bring in another judge, no matter how good, we run the risk of distorting the scores. That will work in favor of some bull riders, against others. Whoever wins either the event title or the World Championship title will be tainted."

"We've already had two murders connected with the PBR," Kyle Nash reminded. Having escaped the hospital, he was seated in a chair with his arm propped on the long wooden table. I sensed, in his mannerisms and tone, that he was decidedly disenchanted with me. Believe me, that was putting it mildly. Did his disenchantment have anything to do with the disclosures he'd surrendered the night before?

"One murder," Daryl corrected. "Only Wanda was connected with the PBR. Jodi had nothing to do with us, officially."

"One, two. It's academic. Right now, we're tainted," Kyle resumed forcefully. "I think Chance should disqualify himself and actually..." Here, he looked at me with meaning. "...I think he ought to resign as vice-president and go home. Get as far away from the PBR as he can. We can't have the PBR associated with someone who's been charged with burglary.

I'm told we have this Washington Post reporter after us now. She's going to be big trouble. Could ruin us. With Chance out of the way, that's one less issue for her to write about."

"Charged is the key word," Russ stressed, stabbing the air with his forefinger. "He's only charged with burglary. In our country, we make a big deal of saying a man is innocent until proven guilty. Right now, he's innocent. He's given us his explanation as to what he was doing. We appointed him liaison. He's taken the matter a little too personal," here he looked at me, "but it shows the PBR is trying to wash its own dirty linen."

"By creating more dirty linen?" Kyle said.

"I bet he beats it," Russ fired back. "In the end, he won't be convicted." (He was right. The prosecutors issued something called a "Nolle Pros." I didn't understand what that was but it kept me out of prison.)

"But in the meantime...."

"In the meantime, we put on a World Finals Championship that is without question."

Kyle was joined in sentiments by Tyler Kennelly. "I think Kyle makes a good point about not creating more dirty linen. We've got to show we're trying to clean up our act. Nothing personal, Chance. I think you're doing a great job. It's the PBR I'm thinking about. And," he hastened to add, "I think we have a real problem with this Washington Post reporter. If the police don't uncover Wanda's killer, we better be ready for a mountain of bad publicity. This would hurt the PBR. Period. Again, nothing against you, Chance."

I nodded. I knew Tyler meant it.

There was unanimous echoing of Tyler and Kyle's concern over the potential fallout from The Washington Post reporter's upcoming article, and then they got down to it.

Daryl ruled that I couldn't vote since I would have a conflict of interest. Since I had no intentions of voting anyway, hadn't said I ought to have the right, that issue was irrelevant.

He surprised me when he took himself out of the process, saying he would vote only in the event of a tie.

There wasn't any. Russ was joined by Jason Moss, who felt we could weather any potential storm. He thought we could issue a press release stating that we upheld the American tradition of a man being innocent until proven guilty and that, in the meantime, we would be upholding the PBR tradition of providing consistency in judging for the World Finals. With Kyle and Tyler squarely against me, that left Casey Applegate to break the tie. A three to two vote however you looked at it.

I was certain Casey would follow Kyle's lead and send me packing. But he hadn't said a word during the discussion, for or against. Surprisingly, Casey chose that occasion to take a position contrary to that of his best friend, Kyle Nash, and voted to retain me. When he cast his vote, he repeated Russ's sentiments about upholding the integrity of the World Finals and left it at that. I had to wonder what was going on, if there was a rift of some sort between the two friends. Anyway, his vote proved decisive and I held onto my job. Make that jobs.

Shortly after the meeting had been called to order, Daryl had given me the opportunity to tell my side. I'd spooned the same dribble to the board that I'd fed Daryl downtown, indicating in the process that I was ready to accept the decision of the board. I'd actually thought they would kick me out as judge, demanding my resignation as vice-president in the process. Liaison didn't seem to figure into it much. Regardless, I was ready to give them everything. In fact, I wanted to. So after telling them I would abide by their decision, I had no choice after the vote but to remain as judge and vice-president — and liaison. The absolute worst of all worlds. In one sense, I had weathered an earthquake; in another, a dust storm was just blowing up.

If only Elissa had been so forgiving. When I found her in the first aid room at the Thomas and Mack a few minutes after the meeting ended, she was rolling bandages and placing them neatly in a drawer. Seeing me, the first thing she said was, "Give me my keys," and held out her hand. Her body language was as demanding as her words.

I offered them to her with much contrition, decidedly more than I'd felt at the board meeting. Unimpressed, she practically snatched them out of my hand.

"Want to get some dinner before the event?" I asked.

"I'll take care of my own dinner, thank you very much." Yes, the tone was as hard as the words.

Catching which way the wind was blowing, I said I would see her around and started for the door.

"When can I expect the return of the file you took?"

I explained that the police were holding it for evidence, that she wouldn't get it back until after the trial. She harrumphed. Then she turned her back to me and I knew I had been dismissed.

Stepping out of the first aid room, I spotted Casey Applegate heading for the cowboy's dressing room. "Casey," I called and hurried over to him.

He turned, smiled and threw out a friendly, "Hey, Chance. How's it goin'?"

"Fine, Casey. Ready to ride tonight?"

"I'm ready. I drew Dirty Harry. I've seen him but never rode him. Think I got a chance?"

"A good one," I said. "Just wanted to thank you for backing me up today. I appreciated it."

"Don't think I expect any special consideration for that, Chance. I did what I thought was right, that's all. Okay?"

"Sure, Casey. Appreciate the attitude." I paused, and then plunged in. "I was surprised you went against your buddy, Kyle. You two are like two peas in a pod."

He lowered his eyes. "Well, about that. I don't think we'll be such peas for a while, if ever."

"What happened?"

He looked over my shoulder, sighed. "Stupidity. Actually, booze. I got drunk and hit on Lucy."

I couldn't resist a snicker. "Lucy?"

His mouth twisted around in disgust. "Yeah. And you know how uptight she can be."

"Were you serious?"

"Hell no, Chance. I was drunk. Happened Tuesday, my first day back in town. I wanted to lighten up before the final weekend. You know, relax. Drank a little too much. Went crazy, I guess. Anyway, Kyle thinks he has to take up for Lucy, so he's actin' all po'd with me. I think it'll blow over in time. My votin' for you had nothin' to do with that. I voted for you because I agreed with Russ. We have to uphold the integrity of the Finals." Then he grinned mischievously as he added, "But I can't say I wasn't a little pleased to be gittin' back at Kyle for being so ticked at me."

Casey left to get changed and taped up while I grabbed something to eat before picking up my gear from LeAnn.

As I took my position in the arena in preparation for the night's go-round, I spotted Jamie Clarke in the stands again. She looked harmless in her seat. An example of looks being deceiving?

I did an outstanding job (if I must say so myself) judging that night. It was one of the most memorable nights in the history of our sport. After it was over, I looked back and thought about how much I wanted to go on being a part of it. In some way. Any way. Judging would allow me to remain so for a long time. Still, I had to question whether I was ready to retire as a bull rider and become a judge on a permanent basis. Riding still held a strong attraction. Of course, if I were convicted of burglary there would be no choice in the matter. I couldn't very well judge (or ride) from a prison cell, now could I? Remember, at that time, my Nolle Pros was still in the future.

Traditionally, the second night of the final weekend of the World Finals saw the bull riders facing the rankest of the rank. The Eliminators. The bulls of the quality the final fifteen would see in the short-go on Sunday. John Henry was there. So was Kryptonite. And Purgatory.

John Henry threw Jason Moss with a hard turn to the right, right out of the gate. No score. Jason then had to survive a John Henry charge, scampering to the side rail as fast as he could gather himself up out of the dirt and run. John Henry was showing no sign of mellowing. A decision would definitely have to be made as to whether the bull would be allowed to continue on the tour.

All in all, seventeen bull riders out of forty-five rode their bulls. An unusually high number for the eliminator pen when only ten to twelve usually make it to the whistle. It was something to see, something else to judge. And we were on, Rich Nobels as well as myself. Man, it was fun. Casey Applegate rode Dirty Harry for a respectable eighty-eight. Hearing the cheers of the crowd, watching the bull riders give each other high fives, I knew I wanted to go on being a part of that. At one point, I instinctively raised my arm to check how my shoulder was coming along. A twinge of pain combined with noticeable stiffness in the area. No doubt about it, if I wanted to return to the PBR as a bull rider, the shoulder had to do its part. It had to heal completely. I sighed as I realized that my future was still up in the air.

The most spectacular ride of the night was Cody Laws on Regulator. Regulator, bull of the year three years earlier, was approaching the end of his prime and having an off year. A ton of pure Brahma power, he'd been ridden three times during the season—a high number for such a ranked animal. Each time, he'd failed to have the trips like we used to see from him in previous years. Lethargic, half-hearted, all those things you expect from a topnotch athlete having a bad day. He'd put in some ranked efforts, too, and when he did, the cowboys on his back failed to make the whistle every time. So at the Finals, Regulator put together one of his best efforts ever, only this time, the cowboy hung tight for exactly eight point zero one seconds. Long enough.

Regulator broke from the gate with a hard turn to the left, snot streaming from his nose. Then he kicked his rear end up so high that for a second I thought he was going to flip right over. The downdraft following was hard enough to toss even the best rider not ready for the move. Somehow, Cody was.

After Regulator's first hard buck failed to eject the foreign object clinging to his back like a leach, he turned back to the right and proceeded to spin half a dozen times at a rate of speed unbelievable for a bull his size, or of any size for that matter. But it wasn't just the speed of the spin; throughout, he was bucking and kicking like a demon. Then he broke from the spin and threw several high and hard bucks, twisting and turning in any and every direction with the kind of alacrity reserved only for the most supple of children. Regulator had the trip of his life, and he got rode in the process.

Of the two kinds of riding styles, this was a scramble all the way. Cody, whether by design or by divine accident, seemed in control throughout the entire ride. I know it seems a contradiction to say the rider was scrambling but in control. In bull riding, it's not only possible but happens all the time. In fact, in this case, had Cody been trying to make-it-look-easy, he might not have scored as high as he did. Truthfully, I doubt if he would have ridden ole Regulator at all.

Cody, during the ride, kept shifting and moving and sliding and somehow stayed on. But he didn't *just* stay on, he rode Regulator with style, whipping his free hand all around for balance, somehow managing to spend four of the eight seconds spurring Regulator in the side with his dull rowels as if purposely adding insult to injury. It was the ride of the event—

up to that point.

Then, one one hundredth of a second after the whistle spelled the end of the ride, it got exciting. For at that point, Cody lost his bull rope. Out of control, holding on to nothing but bare air, the bull entering yet another dizzying spin, Cody was flung out of there like an Olympic hammer. He must have sailed twenty feet before making a wonderful one point landing on his back in the arena dirt, fortunately thick and soft in the spot where he came down.

Cody tried to rise but stunned, as if thrown from a wrecked automobile, fell back. He lay there helpless. Regulator, coming out of his spin, espied the vulnerable cowboy prostrate in the dirt — and charged.

This sent the bullfighters into motion. Judd Blanchard, to one side of Regulator, grabbed the brown fedora from his head and, in an effort to distract the bull's attention away from the unfortunate bull rider, frisbeed it across Regulator's face. The effort was in vain. Although the hat went sailing right through his line of sight, Regulator, as if blind, ignored the spinning sphere and continued straight for his prey.

Travis Nokes, from his position behind the bull, reached out and grabbed Regulator's tail and yanked it hard. Without so much as a glance backward the bull dragged the bullfighter along with him for several steps before snapping his tail out of Travis' hand, sending the man sprawling in the process.

It was Buddy Bach who saved Cody's hide — and paid the price. He had been standing about the same distance from Regulator as Judd Blanchard, but on the opposite side. From his position, he ran straight at Regulator in a desperate attempt to place his body directly between Regulator's threatening horns and Cody's flat form.

It worked. Regulator seized on his new target, lowered his head and slammed it squarely into Buddy's chest. Fortunately, like the bull riders, the bullfighters wear protective vests; the bull riders outside their shirts, the bullfighters beneath their mesh tops. Regulator's blow doubled Buddy over so that when the bull raised his head, he lifted the bullfighter off the ground and sent him spinning ten feet above the arena dirt.

Buddy must have helicoptered one and a half times over Regulator's wide eyes before taking another shot in the chest, a blow that sent him sailing through the air like Judd's fedora a few moments earlier. The crowd "Ooohed" loudly while Buddy spun and sailed, and then "Aaahed" with equal heartfelt emotion when he struck the ground several feet from where Cody still lay on his back.

Regulator now spotted his original subject—and sprang for him. Catching Regulator's intention, Judd Blanchard ran over and threw himself on Cody, covering his body with his own. Travis Nokes, having gathered himself out of the dirt, was running around to Regulator's front side. Here, it wasn't his object to attract the bull. Instead, he ran to where Buddy lay in the dirt and threw himself on top of the prone bullfighter like Judd had done to Cody. That meant there were no bullfighters trying to distract the raging bull. Lance Miles, the gateman, and others near the escape chute gate were jumping and shouting in a futile effort to draw Regulator's attention. Tyson Roberts, swinging a rope from astride his horse, was doing his best to urge the bull to leave the arena. But Regulator had tunnel vision and used it in a mad dash for Cody and Judd. He slammed his head into Judd's side and thigh, rolling him over in the dirt and off of Cody.

Then the ballet commenced. Regulator jumped over the motionless Cody Laws, his bony hooves landing in the dirt, barely inches from Cody's legs—and crotch. Next, he jumped over Judd Blanchard, missing him by the thinnest of whiskers. Then, like a child playing leapfrog, he hopped over Travis Nokes who was holding his cover over Buddy Bach. Through it all, Regulator somehow missed them all.

Now, the waving and shouting at the end of the arena had its desired effect. Regulator, glancing up, caught sight of the waving arms hailing around the open escape chute gate. A couple seconds later, he was out of the arena and making for his warm waiting pen.

Despite the entertaining spectacle, no one was seriously hurt. Cody, along with the bullfighters, rose from the ground to rousing applause. Cody left the arena unassisted while the bullfighters resumed their positions near the bull riding chutes. And the show went on.

I paused a moment before writing down my score for Cody's ride. I didn't pause because I felt any doubt of what score I wanted to give him. Even if Rich Nobels hadn't seen the ride as I had, I felt confident in what I was going to mark—a twenty-three and a half for the bull, the same for Cody, an equivalent of a ninety-four, if Rich agreed with me.

No, the reason I paused before jotting down any numbers was because an idea had struck me like a kick in the chest. Inspiration? I don't really know where it came from, maybe from something in the way Buddy had saved Cody. The move, so self-sacrificing, had planted a seed, maybe a mere germ—this one not on the corrupt side of my brain. Followed through with, it just might lead to the solution to Wanda Sirett's murder.

# CHAPTER THIRTY-FIVE

As it turned out, Rich did agree with me, exactly. Hence, Cody's well deserved ninety-four. The crowd loved it, stood, roared and applauded for nearly half a minute. With Red Parham riding Kryptonite for a ninety-one and a half, followed by Cody's sensational go on Regulator, the two friends were running one-two, Cody in the lead, for the event title. As for the race for World Champion, Justin Diver was thrown four seconds into his ride by Humdinger, the young Clete Fassel bull that the stock contractor had gone to Twin Falls to see the weekend Jodi Hall was killed, while Chad Michaelson, flashy duds and all, garnered an eighty-nine and a half on Dirty Duty. Chad still had a chance.

When the night was finished, I hurried over to LeAnn to turn in my judging equipment.

"You did another good job out there tonight," she commented. "I think you've found your future career, Chance. I really do."

I thanked her and handed in my gear.

I'd spotted Detectives Marks and Hornblower in the stands before the go-round was five minutes old. Leaving, I offered them a wave. Marks motioned me over to the rail where he told me he'd heard about my little trouble of the night before, grinning gleefully as he spoke. I said nothing. He then asked me if I had anything to tell him. I replied in the negative. He told me to keep in touch and without waiting for a reply turned and headed out, Hornblower on his heels like a puppy padding after a child.

I slipped by the first aid room hoping to find Elissa. Despite the ranked pen of bulls, it had been a light night for the sports healers. Sure, a couple of cowboys got banged up pretty good, strained arms, bruised legs, fat lips, but, all in all, nothing major, nothing that would keep any of them out of the next night's go-round.

Elissa was nowhere to be seen. I surmised she'd expected me to stop by and had beat it out of there as fast as a gambler trying to avoid a loan shark he was in debt to.

Was it over? Hardly before it had begun? I hoped not. I had grown more than fond of Elissa. I was regretting what I'd done. But even with a worthy motive, betrayal is still betrayal. I decided I had to give her time to get over it. Maybe she would, maybe she wouldn't. But isn't life always something of a crapshoot?

Without Elissa I wasn't interested in partying (even in Vegas) that night. I turned in early, and the next morning, I found myself up and on the road by six A.M. I wanted to clear my head and play around with the idea that had struck me the night before while judging.

It was a cool, crisp, cloudless morning, the early sun spraying a rich cobalt sky. Although clipping along in the light traffic at speeds between eighty-five and ninety (not bad for a "vintage" pickup), I still had time to view the spectacular scenery flashing by me like asteroids at warp speed. Spectacular doesn't begin to describe it — sublime comes closer. The flat but not flat, smooth but serrated landscape, dry, dressed in shades of ochre, sand and rust, stretched for the distance of several New England states. The road heaved and dropped like a kiddy roller coaster, skirted buttes and promontories, skimmed small towns (even when splitting their centers) and occasionally broke into sights of a tree. Wild, barren country — and fabulous.

I maintained my speed all the way to the outskirts of

Fallon, Nevada, reducing a recommended eight-hour drive to five. Oh, well, that's the cowboy way. Fallon is a small town an hour's drive west of Reno. It can claim a Naval air station, a large impounded lake, a stretch of the old Pony Express route and a singing mountain—shifting sands emitting an eerie moan. South of Fallon, just off US 95, in some weirdly laid-out subdivision, the John Markley family resided. John is married to Leona, LeAnn's mostly—but not completely—estranged sister.

I found her—though it wasn't easy.

At first, I got lucky, and recognized the entrance to White River development. Actually, this part was easy because there was a gray brick marquee that spelled out WHITE RIVER in bold black letters. The place is a five hundred acre winding residential community with hundreds of exactly replicated two-story, gray-sided, white-trimmed boxes with fireplaces, in which a few thousand people have decided to call home. To each his own. I'll keep the place my parents left me in Uvalde.

Getting into White River was the easy part; finding Leona's place was the trick. I couldn't remember her street name or her house number. I knew I had to take either the third or fourth left off the main drag, and then either the second or third right, which should have been a cul-de-sac. Hers was the third house on the right. Turned out, I should have taken the second left off the main street, the third right and the fourth house on the left. Close, just no cigar.

I'd first taken the third left off the main street and then the second right. There was no cul-de-sac. Returning to the main street, I took the fourth left followed by the third right. It, too, failed to meet the requirements. I missed one of my turns getting back to the main street and became hopelessly lost. Being of the male gender, my inclination was against seeking assistance; I was certain I could find my way out on my own. But time was an issue. I had to be back in Las Vegas by eight—actually sooner. With sufficiently bruised ego in harness, I stopped at a house where some small children were playing in the front yard. The woman who came to the door, while far from elderly, seemed a little old to be the mother of such young children. Turned out she wasn't. She was their grandmother (for which she seemed a little young). She watched her grandchildren for their working mother, her daughter-in-law. She deemed it a perfect arrangement since it allowed her to see her grandchildren five days a week — sometimes more.

She gave me directions back to the main road, but then asked me the name of the people I was seeking. I told her.

"Why, they're my neighbors," she exclaimed excitedly.

The coincidence of coincidences soon had me pulling into Leona's macadam driveway where a silver MPV was outside the open garage. Pure gas hog. Although the house was the same as the others in White River, it was landscaped nicely and lavender aster and yellow yarrow competed with thorny cacti through a thick layer of brown mulch.

I got out of my pickup and stood there with the door open, peering around. I wondered what I was doing there, thinking I ought to just climb back in the truck and drive away. The decision was made for me when I heard the front door open and a female voice cry, "May I help you?"

I turned and stared into a pair of familiar green eyes. I had seen those eyes before, many times, though not set in this woman's ocular cavities. Eyes were about the only thing LeAnn and her sister shared in common. Well, that and the fact that their first names began with the letter L. Leona had a lighter complexion than LeAnn, same with the hair that glistened under the blazing Nevada sun. She seemed to have put on a little weight.

Leona did not recognize me so I said, "Hi, Leona. Chance."

Her gaze turned intense. "LeAnn's ex?"

I nodded.

A look of incredulity crept across her face like a cautious cat as she said, "Why you *are* Chance, aren't you? You do look like I remember. I mean, how many times did we ever meet? Three?"

I didn't bother to correct her, just nodded. That was close enough.

Then her expression metamorphosed into one of suspicion. "What are you doing here?" she asked.

I walked over to the edge of the cement stoop that served as a front porch where I said, as casually as I could, "Oh, I was in the area and thought I'd drop in and say hello."

She was wearing a pink short-sleeved top over black slacks and black loafers. A little dressy for a housewife, I thought, especially since I remembered her in jeans and western shirts.

"Why I...I'm glad you did. Though you must admit, you've taken me by surprise."

I smiled my agreement.

Then she explained her dressy attire. "John's working, the girls are visiting classmates in town. I'm picking them up after lunching with some friends," she said. "Believe it or not, I've joined the garden club set." She laughed. "Who would have thought, right?"

"Oh, we all change and grow, Leona," I patronized. "You're just going through your garden club period."

"That was nice, Chance," she said, smiling. "Would you like to come in?"

"I don't want to hold you up," I said.

She swiped the air with her hand. "Oh, I've got a few minutes yet. Besides, most of the others will just drink a martini or something. Since I don't drink, except occasionally a little wine for dinner, it won't matter. Come on in."

I followed her through the front door into the foyer and then into the living room, noting the dining room to one side. While the downstairs was laid off as I remembered it from my one visit years before, the rooms had been repainted (from oyster to Russian white) and all the furniture was new, or fairly so. I sat on the sofa, forest green and firm.

"Would you like something to drink?" she chirped.

I said I would and she retreated to the kitchen. I was feeling stiff from the long ride so I meandered around the room, tossed casual glances at the family pictures scattered about like wildflowers in the desert. I peered out the large double living room windows at the sunburned backyard—a swing set looking as if it hadn't seen a youngster in a decade, a well-used barbecue pit with an absent brick on one side, a tarp-covered object of some sort next to a straggly red oak. I had regained my seat on the sofa by the time Leona returned with a tall glass of Dr. Pepper over ice.

"John still plumbing?" I asked politely after sipping a taste of the cold soft drink.

"Oh, yes," she returned, seemingly happy to talk about her family. "He has his own business now, you know. Three years. Since we last saw you, anyway. Though I don't know if that's any great thing. He has to leave by seven every morning. Sometimes doesn't get home until after eight. Can't call in sick." She laughed, high-pitched, nice sounding. "Still, it has its perks. And he likes being his own boss."

"Seems to be doing all right."

"We are," she said in a tone that clearly said You-can-bet-your-boots. "When John worked for others, he was such a spendthrift. But now that he works for himself, we're actually saving money. Have a retirement fund and everything. The only debt we have is this house and my car." She tilted her head toward the garage and I took that to mean the silver thing I'd parked behind after I'd pulled in.

"How are the girls?"

Leona beamed. "Clarissa is now thirteen." She swiped the air with her hand again. "So you know what that means.

Wants to date. John says not until she's sixteen. She's his pride and joy." She scrunched up her nose, and in a conspiratorial voice added, "I think he'll relent before that." She sighed. "Still, I liked it when she went to ballet and piano lessons. It was a chore driving her around, but looking back now, I wish she were still in those activities. Dating. It's scary."

"And..."

"Melissa's in the sixth grade. She's only one year younger than Clarissa. Just like LeAnn and me. She's the tomboy. She didn't want to have anything to do with ballet." She laughed again. "I remember the first—and the only time—she wore a tutu. She wasn't in it twenty seconds before she wanted out of the thing. But a baseball uniform.... We can't get it off her. At school, she's the best in her class at sports. Has one more year of Little League. Then I don't know. She's definitely not good enough to play with the boys at a higher level. Too small, John says. Won't be able to get the ball out of the infield. I don't know, though. I think if given the chance...."

"She ought to at least be given the chance."

"That's what I say."

I smiled. "Have you seen LeAnn lately?" I asked.

The smile fell from her face. Then she wagged her head, almost defiantly. "Oh, no. LeAnn and I love each other dearly, but...that sibling thing. We don't see each other much. You remember how we were. Cards at Christmas and birthdays. That's about it. I don't even know what she's doing now or where she is. That is, I know she's with the PBR still, but that's about it. I mean we do talk on the phone occasionally." Then hastily she asked, "How long has it been since the two of you divorced?"

"It's been a while."

"Too bad you two busted up. I thought you were good together, Chance. I really did." Then she quickly added, "I...I've heard the man she's going to marry is very nice. I...I've never really met him."

"You know she's going to have a baby?"

Leona's eyes dropped to the stone-shaded carpet. "Yes, she told me. I think it's exciting," she said without excitement. "Oh, sorry. I don't remember much about you...and LeAnn, but I remember you were the one who wanted children. LeAnn wasn't all that keen about the idea. Sorry."

I told her it was all right. I finished my soda, handed the glass back, stood and said I would had to be going.

"You're still bull riding, I assume," she said.

I told her about my injury and how I had been relegated to serving as a judge. She said she hoped I recovered soon. Together, we walked outside, Leona locking the door and pulling it closed behind her. Standing next to my pickup, I said, "I'm a little low on gas. Where's the closest filling station?"

"It's out on the main highway. Turn north." She swiped a hand again. "Oh, why don't you just follow me? We'll go by several. The first one will be on the left, but I go a little farther and get it a few cents cheaper at a place on the right."

I agreed to her suggestion and let her lead me back to the main highway where we turned north toward Fallon. I bypassed the first station, the one on the left, per her recommendation, and then turned in at an off-brand station that soon came up on the right. Pulling next to the low price pump, I watched as Leona proceeded up the highway toward the center of Fallon. I filled the tank and was soon headed south toward Las Vegas. Before having gone far, I found myself in a bull ride of a conscience sort. I considered that I was under indictment for burglary and didn't need anymore criminal charges from the State of Nevada. I have to give myself some credit — my conscience bucked hard before flattening out like a rode bull.

# CHAPTER THIRTY-SIX

I made equally good time on the return trip as for the drive to Fallon and was south of Las Vegas by four-thirty. I knew I'd be cutting it close, but since I was already on US 95, I decided to slip on down to Laughlin, where I figured I had just enough time to locate Ray Bridges and have him confirm (or dispel) a suspicion I'd formed, before beating it back to the Thomas and Mack by eight to judge the sixth do-round of the PBR World Championship Finals.

It was a quarter to six and dark from the shortening days when I motored onto Casino Drive. A few years back, Laughlin was little more than a bait stand on the Colorado River not far from the confluence of the Mojave River. Now, it's a miniature Las Vegas, each year drawing millions of people looking for another venue to satisfy their gambling itch. Officially, its population is little more than a few thousand. It doesn't need to be any bigger because nearby Bull Head City, Arizona, supplies most of the personnel for the ten large casinos and dozens of smaller ones dotting the town.

I pulled into Harrah's parking lot, and then slipped into the casino, quickly locating the blackjack islands. I wasn't sure if Ray would be working, but I could hope. I found a pit boss who told me Ray had just gone on a break and wouldn't return for half an hour. When I told him I was under some time pressure but only needed to speak with him for a minute, he offered directions to the employee's lounge, though declining to guarantee Ray would actually be there.

From attending PBR events in Reno, Atlantic City, Las Vegas and Laughlin, I had always supposed that blackjack dealers held pretty lucrative positions. Tips from winners could exceed their pay from the casino by a huge margin. I guessed the only ones who have a hard time making it are the ones who gamble it all back during their off hours.

Ray was not gambling. He was in the carpeted employee's lounge, ensconced comfortable in a thickly padded chair, sipping a soft drink and reading a national business newspaper. Most of the dozen or so other people in the large windowless room were women. Man or woman, Ray was the only one reading, the others watching television or chatting quietly.

I reintroduced myself to Ray and watched his mien brighten. He invited me to sit down, so I pulled a cushioned chair close and sat facing him, a small coffee table between us. He asked me if I wanted anything to eat or drink.

"I'm in a bit of a hurry," I said. "Have to be in Vegas by eight."

"Have they found the killer?" he asked hopefully.

"Not yet. But I know the police are running down every lead in the case."

"Jodi's too?"

I nodded.

"The police theory that it was a rape attempt gone sour going to end up the official position?"

"That could very well happen, but I don't believe it." When he didn't say anything to that, I continued, "I've dropped by because I think you can possibly help."

"Me? How?"

I showed him the official PBR World Finals program and said, "By telling me if you recognize any of the people in here."

He took the magazine from me, dropped it on the table

before him, leaned forward and began turning pages. He took his time. He knew what I wanted and took the task seriously. Finally, he pointed to two people on different pages and said, "I'm not a hundred percent sure but I think these two might be them."

I looked at him hard for a long moment. I could see from the pleading in his eyes that he wanted to be helpful, but he also wanted to be honest about it. He knew I wasn't asking him to point out Jodi Hall's killer, but he sensed that the people in question might just lead to that result.

I decided to force the issue by having him look at some more pictures. After he did so, I thanked him for his time, assured him I would let him know if I learned anything definite and left.

I drove back to Las Vegas and pulled into a vacant parking spot next to Craig Kelton's two-year old black Silverado in the employee's lot at the Thomas and Mack. Two minutes to eight — plenty of time to spare.

While picking up my clipboard from LeAnn, she said coyly, "You cut it awfully close, Chance."

I replied with an eloquent, "Huh?" before taking my place in preparation for the first bull ride of the night.

Jamie Clarke was sitting in what had become her usual seat. For the first time, she seemed to have come possessed of the spirit of the thing. She was wearing a colorful western style shirt over her jeans and, unbelievably, a shaped cowboy hat, brown. I wondered if her article would say anything about Justin Diver winning the PBR World Championship when he rode a little black Mexican bull named Heartless.

Heartless, a spinner, broke from the gate and turned to his right, and then, like a child's top, kept on turning in that direction for the full eight seconds. He was fast, which justified the eighty-six point score Rich and I bestowed for the ride, but he didn't buck high, nor with much power, which kept Justin from garnering a score in the nineties, or even close. But then these were not the eliminator bulls. No doubt about it.

Justin had failed to ride his bull, Humdinger, a true eliminator the night before, let himself be thrown by Calculator Thursday night, while Chad Michaelson, ponytail flopping, had ridden both of his bulls in the two earlier go-rounds. But Justin needed to ride only one bull in the final weekend of the event to lock up the World Championship. Riding Heartless for that forgettable eighty-six point score served him perfectly.

After Justin won the PBR World Championship, Chad, probably somewhat disheartened, was thrown by Unrepentant, a bull he should have ridden with little trouble, and would have any other night. That's bull riding.

Despite the weaker pen, there were more injuries in the third go-round of the final weekend than the night before when the eliminator bulls were doing their thing. But that's how it goes in bull riding, too.

Three cowboys, both Brazilians and a Montana rookie, were hurt so bad they were out of the competition. That was a break for three standby bull riders who, while having no chance to win the event, were now given the opportunity to earn money on the last day by placing in the go-round. The winner of each go-round would see twenty-five thousand dollars showered on him. Not a bad payday for eight seconds work. Then, too, there was money down through tenth place — each day. But the substitute cowboys still had to get lucky. First, by drawing a bull they could score high with, and then by riding the critter.

Standing out there watching it rain cowboys, all I could think about was how Elissa wouldn't be able to get out of the first aid room so quickly that night. I'd see her, talk to her.

When the go-round ended, I dropped off my clipboard with LeAnn, who took it without a word.

Detectives Marks and Hornblower headed me off again but, this time, I was able to dispatch them quickly. Marks said,

"Where were you today, Boettecher? Was looking for you."

"I've been around," I said as I kept walking.

"Don't you want to know why we were looking for you?" Hornblower asked.

"No," I called back over my shoulder, as proud of myself as if I'd just ridden an eliminator bull for a score in the nineties.

When I got to the first aid room, I found Carlton Brazeau in the process of taping Cody Laws wrist—but no Elissa. I complimented Cody on his ride that night, an eighty-eight on Dr. Pepper. That coupled with Red Parham's eighty-nine on Durango, kept the two friends one-two for the top money in the lucrative final event. Neither was going to be PBR World Champion—that title now belonging to Justin—but either would be happy to hold the title PBR World Finals Champion and spend the big paycheck that went with it. Of course, second place paid a pretty penny as well. Regardless of which man won, the pair were putting on quite an entertaining battle in the process.

I asked Carlton about Elissa. He said she had gone to the hospital with a cowboy who had suffered a concussion when a bull kicked him in the head after bucking him off right out of the chute. I remembered the trip photographically; bull riders do that. It had definitely seemed serious at the time.

I decided to follow Elissa to the hospital, hoping to catch up with her there and find out if I stood any chance of being forgiven. I hurried down the concourse to my pickup. Inching along behind the departing crowd, it took some time to get out of the Thomas and Mack, and it was pushing midnight before I pulled into the hospital parking lot. Then I spent twenty-plus minutes trying to locate Elissa only to be told by a surly nurse that she'd left sometime before, leaving her to believe she was going to return to the arena.

I climbed back into my pickup and twenty minutes later

pulled back onto the lot at the Thomas and Mack. The place was nearly deserted now, but Craig Kelton's pickup sat in the same spot where I'd seen it parked earlier. Good, I thought. He was still there. I would find him and clear up a few details about the money Wanda owed him.

I parked alongside his truck and got out. The door to the arena was unlocked so I wasn't adding a second count of burglary to my criminal record by entering. I hurried down the concourse to the first aid room. The place was dark, the door locked. Finding Elissa was turning into a bust.

Suddenly, from around the corner came the same security guard who had walked in on me two nights earlier.

"Not you again," he whined, through an idiotic grin.

"I didn't break in. The door was unlocked."

"Not now it ain't. I just locked it."

"I can't get out that way?" I said, asking the obvious.

"You'll have to leave through the main entrance." It was at the opposite side of the building.

"Did you see Craig Kelton around?" I asked.

He shook his head. "Don't know him. Though I might recognize him if I saw him."

"I saw his truck outside, so I guess he's here somewhere. I'll slip back to the pen area and look for him. When I'm ready to leave, I'll cut straight across by going through the arena."

He shrugged. "Okay by me if you want to get your boots dirty." Then he grabbed the doorknob of the first aid room and tried to turn it. When it wouldn't move, he smiled and said, "Just checking."

"Doing your job."

"Yes, doing my job." He grunted a parting salutation, and then proceeded down the concourse, soon disappearing into the darkness like a specter.

Except for the lounging bulls farther back, the area behind the chutes was deserted, the lights down low so that visibility was poor. I called out for Craig but the only answer I received was a low bellow from an aroused bovine. Guessing that the wrangler must have walked back to Caesar's Palace, I decided it was time to forget about questioning anyone. Solving murders or love-life issues didn't seem to be in the cards for that night. I climbed over the railing and started making my way through the soft dirt parallel to the bucking chutes. I didn't mind stepping there. As far as I was concerned, dirt was what cowboy boots were made to walk on.

I could still hear people in the arena, vendors cleaning their food and drink and merchandize stalls, cleaning people putting last touches on the place to make it spick-and-span for the next day, probably other security guards bothering those actually working.

I was approaching the center of the arena when suddenly I heard a sound. "Craig?" I called. Then I heard the sound again, and I knew it wasn't Craig. This sound was a familiar one to me, though. Depending on circumstances, it was nothing to be concerned about. But standing in the wrong place at the wrong time, it could be downright terrifying. The sound I'd heard, twice now, was nothing more, or less, than a snort. And it came from off to the side and slightly behind me. I turned and saw none other than John Henry standing in front of the escape chute gate. As far as I was concerned, he was standing on the wrong side of that damn gate. Of course, which side of the gate John Henry was standing on was something of an irrelevant issue since it was wide open.

# CHAPTER THIRTY-SEVEN

The Thomas and Mack is a huge facility, but the arena itself is not all that large. On top of that, it is divided into two sections for the event. I was standing in the approximate middle of one of the sections, dirt on my boots. John Henry stood near the edge, just inside the open escape chute gate. How he got there without my noticing him was beyond me. I must have been so absorbed in finding and speaking with Elissa and Craig that I was afflicted with some form of tunnel vision.

There was a theoretical fifty-fifty chance the bull would simply turn around, proceed back through the gate and return to his pen. Because of his recent penchant for charging anything that breathed that he found in his sights, I didn't think the true odds were anywhere near that good.

The distance between us was twenty feet, give or take. I judged that if John Henry should start running at me right then and I made for the nearest side rail, he would probably catch me just as I reached that rail.

With some kind of bovine consideration, he offered me a warning, taking a moment to paw the ground once with his left front hoof. Then he charged. I'll always wonder if I would have won that footrace. I'll have to settle for guessing, but I did try. Just as John Henry charged, I turned and bolted for the rail, except cowboy boots (whether clean or dirty) are not the best footgear for quick starts. I guess that's why they make track shoes with spikes. With my first step, the dirt, thick but loose, broke away beneath me, and I fell flat on my face.

I lay there like some animal that had just given birth, waiting for my brain to authorize me to scramble to my feet and try again. As if experiencing the initial phase of a major earthquake, I felt the ground tremble beneath me. It vibrated through my torso and all the way out to my extremities. However, it was no earthquake causing the tremors. John Henry, all two thousand pounds of him, was coming.

Catching a glimpse out of the corner of my eye, I saw he had a perfect bead on me. He was close enough that as soon as I made it to my feet, he would plow into me. That could leave me seriously hurt. All I could think to do was stay down, roll myself into a ball, wait—and pray. Snorting noisily, his nose dripping a thick glob of steaming snot, he lowered his head to strike. From where I lay, I could see that if I didn't do something real soon, he was going to butt me squarely in the shoulder, the injured one, thereby destroying all the mending that had taken place to date and permanently ending any thoughts of my resuming my bull riding career, waning though it was. Oh, how I wished I were wearing a vest.

But I wasn't. In truth, I don't think it would have protected me all that much from even the minimum of what John Henry was capable of. Still, I had to do something fast if I didn't want him…to kill me.

Yes, at that moment, I thought John Henry was going to kill me. Meaning, the thought that a bull could kill me in an arena flashed through my brain, something I had never believed before then. It was no consolation that it was not during an event in which I was riding before twenty thousand wildly screaming fans. In a near panic, all I could think to do was move. Move in some way, somehow, somewhere.

Stifling raging sensations of fear, I dug the heels of my boots into the dirt and shoved, one at a time. But I didn't want to get struck in the back either, especially without a vest. So I kept shuffling until I had squirmed around far enough that if

John Henry did not alter his course, he would not strike me in the shoulder or the back but in the most padded part of my anatomy — the ass.

And that's where he caught me — though he caught me good. The blow he delivered sent a jolt all the way up my spine so that all parts of me tingled as if I were one giant funny bone. Let me tell you, it hurt.

Painful though it was, I have to say I was lucky. John Henry butted me with the center of his head. Believe me, it was rock hard. But he had not gone after me with a horn. That could have been (please pardon the horrible pun) pointed in all the ways you can imagine. Anyway, after butting me in the butt and shoving me at least five feet through the arena dirt, he proceeded to run directly over me. Again, I was lucky. He didn't lay a hoof on me. Stepping adroitly, he continued on, only to turn around, seemingly on a dime, less than ten feet away from where I lay.

Fortunately, his momentum was still going away from me. And though my buttock throbbed like you wouldn't believe, the tingling had stopped. Gathering my wits, I leaped to my feet before John Henry could dig in with his. Then I threw a handful of dirt in his face, yelled, "Get away" and broke for the railing.

This time, I made sure of my footing, which meant I couldn't go hell-bent-for-leather. My taunt at John Henry only served to infuriate him more, because before I'd made two steps he was after me again. Snorting and slobbering, he thundered the earth.

I was still fifteen feet from the railing when he was on me. But I knew what to do. It was something all bullfighters have to learn in order to survive their dangerous jobs. Bull riders learn it also. They better. It comes in handy from time to time. It sure came in handy then. Actually, it's a football player's maneuver. Ends and backs, anyone who carries the ball, knows it. All I did was reach back and put my hand on John Henry's head. Then running as if treading water, I kept my arm straight and stiff, letting him push me away from himself. It's nice when it works. It would have worked perfectly this time had John Henry turned his head like most bulls do when this is done to them. When they turn their heads, bulls are usually distracted and run off in a new direction, letting the one they are chasing escape their onslaught.

Except John Henry did not turn his head. Instead, he ran faster. This caused me to be lifted to the points of my toes. Now, I was in real trouble. If I didn't run just right, with my feet pedaling at just the right speed, I would certainly stumble, and John Henry would run over me again, maybe trampling me good this time. Could I expect to get lucky a second time?

Now I'm not a world-class bull rider for nothing. When the soles of my boots touched the ground, I had them moving, as fast as I could make them go. Of course, John Henry is a world-class bull and in world-class fashion he kept right after me, on my tail—literally. Running as fast as I could, I kept my hand on his head. Thus, a second time, he shoved me away from him. Only this time, I was very close to the side rail. (The Thomas and Mack hadn't grown any larger in the interim.)

This time, John Henry lifted me completely off my feet—and tossed me, right into the arena railing. My upper arm struck the middle bar of the railing, dangerously close to my injured shoulder. Pain, running in both directions, shot through the arm, the bad one. Fortunately, I heard nothing break. I fell into the dirt at the foot of the railing next to what most fans would consider the best seats in the house, unable to breath. The blow had knocked the wind out of me.

Lying there, gasping for air, frightened, I watched the most amazing sight. Unable to catch my breath, pain running through my shoulder, arm and backside, my legs weak and shaking, John Henry had me just where he wanted me. I was as vulnerable to his next charge as a sparsely populated island was from an attack by a corps of US Marines. After tossing me into the rails at the side of the arena, John Henry just stood there — and stared at me for a long moment. Then, instead of taking advantage of the situation his hapless quarry found himself in, the big animal just snorted, lowered his head and turned away. Just like that, he'd lost interest. I couldn't believe it. I guess he figured he'd won. Truthfully, as I watched the proud brute prance off, like royalty, toward the escape chute gate, that's the way I had it figured, too.

Then I heard voices.

"What's going on in there?" bellowed a voice I was coming to recognize all too well. My favorite security guard, the one who liked to find me in places where he thought I shouldn't be. He was running down the aisle directly above me, his shoes clattering noisily on the concrete steps.

Still unable to speak or rise, I just lay there for what seemed the longest time. Suddenly, the wind poured back into my lungs and I was able to gasp, "Over here."

"What's going on?" he repeated, as I staggered to my feet.

Then another voice called out from the shadows, this one even more familiar than the security guard's, and it uttered the same words that the security guard had used a moment earlier. "What's going on?"

The second voice came from behind the chutes. Craig Kelton was peering over a chute gate. Then he turned his head slightly and spotted John Henry. "Oh my. John Henry, what the devil you doin' in there?" That said, he disappeared behind the chutes, only to reappear a moment later at the escape chute where he took up a position safely behind the opened gate. John Henry snatched a last forlorn look back at me, and then lumbered down the open passageway. As soon as he was through, Craig shut the gate behind him, climbed over the railing and made sure John Henry returned to his pen. A few moments later, he was back to the railing, scaled it adroitly and then jogged over to where I was standing, the security guard beside me.

"Are you all right? Why, Chance, what're you doin' here?"

Just then, another voice was heard. Royce Sirett was standing next to the gate. "Craig, did I just see you puttin' John Henry away?"

"Yeah, Royce," Craig replied. "He was here in the arena."

"What's going on?" Royce demanded as he climbed over the railing, sprightly for a man of fifty-whatever, and half-jogged over to where we were congregated.

I offered a quick synopsis of the previous fifteen minutes. Then I said, "Now, though, the better question might be what was John Henry doing in the arena?" That said I looked back and forth between the two men.

Royce spoke first. "I...I don't know. I left but decided I ought to come back to make sure Craig had taken care of everything." He glanced back at the pen area. "Guess I'm goin' to have to retire that bull. Can't have no killer bull in the PBR. It'll have to wait till after the short-go tomorrow, but I will."

I swiped the dirt off my clothes, though, because of the pain I was experiencing, not all of it. Then, peering at Craig, and purposefully letting a note of suspicion enter my tone, I said, "Craig, are we to think you haven't been taking care of everything like you ought to?"

The cow wrangler just smirked. "Think what you like, Boettecher. I know how to do my job. And I do it." After a short pause, he added, "Because I do my job, I came back to check on everything." Then turning to his boss, he said, "You didn't need to come checkin' on me, Royce."

"I know, I know," Royce sputtered defensively, lifting

his black cowboy hat and swiping a chubby hand through his thinning hair. "You do your job. Do it great, in fact. But I always check on things myself every now and then. That's why I'm here."

Now the security guard thought he ought to get into the picture. "How did you get in here?" he asked, adding, "I locked the doors."

"I used my key," Craig said, pulling a small ring out of his pocket. "I always come by 'bout now. Seen you a time or two. Don't you remember?"

The security guard nodded warily. Then turning to Royce, he asked, "What about you?"

Royce gave him a look that clearly said, I-am-Royce-Sirett-and-there-is-no-reason-in-the-world-you-shouldn't-know-me. But he said, "I'm a stock contractor. I have a key, also," though he didn't bother to show it to the guard.

We were silent for a few moments, each of us eyeing up the other like wary boxers. The security guard must have felt left out for he said, "Something going on here?"

"What's going on," I said, continuing to eye Royce and Craig in turn, "is attempted murder."

I was about to say more but before I could, the security guard took over. "I think you three had better come to the office with me," he said, pointing with his thumb back over his shoulder. "We're not going to have no talk about attempted murder without bringing in the police."

The security guard had taken control with such authority that neither Royce nor Craig felt he had any other option but to comply.

"What's this crap you're spittin' out, Boettecher?" Craig demanded as he followed the guard.

"Stay calm, Craig," Royce advised, walking behind him. "It'll be all right. You'll see. Chance has just gone through a frightening experience. Let him calm down. He'll see that nothin' as dramatic as attempted murder has happened."

We traipsed up the aisle to the main concourse and then around to a gray metal door located at the west side of the building. The guard opened the door with a key and then ushered us in. Craig sat on a stool next to the lone desk, while Royce took the padded office chair. I was left standing near the door, which suited me just fine. From there, I could easily keep an eye on the two. Meanwhile, the guard had picked up a black telephone receiver from a black telephone base that sat on the desk and was dialing a number he apparently had committed to memory. I suggested he ask for either Detective Marks or Hornblower. He claimed to know them.

"They're on their way," he announced a moment later, while replacing the receiver on its base.

I took a moment to look around. The room was small and windowless, consisting of the desk, chair and stool, as well as a time clock that hung on the wall near the desk. Waiting, we all eyeballed each other again, nervously — or was it malevolently?

Royce left off eyeing me after a few moments and asked the guard if he could make a telephone call. The guard looked at me. (Were we becoming confederates through all of our crime and trials together?) Since I made no objection, he nodded to Royce. The stock contractor used his cell phone and called LeAnn who arrived just seconds before Marks and Hornblower, leaving the two no time to confer.

Marks stepped into the room behind LeAnn, took one look at me and wrinkled his nose with disgust; Hornblower practiced his straight face.

"What's this all about, Jerry?" Marks asked the security guard. In my previous interaction with "Jerry," I'd never heard his name mentioned — either surname or Christian.

"This guy," he replied, indicating me, "is accusing these fellows," pointing first at Royce and then at Craig, "of trying to kill him."

LeAnn's mouth dropped wide open; she looked from Royce to me, said, "Chance!"

"It's all nonsense," Royce exclaimed, shrugging, smiling sheepishly at Marks.

"Damn straight," Craig agreed. There was anger in his tone.

"We'll decide what's nonsense," Marks claimed. "Now, what happened?"

All eyes settled on me so I was to begin. I knew what I was about to say was going to sound ludicrous. I mean the words *One of these men tried to kill me with a bull* were going to make me look ridiculous. Still, I knew they were true, which meant they had to be said. To buy myself some time, I said, "Before I begin, I want to ask a question." When no one objected, I continued, "Craig, how did you get here tonight?"

Surprise washed over the foreman's face. He looked first at me and then at Royce, then at the two police officers in turn. "Why, I…I walked," he said.

"But your pickup is parked out on the lot. I saw it."

"I'm staying at the Mirage," Craig said, his hands open in a pleading gesture. "It's an easy walk from there to here."

It was the answer I expected. Unfortunately, I was left with the question of how to avoid looking like a fool. I needed credibility for the accusation I wanted to make. To get that, I needed to explain my theory. It was the only way everything made sense.

Then I thought: *What if I changed tactics?* I could still make my point. With only a cursory consideration as to the best way to say it, I spurted out, "Royce killed Wanda Sirett in Atlantic City and tried to kill me just now because he knew I was about to expose him."

"Royce killed Wanda!" LeAnn cried, swinging her gaze from the man she had been married to, to the one she was planning to.

"That's a crock," Royce spouted. "You can't prove it."

Marks' eyebrows lifted noticeably. The policeman was all attention. "Interesting choice of words."

Yes, they were, but Royce was right. I couldn't prove my allegations. No evidence. Just theory. Still, I thought the theory was pretty sound, and when I explained it, I was sure everyone would understand the reasoning behind it.

I was all set to give it a go when Marks bucked me off. He did that by asking a frivolous question right out of the gate. He looked at me and said, "Where's the weapon he tried to kill you with?"

Royce nodded knowingly at that.

Trying my best not to sound defensive, I said, "He tried to kill me with a bull."

"A what?" Marks rasped.

"A bull," I repeated. "He let a mean bull loose in the arena when I was walking there."

"Did not," Royce said, shaking his head.

Craig Kelton's mouth fell open, but he merely sat on his stool while staring speechless at the man he worked for.

Although anxious to explain my theory as to Wanda's death, I felt I was being pushed into a cow pie where I would have to wallow in stinking (read: irrelevant) details. "How did he get loose then?" I asked, peering at Royce, though expecting no answer.

I paused before saying anything more. I was in trouble — and I knew it. Marks and Hornblower were eyeing me as if I were a lunatic. To them, it would be one for the books. Murder attempt by a bull. To me, it was a senseless detour. I'd never get to Wanda's death if I had to prove that Royce had just tried to kill me with John Henry.

Then LeAnn, wonderful ex-wife that she was, charged to my rescue. I'm sure she never meant to, would have certainly pushed the words back into her mouth if she had known the consequences of their utterance. But it was obvious to me, too, that just her voicing them proved she had not known Royce killed Wanda. She hadn't been there when it happened because Royce had sent her off on an errand before doubling back to where Wanda was waiting for him at John Henry's pen. And LeAnn's saying them proved Royce never told her.

LeAnn's magic words, bursting into the void created by my silence, were no other than, "Chance, how could you think Royce killed Wanda?"

Royce heard those words from the woman he'd come to love and adore. At their sound, his face crinkled in horror. "No," he cried, "Let's bring this charade to a merciful end. Chance is right. I killed Wanda."

# CHAPTER THIRTY-EIGHT

"Why?" LeAnn cried.

"Because…" I began.

"Cause she humiliated me one time too many," Royce spewed, eyeing me with the frigidity of an upright freezer.

We were still in the Thomas and Mack security office, packed in like bolts in a jar, mere moments after Royce had unloaded his confession. We, all, had been staring at him, waiting, waiting for more. But LeAnn had spoken first.

I decided to let Royce have his chance, let him tell it his way. Maybe, it would work out for the best.

He continued eyeing me—pointedly, stroked his goatee a couple of times and then picked up where he'd left off. "I killed her because I was damn sick and tired of her constantly making a fool out of me."

"Hold on a second," Marks interrupted, as if snapping out of a daze. Then he recited the famous Miranda rights to Royce and asked him if he understood them. Royce tried to get away with just a nod, but offered a soft, "Yeah," when Marks insisted on something verbal.

When allowed to continue, he said, "She made a fool out of me one too many times. Chance, you were there in Fort Worth; you, too, Leann." He shot a glance at LeAnn as he spoke her name but returned his hard stare to me when he continued. "In Atlantic City, she came to me in the pens and demanded money, claimed she was broke. Well, we was divorced, weren't we? As far as I was concerned, I owed her nothin'. I'd honored the divorce agreement to the letter, gave her more besides." He looked around beseechingly. "I had no obligation to bail her out. I tell you after all I'd put up with from that woman, I wasn't going to give her one damn thing more. Besides, I have LeAnn to think about now." He'd grown animated as he spoke, to the point where I thought he was going to leap out of his chair like a jack-in-the-box.

He calmed down, peered around at everyone in turn, again settled on me. Resuming, he said, "I did offer to buy John Henry for a fair price, but she refused to sell. Then I said I'd lend her some money if she promised to stop makin' me the butt of her jokes. She just laughed at that, claimed life wouldn't be worth livin' if she did that. That was the straw that broke the camel's back. Angered, I grabbed her by the neck. I only meant to scare her. I didn't mean to go so far but I couldn't stop myself. And I…choked her." He stopped, looked at LeAnn for a moment and then dropped his gaze.

"You want to say anything more?" Marks asked.

Royce paused a moment as if thinking, shook his head once.

"Guess we'd better call Atlantic City," Marks said, nodding to Hornblower.

Marks cuffed Royce and he and Hornblower led him out, LeAnn following.

As did Craig Kelton who said, "I'll check on the stock 'fore takin' off. I'll see that everythang is takin' care of tomorrow, Royce."

Royce turned and nodded gratefully but said nothing.

As I stepped into the elevator at Caesar's Palace, I thought about Elissa and almost pressed the button for her floor. Then I thought better of it. Even if I told her I'd uncovered Wanda's killer, who'd confessed no less, I don't think it would have helped. If she were to ask me how I concluded that Royce had killed Wanda, I would have had to tell her I'd gained a valuable clue from the file I'd pilfered from the first aid room with the use of her keys—a sad reminder of my betrayal. I didn't think she'd want to hear that.

I should have slept the sleep of the innocent newborn. Instead, I suffered through a restless night. Full of nervous energy, I woke early the next morning, showered, shaved, grabbed a quick breakfast and then left for the Thomas and Mack and the final go-rounds of the PBR World Championships. I saw no one I knew until I arrived at the arena.

The event started at one P.M. before a sold-out crowd. By four, Cody Laws had been crowned the event winner. He and his buddy, Red Parham, were the only two cowboys to cover all eight of their bulls over the two weekends. Cody made a spectacular ride on none other than John Henry, garnering an unbelievable ninety-five for his effort. John Henry did not have an off day either. Chasing me around the arena like a cat after a rat the night before must have served as a perfect tune-up for the finals.

He broke from the gate and spun to his left, bucking and twisting for everything he was worth. Then after drifting twenty feet down the arena, he turned back to his right. Cody anticipated the move all the way but still had to scramble to beat him around the corner and keep from losing his seat.

John Henry remained in his spin for only two circles before reversing course again and turning back to his left. Five seconds into the ride, the crowd was on its feet, yelling and clapping. Everyone in that packed auditorium sensed Cody was going to ride the son-of-a-gun.

At seven and a half seconds, John Henry, all two thousand pounds of power and meanness, had Cody stretched back on his arm to the point where I was sure either he would lose his grip or his arm would pop out of its socket. But somehow (pure determination was what it was) the tough little bull rider hung on for that extra half second—and made the ride of his life. At the whistle, his hand opened, and he was flung out of there like a boulder off a catapult. After sailing a good fifteen feet, he landed in the dirt squarely on his back. Unhurt, he was on his feet in an instant and pedaling for the railing.

John Henry was another story. Something had come over the usually ornery critter. Ignoring Cody, he took one look at me, snorted, and then turned and headed for the escape chute. I guess "getting rode" for the second time that year was humbling to the point of embarrassment for the big fellow. Either that or he'd had enough of chasing cowboys for one weekend. Anyway, it didn't look as if John Henry would be headed for early retirement after all.

Red Parham's ride on Crime Dog was spectacular too, enough for a well-deserved ninety-two, and a second place landing for the event. Still, I knew he was happy for his friend, and he proved it by giving the bull rider a big cowboy hug behind the chutes after Cody had completed his ride on John Henry.

When I'd arrived at the arena, everyone I saw greeted me cordially. But no one congratulated me for uncovering Wanda Sirett's murderer. LeAnn wasn't there. Had she quit her job? I was sure she would go wherever Royce was taken. Of course, Royce wasn't there and, other than LeAnn, him, Craig Kelton and myself, there had been no other PBR people present at the confession. Detectives Marks and Hornblower weren't present either, and the security guard worked at night, was probably home asleep. Jamie Clarke couldn't hurt the PBR now, whatever she wrote. I'd caught a glimpse of her in the stands, garbed in another western wear outfit, this one a little too flashy for my taste.

So when Daryl spotted me on the way to the men's room during intermission, all he said was, "Way to go, Chance. Doing another great job out there." Without pausing for breath, he raced on, "Did you hear? Craig told me. Royce is in jail, confessed to Wanda's murder. Said you had something to do with it. Whatever it was, way to go. Can you believe it? Royce! Makes sense though. After all, aren't we told all the time most murders are committed within the family? If anything, he and Wanda, though divorced, were still like family. By the way, how's the shoulder coming?"

I told him it wasn't quite back to normal but it was coming along. No, I didn't bother filling him in on how it had been aggravated the night before.

"Can't help but wonder what's going to happen with LeAnn. Royce being the daddy of her baby and all."

I was curious about that myself.

# CHAPTER THIRTY-NINE

Which was one reason why I called her early the next morning and pressed her to join me for breakfast. I picked the least popular restaurant the casino had to offer. The Dungeon Café. Can you believe it? In keeping with the hotel's first century Roman décor, it was somewhat on the dark side, with shackles dangling from the walls and one whole side a large drab painting of a long and ominous-looking rack.

Arriving first, I scrounged a far corner booth and ordered coffee, informing the poker-faced waitress another person would be joining me shortly. Sure enough, LeAnn ambled in a few minutes later and slid onto the seat across from me. She was wearing red jeans and a black top. Without her jean jacket, hat and make-up, I knew she would return to her room before visiting Royce in jail.

"Sorry to wake you up so early," I said as the waitress sidled over carrying a coffee pot.

"I was awake," she claimed wearily. "Just lying there. Haven't gotten ten minutes sleep either of the last two nights."

The waitress turned up our coffee cups, poured some of the delicious smelling brew into each and then took our orders. LeAnn was going to settle for the coffee (black at that), but I insisted she eat something. I was certain she hadn't eaten much since Saturday night and needed something substantial in her system. Reluctantly, she let me order waffles and ham for her, same as I'd ordered for myself.

After the waitress left to hand in our orders, we sat

quietly and sipped our coffees for a few minutes, like a long married couple.

"Elissa talking to you yet?"

I wagged my head.

Bitterly, she said, "After all, aren't you the savior of the PBR?"

*That won't garner me a single point for my next ride if I don't stay on for eight full seconds.* I sighed.

"She'll come around."

I was doubtful. By now, Elissa had to know that Royce had confessed to Wanda's murder. Was she aware of my role? Whether she was or not, I don't think it mattered. If she wasn't going to forgive a hero, she certainly wasn't going to forgive Chance Boettecher. It was my opinion she'd already moved on.

"So have you made a decision about what you're going to do?" LeAnn asked.

I nodded, said, "I'm going to give it one more shot."

"Even though the judge position probably won't be there if it doesn't pan out for you?"

I nodded again. "I know. But I can't give up bull riding just yet." I smiled my best sardonic smile as I added, "I'm too young."

LeAnn's pressed mouth made it clear she thought I was living on cowboy hope — false all the way.

"I know," I said. "But last night I watched the guys congratulating Cody for winning the Finals, Justin the night before for winning the World Championship. I found myself longing to be a part of it. That tipped the scales. I'm telling Daryl I'll be riding come first of the year. Despite what John Henry did to me Saturday night, my shoulder is getting better."

"You're not going to press charges against Royce for that, are you, Chance?" Her eyes were employing. "It was like a reflex action. He didn't know you were going to go to the arena that night. And you know Royce has always liked you."

Royce had dropped by the Thomas and Mack to check on his bulls and make sure Craig and his other people were doing their jobs—just like he'd said. He'd heard me calling Craig's name and decided to sic John Henry on me. While he'd recognized the threat my inquiries represented, his act was more spontaneous than premeditated. He'd said it shortly before the police took him off to jail and I believed him.

"No, I'm not pressing any charges," I assured her. "He's in enough trouble as it is. Besides, I never thought John Henry would actually kill me. He just wanted to rough me up a bit." For some weird reason, right then, I actually believed that, too.

LeAnn smiled her thanks.

The waitress brought our orders and set them before us. As we nibbled on our ham and buttered our waffles, I said, "When is Royce being returned to Atlantic City?"

"Probably tomorrow," LeAnn said. "He's waving extradition."

"That's probably smart."

"Yes. His lawyer figures the authorities will look kindlier on him." LeAnn took a sip of her coffee and then said, "So what's the reason for dragging me out of bed at the crack of dawn?"

"Just nosiness, I guess," I said, and then took my first taste of waffle. It was heavenly, melting in my mouth, the syrup's sweetness setting it off perfectly.

"You're wondering what's going to happen to me?"

I was in too big of a hurry to fork more of my delicious waffle into my greedy mouth to offer more than a silent nod.

"I'm going to stand by Royce, of course. I've already quit my job. We're still getting married. Maybe as early as Wednesday. In Atlantic City. The lawyer thinks he has a good chance of plea bargaining manslaughter. Ten year sentence, out in five, maybe less. Sounded to me like manslaughter was what it was anyhow."

I swallowed the mouthful of food before saying, "From his confession Saturday night?"

"Yes. Don't you agree?"

I could see she was hoping she'd have her soon-to-be husband back in five years rather than…a number far higher.

I nodded. "From what he said, yes. Manslaughter sounds plausible."

"What do you mean from 'What he said?'" She was eyeing me warily.

"Come on, LeAnn," I said. "You don't want to go there."

She set her fork on her plate and sat back in her seat. "I think I do. Don't you believe Royce?"

"Let's just say I know you believe him. Let's let it go at that."

"No, I won't let it go." She was getting quite indignant now. "Explain yourself, Chance Boettecher."

I gobbled another mouthful of my breakfast and then stared at my ex as if hypnotized. Up until then, I had been ambivalent about how far I wanted to take it with her. I think, though, deep down, this is exactly where I had hoped she would push it.

I set my fork down, too, and then leaned forward. "You know how on television," I began, "at the climax of a mystery whenever the murderer is confronted by the detective, the detective throws out a few pieces of evidence and the murderer suddenly confesses?"

Like a criminal sensing a trap, LeAnn nodded dubiously.

"Well, I always thought that phony. Unrealistic. Of course, I know that on television they have to get the show over within the allotted time, so the confession is a device to bring about a timely conclusion. And I accept it for television. But in real life, I always doubted that it worked that way. From the newspaper accounts of all the murders I've ever read about, the murderer stonewalls it. Criminals know their right to remain silent. Most anyway."

"Where are you going with this, Chance?"

"Didn't it strike you as odd how fast Royce confessed?"

"Odd?"

"Yes. At first, he seemed about to stonewall it, just like I thought he would. But after you asked me why I thought Royce killed Wanda, he suddenly blurts out that he killed her and told us it was because she was hounding him for money and humiliating him to the point where he couldn't take it anymore."

She wiggled in her seat, smiled smugly. "That's where the lawyer thinks he can get the DA to go along with manslaughter."

"Right. I figured Royce thought that, too. Which is why he didn't want *me* to answer your question."

"Huh?"

"LeAnn, you're forgetting something."

"What's that?"

"I was arrested for burglary."

"So?"

The waitress chose that moment to materialize and refill our coffees, ask if everything was all right and if we needed anything else. LeAnn gave her a sharp "No" that left the poor woman perplexed. When she looked at me, I just shook my head. She nodded and walked away.

With the waitress out of range, LeAnn repeated her "So?"

"They caught me red-handed holding a file, a medical file."

"Whose file?" she queried, tilting her head in a way that said she'd already guessed whose it was.

"Have you wondered why Royce fainted when he did?"

"It was Royce's file?"

I confirmed it was.

She looked down, picked up her fork. She cut a wedge of waffle and stabbed her fork into it, dabbed it into a glob of syrup, sent it to her mouth.

"Royce spotted Elissa with me on Monday. The sudden anxiety of wondering what she might tell the PBR's handpicked police liaison was too much for him and he collapsed. But Elissa hadn't told me anything, though she'd made the mistake of dropping a couple of hints. I had to commit burglary to find out what I needed to know. And yes," I continued while she munched, "I'd already gleaned something important from that file by the time the security guard walked in on me."

"Which was?" she asked between chews of waffle.

"Remember how Wanda, after the death of her little girl, used to say motherhood was not for her and how she'd had the appropriate tubes attended to?"

LeAnn nodded.

"We all thought she'd had her own tubes tied. Turned out that wasn't the case at all. Guess she didn't want anyone messing with her equipment. Well, it turned out that instead of *her* tubes having been attended to, it was Royce's equipment that got tied or snipped or whatever. Royce had a vasectomy some time back."

"Vasectomies can be reversed."

"I doubt if you're going to make that fly in this case," I said. "When I put two and two together, I came up with Royce is not the father of your child. And he knows it."

While her look said *Of course, he knows it,* her mouth said, "Then if not Royce, who could possible be the father?"

She was staring at me slit-eyed, as though throwing down the gauntlet. But hadn't I come looking for some kind of closure? Pouring my gaze directly into LeAnn's challenge-filled eyes, I said, "My guess is Lane Lowick is the father."

As if slapped in the face, she looked away. Quickly recovering, she returned her stare to me. She made as if to laugh, as if trying to foster an image that the idea couldn't be anything but preposterous. "And where did you come up with that wild idea?"

"It all fits."

"Fits?"

"Yes. Saturday afternoon, after returning from my little visit with your sister…"

"Did you really think I didn't know about that?"

"Royce's little ploy with John Henry Saturday night told me you did. My guess is Leona called you after I left."

"You think? My ex shows up on her front porch, she's not going to let me know? She's my sister."

"Anyway, I didn't return directly here. Instead, I slipped down to Laughlin where I carried a PBR World Finals program to a certain man. I had him look through it, asking him to point out the pictures of a man and a woman who were dining together in a restaurant the night before Lane was killed. That man was having dinner with Cauy Hall in the same restaurant at the same time. Cauy recognized the two people and pointed them out to him."

"And…?"

"He looked at the pictures in the program, turned the pages slowly. He looked carefully at every picture in there. Finally, he pointed to two people. They were on different pages. Then he said, 'I'm not completely sure, but I think these are the two.'"

LeAnn regarded me with curious eyes. I could see she was more than a little anxious to hear the names of the people the man had targeted. She was biting her tongue as if to keep from screaming at me to get on with it.

"I also showed him two pictures I always carry in my wallet. This time, he confirmed them definitely as pictures of the two people Cauy had pointed out to him in that restaurant. They were pictures of the same two people he'd pointed out from the program but wasn't sure of. The pictures were of Lane and you."

"If I had been in a restaurant with Cauy Hall, don't you think I would have recognized him?"

I shook my head. "Not this time. He sat several tables over from you. Had a direct view of both you and Lane. You had the same clear view of him as well. But despite that, you didn't recognize him."

"And why didn't I?"

"Because he was dressed up as a woman."

"A woman?"

"Yes. Cauy was both gay and a cross-dresser. And that night, he was on a date with a man who had no connection with the PBR. He pointed both you and Lane out to his date. Got a big kick out of watching the two of you together without either of you recognizing him. He did this more than once, I've learned. He told the man someone was going to be surprised to learn his wife was out with his best friend. It was the words "his wife" that threw me off for the longest time. Had me suspecting other happily married bull riders and their wives who weren't the least bit involved. What Cauy actually meant was 'his ex-wife.' Cauy was buried in a Catholic cemetery. He and Jodi must have been raised Catholic. Catholics do not believe in divorce. At least in theory. So I guess he saw you and me as still married. Anyway, because of his sexual preference and his penchant for dressing up like a woman, he could tell only one other person what he saw."

"Who was that?"

"His sister."

"Jodi? Wait a minute." Her eyes grew wide. "You're not

going to try to pin Jodi's murder on Royce, too, are you? He never went to Twin Falls that weekend. We were together the whole time. I can vouch for that."

"I'm sure you can. No, I'm not trying to pin Jodi's murder on Royce."

"Who killed Jodi, then? Some rapist as the police think?"

"I don't think so but I can only guess."

"So, what's your guess?"

"I think Wanda killed her."

"Wanda?"

I nodded. "She was certainly strong enough. Jodi being the petite thing she was. As I see it, Cauy told Jodi he saw you and Lane having dinner together. Jodi probably made nothing of it at the time. Then Cauy was killed by John Henry on the same day you announced your pregnancy. Jodi remembered what Cauy told her several weeks before. If Cauy were alive, she couldn't do anything. To do so would push Cauy out of the closet and Jodi wouldn't do anything to hurt Cauy. He was her brother, after all, but he was also her bread and butter. He took care of her. And under normal circumstances she wouldn't hurt a soul. But Cauy was dead. She'd lost her source of income. So she felt free to act. Needing money, she…now here I'm *really* guessing…went to Wanda to get her to blackmail Royce."

"Why Wanda?"

"Because, despite needing money, Jodi really was a sweet kid who wouldn't hurt a fly. At least directly. But she knew Wanda was just ruthless enough to go after Royce for everything she could get. Her idea was to split whatever Wanda got out of Royce. Jodi probably thought she and Wanda could milk that cow for years."

"But why did Wanda kill her?"

"Because Jodi was right about one thing—Wanda was ruthless. Worse, Wanda, heavily in debt, was growing desperate.

And the roof was about to cave in, as the saying goes. Once she learned what Jodi told her, she didn't need her anymore. Without Jodi, she could keep everything she could milk out of Royce for herself."

"But what did Jodi have to blackmail Royce with?"

I paused, sat up straight in my seat. "Well, there are two potential theories on that."

"There are?" She was all ears, green eyes sparkling.

"There are two reasons Jodi couldn't move on her blackmail scheme while Cauy was alive. The first, I've told you. She couldn't push Cauy out of the closet. But the second reason was because, until the night Cauy was killed, she never suspected who killed Lane by running over him with a motor vehicle."

"What gave her ideas?"

"Your announcement that you were pregnant." LeAnn was about to say something but I cut her off. "And not just pregnant, but six weeks pregnant. Six weeks would take it back to your dinner date with Lane. And she put two and two together."

"So why did she want to blackmail Royce?"

"Because he had money and she believed he was the one who ran Lane down."

"Why did she believe Royce capable of such a thing?"

"Because, like everyone else, she knew you and Royce had been dating for some time. Then you're out on a dinner date with Lane Lowick. Six weeks thereafter, you and Royce are announcing that you're pregnant and Royce is the father. In putting two and two together later, she must have thought Royce ran Lane down because he'd learned of your date and was jealous. Makes sense to me."

"Yes. But, of course, Royce is not the type. He wouldn't have killed Lane."

"Well, he killed Wanda, don't forget."

"He explained that. It was manslaughter."

"And, of course, the fact that Royce couldn't commit premeditated murder shoots Jodi's theory all to hell."

"Exactly."

"So we have to conclude Royce did not kill Lane."

"Right."

"Otherwise, he never would have confessed to Wanda's murder. He would have stonewalled it."

"So if Royce didn't kill Lane, who did?"

"Well, that brings us to the second theory of the matter."

# CHAPTER FORTY

"So, what's your second theory?" LeAnn asked.

I looked at her without answering. She peered back at me expectantly. Now, I hadn't forgotten that LeAnn was possessed of a certain blessed affliction. I did not hold with Detective Washington's reasoning concerning the irrationality of pregnant women. As far as I was concerned, her condition did not explain why she wouldn't drop it. Was she seeking a purging of some sort? Or was she a glutton for punishment? I certainly didn't think my explanation would prove cathartic to any degree. But she'd asked so I decided I wouldn't hold back. She would get it full blast.

"It was only when I started thinking about this from the point of view that Lane's death might be important in this sequence of events, at the root of everything in other words, that I began to make some sense of it all. By this theory, Lane's death was the catalyst that led to both Jodi's and Wanda's murders, and all the subsequent events that almost destroyed the PBR."

"That significant?" she said.

"Yes, it was."

"So, according to your second theory, who ran over Lane?"

I sat there and stared at her for a long moment. Finally, I said, "You did, LeAnn. You ran down my best friend."

LeAnn brought a hand to her throat. "Me?" she said. "What makes you think a thing like that?" Then hurriedly, she added, "Of course, this *is* just a theory."

"No, LeAnn. It's more than a theory. I remembered while we dinned in Billings, you told me your Bronco was getting a tune-up and an oil change. But I haven't seen you driving it for some time now. You've been riding with Royce. All the time. That's not like you. You love that toy of yours. Have to be driving it wherever you go. So, I started thinking. Why wasn't she driving it? That had me wondering where it could be. Then I remembered your sister. While I was there I didn't see much. But I did see one thing. Something from her living room window that made me want to take a closer look. Not with Leona present, however. Leona and I left her place at the same time. But I dropped back and had myself a better look. There was something covered with a tarp sitting in her back yard. Any guesses what was under that tarp?"

LeAnn did not answer, just stared at me coldly.

Expecting no reply, I continued, "Turns out it was your Bronco. I'd recognize it anywhere. Right down to the chipped American flag decal on the rear window directly behind the driver's seat and the United We Stand bumper sticker on the right side of the rear bumper. You'd suffered some damage and hadn't had it fixed yet. Your front bumper has a major dent and the grill has been smashed in as if you'd run into something — or someone."

"So I have some body damage to my Bronco. That doesn't explain anything."

"It does to me. You can't have it fixed just yet because you've probably guessed that every body shop in Nevada, Arizona and California, has been alerted by the police to be on the lookout for a vehicle with just that kind of damage."

"And that tells you I ran over Lane?"

"Yes, it does."

"And why would I do that?"

"Because…because of what he did to you."

"What do you think that was, Chance?" she asked

with an edgy calmness, like that of a time bomb just before it explodes.

"He…he forced himself on you, is my guess."

LeAnn leaned forward, gritted her teeth. "He raped me, Chance. Raped is the word. Not something so gentle as 'forced himself' on me. He raped me."

"They call it date rape," I agreed.

"Yes. Date rape. But it's rape all the same. And don't you forget it."

"Why didn't you go to the police?"

She bobbed her head as she said, "What good would it have done?"

"It's what you should have done."

"Maybe in a perfect world," she spurted, "but not in the real one. And when did you acquire this strong sense of what's right? It was never you before. Think about it, Chance, if I had gone to the police in Laughlin, those rednecks would have just laughed at me. They're nothing but good ole boys. Lane is…was a good ole boy. A world-class bullfighter in the PBR. That's macho stuff in their eyes. He's a celebrity. Who am I? A woman. Men taking us whenever they want is what good ole boy rednecks think women are for. Come off your high horse. I've lived in this cowboy world all my life. The police would have done exactly nothing. Except congratulate him. I had no chance."

As she spoke, like déjà vu, Lena Atkins' sentiments on the subject came roaring into my mind.

I climbed off my high horse and said, "So why were you out with Lane? I thought you'd given up the type when you divorced me."

"Royce and I had been dating. You know that. Well, he was concerned about the difference in our ages. And that he couldn't give me children. The age difference never bothered me. But, of course, I wanted children."

"Not with me."

"Even with you. But not while you were riding bulls. After."

"You never told me that."

She shrugged. "If I had, you would have assumed I was open to having them then. Let's let it go that I *did* want them with you. Anyway, with Royce, I was willing to forego children altogether. Despite a ticking clock, our being together was more important."

"Did you tell him that?"

"Of course. Still, there was the possibility I would change my mind before it was too late. Anyway, he kept harping about the age difference thing so much that I told him maybe we should stop seeing each other for a while and see how we felt. He agreed. From his manner, I could sense that was not what he wanted to do, but if he wasn't going to shut up, he had to put up. Anyway, on Thursday afternoon in Laughlin, I ran into Lane who asked me out to dinner. Having broken up with Royce the weekend before, I accepted. Big mistake. While we were having dinner, I realized I didn't want to be there. I loved Royce. The difference in our ages be damned. I didn't want to be with anyone else but him. After dinner, Lane drove me back to my motel. Then he wouldn't leave. He pushed his way into my room and then wouldn't take no for an answer. In his mind, he probably thought I wanted to say yes. Was just playing it coy. After all, I had agreed to have dinner with him, hadn't I? You know how he could think. In the end, if I didn't want to get hurt, I had no choice but to submit. In his warped mind, it probably wasn't rape at all. But it was. You've got to believe that, Chance. It *was* rape. When he was finished and was leaving, he said, 'Let's plan on dinner tomorrow, too.' See what I mean?"

"Why didn't you have an abortion?"

"Because Royce and I both saw it as our chance to have

a family. Although the child wasn't Royce's, I wanted to keep it. Finding out I was pregnant made me want to be a mother regardless of whose child it really was. Royce agreed."

"So how did it happen that you killed Lane?"

"That was pure chance. All day Friday, I kept dodging him. Naturally, I was still infuriated with him for what he'd done to me. So I didn't want to see him, much less speak to him. Of course, I didn't know then that I was pregnant. With Royce, I hadn't needed to take any precautions. Anyway, as soon as the go-round was over, I hid out until I thought everyone was gone. Then I went to my Bronco. I'd just started my engine and put it in gear when, suddenly, he was there. He was walking across the parking lot. I assumed he'd hunted all over for me, and then gave up and was going to his pickup. Alone. Most of the cars had filtered out by then and there were only a few left. I didn't see anyone else around but I wasn't really looking. He continued across the parking lot until he was almost in my line. Without thinking, I stomped on the accelerator and drove straight for him. I didn't bother turning on my lights. He heard me coming but he couldn't figure out from which direction. That was one time his bullfighting skills didn't come to his aid."

"He'd been drinking wine the night before," I reminded. "He had to have had some lingering effects from that. Probably slowed him up."

"Yes. I'm sure it did," she agreed with a nod. Then zeroing in on what she was saying, she reached over the table and placed her hand on the back of mine. "I didn't mean to kill him, Chance. Looking back, I see I wanted to hurt him—bad. But kill him? No." She removed her hand from mine and backed up in her seat. Lowering her gaze, she said, "Though I believed he deserved some punishment for what he did to me, I'm truly sorry he's dead."

"After you ran him down, you went back to your motel and called Royce."

"How did you know that?"

"The two of you were heard arguing."

"He was so angry with me. He must have yelled at me for two hours straight. Asked me over and over what could I have been thinking? But in the end he helped me. And later, he understood my getting pregnant. He knew that wasn't my fault."

"What was he so angry with you about then?"

"That I had accepted a date with Lane in the first place."

"Because it was Lane?"

"Not really." She shrugged. "Anyone."

"He saw the two of you as an item."

"Yes. Wasn't that sweet?"

"You say so. Anyway, after the argument you drove your Bronco to your sister's place, Royce following."

She nodded. "We had to get it out of sight because of the damage."

"Then you returned, took up with each other again and kept quiet, riding in his pickup."

She nodded.

"You took to drinking a little to deal with the guilt. Until you found out you were pregnant."

Contritely, she nodded again.

"And when you learned you were pregnant, you both agreed to pass the child off as his."

"Yes. I'll always love him and stand by him for saying the child was his."

"Which got Jodi Hall to thinking after Cauy was killed."

"I guess you've got it all figured out."

"And Royce knew I'd figured it out."

"Huh?"

"Which is why he blurted out that he'd killed Wanda.

You didn't know he'd killed her. He never told you."

"Guess he didn't want two hours of me yelling at *him*."

"Guess not. Anyway, in your innocent ignorance Saturday night, when you asked me why I thought he killed her, he had no choice but to confess and give *his* reasons for doing it. He didn't want me to tell everyone the *real* reason."

"That he was protecting me?"

I nodded. "He was watching me, gauging me. He wanted me to keep silent. So he confessed before I had a chance to speak, telling that half-truth fairy tale."

"Half-truth?"

"Wanda did want money She *was* trying to blackmail him."

"All of which proves he loves me."

It's some consolation, I thought.

LeAnn sat in her seat, pensive for a moment, while I finished off the last of my breakfast. It was cold now. She'd downed about a third of hers. Not bad, considering.

The waitress appeared, asked if there was anything else. When I said no, she dropped off the check and left.

"So what are you going to do, Chance?" LeAnn asked, sparkling green eyes directed at me.

I stared at her for a time. We had come down to it, of course. I thought about how she'd run over my best friend in cold blood. The thought steeled me. Certainly Lane hadn't been innocent. And LeAnn was right. He probably never considered that she truly meant it when she told him she didn't want to engage in a little horizontal delight with him. I know because I remembered how he was after he returned from that date. He'd thought he'd found his new ladylove. Practically told me so when he'd said he didn't want to tell me the name of the one he'd been with until he was sure wedding bells were in the offing.

Could that have happened? Ha. Lane never had a clue.

But did he deserve to die for his blindness, or even his actions? LeAnn was right that he probably never considered that what he'd done was rape. But it was. I couldn't deny that and didn't want to. At one time, they put men to death for that crime. It had been decades, though, since that was stopped. So, no, he didn't deserve to die. But he was dead just the same. And the one responsible for his demise — in less gentle words, his killer — was sitting across the table from me.

Fictional murder mysteries are supposed to be moral tales, where in the end, the killer is caught, justice rendered and world balance restored. I was sure I could prove some of LeAnn's culpability in Lane's death. Her dented car, for one. Blood type and DNA of her fetus, for another. Even so, there were still some pretty big holes that needed plugging — and time had worked in her favor.

Too, she had the right to remain silent. In fact, that would be her best tactic. For if she did, my guess was they'd never buck her off. All during my recap of events, she'd displayed such an astonishing poise and strength that I took it as her planned design to stonewall it. Because the evidence was so flimsy and LeAnn too tough to confess, I knew this case would never see the light of a courtroom. That meant I had to be jury and judge. It was a heavy responsibility. I can proudly announce, here and now, that, without hesitation, I did my job. I judged her guilty and gave her a life sentence.

"Nothing," was what I said.

Her face filled with surprise at the "Court's decision." "Why?" she asked.

Almost cheerfully, I said, "I can't be responsible for sending the mother of my best friend's child to prison."

"It truly was without thought."

I didn't buy that for a second, though I refrained from saying it. Hadn't LeAnn known exactly what she was doing when she stomped on that accelerator? Of course she did. Which was why I judged her guilty and gave her a life sentence.

You see there was another consideration—a more important one than seeing that LeAnn actually went to trial and served time in prison for the death of my friend. And this consideration meant, for me, the die had been cast. In fact, it was cast the instant I'd put it all together.

That other consideration was the child. Not just any child. Lane's child. His son. A son he would have been proud of. And I wanted LeAnn to remember her crime and see Lane in that boy's face every day for the rest of her life. Hence, the judgment and resulting life sentence. There would be no time off for good behavior—not one day—which meant she would not sit in some woman's prison while someone else, probably Leona, raised Lane's son. No, everyday for the rest of her life, when she breast fed him as an infant, played with him as a toddler, sent him off to school, watched him learn to drive a pickup, go on his first date, go off to college (or bull riding school), get married, have his own child, she would see Lane Lowick and remember what she'd done. Maybe it was an act committed in haste (I'll give her that much), but it was an act committed all the same and now she would repent at leisure.

Moreover, *because* it was Lane's, I saw my best friend's son needed his parents. Not Leona and her husband, or, worse, foster parents. Certainly not yours truly even if he were hooked up with a good woman. Only one parent would be there in the beginning. But Royce would join the family later. That was all right by me. He would be a fine "Dad," even if one with a prison record.

Yes, I reasoned, the child had to be considered. So my verdict and sentence had already been rendered, rendered before I ever invited LeAnn to breakfast.

We were silent for several minutes, sipped coffee, looked at each other. Then, her cup empty, she set it in its saucer, sighed deeply and, moist-eyed, leaned in toward me. As tears started trailing down her reddened cheeks, she stared me squarely in the face and said, "I know you're doing this because of the child. He'll be Lane's son. You know it. And so do I. Well, I'm going to love this baby with all my heart, Chance. I promise I'll give him the best upbringing I possibly can."

Maybe it was because she was my ex, maybe it was because deep down I knew LeAnn's genuinely good character, maybe it was because I sensed some measure of contrition in her — whatever---all I knew was I believed her.

Also by Aberdeen Bay

# Reticence of Ravens

Author: M. M. Gornell

ISBN-13: 978-1-60830-039-6

ISBN-10: 1-60830-039-0

Publisher: Aberdeen Bay

Time and events have turned Hubert James Champion III into a morose man trying for the last year to escape into California's Mojave Desert—*somewhere a little north of Route 66 on the way to Arizona.* No longer a practicing psychologist and FBI collaborator, Hugh now owns Joey's mini-mart, a half-defunct gas station with no gas, no supplies, and little food for customers. *Opening hours variable.*

He has become a man hiding out from the world, and himself—trying to seek redemption among the Creosote and Palo Verde trees. His main companions these days are an aged desert dog, and the unkindness of sometimes raucous, but usually reticent ravens.

But Hugh soon senses that he can't escape—especially when a "special" young woman with red Medusa-like hair, and covered in her father's blood is brought to him one Sunday evening. Turner Jackson has been murdered, and LoraLee Jackson is the main suspect. In quick order Hugh is drawn into proving LoraLee's innocence by both locals and unwanted East Coast intruders. Add the sudden appearance of LoraLee's previously unknown brother, a bulldog FBI agent with an agenda of his own, and Hugh's cousin Della's love-sick ex-husband—not to mention multiple shootings, exploding drug-labs, and most importantly, Hugh's past demons rearing their ugly heads once again.

No, Hugh cannot escape having to find a murderer—*or his own past.*

## *A Route 66 Mystery*